W9-CEB-149

MISS JULIA STRIKES BACK

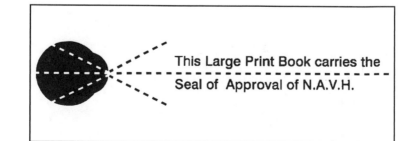

This Large Print Book carries the
Seal of Approval of N.A.V.H.

MISS JULIA
STRIKES BACK

ANN B. ROSS

THORNDIKE PRESS

An imprint of Thomson Gale, a part of The Thomson Corporation

Detroit • New York • San Francisco • New Haven, Conn. • Waterville, Maine • London

BOCA RATON PUBLIC LIBRARY
BOCA RATON, FLORIDA

Copyright © Ann B. Ross, 2007.

Thomson Gale is part of The Thomson Corporation.

Thomson and Star Logo and Thorndike are trademarks and Gale is a registered trademark used herein under license.

ALL RIGHTS RESERVED

This is a work of fiction. Names, characters, places, and incidents either are the product of the author's imagination or are used fictitiously, and any resemblance to actual persons, living or dead, business establishments, events, or locales is entirely coincidental.

Thorndike Press ® Large Print Basic.

The text of this Large Print edition is unabridged.

Other aspects of the book may vary from the original edition.

Set in 16 pt. Plantin.

LIBRARY OF CONGRESS CATALOGING-IN-PUBLICATION DATA

Ross, Ann B.
    Miss Julia strikes back / by Ann B. Ross.
      p. cm.
    ISBN-13: 978-0-7862-9112-0 (hardcover : alk. paper)
    ISBN-10: 0-7862-9112-5 (hardcover : alk. paper)
      1. Springer, Julia (Fictitious character) — Fiction. 2. Jewel thieves —
    Fiction. 3. North Carolina — Fiction. 4. Palm Beach (Fla.) — Fiction. 5. Large
    type books. I. Title.
    PS3568.O84198M573 2007b
    813'.54—dc22
                                                                2007004147

Published in 2007 by arrangement with Viking,
a member of Penguin Group (USA) Inc.

Printed in the United States of America on permanent paper.
10 9 8 7 6 5 4 3 2 1

BOCA RATON PUBLIC LIBRARY
BOCA RATON, FLORIDA

This book is for my girls:
Marian, Claudia, Jennifer,
Alice, and Ramsey

CHAPTER 1

"Lillian!" I tore out of the bedroom and flew down the hall as fast as my feet would take me, my heart thudding like a wild thing. *"Lillian! I need you."* Swinging past the stairs, I slid into the living room and on through the arch into the dining room. "Where are you? *Lillian!"*

A pan clattered to the floor in the kitchen as I skidded past the dining-room table. I heard the flap of Lillian's shoes as she hurried to meet me, shrieking as she ran, *"What? What's the matter?"*

Pushing through the swinging door into the kitchen, I ran smack into her on her way out. We both came to an abrupt halt, staring at each other, our mouths open. She grabbed my arms and yelled in my ear, "What's the matter? What's the matter?"

"Oh, Lillian, they're gone," I gasped, clinging to her for fear I would fall. I was in such a state that I could hardly get the words out. "They were here the other day, I mean, yesterday, I think, but now they're not. I can't find them anywhere, Lillian, and I've looked and looked everywhere, under and over everything, and they're just . . . *gone.*" The breath rasped in my throat as I trembled against her. "*Both* of them."

She took me by the shoulders, put her face up close to mine, and studied me intently. Then a funny look swept across her face as she put her arm around me. "You come on over here, Miss Julia, honey, an' set yo'self down. You feel better when you rest awhile, see if you don't."

I let her lead me to a chair, but I didn't feel any better for it. I was so done in that it was all I could do to catch my breath. "Oh, Lillian, what am I going to do? I've looked everywhere."

"Now don't you worry," she said, patting my back. "You jus' havin' a little spell an' it be over pretty soon. How 'bout I fix you some hot chocolate? Something to warm you up? See there, now," she crooned, "you feelin' better already. You jus' forget for a minute, but I bet you recollect everything if you think about it."

"No, I won't," I said, shaking my head. "I've already gone over and over it, and they're just not here."

"I know, honey, but it be all right. Mr. Sam, he be back 'fore you know it, and Miss Hazel Marie, too. They won't be gone long, and they be comin' in the door 'fore you turn around good. You 'member now?"

I sprang from the chair, staring at her with my mouth open. "What in the world are you talking about? I *know* Sam's coming back, and I *know* Hazel Marie is, too. I've not lost my mind, Lillian, and I'm not having a spell, little or otherwise. And futhermore, I know that good-for-nothing Mr. Pickens is with Hazel Marie, in spite of their efforts to keep it from me." I took two paces, then spun back around, my arms flying wide as I wailed, "And wouldn't you know he'd be gone just when I need him!"

Lillian squinched up her eyes and gave me a careful going-over. "I might oughta call the doctor. You need something to settle you down."

"I don't need a *doctor* or any hot chocolate. I need Mr. Pickens or the police or the sheriff or Deputy, I mean Sergeant, Coleman Bates or *some*body!" I clasped my head in my hands, trying to make her understand. "Don't look at me like that, Lillian. I'm not sick, and my faculties are working just fine, and when I say they're gone, I mean they're *gone*."

"See," Lillian said, reaching out for me. "You gettin' yo'self all worked up again."

I flapped her hand away, not wanting any well-meant soothing. "You'd be worked up, too, if your rings had all of a sudden disappeared."

"What rings? I don't have no rings."

"I'm talking about my wedding band and . . ." I had to stop a moment to quell the tightening in my chest. ". . . and my *engagement* ring! The one Sam gave me that is almost an exact replica of Princess Diana's, only mine is better and can't be replaced. Oh, Lillian," I cried, as the tears welled up, "my precious rings are gone, and I know they were here yesterday, and now I can't find them anywhere."

CHAPTER 2

Exactly one day before I made that awful discovery, I'd stood shivering in the open door of my house, bidding the last of my guests good-bye as they strolled across the porch and down the front walk. Clutching their coats in the bitter cold, they'd laughed and chatted as the wind swirled through their carefully done hair. I'd lingered in the doorway, wishing they'd hurry and be gone because I was freezing to death. LuAnne Conover, my friend for many years, had broken away from three other guests when she reached the row of boxwoods that bordered the lawn, and had turned to wave at me as she opened her car door.

To tell the truth, I'd been ready for them to leave thirty minutes earlier. Ordinarily, I would have been pleased that they'd enjoyed themselves enough to overstay their welcome, but two hours of chitchat is about all I can take at one time. Now that they were leaving, though, a wave of dread swept over me as I watched and waved at the several groups of well-dressed women talking and laughing together on their way to the cars parked along the curb.

Sighing, I closed the door and turned to the living room, where used coffee cups and saucers sat abandoned on occasional tables. One set had been left on the floor beside the Hepplewhite chair — wonder who'd done that? I'd used my second-best Spode china, the Buttercup pattern, because the yellow flowers are so cheerful, and the saucers are curved enough to keep cups from sliding off.

I glanced across the room at more evidence of departed guests. Linen napkins, some with lipstick stains, had been left crumpled on chair arms. And the chairs themselves had been moved just that little bit out of line, as tends to happen when people gather to visit and share the latest news. The dining room table held the remains of my offerings — half-filled trays of fruit and finger sandwiches and coffee cake, along with cooling pots of tea and coffee. Crumbs littered the polished mahogany under the centerpiece that I'd paid a fortune for. Fresh flowers are costly in the middle of January, but they add an air of festivity to a party so I hadn't begrudged the expense.

I carefully picked up a cup and saucer from the lamp table by the sofa, hoping my hand wouldn't give out on me. Having begun to suffer a few aches and twinges in the joints of my fingers lately, as well as a little swelling, I'd finally broken down and gone in to see Dr. Hargrove. After pulling and prodding my sore digits, he told me I had some localized arthritis, although not enough to worry about. But he couldn't leave it at that. He had to go on and say that a little arthritis here and there was only to be expected at my age.

I don't know why I keep going to him. I know exactly what he's going to tell me. It doesn't matter what my complaint is, it's always caused by age. The man has an obsession, that's all there is to it.

Standing there with one cup and saucer in my hand, I looked around again at the remnants of my party. One thing was certain — inviting twenty-five of my closest friends for morning coffee had not lifted my spirits as I'd hoped it would.

I'd made my plans and issued my invitations two weeks before, when I'd realized that I was going to need something not only to do but to look forward to. This little get-together was meant to take my mind off those who were gone. Yet now that the party was over and done with, I realized that it had only reinforced the emptiness of the house.

I picked up another cup and saucer and with my hands full, walked into the kitchen, where at least Lillian remained with me.

"They're gone," I said, putting the china on the counter.

Lillian wiped the coffeepot dry and put it back in the corner out of the way. "I figured, else you wouldn't be bringin' them things in here. Them ladies enjoy theyselves?"

"I think so. At least they stayed long enough." I tapped my fingers on the counter, wondering what to do with myself for the rest of the day. "I declare, Lillian, I don't know how I'm going to get through this. It's only been a few days, and already I'm floundering around like I've never been alone before." I couldn't admit, even to her, the other matter that was bothering me.

"Why don't you have another party? That take yo' mind off of it, 'cause you have something to do and won't be lookin' for something else."

"I don't want to have another party. This one didn't help matters, so what's the use of trying again? Besides, I'm tired of hearing the same old stories and listening to the same old gossip told and retold."

"Them ladies didn't come up with nothin' new?" Lillian smiled, trying to tease me out of my mood. "They's us'ally something goin' on 'round town to talk about."

"Not lately, apparently. Or if there is, nobody's heard it yet. Oh, Dub and Clara and her electrician are still a source of interest, but not to me. I could care less who's living with who. Or whom."

Lillian narrowed her eyes at me. "That don't sound like you. You better perk yo'self up 'fore Lloyd get home from school. He see you mopin' 'round, he start in doin' it, too."

"I know. And I will. But, to tell you the truth, I just don't know what to do with myself."

"Well, I give you something. Come on and he'p me pick up in yonder. I got to get them leftovers in the frigidaire."

I followed her into the dining room, and we began to clear the table.

"These sandwiches were lovely, Lillian," I said. "You can see there's only a few left. Why don't you have them for lunch?"

"They's enough for me and you, 'less you already eat some an' don't want no more."

"I had one or two, and they were good. But I've had my fill of cream cheese and nuts, and cream cheese and pineapple, and

15

cream cheese and cucumber."

Lillian picked up a large silver tray and headed for the kitchen, shaking her head. "Don't nothin' please you when you get like this."

"Well, I can't help it." I followed, carrying the silver coffeepot and teapot and a handful of used napkins. "I didn't know it'd be so lonesome, and I could just sit down and cry." So I put the pots on the counter and sat at the kitchen table, where I dropped the napkins to await washing. But in spite of my dejected spirits I couldn't work up a tear. Which was well and good, because there's nothing worse than a mature woman allowing herself to fall apart.

Lillian put the tray next to the sink and came to sit across from me. "You better git hol' of yo'self and set yo' mind on something else. Tell me what them ladies say 'bout Miss Hazel Marie's room. I hear 'em going up an' down the stairs carryin' on an' on 'bout her decoratin'."

I had to smile. "Oh, they loved her room, and of course Opal Nixon was just beaming. I'm glad I invited her, even though Hazel Marie wasn't here to get her share of compliments." Opal Nixon was the decorator Hazel Marie had engaged to help her redo her upstairs bedroom. They'd done it in pink with gold accents, which didn't reflect my taste, but it had impressed any number of my guests. Opal would undoubtedly get some decorating commissions from the morning's viewing, and I hoped she remembered who to thank for it.

"And," I went on, "everybody had to see mine and Sam's room, too, although it doesn't come anywhere near the opulence of Hazel Marie's. Have you ever noticed how interested people are in other people's sleeping arrangements?" When Sam and I married, Hazel Marie had moved out of her large bedroom downstairs and taken the upstairs room that I'd once shared with Wesley Lloyd Springer, my first and now-deceased husband and her, well, *whatever* he was. Hazel Marie had never said anything, but I was sure that her decorating fit was an effort to erase any reminder of Wesley Lloyd from the room. Not that there'd been any reminders left, since I'd occupied it alone for a few years and had done all the erasing I could think of.

"I declare," I said, picking up where I'd left off, "I think every woman here this morning made the trek to both rooms. I know LuAnne Conover went upstairs twice, she was so taken with all that pink. Then she asked me if I thought Leonard would like a

17

pink bedroom." I laughed at the thought of LuAnne's morose husband ensconced in a pink silk, satin, and velvet bedroom similar to Hazel Marie's. "Now, why in the world would I know what he'd like? As far as I can tell, Leonard Conover wouldn't know the difference between a bed at the Ritz-Carlton and a cot in an army tent."

"Well, me neither, since I never been in either one. But that's something you can do," Lillian said. "Why don't you get Miss Opal to fix up yo' room?"

"Lord, Lillian, I wouldn't let her get within a mile of that room. Her ideas are too fancy for me."

"Well, you could do it yo' own self. That give you something to do, wouldn't it?"

I nodded. "It would, if it was something I wanted to do." I propped my elbow on the table and leaned my head on my hand. "Oh, Lillian, I am just heartsick with loneliness, and about half-mad, too. I feel as if I've been abandoned, and don't think that everybody else didn't think the same. Nobody would come right out and say so, of course, but they were so concerned and *pitying*. I'm sure they thought all was not well with Sam and me." I rubbed my forehead, trying to forestall a headache. "I didn't know it'd be this bad, so how in the world am I going to get through two more weeks?"

"Too late to be moanin' now, 'cause you coulda done something about it."

"Yes, and it's a little late to be reminding me of it, too." I had to clear my throat before going on. "You want to know what the ladies talked about this morning? Well, I'll tell you. They whispered about Sam going off and leaving me hardly six months after our wedding. Among themselves, not to my face, but I knew. And they wanted to know how I'm taking it, and they wanted to know where Hazel Marie is and who she's with and why she went off, and why I'm here all by myself with just you and Little Lloyd. And it was such an effort to put a good face on it all and try to pretend that I don't mind that my husband of less than a year is halfway around the world all by himself." I wiped my eyes with somebody's napkin. "And of course, they wanted to know why I didn't go with him, or at least with Hazel Marie."

"Well," Lillian said, not as sympathetically as I would've liked, "that's what I want to know. Why didn't you?"

I sniffed. "I haven't lost a thing in Mexico, and certainly not in Russia. I wouldn't go flying off to either one for all the tea in China."

CHAPTER 3

"That's what you keep on sayin'," Lillian said. "So you got no call to be moanin' 'bout it now." Lillian heaved herself out of the chair, sighing as she did so. "Well, lemme get up from here an' get busy. Them plates an' things not gonna wash theyselves."

"They're not going anywhere, either." I reached across the table to forestall her. "Stay and talk to me. I want you to know that I might've reconsidered if I'd realized that Sam and Hazel Marie would both be gone at the same time. It just did not occur to me to check the dates. I mean, who would've thought that she'd win a trip to Mexico at the same time that Sam was going to Russia? I knew when *he* was going, because he'd made his plans a long time ago, way before either of us thought of getting married. But I never dreamed that Hazel Marie would sign her name to some raffle ticket in a store and actually end up winning a trip. And at the exact same time."

"You got to think about them things," Lillian said, offering not one iota of sympathy. "An' both of 'em wanted you to go with 'em. You know they did. They begged and pleaded, but would you do it? No, sir, you wouldn't."

"Well, even if I'd wanted to go with Sam, I couldn't have gotten on the same tour. Those things are planned down to the last detail long before they actually leave, and I happen to know that his tour was full. It would've changed all his plans if I'd decided to go at the last minute. And you know how he was looking forward to seeing all the sights in Russia — the Hermitage and the palaces and the churches with those Oriental domes and things. And you know what that sweet man did? He offered to back out and not go at all, but I couldn't let him do that. I mean, he'd already paid his money and everything." I wiped my hand across my face and sat up straighter. "So it's only two more weeks and surely I can manage without him for that length of time. I did fairly well without him before this."

"Well, it diffrunt once he be a husband an' then go off."

"That's the truth. And I guess that's why I'm so done in now. I just didn't realize how much I'd miss him. If we weren't married, I'd still miss him. I know that, but I don't think I'd feel as lost as I do now. Marriage does strange things to you, Lillian."

She laughed. "Don't nobody know that better'n me, which is why it don't figure in my plans no more. But I miss Mr. Sam, too. He the nicest man, an' no trouble at all to have around. But you don't have no excuse for not goin' with Miss Hazel Marie. You know she wanted you to."

"Yes, and she probably meant it," I said, nodding. "At the time, that is. Now, Lillian, don't say anything about this, but I will bet you money that if we called Mr. Pickens we wouldn't find him. Because I think he's with her. Why else would she extend the one week she won to two?"

"How you know that? She didn't say nothin' 'bout him goin'."

"Well, of course she wouldn't. Hazel Marie's not one to go around telling everything she knows." I stopped and considered what I'd just said. "Well, actually, she is, but she's picked up some self-restraint since she's been with us. So she wouldn't say anything, knowing how I feel about them not being married and all. But do you think she'd have been so excited if she'd been going to a foreign country all by herself? No, she wouldn't. She'd have been scared to death, and probably wouldn't even have gone. You know how she is, and at heart she's just a little country girl and would no more fly off to some Mexican beach resort on her own without any tour group or anything than she'd, well, fly."

"You took her to the airport, didn't you? Did you see Mr. Pickens steppin' on that airplane with her?"

"No, but she had to change in Atlanta, and I'll bet you anything he was there waiting for her."

"I'm not no bettin' woman, an' you not, either."

"Well, I'm just saying," I said.

"'Sides, even if you right, it's her business. An' his, I guess, if they want to go off on a vacation. You ought not be settin' up to do no judgin', 'cause least they go outta town to do it."

"Lord, Lillian, I'm not judging anybody. For all I know, they're staying in separate rooms, but far be it from me to speculate about that. Fact of the matter, I'm glad he's with her. I'd really be worried if she was off by herself. At least he'll look after her and not let her get involved with some smooth-talking foreigner who'd take one look at her in that skimpy bathing suit I couldn't believe she bought, and, well, you know what could happen then."

"That's what I been tellin' you. She be safe with Mr. Pickens, so you ought to be thankin' him 'stead of moanin' 'bout him."

"I am not moaning," I said with some asperity. "What I'm doing is explaining why I didn't go with her or with Sam. My presence would've spoiled everything. Sam and I would've had to tour Russia alone since the group was full, and can you see us trying to get around in all that snow by ourselves? And how much would Hazel Marie and Mr. Pickens enjoy Mexico if I'd been tagging along? Talk about your fifth wheel."

"Yessum, I 'spect you done the right thing to stay home. But that don't mean you got to set here whinin' an' feelin' sorry for yo'self. You got to git over that an' be glad they havin' a good time."

"I'm not whining, and I'm not feeling sorry for myself. At least not much. I just didn't realize how badly I'd miss them. It surprises me, because you'd think I'd be able to entertain myself for a few weeks. I did it long enough after Mr. Springer's passing to know how to do it." I stopped and considered my first husband's passing and my entrance into the world of business and high finance when Little Lloyd and I had inherited his estate.

"Of course, I didn't have to put up with missing him like I miss Sam. Well," I went on, "I'd better not get into that. You need your lunch, Lillian. Let's finish clearing up so you can eat."

"Don't you want nothin'?"

"Goodness, no. I've been snacking all morning." I started out of the kitchen to finish bringing in the remains of the party. Upon consideration, though, I turned and said, "Well, maybe a cup of soup would hit the spot. And a salad from that leftover fruit. But eat up everything, Lillian, you know it won't keep."

We made several trips from the living and dining rooms, bringing in trays and china and silver to stack on the kitchen counter. On my last trip, I had a sudden inspiration.

"I know what I'll do today," I said. "When Little Lloyd gets home, I'll take him shopping."

"Oh, he enjoy that," Lillian said with a slight roll of her eyes.

"Well, it seems to work for Hazel Marie. No matter what kind of mood she's in, shopping is the answer. So I think I'll try it. Besides, Little Lloyd said he needs some new tennis shoes, and it'll get us out of the house. We can go over to that new mall near Asheville and make an afternoon of it."

Lillian looked up from the pan of soup she was stirring. Then she looked back down. "If you ast me, I think it 'bout time for all us to stop callin' Little Lloyd 'Little.' He gettin' to be a big boy now, an' a baby name don't suit him no more."

"Why, Lillian, that's not a baby name. It's just a normal way of doing things, and lots of people're called 'Little' something or another all their lives. Why, think of Dora Benning — you know, her husband has that insurance agency? Her daughter is known as Little Dora and ever since that child was born her mother's been called Big Dora."

"Yessum, an' I bet she don't like it, neither."

"Well, she has put on a little weight, but nobody thinks about that. They just call her Big Dora because she's the oldest and the first one with that name. It's just habit." I gathered the soiled napkins and walked into the laundry room. I dumped them onto the washing machine and went back into the kitchen. "But, you know, Lillian, there's not a reason in the world to continue calling Little Lloyd 'Little.' I mean, it's not as if we need to distinguish him from his father who's dead and he's not. Who would ever mix them up? Besides, when Lit . . . , I mean, when Lloyd comes of age, it won't do

26

to have 'Little' tacked on to his name. How would it look when he's managing money and property, and dealing with lawyers, and making a real name for himself in this town? Maybe in the whole state and beyond? Why, nobody would take him seriously."

"You don't have to tell me," Lillian said, putting the soup and salad on the table. "Now, come on over here an' eat."

"Thank you, Lillian, and I appreciate your calling this matter to my attention. From now on, it'll be Lloyd, and Lloyd alone." I sat at the table and picked up the soup spoon. "If I can remember."

"Well, I call something else to yo' attention, if you a mind to hear it," Lillian said, as she began to run water in the sink to hand-wash cups and saucers. We never put my good china and silver in the dishwasher.

"I'm always interested in what you have to say," I said, stabbing a chunk of pineapple with my fork. "This salad dressing is delicious, Lillian. Is it your poppy seed dressing?"

"No'm, it's sto'-bought, but it 'bout as good as homemade."

"I thought it was yours." I continued to eat while Lillian made short work of washing the Spode. "Well, go ahead. What else do you want to call to my attention?"

She flicked soapy water from her hands over the sink, then dried them with a towel. I thought for a minute that she wasn't going to answer me, but then she turned around and leaned on the counter, facing me.

"I know it not my place to say this to you, but I don't wonder them ladies talk about you and Mr. Sam. You let him go off here, there, and yonder all by hisself, an' I know he not the kind to get in trouble on his lonesome, but they's lotsa women on the loose jus' lookin' for a fine man like him. An' since I done started, I might as well finish it up. Look like to me you ought to treat that good man better'n you do."

I let my fork drop onto the salad, stunned that anyone would presume to tell me how I should conduct myself, especially in matters matrimonial. Then I laughed, trying to pass it off. "Well, Lord, Lillian, if I thought I needed advice on that subject, I'd go to a professional. But you don't see me making an appointment, do you?"

"Maybe you think I'm meddlin'," Lillian said without cracking a smile, and I quickly sobered up. "But I know how you was when you thought somebody be after Mr. Sam, an' you not even close to married then. What it be like if somebody come after him now? All I'm sayin' is you ought to change yo' ways an' be nice to him."

"I *am* nice to him! When am I not?" I stopped then, recalling a number of times when my sharp tongue had gotten the best of me. "Besides," I mumbled, "he likes it."

"He don't like goin' off by hisself, I know he don't. A man want his wife with him, I don't care where he go, 'specially when he beg her to."

"Well," I said, somewhat defensively, "lots of people do it these days. Take separate vacations, I mean. Besides, I might want to go off on my own sometime, too. You never know."

"Well, I guess you know what you doin', but he might get tired of it, too. Then you be stompin' an' stormin' 'round here, worriet to death 'bout who be after him."

"Why, when do I ever stomp and storm around? I declare, Lillian, I am the most easygoing woman in this town, and you know it."

"Yessum, I guess so, but I'm jus' sayin'."

CHAPTER 4

When Lloyd, as I made a conscious effort to call him, came home from school that day, we began preparing for a trip to the mall. He didn't seem especially thrilled with the prospect, but he was his usual amiable self and didn't complain.

"Now, Lillian," I said, as I put on my coat and checked my pocketbook to be sure I had all the necessities, "you take the afternoon off, too. There's no need for you to sit around here all day. You can pick up Latisha early, and . . . I can't find my car keys. I must've left them in the bedroom." I started out of the kitchen, but kept on talking. "I mean it, Lillian, I want you out of here. Lloyd and I will get supper at the mall. Maybe even go to a show, so we'll be late."

"Well, that be the case, I think I will. Latisha love to be picked up early. She get tired of that after-school program." Lillian headed for the pantry to get her coat, shaking her head at the thought of her great-granddaughter who'd come for a visit and stayed for the duration. "You gonna lock up, or you want me to?"

I stuck my head back through the dining room door. "I will, since Lloyd's not ready yet. You run on, and I'll see you tomorrow."

"If I any shape to get here," she mumbled from the pantry. "Latisha stay wide open all the time."

I stopped at the foot of the stairs and called up to Lloyd. "You about ready?"

"Yessum, I'm coming," he called back.

I smiled, beginning to look forward to spending a few hours in his company. He was getting on in age, about to hit his teens, and everybody says that's when you begin to lose a child. They say that's when children begin to close themselves off and stop listening to good advice. I didn't intend to let that happen. Whenever I had the opportunity, I discussed with him the duties and responsibilities of inherited wealth, telling him where certain funds were invested and what properties he owned — or would, when he came of age — and I'd never had any problem at all holding his attention.

"I'm ready, Miss Julia," he called, as I heard the clatter of his footsteps coming down the stairs.

Snatching up the keys from my dresser, I thought to myself that a trip to the mall might not have been one of my better ideas. The only redeeming factor was having the time with Lloyd and, of course, filling up the day. I didn't enjoy shopping all that much — when I need something, I call and have it delivered — but an afternoon of looking for shoes and into store windows and having a meal out and maybe taking in a picture show, if anything tasteful was on, should pass the time fairly pleasantly. And I needed a pleasant pastime since Lillian had brought me up short by criticizing my treatment of Sam. The whole discussion had been burdening my soul, adding another worry to all the others I had. I wouldn't admit it to Lillian, but as soon as Sam got home, I was determined to bend over backward to treat him nicer. Whatever that meant.

We wandered around the mall and through a few shops, stopping now and then to discuss an item of merchandise. As we strolled along, dodging shoppers as we went, Lloyd suddenly darted toward a store.

"There they are," he said, pointing at a window display in a sporting-goods store. "That's what I'm looking for. See, they're

Adidas Samba Indoor Soccer Shoes."

"My goodness," I said, impressed with the information. Then realizing what he'd said, my heart lifted. "Does that mean you're going to try out for the soccer team again?"

"I'm thinking about it," he said. "You know, if at first you don't succeed. And so on." He grinned as he teased me with what I'd said to him so often.

The store was filled with what seemed to be every kind of tennie pump known to man, and I couldn't distinguish one kind from the other. But he told the salesman exactly what he wanted and only had to try on three pairs to find the right size. Children's feet grow out of proportion to the rest of them, you know. I sat back and watched as the salesman offered pair after pair, as Lloyd stood up and wiggled his toes in each one. Finally, he gave me a smile that barely hid his pleasure. "These feel good," he said as he admired himself in a mirror, "and just what I wanted."

I was careful to keep my opinion to myself, but I'm here to tell you that those shoes looked like twin boats on his feet.

He wore the new pair out of the store, the old ones in a sack under his arm. "Miss Julia," he said as we braved the crowds again, "I wish you'd get some tennis shoes. Let's go back, so you can try some on."

I laughed. "Can't you just see me in a pair of tennis shoes? No sir, I'll stick to my Red Cross oxfords and Naturalizer pumps." We sidestepped away from a woman pushing a baby stroller. "There're two things I intend to steer clear of: blue jeans and clunky tennis shoes. They're unseemly for someone of my age."

He grinned up at me. "Okay, but I think you'd like 'em. You can really flit around in them."

"My flitting days are over. Are you hungry?"

"Oh, man, I've *been* hungry. Where're we going to eat?"

As it happened, we were near a cafeteria in one of the side halls of the mall and decided to have our supper there. I much prefer to be seated and served, but Lloyd considered it a treat so we pushed trays and filled them from a steam table. You'd think he'd get enough of that in the school cafeteria, but he told me the school didn't have much of a selection.

By the time we finished our meal, I was ready to go home. My feet felt as if I'd walked ten miles around that mall, and I may well have, for Lloyd was interested in seeing everything.

"Miss Julia," he said, as we walked out of the cafeteria, "there's a good movie on right here. If you want to see it, we won't even have to move the car."

"What's it about?" You can't be too careful these days, especially when the television is even showing commercials about all kinds of intimate matters. And so-called comedy actors come right out and say things over the airways about human anatomy that I wouldn't say in my sleep.

"It's about a Little League baseball team, and it's supposed to be funny."

That sounded harmless enough, so we went. But let me tell you, it was not funny to me. I'd never heard such language in my life, and after being subjected to it for about ten minutes, I grabbed Lloyd's hand and left. But not before giving an usher we happened to meet on our way out a piece of my mind.

After we'd traversed the windy parking lot and got into the car, I had a few second thoughts about my tirade. "I hope I didn't embarrass you, Lloyd, but lines have to be drawn." I turned on the ignition and carefully backed out, dreading the trip home in the dark. It was a sign of the desperate need to distract myself that I'd been willing to risk driving at night in the first place.

As we drove down the wide street that

would lead to the interstate, I continued my explanation. "I have long held the firm belief that the language we use reveals our inner selves, and you and I are not foulmouthed people who can't express themselves in correct and decent English."

"No, ma'am, you didn't embarrass me." His grin flashed in the headlights of an approaching car. "But I'll have to say that you used such correct and decent English to that usher that I'm not sure he understood a word you said." Then he laughed out loud. "You blessed him out good and he didn't even know it."

I laughed, too, and said, "Maybe he'll figure it out one of these days."

I never liked going into a dark house, and the one small light I'd left on over the kitchen stove only made the house seem lonelier. But having someone with you, even if it is a child, makes it somewhat easier. For one thing, you have to pretend you aren't afraid, and that, in itself, gives you some backbone. At least, I was trying to act as if it did.

I led the way in, unlocking the door and quickly switching on the overhead lights. The house seemed to be just as we'd left it, and I made sure of that by turning on lights and looking into every room, all the time chattering away to Lloyd, trying to cover my nervousness with conversation.

"It's late, Lloyd," I said, standing with him in the upstairs hall after my house search. "We should be in bed."

"Yessum, but I have to look over a Social Studies chapter first."

"Well, don't be long." I walked around upstairs turning off the lights I'd just turned on in Hazel Marie's room and in the room Deputy, now Sergeant, Bates used to rent. Going back downstairs, I recalled how comforting it had been to have Coleman Bates in the house. There's nothing more reassuring than having a sheriff's deputy living under your roof. But now he was both a husband and a father, and no longer around to provide me with protection and security.

I turned off the lights in the kitchen and the living room, pausing to check that the doors were locked. I was tempted to leave a few lights on, but resisted the urge since I didn't want Lloyd to know how edgy I was. Actually, I wasn't just edgy. I was downright scared, even more so than usual.

And that had been a good bit of my problem with the loneliness I'd complained to Lillian about — a big, half-empty house at night is a spooky place. Even though it looked the same, it didn't feel the same. I had kept my dread of the nights to myself, though, because I'm a grown woman, for goodness' sake, and old enough not to give in to foolish fears. Or at least, old enough not to tell anybody about them.

But the fact of the matter was, I hadn't slept a wink since Sam and Hazel Marie had been gone. Lying in bed alone and wide awake, I listened for every creak and thump in the house, picturing dark, hooded prowlers creeping along the hall, bent on carrying out terrible acts of mayhem and bodily harm.

Each night I had considered closing my bedroom door and pushing a chair, or maybe two, against it to give me a few minutes' grace if someone was already in the house. I couldn't do it, though, because I needed to be able to hear Lloyd if sneak thieves went to his room first. So I left the door open and went quietly to my closet. I searched in the far corner, moving clothes around, until I found Lloyd's old baseball bat. I declare, you have to hide everything from Lillian. When she gets into a cleaning frenzy, nothing will be where you left it.

I laid the bat under the bed on my side, right near the edge so I could quickly reach down and get it. I didn't know how much good a bat would do me, since it was a stubby little one, but any kind of weapon is reassuring when you're as scared as I was.

I undressed then and got into bed. Removing my watch, I laid it on the bedside table and clicked off the lamp. I turned on my side so I could watch the open door, expecting any minute to see a stealthy shadow lunge into the room. How in the world I was going to get through another wakeful night, I didn't know.

But I did, and there's nothing more welcome than the light of day when every minute of the nighttime is fraught with terror. I hid the baseball bat in the closet again and hurried to the kitchen. After getting Lloyd off to school and having a second cup of coffee with Lillian, I returned to the bedroom to finish dressing, promising myself that I would take a nap later on. That would have to wait until the afternoon, though, for I knew everybody would be calling this morning to thank me for the lovely party.

After doing a little something with my face and hair, I put on the garnet wool dress that Hazel Marie said looked so good with my coloring. Then I looked at my hands, pleased that the little swelling around the knuckles had gone down.

Brushing off the shoulders of my dress, I

took one last look in the mirror, then walked over to the bedside table where I'd left my watch before retiring. I clasped the watch on my wrist, then with a sudden stab of fear, I stopped. Hurrying back to the dresser, I leaned over it, scanning across the top. Quickly moving perfume bottles, hairbrush, comb, and hand mirror, I searched frantically, my hands scrambling over and under the dresser scarf.

The breath rasping in my throat, I knelt down, knees creaking with the strain, and looked under, around, and behind the dresser. I could feel my heart thumping in my breast, as panic nearly overwhelmed me.

"Oh, my Lord," I gasped, running my hand back and forth under the dresser. "They're not here. Oh, my goodness, where did they go? They have to be here, they just have to." I pulled myself upright and leaned heavily against the chest, hardly able to comprehend the loss. *"Lillian!* Oh, my goodness," I sobbed, desperately holding on to the chest. *"Lillian!"*

CHAPTER 5

I tore out of the bedroom and flew down the hall as fast as my feet would carry me, my heart thudding like a wild thing in my chest. "*Lillian!* Where are you?"

I heard a pan clatter in the kitchen, and, well, I've already told what happened then, but if Lillian hadn't been there I don't know what I would've done. She immediately took charge of a search party, consisting mostly of herself since I'd already looked high and low without finding my precious rings.

"No, now," she said when she finally understood what, and not *who,* was missing. "They can't be lost. You wear 'em all the time, and they too tight to fall off, so you got yo'self all upset over nothin'. You prob'ly jus' put 'em down somewhere, an' they still there. Where'd you put 'em?"

I wiped my eyes with the sleeve of my dress, then pointed toward the bedroom. "Right in there on my dresser in that little Haviland candy dish. It's where I keep my rings when I'm not wearing them. And they were still there yesterday, I mean I think they were, because I didn't wear them yesterday. And now they're gone."

"Le's go look again," Lillian said. "If you say they in there, then they be there somewhere."

I followed her back to the bedroom, hoping against hope that she would find what I hadn't been able to.

She walked straight in and began searching among the items on top of the dresser. "You jus' overlook 'em. I bet they here somewhere."

"I've looked everywhere, and they're not." I stood wringing my hands as I watched her go through the same search I had made. "Oh, Lillian, what am I going to do? I wouldn't lose those rings, especially my engagement ring, for anything in the world. Sam made a special trip with Little — I mean, with Lloyd to Charlotte to get it. And you know what it means to me. I'll never be able to tell him I was careless enough to lose it."

By this time, Lillian was on her hands and knees, looking under the dresser and sweeping her hands across the carpet. "They got to be here somewheres."

Then, groaning with the effort, she got to

her feet. "Lemme go get a broom an' swish this room good. They prob'bly fall off an' roll under something."

While waiting for her to return, I searched under the chair cushions, checked both bedside tables, and looked in the dresser drawers. "They're just not here," I said as Lillian came back with the broom.

"Yessum, they is. An' we find 'em if we have to tear this whole room up." She commenced sweeping the broom across the carpet, under the bed, and in the closets, as we both watched for a flash of the diamonds and sapphires that made up my precious rings.

Finally, we both slumped into chairs, defeated and empty-handed. Or empty-fingered. Lillian had lost her confidence and was looking almost as bereft as I was feeling.

"Think back," she said. "You come home las' night with Lloyd, an' what you do then? You get ready for bed, an' you put them rings in the candy dish, then . . ."

"No. No, I didn't." I sat up, frowning as I went over in my mind the last time I'd worn the rings. "I wore them to church Sunday, but they bothered me because the stones in my engagement ring were rubbing against the sore knuckle on my little finger. So I took

43

them off as soon as I got home, and yes, I clearly remember now, I put them both right there in the candy dish, and I haven't worn them since. Not even for the party yesterday, which come to think of it, probably caused some of the strange looks I got. But when I went to put them on this morning, they weren't there, and they *have* to be because I didn't move them. They couldn't just get up and walk off."

I could've cried, thinking of Mildred Allen, who had just had the stones in some of her favorite rings made into earrings. She said that she had arthritis in her fingers, too, but that wasn't what was causing her swelling. Anyway, I had discounted that solution, because I could just see Sam's face if his rings ended up on my ears and not on my finger.

"Well, they not in that candy dish now, so they got to be somewhere else. You sure they there yesterday?"

I frowned, intent on recalling every minute of the previous day. "I think so. I assume they were, because everything's always been safe in this house. I didn't even think of making sure. Wait, Lillian, who all came to the house yesterday?"

"You mean, 'sides all the ladies come for yo' party? Nobody but that florist lady what brought the centerpiece. But she don't never come in. She jus' ring the do'bell, an' I take it from her an' put it on the table."

"That's right. I remember. And Lloyd didn't have any friends over. Was there anybody else?"

"No'm, they not been a soul in this house 'cept yo' lady friends what come to the party."

We sat quietly for a minute, going over every minute of the previous day. Then we turned to each other as an unthinkable possibility dawned on the both of us.

"No," I said. "Absolutely not. It couldn't be."

"No'm, I don't think so, neither," she said. "You been knowin' most of them ladies for years an' years. None of them do any thievin' in yo' house, so don't even think about it."

"Oh, Lillian, I don't *want* to think about it, but what else can I do?" If I'd thought I was utterly dismayed by the loss of my rings, it was nothing to the way I felt at the thought that one of my friends might be responsible. "Are we sure nobody else could've been in here?"

"Sure as I can be, 'less you entertain somebody at night after I go home."

"Lord, Lillian, who would I entertain at night? No, as soon as you leave, I lock all the doors and won't even let Lloyd go out again.

And I certainly had no one in last night. Why, it was all of eight-thirty by the time we got home from the mall."

"Maybe you forget and wear 'em yesterday, and they fall off at the picture show, or when you walkin' 'round the mall. Call them mall folks an' see they find 'em."

"I didn't put them on yesterday at all. I remember that clearly, Lillian, because I wanted to wear them for the party. But my fingers were still sore, and I was afraid I wouldn't be able to get them off again. Oh," I said, as a sudden mental image came to mind. "They were definitely in the candy dish yesterday morning. I remember now, because after I got dressed for the party, I walked over to get them, then decided not to risk having to have them cut off. Yes, they were there yesterday morning, I know it just as sure as I'm sitting here."

"Then I guess that mean we better think about what you don't want to think about."

"I can't bear to think it, Lillian." I could've cried at the idea that one of my friends — faithful churchgoers, one and all — could've given in to the temptation to pick up something that didn't belong to her. Even if it was sitting out in plain sight. I would've trusted any one of them with everything I owned, but now the awful possibility that a thief

46

lurked among us was beginning to fill my mind.

"I know you don't want to think it," Lillian said, "but nobody else been here. And them ladies went all over this house, an' some of 'em you don't know too good."

"Only Opal Nixon, but it couldn't be her. Why, she was in and out of the house for weeks doing that decorating, and nothing has ever been missing. No, she wouldn't be in business long if she had a habit of picking up things."

"Maybe she one of them klepto people, what can't help theyselves. Or maybe somebody else is, an' it come over 'em without nobody knowin' it."

I waved that off and said, "Maybe we ought to really scour this room good and search through everything. They could still be underneath something. Would you mind calling James and asking him to help us move the furniture?"

"No'm, I don't mind callin' him. I jus' mind bein' 'round him. But I think that the best thing to do." She heaved herself out of the chair and started toward the phone to call Sam's housekeeper. Sam had kept James on to see to his house, even though he no longer lived there. Sam used his house as an office where he piddled with first one thing and another, giving him an excuse to keep James on the payroll.

Lillian got to the door and stopped. She held on to the sash with one hand and turned to look at me. "Miss Julia, them ladies all went up to Miss Hazel Marie's room, too. If somebody pick up yo' rings down here, then . . ."

"Oh, my word!" I sprang from my chair and headed toward her. "Come on, Lillian, hurry."

CHAPTER 6

We scrambled up the stairs as fast as my creaking limbs and Lillian's flopping shoes would carry us, only to run into each other in the door to Hazel Marie's room. Turning sideways, we both managed to squirm through and pop out into the pink room.

"Where she keep her jew'lry?" Lillian asked, looking around. Then she went to the bed and smoothed the wrinkled spread where someone had sat on it during yesterday's visitation. "Look like people wouldn't set on somebody else's bed, 'specially when that somebody not at home."

"Over here, Lillian," I said, walking over to Hazel Marie's pink-skirted dressing table. The glass top was covered with perfume bottles and all manner of jars and cosmetic containers. A gold-plated hairbrush and hand mirror flanked her large pink leather jewelry chest, one that I knew contained several layers that could be lifted out to display all her rings and bracelets, pins and necklaces.

Before touching the chest, I carefully scanned the top of the dressing table. Nothing looked disturbed, but even so, I caught my lower lip in my teeth as I reached to open the chest.

"Oh, I hope it's all here," I said, undoing the clasp.

"Might not be," Lillian said.

I took back my hand, afraid to look. "Don't say that. It has to be. Because if it's not, that means we had a premeditated thief among us. It's one thing to steal something on the spur of the moment, something in plain sight like my rings, but another thing entirely to ransack a closed jewelry chest. Besides, whoever it was would've had to make sure to bring a large pocketbook to hold everything." I frowned, trying to bring to mind who among my guests had brought what size pocketbook. Emma Sue Ledbetter was out. She never carried anything but a little clutch for her keys, driver's license, and comb. It really cuts down on the size and weight of your purse when you don't wear makeup.

"I jus' mean we don't know what Miss Hazel Marie take to Mexico with her," Lillian said.

"Yes, we do. She asked me about it when she was packing. She was concerned about leaving anything in a hotel room. I told her that the finer hotels have safes in the rooms, or she could always use the manager's safe. But I recommended that she not take many pieces in the first place. Less to worry about and keep up with."

"So what she take? You 'member that?"

"Just her everyday jewelry. That big dome ring, the charm bracelet I gave her and that Mr. Pickens keeps adding to, so that there're two rows of charms on it — I remember it clanking on her arm as we drove to the airport — and one long and one short gold necklace, which is a gracious plenty for any-body. Besides, she said gold looks better with a tan, and she intended to get one. Tan, I mean."

"Well, look in that box an' see everything else still there," Lillian said.

I opened the lid and nearly fainted. The top layer was empty. With shaking hands, I lifted it out. The second layer held nothing but a bobby pin and half a piece of chewing gum. I snatched that layer out, and in the very bottom there were a small gold ring, an anklet that she'd learned better than to wear, and two pairs of silver earrings that weren't even sterling.

"Well," Lillian said, looking over my shoulder, "least they didn't take everything."

"They might as well have," I said, feeling sick to my stomach. "This is her high school ring. It's only ten-karat gold, and not worth the taking. And this ankle bracelet and these earrings are costume jewelry. Oh, Lillian, somebody has cleaned her out."

"Maybe she put it in a lockbox at the bank, since she know she won't be home to wear it."

"I don't think so." I had to sit down, so I did, just done in by being the victim of a crime in my own home. "I mentioned that to her once, but she said she liked to have it near so she could wear it anytime she wanted to. Oh, Lillian, those beautiful pearls I gave her are gone, and the diamond pin she bought at Neiman Marcus. And that gorgeous Judith Ripka necklace, and I can't even think what all else. Oh, and her diamond watch is gone, too. Hazel Marie's never going to get over this. She gets more pleasure out of jewelry than any woman I know, and that's saying something. And now I'm going to have to tell her it's all gone."

"She got insurance, don't she?"

"Yes, we both do," I said, rubbing my hand across my face. "But that won't make up for the loss. Hazel Marie bought most of her things herself. She says it's her investment fund that lets her have her enjoys at the same time. But for me," I said, stifling a sob, "insurance can never replace what came from Sam."

I caught my breath at the thought of what my exquisite ring meant to me. Sam's gift, the one that was a replica of Princess Diana's — at least, as far as I knew, having never seen hers in person — the one he'd chosen himself. Another one could be made and purchased with insurance money, but it would never have the same significance as the original. Which was now in the grasping hands of a homegrown thief.

Lillian glanced around the room, then said, "I don't like thinkin' somebody been in here rootin' 'round in that jew'lry box. No tellin' what else they been up to."

"I don't like it either, Lillian." I closed the chest and put it back on the dressing table. "Oh, my," I said, whirling around and heading out of the room. "Other things could be gone, too."

We rushed across the hall to Lloyd's room, but it was as neat as he always left it. Or, rather, as neat as it always was when Lillian went behind him. All his electronic contraptions were right where they were supposed to be.

"No need to search in here," I said. "He only has that big watch he wears to school. Let's go back downstairs."

On our way to my bedroom, we scanned the dining room for evidence of further theft, even though I thought I would've noticed if anything had been missing there. I'd used the silver urn and trays for the party, and they were right where they should be, there on the sideboard. The silver candelabra were on the table, and the flatware was in the drawers of the breakfront.

Lillian said, "Guess they couldn't get any of this in they pocketbook."

We rushed back into my bedroom where I threw open the closet doors and reached up to the top shelf where I kept a row of pocketbooks. Taking down an old macramé one that I never used, I opened it and, with a sigh of relief, pulled out two velvet pouches. Untying them and dumping out the contents on the bed, I sagged down beside them.

"Look, Lillian, my diamond brooch is still here, thank the Lord, and so are my pearls. And here's my gold pin with the jade stone and the wedding rings from Mr. Springer, the only jewelry he ever gave me. He didn't believe in throwing money away on show. I wouldn't mind losing them, except the diamond solitaire was his mother's, and I thought Lloyd might want to have it reset for an engagement ring someday."

"Well," Lillian said, with satisfaction. "Least that thief didn't get everything in the house."

"It looks as if they took only what was easily accessible. And, Lillian, I think this proves that it wasn't your run-of-the-mill regular thief. I mean, like vandals or professionals. I know the house was empty yesterday afternoon, but it couldn't have been vandals because the house isn't torn up. And it couldn't have been professionals, because they would've taken all our televisions and computers and silver and everything else."

"Maybe they didn't have no truck to haul it off in."

"No, Lillian," I said, with a heavy sigh. "It had to be somebody we invited in."

"Don't say *we*. I don't invite nobody to yo' house, 'cept Latisha, an' she don't take nothin'."

"Oh, Lillian, of course not. I didn't mean to imply . . . No, I meant *we* in the sense of you and me together when we have a coffee or a dinner party." I gathered the jewelry up and put it all into the pouches, and then back into the pocketbook. After I stashed it up on the shelf, I turned to her. "What we have to do now is look over my guest list. I tell you, Lillian, I'm not going to stand for this. The more I think about it, the madder I get. Why in the world would a guest steal from me? Or from any of us, for that matter? They could never get away with wearing it. It'd be recognized in a minute. I mean, who else in town has anything like my ring? Or like Hazel Marie's things, either?"

"Maybe they sell it, an' take the money to buy something else," Lillian said. Then she studied on it for a minute. "I 'spect this mean yo' rings and Miss Hazel Marie's things be gone an' not lost under something or hidin' in a corner somewhere. So James can stay where he is."

"I guess so," I said with a sigh. "No need tearing up the house to look for something we know is gone."

She wrapped her arms around herself and shivered. "I don't wanta hope it one of yo' friends, but I don't like thinkin' somebody we don't know come in here an' take things, neither."

"It scares me, too, Lillian. But it makes me mad as fire to think that it's somebody we *do* know. I'll tell you one thing, I won't be fretting anymore about what to do while Sam's gone. Believe me, I am going to find out who accepted my invitation, and who then, with malice aforethought, planned ahead enough to bring an extra-large pocketbook so they could take advantage of my hospitality and rob me blind." I started out of the room. "Come on, Lillian, let's find that guest list."

CHAPTER 7

We shifted our chairs at the kitchen table, spread out the two pages of names and addresses between us, and began to scan them. Lillian shook her head and said, "I won't never b'lieve these ladies do such a thing, Miss Julia."

I propped my elbow on the table and leaned my head against my hand. "Me either, Lillian, but who else could it be?" I straightened up and turned the paper so I could read the names. "Nobody, that's who, because nobody else has been here. Now, look this over and see if anybody jumps out at you."

"Nobody gonna jump out at me. I been knowin' these ladies long as you have, an' none of 'em been thievin' far as I know."

"Well, that's just it. As far as we know. Maybe other people have missed things, and it just happened to be my turn this time."

"No'm, you hear 'bout it, if something

come up missin' in yo' friends' houses, 'cause they be tellin' everybody."

"You would think so. But maybe the thief has gotten away with it so long that she's going for the big stuff now. I don't know, Lillian. All I know is that the thought of one of my friends stealing anything is doing me in. And," I said, drawing the page closer, "there's not a person on here that I could possibly suspect. Yet it has to be one of them."

We canted our heads so we could both study the guest list. I moved my finger down the list, carefully considering one woman after the other. Each name brought to mind a face and a personality, and each name brought a shake of my head as I considered and discarded the possibility of that woman being a thief.

"Mildred Allen, no. Helen Stoud, certainly not. Opal Nixon, we've already passed on her. Margaret, no. Louise, Harriet, Tina. No, no, no. Lillian, there's just nobody here who would've done such a thing."

Lillian sat back and rubbed her face. "Maybe you just got to wait till something else happen, 'fore you know who it is."

"I'm not about to do that. Those rings, especially my engagement ring, mean the world to me, and I'm going to get them back if it's the last thing I do. And get them back before Sam comes home, too. I'm calling LuAnne."

Lillian reared back in her chair. "Not Miz Conover! You can't think she done it."

"No, no. Of course not. LuAnne, bless her heart, doesn't have as much as some of us, and she never lets us forget it. But she would never in this world take something that didn't belong to her. No, I'm calling her because I know she didn't do it. Besides, I want to get the word out that I'm going to find the thief, no matter who it is, if I have to turn this town inside out." I walked over to the telephone, picked it up, and prepared to dial. "I can count on LuAnne to tell everybody she knows. And some she doesn't."

I dialed and as soon as LuAnne heard my voice, she started in telling me how much she'd enjoyed the party and that she had just been getting ready to call me.

"If you'd waited a few minutes, Julia," she said, and I could almost see her wagging a finger at me, "I would've made my manners and called you first. Because I thought it was a lovely party."

"Thank you, LuAnne. I enjoyed having you, but that's not the reason I called. When you were here yesterday, did you notice anything unusual?"

"I sure did," she said, and my heart jumped. "That blouse Tina Doland had on was cut so low, I thought to myself she'd better not lean over or everything would fall out. Have you ever seen the like?"

"It was certainly inappropriate, but that's Tina for you. But listen, LuAnne, did you see anybody acting, well, unlike themselves?"

"No more than usual. Why? Oh, I know. Barbara Maddox was kinda out of it. Did you notice? I think she's on something, if you want to know the truth. She's been having a hard time lately, and I think the doctor has her on tranquilizers. Poor thing, she needs them, what with that houseful of children, and having to take in her mother-in-law on top of that. Why, Julia, she hardly got out of your Victorian chair the whole morning. Just sat there, resting, I guess. Wouldn't even go upstairs to see Hazel Marie's beautiful bedroom, even when I asked her to go with me."

"I guess that lets her out," I mumbled, drawing a line through Barbara's name on my guest list.

"What?"

"Oh, nothing. I'm just trying to make sure everything went well yesterday, and everybody had a good time." Then I was suddenly inspired on how to narrow my investigation.

"Actually, LuAnne, somebody left a, I don't know what you call it, a little cosmetic bag, I guess. You know, one that you carry in a large purse, and I don't know who it belongs to."

"Where was it?"

"In somebody's pocketbook, I guess."

"No, Julia. I mean, where did you find it?"

"Oh, well, in, uh, Hazel Marie's bathroom or mine, one. Lillian found it, and she just said in the bathroom." I flapped my hand at Lillian, who was shaking her head at me. "She said it was on the counter by the sink. I mean, on the floor by the wastebasket, like it had fallen off the counter by the sink."

"What was in it?"

"Well, uh, cosmetics," I said, trying to remember what Hazel Marie kept in hers. "Like, let me see, lipstick, a comb, a compact, things like that."

"What brand?"

"For goodness' sake, LuAnne. I don't know. What difference does it make?"

"Why, it makes plenty of difference. I know for a fact that Helen won't use anything but Estée Lauder, and Angie Wilmot goes all the way to Asheville for Bobbi Brown. It's a process of elimination, Julia. Look and see what brand those things are, and I'll bet you'll figure out who they belong to." She stopped for a minute, then said, "Or just wait till somebody calls and asks if you found her cosmetic bag."

"That's what I'll probably do," I said with some relief, since I didn't want to go into any more detail about something I knew so little about and which didn't exist anyway. "But I thought you might've seen somebody searching through a large pocketbook, you know, like they were looking for something they'd misplaced." I paused, inspired by another line of thought. "Who all had large pocketbooks, LuAnne? Did you notice?"

"Good grief, Julia, I'm not in the habit of measuring people's pocketbooks. But big bags're in style now, so a lot of people carry them. You know, totes and hoboes and things like that. Actually, I had to carry my brown hobo, and I know I'm too short for such a huge purse, but it's the only one I have that goes with the tweed suit I wore yesterday. But I didn't lose a cosmetic bag, because I don't have one. I just dump every-thing in the big one."

"Well, maybe I'm on the wrong track here. Just think back, LuAnne, did you see any-thing out of the ordinary when you were in my bedroom or Hazel Marie's?"

"You mean, in comparison? I noticed that

hers was a lot more *House Beautiful*–looking than yours, but that didn't surprise me. Why? Did I miss something?"

"No, but I did, or rather, I'm missing something now. LuAnne, I am just sick to have to tell you this, but some of my jewelry and all of Hazel Marie's have been stolen."

"What! And you think *I* know something about it!"

"No! No, I don't think that. I wouldn't be calling you if I thought that."

"No, I guess you wouldn't," she said, a sharp edge of sarcasm dripping in her voice. "You're just calling to talk about the party, aren't you? And to ask questions about what I know without telling me why." She took a deep breath. "Julia, you and I have been friends forever, but if you think I would steal from you or from anybody else, then this friendship is over!"

She slammed down the phone, leaving a buzzing noise in my ear.

"Well," I said, as I turned to Lillian, "that didn't go so well. Would you believe she thought I was accusing her?"

Lillian didn't say a word. She got up from the table and started scrubbing the counter. I continued to sit by the telephone, trying to decide how to repair a friendship that I had unwittingly broken.

The more I thought about it, though, the more I began to feel that it had not been my fault. LuAnne should've known that I would never suspect her. She should've understood that my call had been for help in finding the culprit, not to imply that *she* was the culprit.

"Lillian," I said, my mouth tight with a building anger, "she was too quick to take offense. Too quick to get off the phone, like she didn't want to talk about it. Do you think she might know something?"

"No'm," Lillian said, turning her back to me and busying herself at the sink. "I don't say nothin' 'bout yo' friends."

"Well, I don't want to say anything about them, either, so there's only one thing left to do."

She glanced over her shoulder at me. "I hate to ast, but what?"

"I'm calling Deputy, I mean Sergeant, Coleman Bates."

65

CHAPTER 8

As I reached for the phone, it rang. I barely got a hello out of my mouth before Mildred Allen started in.

"Julia!" she shrieked. "LuAnne just called me, and I've been robbed, too! What're we going to do?"

"Slow down, Mildred," I cautioned, even as I marveled at LuAnne's rapid information-delivery service. At the same time, a thrill of fear stabbed me at the thought of a thief rampaging not only in my home, but throughout the town. "I don't know what we can do, but believe me, it's going to be something."

"Oh, Julia, who's doing this?" Mildred wailed. "I am scared to death, just thinking about somebody coming into my house and taking all my beautiful things. I'll never get to sleep tonight. What if they come back?"

I hadn't thought of that, and it stopped me for a minute. "I think we're safe, Mildred. At least, I hope so. For one thing, I don't have much left to steal. What did they get from you?"

"My jewelry!" she wailed. "That's all they took, but every last piece is gone!" She had to stop as sobbing overwhelmed her. Then in a choked voice, she went on. "All my mother's pieces that I've added to over the years. Oh, Julia, you know what I had, and you know it's irreplaceable."

Jewelry, again, I thought. That ought to tell the police something.

"You have to report it, Mildred, just like I'm about to do. Have you called the police?"

"No," she sobbed. "But I've called my insurance agent. I've got pictures of everything. I hope you have, too."

That really stopped me, because I didn't. I wiped my forehead with my hand, regretting my lack of foresight. "I guess I don't. But Mildred, when were your things taken?"

"During your party! That's why I'm calling you. To let you know that your party provided a thief with the perfect opportunity to steal! Because that was the only time that nobody was home."

"Oh, no, Mildred, that couldn't be. Because I think my things were taken during the party, too. The thief couldn't be in two places at the same time. Besides, Ida Lee was there, wasn't she, and she'd know if anybody came in."

"The house was empty, Julia. Ida Lee went to the grocery store while I was gone. But how did they get in? Ida Lee said she had to unlock the door when she got back with the groceries." She didn't say anything more for a minute. Then, as if she'd just realized what I'd said, Mildred whispered, "You think somebody at the party stole from you? Somebody we know?"

Anxious to quash that line of thought now that I was thinking better of it, I said, "I did at first, but not any longer. I'm sorry I even considered it, because the theft at your house proves it had to be somebody who *wasn't* at the party."

"Who didn't you invite?"

"I only invited about twenty-five, so that leaves the rest of the town. But listen, it had to be somebody we don't know, maybe a robbery ring or something." At the mention of any kind of ring, my breath caught in my throat. "We've got to get off the phone and report this, Mildred. I'm calling Coleman right now."

I hadn't seen Coleman since Christmas Day, when he'd brought his little family by for a visit and an exchange of gifts. It had been

68

a pleasant afternoon, with Sam, Coleman, and Mr. Pickens commenting on the football games, Binkie and Hazel Marie discussing the highs and lows of motherhood, and Lloyd and Latisha playing with the baby. Things had certainly changed since Coleman had lived right here in my house, at my beck and call, on and off duty, day and night. But these days I generally saw him only when I needed police protection. Like now.

But when he walked into my kitchen, using the back door as he normally did, I had to catch my breath. He'd always been a handsome young man, looking somewhat like a blond Tom Cruise, only taller, but now there was an air of maturity and authority about him that only added to his manly attributes. His navy uniform with its badge and emblems, and the creaking leather attachments on it, didn't hurt, either. A man in uniform does something to a woman, don't you think?

I can't describe the relief I felt to have him in my house. He'd responded to my phone call in a matter of minutes, dropping whatever he'd been doing to come to my aid. Like I always say, it's not what you know, but who.

And not only had he come to my aid, but

another patrol car had pulled in behind his in my driveway. Lillian and I had watched as two officers jumped out of the car and began to circle the house.

"Y'all all right?" Coleman asked, as he ran into the kitchen, his eyes darting around. One hand rested on the gun at his waist. "Anybody still in the house?"

"No, we're fine," I said, somewhat taken aback by what I'd set in motion. "The danger is long past. We think the theft happened sometime yesterday, we're not sure when. I mean, we thought ours happened during the party, but since we now know somebody robbed Mildred Allen during the party, they couldn't have happened at the same time. Unless there were two of them. Or a whole band of thieves, which it could have been, especially if anybody else has been robbed, too."

Coleman let his hand fall away from his weapon, his whole posture visibly relaxing. "I thought you said a robbery was in progress."

"Well, it was. I mean, it is, because until we get our things back, it's certainly ongoing."

Coleman stared at me for a minute, then grinned at Lillian. "Hey, Lillian," he said, then turned back to the door. "Let me call off the dogs. I'll send them on over to Mrs. Allen's."

He went outside, letting a rush of cold air in as he left. Watching as he called to the officers who'd accompanied him, I could see white clouds of their breath float between them as they spoke together. When Coleman came back in, the second patrol car cranked up and left the premises.

"Okay," he said, hunching his shoulders under the thick nylon jacket he wore. "Let me get this straight." He pulled a spiral notebook from his pocket and clicked on a pen. "What's missing, and when do you think it happened?"

Lillian set a cup of coffee and a slice of chocolate cake before him, and he managed to take notes and eat at the same time. I told him everything we knew, including a detailed description of my precious rings and as much as I could remember about Hazel Marie's possessions. I also passed along what Mildred had told me about her devastating loss.

"All right," he said, pushing his plate away, "I think I've got it. You and Lillian were gone yesterday afternoon and early evening, and Mrs. Allen was over here yesterday morning at the same time Ida Lee was at the store. So both houses were empty at some point yesterday, when somebody could've gotten in." He glanced up at me. "Let's check the doors and windows."

"I checked them all last night," I said. "And every last room, too."

He smiled. "I'll just double-check."

Lillian and I followed him in and out of the rooms, watching as he looked over every window. He tried the latches, carefully checked the locks and hinges on the doors, and while Lillian and I waited, he even went up in the attic and down in the basement.

When he came back up the stairs and closed the basement door behind him, I asked, "Did you find anything? Oh, Coleman, what if somebody broke into the house while we were asleep?"

He shook his head. "I don't think you need to worry about that. Everything looks fine. No windows broken, no scratches on the doors. No, I hate to tell you this, Miss Julia, but it looks like a professional job."

"Well, can't you look for fingerprints or something? If you know they're professionals, you must have them on record somewhere."

He shook his head. "I'll send somebody out to do that, but they haven't left any evidence yet. There's been a string of robberies with an MO pretty much like this all over the Southeast. This crew or crews, we don't know how many there are, hit small towns and suburbs, low-crime areas where slick in-and-out operations aren't expected and don't get compared with reports from other towns. We're just beginning to see a pattern, now that we're trying to get some coordination going. Funny thing, though," he went on, "they've never hit a jewelry store, never held up a commercial place. So far, they've only targeted specific houses in one town or another and take only jewelry. Then they move on."

"Jewelry heists!" I said. "That's what they're doing. But how do they know who has something worth stealing? Or when people aren't home, and how do they get in without *breaking* in?"

"Lots of theories, like maybe they read the newspapers to see which homeowners have been written up or pictured wearing a lot of jewelry on a society page somewhere. And to see who's going to a big party or on a cruise or whatever."

"I would've never thought of that," I murmured, with a sinking feeling.

"And," he went on, "once you have names, it's no trouble to find addresses."

"Newspapers," I said. "Lillian, remember that picture of Hazel Marie in the paper right before Christmas? Coleman, she'd just been elected secretary of the Garden Club, and they had a picture of all the officers."

"Yessum," Lillian said, "an' Miz Allen in it, too. She y'all's new president."

"That's right! And oh my goodness, Coleman, Hazel Marie had on almost every piece of jewelry she owned. I tried to tell her a little goes a long way, but she was excited about having her picture in the paper." I stopped and rubbed my brow, struck by the realization that Hazel Marie had been the real target, and my rings were gone simply because I'd had a little arthritis and left them in a candy dish. "Of course, Mildred always wears too much."

Coleman nodded. "That could've been how they knew where to hit. But as far as how they get in, the only thing we can figure is that at least one of them is a master locksmith. Somebody who can pick a lock without leaving any evidence of a break-in." Coleman gave me a rueful smile. "If it's any comfort, you're in a pretty exclusive group. They know what they're looking for, and they know where to find it."

"That's not a bit of comfort," I said. "But why just jewelry? They passed up my silver and all kinds of things that could've been resold. Not that I'm complaining, but if I was going to steal, I think I'd do a better job of it."

He shrugged, then leaned his hand against the back of a chair. "Don't know, Miss Julia. But this thing is getting so big that a task force is being formed, so we'll know more as soon as they're up and running. The only reports we've gotten is that the focus is on Florida. Not sure why, because none of the stolen items have ever surfaced. Nobody's reselling them and, believe me, every pawn shop and jewelry store in a dozen states have been alerted."

"Well, my goodness," I said. "What will those thieves do with it, if they're not selling it? Who'd want to just sit and look at it and not wear it or get money for it?"

Coleman shook his head. "Beats me. But some of the DEA guys think that somebody in one of the drug cartels in Central America — maybe operating out of Miami or somewhere — may be buying it up to put aside for a rainy day. Maybe he's thinking ahead for when it gets too hot to stay in business. Jewelry, especially loose stones, is more portable than large amounts of cash."

"Well," I said, entirely unsympathetic to the financial problems of thieves, "I just want my rings back, and I don't want them going out of the country where I'll never see them again." I shuddered. "The idea of a drug cartel from South America or Miami sneaking around in my house is more than I can stand."

Coleman smiled. "Well, actually, the latest focus is on Palm Beach, which probably has the largest concentration of jewelry on the East Coast. Except none of it's missing, which might mean something. Anyway," he added, "that's one theory."

He started toward the door, then turned back. "Listen, I hate to be pessimistic, but I know you'd rather have the facts. We don't know who these people are. For all anybody knows, it's a few homegrown burglars who're just smart enough to fly under the radar and sell out of the country. It's all guesswork at this point, nothing more, and I'm as sorry as I can be about it." He gave me a sympathetic look, settled his hat on his head, and opened the door. "I better get back at it. We'll do what we can, Miss Julia, but I have to tell you that your rings and everything else are probably on their way to a Florida port where nobody'll ever find them."

"It looks to me that you'd be going after them if you know where they are." But I was thinking, *Florida.*

"It's just a theory," he said as he shook his head, "though a pretty strong one. Look,

76

I've got to get on over to Mrs. Allen's, then I'll be faxing reports to the task force. We're working on these guys, and we'll do the best we can to get your things back."

As he closed the door behind him, I looked at Lillian. "I don't think their best is going to be good enough, do you?"

CHAPTER 9

As I pondered all that Coleman had said and tried to overcome the sinking feeling in my insides, something hit me full force. "Loose stones!" I said. "Is that what he said? Oh, Lillian, they're going to break up my rings and just ruin them!"

"Now, Miss Julia," she said, taking my arm and leading me to a chair. "You can't be gettin' all upset an' makin' yo'self sick. I know that one ring mean a lot to you, but, like the Reverend Abernathy say, it jus' a *thing.* When you get to heaven, you won't even 'member it, you be so happy."

I wiped my eyes and looked up at her. "I know that, Lillian, and I know what's important. After all, we have our health, and we aren't going hungry or without a roof over our heads. I should be thankful for that, and not so torn up over being robbed right under my nose."

I jumped up from my chair. "I know that a

ring, no matter how dear it is, can't compare to eternal matters. But it makes me mad as fire for somebody to just take it — as if it belonged to them — and not suffer the consequences. And somebody, I don't care who it is, is going to suffer a few consequences, if I have anything to do with it. I am not going to take this lying down, Lillian, and I'm not going to sit around and hope some task force will get it back for me." I stomped over to the counter and whirled around to face her. "You heard Coleman. He wasn't a bit surprised that we'd been robbed. You heard him say that these jewelry heists have been going on in other places, and tell me this, just what're the authorities doing about it? Not one thing, that's what. And while they're waiting to get organized, my rings and Hazel Marie's investments and Mildred's mother's things are on their way to some drug-runner's pocket."

Then, with fresh determination, I headed for the telephone. "I'm calling Mr. Pickens, just in case he didn't go with Hazel Marie."

But Mr. Pickens was nowhere to be found, just as I suspected. Machines at both his home and his office told me that he would be unavailable for another week, which was when we expected Hazel Marie to be back. No surprise, but it didn't hurt to be sure.

I paced back and forth between the counter and the table, about two steps one way and two steps the other. Wringing my hands, I asked, "Who do we know in Florida?"

"Mr. Pickens got a friend what live down there. You know, that man he used to meet in Atlanta havin' some kind of problem, but I don't know him and nobody else do, either."

I stopped in midstep. "That's right! And he's a private investigator, too, and if he's half as good as Mr. Pickens, I could have my rings back in no time." I started toward the telephone. "What's his name, Lillian?"

"How I s'posed to know his name? I never hear no name. All I ever hear was Mr. Pickens's friend, an' that's all I know."

"Well, I don't know any more than that, either." I let my hand fall away from the phone, overcome again with despair. "I guess I could call every investigator in Florida and see if they know Mr. Pickens, but by that time my rings could be in the drug-infested jungles of Central America."

"Maybe Lloyd know his name."

"Mr. Frank Tuttle," Lloyd said. I'd sprung the question on him as soon as he got in the door. "And he lives in West Palm Beach." He let the heavy bookbag fall from his shoulder to the floor, then shrugged out of his coat. "Why?"

"I think we have need of him," I said, thinking, *Palm Beach, just where Coleman said.* Then I proceeded to tell Lloyd of our heartrending losses. "Your mother is going to be so torn up over this, she may never get over it. I want to put a recovery operation in motion right away so she'll know we're trying. It's a settled fact that the authorities aren't doing anything."

Lloyd's eyes grew big behind his thick glasses, as he took in the fact that we'd been robbed. "A thief in the night? Right here in our house? I better find my baseball bat."

"No need for that, Lloyd," I said, hoping he wouldn't look for it too hard. "Coleman thinks they picked our locks and came in while we were at the mall yesterday," I said with a surge of anger, "and did it without leaving a smidgeon of evidence behind."

"Wow," he said, pushing his glasses up on his nose. "Pretty slick operation, if you ask me."

"Well, let's don't compliment them. They're evil and ought to be strung up for taking what doesn't belong to them." I took a deep breath. "I'm going to call that Mr. Tuttle and see if he knows anything about anybody collecting a pile of jewelry in case the banks fail or the bottom drops out."

A sudden gust of wind off the mountains to the west of us rattled the window at my back. I looked out at the slate-colored sky, wondering if we were in for worse weather.

"It looks like snow out there. What's the temperature, Lillian?"

"Droppin' like a rock," she said, peering out the fogged-up window at the thermometer. "If that wind die down, we pro'bly get some snow. 'Less it get too cold, which it already feel like."

"Well, I'm not going to worry about that right now. The thing to do is track down Mr. Tuttle and get him on the job. Lloyd," I said, turning to him, "are you sure he lives in West Palm Beach? Or is it Palm Beach, and what's the difference, anyway?"

"Two different cities," he said. "Right across the Intracoastal Waterway from each other. One kinda runs into the other when you cross a bridge. I think, since I've never been there."

"Then the thing to do is call Information and track him down. Do you mind doing that for me, Lloyd? I am so jittery, I probably wouldn't make sense."

So he did, and quite efficiently, too. I watched as he dialed, gave the name, and, after a brief conversation with the operator, wrote down a number on a pad. His little shoulder blades poked through the flannel shirt he was wearing, and I noticed that he seemed to have grown another inch or two. Lord, he wouldn't be a little boy too much longer.

"I got it, Miss Julia," he said, hanging up the phone. "It was under Tuttle Investigations. You want me to call him?"

"I better do that, honey. I want to be sure and impress on him the urgency of the matter."

I took the phone and a deep breath, readying myself to speak clearly and concisely, giving all the details, so as to engage Mr. Tuttle in my employ.

I dialed the number Lloyd had written down — long distance, too, down in West Palm Beach, Florida — with only a bit of hesitation about what it would cost me.

The phone rang six times before a cool, professional voice answered. "Tuttle Investigations. How may I help you?"

"Mr. Frank Tuttle, please."

"He's not available," she said. "Please leave your name and number."

"Please tell him that Mrs. Julia Murdoch from Abbotsville, North Carolina, is on the line, and needs to speak with him on an urgent matter."

She didn't change her tune one whit. I could've been telling her the laundry had his shirts ready. "Please leave your name and number, and he'll return your call."

"Well, would you just tap on his door and tell him I'm on the line? I know he won't want to miss this call."

Lloyd stood beside me, his hands itching to take the phone, while Lillian frowned and shook her head. They knew I was having no success.

"I'm sorry," the woman said. "Please leave your name and number, and he'll . . ."

I'd had enough of cool professionalism by this time. "Now, listen, young lady. I want you to get up out of that chair and go into his office. Tell him that Mrs. Julia Springer Murdoch needs to speak with him. Tell him . . . hello? Miss? Hello?" I jiggled the receiver hook and stepped back in surprise when I got a dial tone.

"Why, that little snip hung up on me! Just hung up in my face." I put the phone down, so done in by the rudeness of a perfect stranger that I could hardly get my breath.

Lillian said, "Maybe if some people act nice in the first place, other people be nice back to 'em."

Lloyd gave her a quick grin, then wiped it away. "Still," he said, "that's no way to run a business."

Lillian nodded her head in agreement. "So what you gonna do now?"

"I don't know. I've got to think about it. One good thing, though, if Mr. Tuttle is too busy to take my call, that means he's in demand. Which means he's good at what he does." I reached over and smoothed down Lloyd's hair, which was waving around from static electricity. "We might as well eat supper, Lillian. I'll call back in a little while, though his office'll probably be closed then. But maybe a machine will answer instead of that discourteous woman."

"I hope he can do us some good," Lloyd said, a worried frown on his face. "I hate to think of somebody else wearing my mama's pretty things. It's just not right."

Since Latisha was spending the night with a friend, Lillian lingered, and I set a place for her at the table. We all picked at our food. Then the three of us sat in silence for a while over the littered table, not knowing what to do next and, speaking for myself, getting more frustrated by the minute. I declare, I hate to delegate duties to other people and then have nothing to do but worry about them getting done.

"Government authorities," I suddenly announced to Lillian's surprise and Lloyd's elevated brows, "like the police and sheriff's deputies and state task-force officers, are all well and good. But it's private enterprise that knows how to get things done. Speed, efficiency, and cost-effectiveness are the attributes of the private sector, and don't you forget that, Lloyd."

"No'm, I won't."

"Well," Lillian said, pushing herself up and beginning to stack the plates. "I don't know nothin' about that, but settin' here's not clearin' this table off."

"I'll help you," Lloyd said, sounding quiet and subdued. He picked up his silverware and mine, and carried them to the counter.

I just sat there, going over and over some possibilities that had been jostling around in my mind.

Later, after Lillian had left and Lloyd had finished his homework, I went upstairs to tell him good night.

Tapping on his door, I looked in, struck again by how much the boy favored his father. His sandy hair, slight build, and bespectacled face came directly from Wesley Lloyd Springer, a fact that I had to constantly shove aside. Easy enough to do most of the time, since the child's inner qualities more than made up for the physical resemblance. Besides, there was still a chance he'd grow out of it.

"Time for bed, honey," I said. "And try to sleep. All is not lost because we haven't been able to reach Mr. Tuttle. I called again a few minutes ago and couldn't get through. But I'll try again in the morning and all day long, if I have to."

"I don't think I can sleep. I'm just worried to death about somebody robbing us." He looked like a little old man, sitting on the bed in his pajamas and bathrobe, wringing his hands. "I'll probably dream about it all night long."

"I know how you feel. But we have to try, if for no other reason than to be ready for whatever tomorrow might bring. Besides," I said, somewhat hesitant to let him in on what had been building in my mind in case it didn't work out, "I may have a plan for tomorrow, and I may need you to help me pull it off."

"What is it?" He lifted his head, eager to hear what I'd decided to do. The child placed so much trust in me it would've scared me, if I hadn't always been able to come through for him in the past.

"I still need to work it out," I told him, "and since it may not even be possible, let me think about it a little more. I don't want to get your hopes up if it can't be done."

He heaved a long sigh. "I just hate for Mama to come home and find out she's been robbed. I want to get her things back before she gets back."

"I do, too. Now, say your prayers, and try to get some sleep." I turned off the overhead light, leaving a lamp still burning.

Going back downstairs, I was sure I wouldn't sleep a wink, what with thoughts of strange people marauding through my house and with the seeds of a plan to bring them to justice fermenting in my mind. I went to bed only as a matter of habit, positioning Lloyd's baseball bat near to hand — which was like locking the barn door after the cows were gone — and figuring I'd lie there in a quandary all night long.

I figured wrong, because I woke at six o'clock, feeling both rested and ready for action. A good thing, too, because sometime in the night my mind had been made up.

CHAPTER 10

I had half a mind to keep Lloyd home the next morning, since you can't get much education when you're worried about break-ins and robberies and evil men creeping around. But I went on and sent him, because he might be missing school for another reason real soon, and I wanted him to get in all the attendance he could while the getting was good.

"Lillian," I said as I marched myself to the telephone. "It's nine o'clock, and I'm going to give Mr. Tuttle one more chance. And if that woman gives me a hard time, I'm . . . well, I don't know what I'll do."

It is the most frustrating thing in the world not to be able to count on people to do what they ought to be doing.

And yes, sure enough, Mr. Tuttle was not in his office and the woman didn't know when he'd be in, and no, he had not called in for his messages. Which meant he did not even know that he'd had an urgent call from Mrs. Julia Murdoch, even if I'd left a number where I could be reached.

"Lillian," I said as I hung up, "something's got to be done, and nobody's doing it. So there's only one thing to do."

She rubbed her forehead as if she had a headache coming on. "I hate to ast, but what?"

I drew myself up straight, firming up my resolve at the same time. "I'm going down there."

Lillian's mouth dropped open. "No, you not."

"Just watch me. I'm through depending on other people to do their jobs and being disappointed every time I turn around. Besides, you have to strike while the iron is hot, which is right now — before the trail gets cold."

"What Mr. Sam gonna say, you go off down there by yo'self an' get in all kinda trouble?"

"I don't intend to get into any trouble, and what Mr. Sam doesn't know won't hurt him. Besides, he's not here to give an opinion one way or another. I need to get down there and locate Mr. Tuttle if I have to scour the city. Then I'll make him an offer he can't refuse, and dog him every step of the way until he locates my rings. And Hazel Marie's things, too. And Mildred's, too, if we have time."

"You don't even know they in Florida," she said, glaring at me. "What if they in Detroit or New York somewhere? You can't go flying off one way when they might be somewhere else."

"First of all, I don't intend to fly. And second, I have to start somewhere, and if Coleman thinks it's Florida, then that's where I'm starting."

Lillian stood and watched me, trying to hold her tongue as she considered everything I'd said. Then she said, "If you bound an' determined, which look like you are, then I'm goin' with you."

"No," I said, "I've thought this out, and I need you here in case Sam or Hazel Marie calls. I'd appreciate it if you and Latisha would stay overnight while we're gone, so you can take their calls. It would scare them to death if they couldn't get an answer."

"What I gonna tell 'em? That you off down yonder, lookin' 'round for thieves? What you think they gonna do then?"

"No, don't tell them that. Tell them I'm indisposed or I have company or maybe I'm at a meeting over at the church. We'll call you every day or so, then I'll call them back if I need to."

"We!" she yelled. "If I can't go, who this *we* you talkin' about?"

"I'm taking Lloyd with me."

"Lordamercy, you can't do that. What about school? What about draggin' that child all over that place, runnin' into jew'l robbers an' cat burglars an' all like that?"

"Now, listen, Lillian," I said. "It's not safe for a woman to be traveling alone, so . . ."

"What you think that chile do, somebody try to get you?" Her voice went right up the scale.

"He'll be company, and who else would you suggest I take? Coleman can't go and neither can Binkie, what with the baby and her law practice, and can't you just picture the help LuAnne would be? And with Sam and Hazel Marie gone, Lloyd is the logical one. Besides," I said, "he's smart and helpful, and he can read a map."

"Lemme get this straight. You plannin' to drive that car down the mountain and I don't know how far to Florida just to track down that Mr. Tuttle when you can't even get him on the telephone, then you plannin' to make him track down them jew'l thieves when none of them police down there been able to, an' you gonna be draggin' that little boy 'long with you while you doin' it?"

Put like that, I had to think it over again,

although I'd done a world's plenty already. I had agonized over exposing Lloyd to the perils of such a trip, but the truth of the matter was, he was safer with me than with anybody else.

So I firmed up my resolve and said, "That's exactly what I'm going to do. Help me get his things packed, Lillian, because the sooner we leave, the better. I don't want the trail to get cold."

"Speakin' of gettin' cold," she said, "you looked out the window lately? They's flurries out there, an' you tellin' me you plannin' to drive on them slick highways when you won't even go to the grocery store when it snowin'?"

I went to the window and looked out. Snow was swirling around in the air and beginning to stick on the grass and along the curbs, but the street was still clear.

I thought about it for a minute, then headed for the phone book. "All I have to worry about," I said, "is getting out of town and down the mountain. We'll be going south, so we'll outrun any accumulation."

I dialed a number and asked for Ralph Peterson, the salesman I'd bought my little car from. I told him what I wanted: the biggest, heaviest car he had, with every up-to-date feature and accessory known to man, including the latest gadgets: like a cup-holder for coffee to keep me awake, a seat warmer for the obvious reason, fancy headlights, and tires that wouldn't slip on ice and snow.

"That'd be your 700 series," he said, "and I've got one that'll fill the bill. Got a limited-slip differential, too, which'll get you anywhere you want to go."

"Just do whatever you have to do — tags, papers, gas, and so on. I want it ready to go, and I want all the maps you can find of the southern states. Detailed ones, too."

"Oh, I'll fix it up for you, you know I will. Now, Miss Julia, how you want to finance this?"

"With a check," I told him. "I want it parked in my driveway within the hour and ready for a long trip. If you can't do it, tell me now and I'll find someone who can."

"I can do it, don't you worry about that. Now, one more question, you want to trade in your present car?"

"Of course not, Ralph. I like that car, but I'm in urgent need of a bigger one with this weather. Oh, and, Ralph," I went on, "you'd better have someone follow you to take you back. I'm not going to have time to do it."

"Yes, ma'am," he said. "I'll be right there, and I'll have just what you want. Don't you worry about a thing."

I heard the frantic shuffling of papers on his desk before I hung up.

Hurrying to the hall closet where my summer clothes were stored, I tried to decide what I should pack for the trip. It'd been years since I'd been to the Sunshine State, and never in the dead of winter with snow piling up on the streets at home. That's when a Florida trip is normally taken, but Wesley Lloyd had always had his two weeks in August, and far be it from him to change his routine. So our one trip to SeaWorld and the wax museum at St. Augustine in the heat of summer hadn't put him in mind to make a repeat visit.

I knew my winter woolens would be too hot where we were going, so I compromised by selecting some long-sleeved cottons and crepes and a few sweaters, with a raincoat to layer over them in case of a cold snap. I didn't intend to be staying long, so my packing went quickly. If I needed something more or different, I could purchase it there.

Pulling out another suitcase for Lloyd's things, I took it upstairs to his room. As I opened his closet, the doorbell rang downstairs, and I heard Lillian's flapping footsteps as she went to answer it.

"Miss Julia," she called from the foot of the stairs, "you got comp'ny."

Pleased that Ralph had my new car ready so fast, I hurried down the stairs. But it wasn't Ralph standing in the living room. It was Etta Mae Wiggins in the white nylon pantsuit that her job as a Handy Home Helper called for, giving her padded nylon coat to Lillian.

"Look who come to visit," Lillian said as I entered the room. "Miss Etta Mae, you need warmin' up. I know you 'bout to freeze."

"No'm, I'm all right, thank you all the same." She turned to me as I extended my hand in a welcoming gesture that I had to force myself to make. "I hope you don't mind me dropping in like this, but Mr. Cal Owens asked me to give this to you."

As I accepted the small envelope she held out, Miss Wiggins went right on. "He's one of my shut-ins? You know, that I look in on every week? And today he was so worried about falling behind on his pledge to the church, and he said since you're always there, he'd like for you to put it in the collection plate for him." She smiled at me. "If you don't mind."

It was all I could do not to stare at her heavily lined eyes, but I did my best. "Of course I don't mind. I'll put it in the very next time I'm at church." I was careful not to say that the very next time might be a while com-

96

ing. Then, hoping to usher her on her way, I said, "It's kind of you to do this for him. I'm sure you're quite busy without having to go out of your way on extra errands."

"Oh, it wasn't out of my way," she said. "I've been wanting to tell you that I haven't had any more problems at the trailer park. Everybody's paying their rent on time, and I get it right to Binkie."

I nodded, pleased that in spite of my reluctance to make Miss Wiggins the manager of the Hillandale Trailer Park, where she lived in a single-wide, she was working out quite well. The trailer park was one of the less salubrious of Wesley Lloyd's investments and, after some rowdy incidents out there, Hazel Marie had recommended her friend as someone who could straighten things out. And she had, I had to admit.

"And you know what?" Miss Wiggins went on. "I haven't had to call the police on anybody in over six months. But I also wanted to see if you'd heard from Hazel Marie. I'm just thrilled that she won that trip. One of these days I'm going to Disney World. That's my dream vacation."

"Hazel Marie's having a wonderful time," I said, thinking to myself that she ought to be enjoying herself, what with Mr. Pickens so close at hand. "And I'm fully aware of all you're doing at the trailer park. Binkie keeps me up-to-date, and we both appreciate the good job you're doing."

Lillian, who'd always had a soft spot for Miss Wiggins, suddenly chimed in. "It cold in here, like I been tellin' you goin' on five years now. Y'all ought to come on out to the kitchen where it's warm. You can do yo' visitin' in there."

So of course I had to follow through, once Lillian had extended the invitation. "I know you have to be on your way, Miss Wiggins, but let us offer you a hot drink before you go."

I motioned her to follow Lillian, which she did, but somewhat hesitantly, I thought. She'd never seemed comfortable in my house, the few times she'd visited. Or maybe it was me she wasn't at ease with, which made sense since I wasn't too comfortable around her. I never knew what to call her, for one thing, aware as I was of her checkered marital history, which had resulted in several name changes. But she'd been introduced by Hazel Marie as Wiggins, which I knew was her maiden name, and I guess I admired her for taking back a name that was well-known in Abbot County for less-than-stellar accomplishments by those who had been born with it. If it'd been me,

I think I'd have stuck with one of the husbands' names just to cut myself off from that family. But maybe she was proud of it or, more likely, the husbands' names weren't any better.

"Have you had lunch, Miss Wiggins?" I asked as we sat at the table near a heat vent.

"No'm, but I don't want to put you out any. I had to come over from Delmont to pick up a wheelchair and a bedpan from the hospital supply place, so I just thought I'd drop off Mr. Owens's pledge since I had to be here anyway."

"We're glad you did," I said, noting one more time that good manners require a good deal of falsification. I had things to do and not much time to do them in, and the last thing I needed was a visit from someone I wasn't too thrilled to see in the best of circumstances. Still, she was Hazel Marie's friend and, as I thought about it, maybe the only close one Hazel Marie had. Except me, of course, and Lillian and Mr. Pickens, but I'd hardly count him as just a friend.

Let's put it this way: Miss Wiggins was the only friend Hazel Marie had from her past life, and I could hardly begrudge her of that. Still, I wanted Hazel Marie to put that life behind her and, with my help, build a new one based on socially acceptable friends and decent living.

But far be it from me to criticize.

"Well," I said, "I need a bowl of soup or something. Surely you'll have one, too?"

"That'd be real nice, thank you. I didn't mean to come right at lunchtime, but it was the only time I had. We're awful busy now, seeing to all the shut-ins we have. Flu season, you know. Then I had to stop and put another quart of oil in my car. It just drinks that stuff, and smoke just boils out the back end every time I drive it. Which," she said with a laugh, "is about all the time, what with my work and all."

The woman was ill at ease, I could tell, and probably would've preferred not to eat with us. Eating gracefully in front of others is a mark of good breeding, but I've found that the harder you try to do it politely, the more likely you are to spill something on yourself. I gave her credit for accepting my invitation when she'd probably rather have had a Hardee's hamburger.

Lillian placed bowls of her thick, home-made soup on the table, properly served on plates with linen napkins and place settings beside them. She put a basket of hot corn muffins between us and glasses of milk and water next to our plates.

"Would you like a muffin, Miss Wiggins?" I asked.

"Don't mind if I do, but Mrs. Springer, I mean, Murdoch, you can call me Etta Mae. That's what everybody calls me." She took a muffin and began crumbling it into her soup. I didn't say anything, of course, even though I'd had to break Lloyd of that unsightly habit.

I mentally shrugged and crumbled my muffin, too. It's strange that in order to have good manners, you have to occasionally engage in some bad ones.

"Thank you, I'll do that, and you may call me Julia."

We ate as silently as soup would allow, as I wracked my brain to think of something to talk about. Miss Wiggins and I had little in common under normal circumstances, and as my mind was taken up with preparations for our trip, I couldn't think of a thing to say.

Lillian, apparently deciding that we needed some help, walked over to the table and proceeded to lay out our current situation. My sharply withdrawn breath didn't do a thing to stop her.

"Miss Etta Mae," she said, "did you know we been robbed? And so has Miz Allen an' no tellin' who else. It been awful 'round here ever since we found out about it, an' Miss Julia, she goin' down to Florida to get her things back, an' Miss Hazel Marie's, too."

Etta Mae Wiggins's eyes got bigger as she listened to Lillian, then she turned them on me. "Really? Did somebody break in? Were you here? That is just awful."

So there was nothing for it but to tell her all the details, including what I planned to do.

"Well, shoot, Miss Julia," she said, laying her soup spoon on her place mat. Then she quickly picked it up after glancing at my spoon and put it on the service plate. I like a quick study, don't you? "I don't blame you for going after them. That's what I'd do. You can't just let people walk in and take whatever they want." Then she leaned across the table, her eyes sparkling. "I could go with you. I mean, if you want me to. I can get somebody to fill in for me at work."

I was touched. I knew the woman didn't have a nickel to her name and had to work to keep herself alive. Which just brought to mind all the women in the same situation who'd made poor choices in husbands. I'd had a husband I wouldn't wish on my worst enemy, but at least I'd picked one who'd known how to make money and leave a sizable amount behind. And don't tell me that love is more important than a healthy bank account: It didn't apply in Miss Wiggins's case because she'd divorced two, leaving her with neither love nor money.

"Thank you," I said, "but there's no need for that. You have your work, and there's no telling how long we'll be gone. But I appreciate the offer."

"Well," she said, dampening her enthusiasm, "I'm here if you need me. What time does your plane leave?"

"Uh-huh, see there," Lillian chimed in with a glare at me. "I been meanin' to tell you myself. If you got to go, you ought to be flyin' an' not do no drivin' in this weather."

"If it's dangerous to drive in this weather, it's doubly so to fly. Besides, I don't like flying and I'm not going to do any of it."

"I've never been on an airplane," Miss Wiggins said, somewhat wistfully, as if there were a lot of things she'd missed out on, although for my money, missing a ride on an airplane wasn't worth mourning over. "Well," she went on, "except one of those little ones at an air show one time."

"We'll need a car when we get there," I said, hoping to settle the matter. "And it's easier to take my own."

"You can rent them cars," Lillian said. "An' not have to go an' buy one like you doin'. You gonna get awful tired, I don't care how good that new car ride."

"We'll stop along the way. Now, Lillian, stop worrying me with it. I'm not going to fly and that's that."

"You jus' scared," she said, "an' won't own up to it."

"All right, I admit it," I said, hoping to end the discussion. Miss Wiggins ducked her head and smiled as I pretended not to notice. "We'd better get Lloyd packed, Lillian. Be sure and put in a few sweaters. It's supposed to be hot down there, but you never know."

"Yessum, I will. I got a load of underwear in the dryer that's about done, so I'll jus' go on up and get him packed. What else 'sides clothes you want me to put in?"

I thought for a minute, trying to anticipate what we'd need. "Something to entertain him on the trip — books, his Game Boy, whatever else you think. He'll have his schoolbooks because I intend to pick him up from school and leave from there."

"You not gonna bring him home first? How I gonna say bye, if you do that?"

"Lillian, we can't linger. It gets dark by four and, with the road conditions, we need to get on down the mountain. I'll tell him good-bye for you."

She didn't like it, but I couldn't help that.

Miss Wiggins looked out the window, then turned to me with a frown on her pretty face. That short, tightly curled blond head of hair of hers made her look like one of those angels on a Christmas card — in certain lights. And if you discounted the blue eye shadow. "Miss Julia," she said, "it looks real threatening out there. You think you ought to try it today?"

"That's what I been tryin' to tell her," Lillian said.

"We might not be able to get out at all tomorrow," I pointed out, laying my napkin beside my plate. "It's either do it this afternoon or not do it at all. Now, listen, you two, I don't want any more arguments about the weather, my driving capabilities, Lloyd's schooling, or anything else. Our property is in the possession of thieves, and I am not going to just sit around and let them keep it. Or Hazel Marie's things, either."

CHAPTER 11

Frowning and mumbling, Lillian went into the laundry room to take Lloyd's underwear out of the dryer. I knew as well as I was sitting there that she'd tell Sam on me if she had any way to get in touch with him. Not that he could've stopped me, being a few thousand miles away, but I was tired of having to defend my decisions to all and sundry.

After slamming the door of the dryer, Lillian took herself up the stairs. But not before giving me another baleful stare on her way.

"Lord, Miss Julia," Miss Wiggins said, "Hazel Marie sure is lucky to have a friend like you. I don't know of anybody who'd go to bat for me like you're doing for her, except maybe my Granny if she could remember what day it is. I mean, I know you want your rings back and all, but you intend to get her things back, too. That's real unselfish of you."

I twisted my mouth, not at all sure that I would have been that determined to go after the thieves if they'd taken only Hazel Marie's jewelry. But they hadn't, so I stopped thinking about it.

"I just try to do what's right," I modestly assured Miss Wiggins, noting the shining admiration in her eyes.

It pleased me to have my efforts on behalf of someone else recognized and praised, although I know we're not supposed to make those efforts for that reason. And I did have a twinge of pity for the woman, knowing as I did what it was like to have no one who'd go the extra mile for you, especially when Wesley Lloyd was among the living. His view had been that if you get yourself in trouble, you have no one to blame but yourself and it's up to you to get yourself out of it: Don't ask him for help.

I thought of Sam and felt a rush of warmth. He'd go as far as needed for me. At least, I thought he would. But whether he'd go to Florida for me, well, that was another matter. Too bad that this young woman had to face the world and all its troubles alone. I hoped someday somebody would come along for her, as Sam had for me. Or, barring that, she'd learn not to miss him if he didn't.

"Miss Julia," Lillian called from the hall upstairs. "I see that new car pullin' in. You want me to go see about it or finish up what I'm doin'?"

I rose from the table and called back, "Finish up there, Lillian, please. I'll see about the car. Miss Wiggins, uh, Etta Mae, why don't you put on your coat and come help me learn to drive that machine out there."

Miss Wiggins jumped up from the table, an eager smile on her face. "I'd love to. And if there's anything else I can do, just let me know."

"There just might be. I'd appreciate it if you'd check in with Lillian every now and then. Just to be sure she's all right and see if she needs anything. But don't tell her I asked you to. I'll be calling in every day or so to see if she's heard from Mr. Murdoch or Hazel Marie, because, see, I don't want them to know where I am or what I'm doing."

She cut her eyes at me as a conspiratorial smile lifted the corners of her mouth. "I get it. You don't want anybody telling you you can't do something, right? Don't worry, I'll be happy to come by every so often. And if you want me to, I can even stay here with her."

"Well," I hedged, not knowing if, from all I'd heard of her social activities, I wanted her

108

sleeping in one of my beds. Which was probably a prejudgment, but there it was. "Let's wait and see about that. I'll tell Lillian to call you if she gets scared at night, or if anything untoward happens, like more prowlers around the house. If anything like that happens, get in touch with Sergeant Coleman Bates at the sheriff's department."

"Yes, ma'am, I will. That won't be a problem at all. I know another deputy I could call on, too."

"That could be quite helpful," I said, "if the need arises." I, however, was not at all sure of the kind of deputy knowledge she had. "Now, let's go see how well I can manage that car."

I put my money-market checkbook in my coat pocket and opened the front door. Clouds hung low and threatening over the town, making the early afternoon feel like dusk. Cold seeped inside my coat as I walked, with Miss Wiggins close behind, toward the long black car waiting in my driveway.

The snow seemed to have stopped, but the wind, filled with specks of ice, stung our faces. We hurried to the car and Ralph Peterson, who was standing beside it grinning and shivering in a plaid sports jacket.

"Ralph," I said, as the wind whipped the words out of my mouth, "you better get back in the car. You're going to freeze in that light coat."

"Jus' holdin' the door for you, little lady," he said. I shot him a look that should've shriveled him, but didn't. He waved me into the driver's seat with a flourish of his hand.

"You get in, too, Etta Mae," I said, as I slid under the wheel. "I'll need help remembering everything."

Ralph opened the back door for her, then ran around and got into the front seat beside me. For the next several minutes, he showed me more than I ever wanted to know about the operating of what he called the best-engineered automobile on the road. I withheld judgment until the car proved itself.

As Ralph rattled on and on, my head began whirling with unattached information concerning antislip devices and differentials; front-, side-, and backseat airbags; navigation system; seat-position memory; panic buttons; electronic stabilizers; net torque; and zero to sixty, though who would want it, I didn't know.

"I just need to know where the lights, windshield wipers, and horn are," I said, about fed up with a useless sales talk, since I had as good as bought the vehicle already.

"Well," Ralph said, leaning over so that I got a big whiff of his cologne, "here's where you turn on your xenon lights. Just leave 'em on automatic, and this here's your wiper control. You got your high and your low and your intermittent. See, like this. Now, right here, if you want to . . ."

"Please, no more," I said, holding up my hand. "My head's already spinning. Let me drive it around the block and get the feel of it."

"Right. We can do that." Ralph smiled down at me. "Have to take care of our special customers, don't we? Now, just turn the ignition, don't pump the gas, and . . ."

"You're making me nervous, Ralph," I said, about ready to smack him for patronizing me and assuming I liked it. "So give me the bill and I'll let you get on back to work."

He whipped out a handful of papers that I had to sign from one end to the other. Then, pointing at an astronomical figure at the bottom of one of them, he said, "Make it out to Abbotsville Motors, and you'll be all set. I'm puttin' your temporary registration and insurance card inside the front cover of the manual. You'll need 'em in case you get pulled for speedin'. Ha-ha, just kidding."

I wrote out the check, covering my balance from curious eyes as I recorded the amount. I knew it'd be all over town as soon as Ralph got back to the showroom that Julia Murdoch had written a check for the full amount without turning a hair.

Well, let them talk.

I held out the check, but didn't turn it loose when he reached for it. "Now, Ralph, I want your word that this car is ready to go in all its particulars. I don't want to get ten miles down the road and discover it needs gas or oil or air in the tires or the tag falls off or warning lights come on all across the dashboard."

"No, ma'am, nothin' like that's gonna happen. Why, I'd drive this car just the way it is from here to anywhere you want to name. It's in top-notch condition, guaranteed."

"I hope so. But give me your home number just in case. If this car's as good as you say it is, you won't need to worry about being called in the middle of the night."

He gave me a sideways look, but he wrote his home number on the back of a card and stuck it in the manual. Miss Wiggins was leaning over the console, grinning at the details of our transaction.

"Thank you very much," I said. "I believe that concludes our business, and I appreciate all you've done. Now, if you'll get on out and let Miss Wiggins take the front seat, I'll try this thing out."

"I'll wait for you," he said. "See if you have any questions."

"No need for that. Your ride's already here, so you can go on back to work. If anything goes wrong, I'll let you know. So don't deposit that check."

He got out, looking none too happy about being dismissed, and Miss Wiggins got in beside me. Bouncing a little, as she did so.

I turned the electronic key in the ignition and started to do it again, since the motor was so quiet I didn't think it had caught.

"Better not crank it again, Miss Julia," Miss Wiggins said. "You'll grind the motor."

"Oh. Well, is Ralph out of the way? I don't want to clip him when I back out. Although he ought to have enough sense to stay out of the way."

"Back on out," Miss Wiggins said, twisting around to look out the back window. "You're clear. Wait, hold it. There's a pickup coming."

"Have you ever driven one of these, Etta Mae?"

"No'm, not this kind. But I've driven some pretty much like it. American-made, mostly, that some of my patients have. They like to get out now and then, and want me to take them in their big cars. More comfortable than mine."

113

As I backed into the street, I glanced at her gray, oil-burning, old car, splotched with rust, parked at the curb. I had a twinge of guilt for paying so much for what I was sitting in, when the same amount of money would've bought two smaller cars, one for her and one for me, brand-new and probably just as good. Though not as comfortable.

But if you think too much along those lines, you could find yourself ending up a Communist or something. Or maybe a Christian, but I had too much on my mind to follow thoughts like that.

When I'd first walked out and seen this new car, it looked to be as wide as a truck and as heavy as a tank. But it drove as easily as my smaller car, especially after I learned that I didn't need to swing wide when I turned a corner. Miss Wiggins proved to be invaluable help. She remembered every bit of Ralph's spiel and showed me a number of helpful conveniences, like how to set the navigation system if we'd had an address to put into it, how to adjust the temperature, the radio, and the CD changer in the glove compartment, although it didn't come with any CDs, all of which had gone over my head when Ralph rattled them off. Like I've said, she was a quick study, and I briefly considered asking her to go with us.

Then just as quickly, I decided against it because I couldn't imagine how we'd get along on a long trip. Perkiness went only so far with me, then I got tired of it. Instead, I laid the groundwork for a future contingency.

"Miss Wiggins," I started. "Oh, sorry, Etta Mae. I've been thinking, just off the top of my head, you know, if you might be available to come help us when we get where we're going. If we should need you, that is. I'd pay your expenses, of course, but I doubt it'll come to that. It'd be a comfort, though, if I could count on you, if I find myself at a loss down there."

"Oh, Miss Julia, I'd love to! Yes, ma'am, I'd come in a minute, anytime you want me. Here, let me give you my phone numbers: work, home, and cell numbers. Just call me anytime, day or night, and I'll hop right down there."

As I pulled back into the driveway, after a cautious two laps around the block, she handed me a thin business card with all her numbers on it.

"In fact," she went on, enthusiastically enough to endear her to me or to put me off entirely, I couldn't decide which, "I'll have a bag packed, so I can leave as soon as you call."

"I don't want you to endanger your job," I cautioned her, "and I seriously doubt I'll need you. But I'll appreciate having you on call, so to speak, since everybody I usually count on is off in foreign fields. Not that I don't have other friends, you understand, it's just that they'd all insist I come home and leave it to those who know what they're doing. As if they do and I don't."

"I know what you mean, Miss Julia," she said, with a firm nod of her head. "And if it helps, I think you're doing exactly the right thing. Because if you're like me, you know the only way to get something done is to do it yourself."

I was beginning to like that young woman the more I got to know her. In spite of her reputation around town.

I put the gear shift into park and opened the car door. "Let's get on in. I need to double-check everything so I don't forget anything, then get the suitcases in the trunk."

"I'll help. Just tell me what all you want." She hopped out of the car and came around to my side to open the door. The wind whipped our hair, and snow swirled around us as we hurried to the porch.

When we got inside, I saw that Lillian had the suitcases lined up in the hall. A shopping bag held books and other entertainment items for Lloyd, and there was another one filled with enough snacks, sweets, fruit, and sandwiches to last us for days to come.

"Let's see," I said, looking at my watch, "it's already close to two o'clock, and I'd intended to be on my way by now. I need to get a move on. What have we forgotten? Lillian, I'm leaving you a couple of signed checks, in case anything breaks down, and here," I said, opening my billfold, "here's some money for groceries or whatever you need." I counted out close to three hundred dollars, which about wiped me out. "Lord, I'll need to stop by the bank. At this rate, we'll never get out of town."

"Traveler's checks," Miss Wiggins said. "That'd be the safest. You can get them at the bank, along with some cash to have on hand. And, Miss Julia, I don't know how you do it, but I always hide some money under the spare tire in the trunk, just in case somebody steals my purse."

"What a good idea," I said, knowing that I would've never thought of either traveler's checks or of hiding money, not being a seasoned traveler or accustomed to being around thieves. "Anything else I ought to do?"

"Cell phone," Miss Wiggins said. "And charger."

"I've never felt the need for one. But Lloyd has his in his bookbag. Lillian, do you know where the charger is?"

"Right here in this sack, and they's a thermos of coffee for you," Lillian said, as mournfully as if we were never coming back. "An' some hot chocolate for Lloyd."

"Thank you, Lillian, and that reminds me," I said, turning toward the bathroom. "I'd better make one more stop."

"I'll take the suitcases out," Miss Wiggins said, hefting up one of the larger ones. "And get the maps folded just right for you. Oh, this is so exciting, just picking up and leaving on the spur of the moment. I know you're gonna find your jewelry in no time at all."

The young woman's confidence in, and enthusiasm for, what I was doing lifted my spirits immeasurably. I was glad that she'd come by to counteract Lillian's lack of both.

CHAPTER 12

Giving Lillian a reassuring pat on the arm as I passed, I hurried out onto the porch. "Now, Lillian," I said, as she stepped out behind me, "don't worry about us. We'll be all right, and if we're not, why, we'll just come home."

"I can't help but worry." She frowned and wrapped her arms around herself. "You never done nothin' like this before, an' you ought not be doin' it now."

"We've been over and over this, Lillian, and I have to. It's the principle of the thing." I took a deep breath, trying to generate another surge of outrage at being robbed since, now that I was about to take off into the unknown, a few second thoughts were beginning to creep in.

Miss Wiggins slammed the trunk shut after placing our suitcases inside, then waited for me as I walked carefully down the icy steps. She reached up and brushed her hair out of her eyes. "Which way you planning to go?"

"Why, south, I guess."

"Well, but there's two ways to get there."

That stopped me. "Which would you recommend? Let's get in the car, and you can show me on the map."

As we got in, snow flurries started again, and I started worrying along with them. If the roads got slick, as they would toward nightfall when the temperature dropped, we'd be in trouble. We needed to be down the mountain before then. I turned on the ignition to heat up the car, as Miss Wiggins spread out the map.

"See, Miss Julia," she said, pointing to a heavy line. "You can take I-26 across South Carolina and pick up I-95 here and go all the way on that. You'll go through Savannah and Jacksonville and on down the coast."

"My goodness, that looks a long way."

"It sure is. You better plan on two days of driving at least. And watch out for a lot of traffic on I-95. That's the way everybody goes to Florida from up north, and it's the way drugs're moved going the other way."

"I certainly don't want to get mixed up in that. What's the other way?"

"Right here. Look, you can take 25-South out of town, and pick up I-85 through South Carolina. It'll run into I-75 in Atlanta, and you can follow that till you hit the turnpike right here. It'll take you on into West Palm Beach."

"Any drug-runners on it?"

She smiled. "Probably, but less likely. The only problem with going this way is Atlanta, and that's a mess. Traffic's just awful. Try not to hit it during morning or evening rush hour."

"You must be an experienced traveler to know so much. You'd take this turnpike way, wouldn't you?"

"Yes, ma'am, I would." She leaned up and began fiddling with the navigation system. "If that's the way you want to go, I'll enter it for you, and you'll always know where you are until you get there. Then you'll need a local address. But there's less traffic this way, except for Atlanta, and it goes right by Orlando where Disney World is. But as far as being a traveler, I've only been to Atlanta once, for a Vince Gill concert, but I'm going to Disney World someday. Maybe, when you find your jewelry, y'all can stop by there on the way back. You'd love it, Miss Julia, I've got all the information on it, brochures and everything. And I know Lloyd would have the time of his life."

"It'd be nice, I'm sure. But this trip is strictly business."

"I know, so I'd better let you get on the road. That snow is looking serious out there. The street's still okay, though. Good luck, Miss Julia, and don't forget to call if you need any help."

I thanked her, trying to still my anxiety now that I was about to embark on such an untraveled road. I'd never been much of a driver, just naturally yielded the wheel to Wesley Lloyd, and now to Sam, every time we went anywhere. But in between my two husbands, I'd done more driving than I'd ever done before and gotten quite good at it, if I do say so myself. Unless it was after sundown or there was too much traffic.

I gave a quick wave to Lillian, who was wringing her hands on the porch, and to Miss Wiggins as she stood in my yard with snow swirling around her. Then I backed out and headed for the bank.

Everything takes longer than you plan for, and it took twenty-five minutes to get the traveler's checks and the cash I wanted. Of course, my transactions were well noted by the teller and by other people in line, even though I lowered my voice and hid the amount on the check I wrote. But everything I did was a source of comment and speculation, the result, I expect, of my financial prominence in town and my unusual living arrangements. And of curious minds with nothing better to occupy them.

I encountered the same kind of delay at Lloyd's school. First, I had to speak to the principal — ask permission, if you please — then to the teacher, and wait for her to explain the lesson assignments we'd take with us. And all the time, the child stood beside me, looking pale and anxious, not understanding why I was getting him out of school and fearful of the reason. I told them all that we had business out of town with no further explanation, it not being anybody's business but our own.

As we walked out of the building, he said, "Has something happened to Mama?"

"My goodness, Lloyd, put your mind at rest. Your mother and Sam are fine as far as I know, seeing that I've not heard from them today. All I'm doing is what I wrestled about doing all of last night, and I need your help to do it."

I led him to the car I'd just purchased and opened the door, glad to have him with me but suddenly fearful of what I was doing. It had all seemed such a good idea the night before.

He stopped, confused at the sight. "Where's our car?"

"This is it. I just bought it for the long trip

we're taking. Now jump in, and let's hope Lillian packed everything you need, because we're leaving from here and not coming back until we find our property."

He took a big, deep breath, his eyes and mouth wide-open from the shock of it. "Cool! Who else is going?" He ran around the car to his side and crawled in.

"Nobody. Just you and me."

"Oh, wow." He would've bounced in his seat if he hadn't buckled himself in.

"Now listen to me, Lloyd. We're on serious business here. I don't exactly know where we're going or how to get there or what we should do when we do get there, and the weather is bad and I'm not too familiar with this car, so I need your help. This is not a pleasure trip, and I want you to be on your toes every step of the way. You're in charge of the map and this thing here." I pointed at the electronic display screen. "I'm depending on you to keep us on the right roads."

"I can do that." And he got right to it, taking a pen from his backpack and marking our route as I pointed it out the way Miss Wiggins had recommended. "And I've got my cell phone if we need to ask directions. So don't worry, I'll navigate for us."

And I didn't worry, except about the

weather. I had complete confidence in anything the boy took on, he was so meticulous and picky with everything he did. Besides the physical resemblance, that was another way that he reminded me of his father, except the child had some redeeming characteristics to balance him out.

By the time we got through town and on the southbound highway, the snow was falling thick enough to require headlights and windshield wipers. It took me a minute to regulate the wipers to the right speed, then noticed that Lloyd, without making any unwelcome comments, began studying the manual.

I drove fairly slowly, getting the feel of both the road and the car. Snow was sweeping across the pavement in gusts, and it was beginning to stick on the trees and banks along the side. Other cars passed us, unmindful of conditions that could get hazardous at any moment, but there're always idiots who reveal themselves when they get behind a wheel.

I recalled another trip I'd taken down this same mountain a few years before, but it'd been on another route with other people and in the dark of night. Better weather, though, yet under equal tension. But maybe I was even more tense now, because I kept wondering if I'd made a bad mistake by not flying. We'd certainly get there quicker, if planes were taking off at all, but I doubted I'd be any less anxious than I was with my own hands on the wheel. You never know who's driving an airplane.

When we finally got to the foot of the mountain, and the road flattened out toward Greenville, the snow began to slack off, and I began to relax.

"Look, Miss Julia," Lloyd said, pointing. "There's a sign for I-85. We better follow that through town."

"Here we go, then. Why don't you get out your telephone and call Lillian. Let her know we made it safely so far."

He grinned, delighted to be the one to check in with headquarters. I could hear Lillian's amazed shriek when he told her he was calling from the car.

"Yessum," Lloyd said, nodding his head. "We're all right. Yessum. Yessum. Yes, ma'am, I will."

He was still smiling when he clicked off the phone. "Miss Lillian said to tell you to be careful."

"I gathered as much. That's not all she said, was it?"

We exchanged a smile at Lillian's propensity to boss everybody around. "No'm," he said, "but she sure is worried about us."

"I know she is, but if she'll just keep her worries to herself for a little while, we'll be all right. I was afraid Sam or your mother would call before we got away, and you know what they'd say about us taking off like this. They'd tell us to stay where we were, then probably come flying home to keep us there. But it's my property — well, and your mother's, too — that's in peril, and I don't plan to sit around and wait for somebody else to get it back for me."

He laughed out loud, a sound so rare and pleasurable that I was immediately confirmed in my decision that what I was doing was the absolute right thing to do. Even if nobody else thought so, and even though I was pretty shaky for daring to do it.

By the time we got through Greenville and on I-85, headed toward Atlanta, the snow had lessened but dark was falling fast. I began to be concerned about my night vision, which wasn't all that good in the daytime.

"What towns are there between here and Atlanta, Lloyd? We may need to pull off and spend the night."

"Nothing much, looks like." He studied the map intently, then said, "There're several off a little ways. Maybe we can find a motel on the side of the interstate and not have to go into a town."

"That's what I'm thinking. You watch and find us a nice place. It's almost full dark and not five-thirty yet, but if we get to bed early, we can get an early start and try to beat the Atlanta traffic."

I drove farther in the dark than I wanted to, but we didn't find a decent-looking motel until we were some forty miles from the big city. We stopped and checked in, taking one room with two double beds since I didn't intend to let Lloyd out of my sight, what with all the strange people I expected to be coming up against.

I declare, when you travel on your own, there's so much to think about and worry with. Lock the car, double-lock your room door, check your money to be sure it's still where you put it, watch the gas gauge, worry about the desk giving you a wake-up call on time, and I don't know what all. I just know that I wished I'd done a whole lot more traveling when I was young so it wouldn't be so strange in my later years.

We ate Lillian's sandwiches, along with Coca-Colas from a machine that Lloyd knew how to work. I didn't ordinarily approve of him drinking carbonated beverages, but there was no milk and it was too late for coffee. I figured that our unusual trip called for unusual relaxation of our normal habits.

When our wake-up call came at four-thirty the next morning, I fumbled with the telephone, then sat up, dismayed at being so far from home. What had seemed a fine and adventurous idea the day before now appeared foolish and frightening.

I staggered across the room, plugged in the coffeepot so conveniently provided by the motel, and proceeded to dress before rousing Lloyd from his bed.

Stunned at our daring, neither of us had much to say, and we ate the fruit Lillian had packed the day before and drank the thin coffee. Since it was too early for the restaurant to be open, I promised Lloyd a big, hot breakfast south of Atlanta. For now, I was anxious to get ahead of that morning rush hour that Miss Wiggins had warned about.

As I pulled back on the interstate, with the headlights on and little sign of daylight, I began to feel quite pleased with myself. We'd outrun the snow, for one thing. And we'd made close to eighty miles on our first day, even with the late start, and that feeling persisted until Lloyd opened up the map and I saw how much farther we had to go.

Still, we'd weathered our first night among strangers without being robbed, wrecked, or swindled, and I could congratulate myself on now being a seasoned traveler.

CHAPTER 13

At least I thought I was, until we were some twenty miles outside of Atlanta, where the road widened out to six lanes, and that was just on our side. On top of that, every last one of those lanes was filled with cars, trucks, and various other vehicles. I couldn't figure out where they'd all come from.

"My word, Lloyd," I said, taking a tighter grip on the steering wheel, "would you look at this, and it's not six o'clock yet. I'd hate to see what rush hour is like."

As we got closer to the middle of that mad city, I began to pray that we could get out of it alive. If those drivers had just gotten in one lane and stayed there, it would've been so much more thoughtful, to say nothing of being safer for everybody concerned. But no, they had to switch, swerve, and cut in and out like they were all on emergency runs. For myself, I stayed under the posted speed limit, which was inordinately high for the road conditions, not wanting to be the cause of an accident. They passed me like I was standing still.

Finally, I came up behind a big truck that was going about my speed and laboring to maintain that, and I got behind him and stayed there.

"Lloyd," I said, easing back on the gas pedal, "I'm going to stay right here as long as I can, and let this truck run interference for us." I sped up just a hair to keep a sports car from cutting in front of us. "But if he's going to California, we may be in trouble."

"Good idea," he said, nodding stiffly as his hand gripped the armrest. Like me, he was amazed at the antics of other drivers.

Letting the huge truck shield us from cross-cutting drivers who didn't know enough to stay in their own lanes, we were swept along with thousands of other cars. We dipped and banked and swooped on the broad interstate, and it was like running along a ribbon that curled through the city. It would've been thrilling, if I hadn't been scared to death.

In spite of my plan to stop for breakfast, Lloyd agreed that we'd do better to stick with our escort while we had one. After we went through the city and passed the airport with planes roaring in and out almost as thick as the road traffic, we settled down to drive on, in spite of our empty stomachs.

Both of us were squirming by the time we got close to Macon, it being past time to stop for nourishment and other necessities brought on by two cups of coffee apiece. Unable to go another mile, I came off on an exit ramp to look for a place with decent food and clean bathrooms. We settled on an IHOP, which I figured would do for either breakfast or lunch, it not being the proper time for either.

If you want to know the truth, I could've stopped for the day and gone back to bed. Driving, when you're unaccustomed to maintaining the same position and to the tension required to stay alive, can mortally sap you. Now that I was feeling the effects of long-distance travel, I began to question my wisdom in not bringing either Lillian or Miss Wiggins to spell me at the wheel.

I was refreshed, however, after a big meal of blueberry pancakes and a few constitutional moments in the ladies' room, and felt good enough for a few more hours of driving. Lloyd entertained himself by listening to the radio, doing his homework, and occasionally resting his eyes.

I declare, the child was a good companion, never complaining of being bored and never commenting on my driving skills, like some people I know. Besides, practice makes perfect, and I was getting more practice than I'd ever had at one time.

We stopped for the night in midafternoon, when I was so stiff and tired I could hardly crawl out of the car. We had barely gotten out of Georgia and into the state of Florida, but even one more hour of driving was more than I could manage.

I made sure to stop at a decent national chain, one I'd heard of, but even then the place we chose appeared hard-used and in need of refurbishing. Pleasantly surprised to find our tub equipped with whirlpool spouts, I had a good long soak in hot, swirling water and felt considerably better.

Dressed again for dinner an hour before serving time in the motel restaurant, I studied the map for a few minutes trying to calculate how much farther we had to go.

"Looks like we have a little over three hundred and fifty miles more, Lloyd. It makes me tired to think of it, and I'm not sure if we can do it all in one day. You think we ought to try it?"

"I sure do want to get there, and as fast as we can, too."

"So do I, but I also want to be able to move when we get there. And if I stay bent up over that wheel for hours at a time, I might not ever straighten up again. Well, let's just see how far we get tomorrow. If you get tired, we'll stop and go on in the following morning."

"I wish I was old enough to drive."

"I wish you were, too. I'd turn the whole business over to you and know I was in good hands." Refolding the map as best as I could, I said, "Now let's call Lillian and see how she's doing."

I told him to use his cell phone, since hotels are known to charge an arm and a leg for the use of theirs. As soon as she answered, Lillian yelled when she recognized his voice. After assuring her that we both were fine and enjoying the trip, he handed the phone to me.

"Lillian," I said. "How're things going there?"

"They goin' all right, if they wasn't four inches of snow on the ground, an' if some people call in like they say they goin' to."

"We've been on the road since before six this morning, and I didn't think you'd want to be called that early."

"Well, I been waitin' all day to hear from you. You coulda been lyin' on the side of the road, dead as a doornail, for all I knowed."

"What is it, Lillian? What's going on?"

"Well, that Mr. Tuttle, he called."

"About time! What'd he say?"

"He say he don't take on no clients over the telephone without they send him some money first."

"Well, I never. Did you tell him we're on the way and expect him to be available as soon as we get there?"

"Yessum, I tried to, but he didn't know what to think about that. But I tell you, Miss Julia, he a hard man to talk to. Seem like he don't understand a word I say."

"Is he a Mexican or something? I can't deal with somebody who can't speak English."

"No'm, he don't sound like that. He sound like his mind on something else."

"Well, if that's the case, I'll straighten it out for him. You did tell him we're on our way?"

"Yessum, I did, an' he say he too busy."

"We'll see about that," I said, my spirits rejuvenated at the thought of getting Mr. Tuttle unbusy in a hurry. "We'll get there late tomorrow or early the next day, and I'll let you know where we'll be staying."

"Well, one more thing 'fore you hang up. Coleman, he come by to tell you somebody done put up a reward for, let me see here, he wrote it down for me, 'information leadin' to the arrest.' He talkin' 'bout anybody goin' 'round stealin' jew'lry, an' he say they's a lot of money jus' waitin' for whoever help the police find them folks. An', Miss Julia, he real bothered 'bout you an' Lloyd goin' off by yo'selves. He say they's no need for that an' you oughta stay home, an' for me to tell you to get yo'self back here soon as you can."

My back got as stiff as a poker at that. "The days of taking orders are long behind me, Lillian, and you can tell him I said so. We are past the point of no return, and I'm not coming back until I sic Mr. Tuttle on those thieves and get my property back. But I'm glad to hear about that reward, and you can tell Coleman I will add a considerable amount to it. It's just what I need to light a fire under Mr. Tuttle."

After telling her that we'd talk to her to-morrow, I hung up and mulled over the prospect of holding out a sizable reward as an enticement to get Mr. Tuttle on our case. Then, thinking over Coleman's orders to re-turn home forthwith, my mouth tightened.

"Lloyd," I said, "it's nice to have people care for you, but sometimes you just have to ignore them and go on doing what you need to do."

"Yes, ma'am." He grinned. "I'm taking lessons as fast as I can."

We had another early night and an early

rising the next morning, and finally drove deep into the state of Florida. I'd forgotten, from my one previous visit, just how flat that country is down there. Not a mountain or a hill in sight. Easy driving, though, on the turnpike — even if you do have to pay for it. Lloyd enjoyed seeing the horse farms and orange groves that we passed as we got toward the middle of the state. I took note of all the signs for Disney World as we cruised past Orlando, and determined to tell Miss Wiggins that if she had all the time in the world she could drive right to it.

We stopped again for the night right outside Fort Pierce, with a little less than a hundred miles to go on the following day. I knew Lloyd wanted us to push on, but, I declare, I just couldn't. I promised him we'd be in West Palm Beach well before noon the next day, we'd find us a decent place to stay, then track down Mr. Tuttle and put him to work.

By midmorning the following day, we drove into West Palm Beach by crossing several main roads, including I-95 that we could've come in on if it hadn't been a drug-running route. Not being familiar with the area, I didn't know whether to turn left or right as we approached the Atlantic Ocean, so I compromised by pulling into a service station. We filled up with gas, Lloyd being adept by now at managing the gas pump. It beats me what service station employees do with their time, now that they no longer pump your gas or clean your windshield or check your tires.

They did have city maps for sale, though, and Lloyd and I parked under a palm tree that offered no shade at all and studied the thing. And while I'm on the subject of shade, that whole entire place could use some. I turned on the air conditioner as high as it would go and came out of my sweater. Hard to believe that we'd left North Carolina with snow chasing us down the mountain.

It took us a while, but by using the telephone directory at the station, we figured out about where his office was located. We went another block and turned left on the Dixie Highway and started looking for numbers. We passed it the first go-around and had to turn and come back at it from the other direction, mainly because it had no numbers. His office was located in one of those strip malls that lined the street from one end to the other. Just a run-down, trash-littered line of shops and business offices with a Publix grocery store at one end. Mr. Tuttle's office was more toward the other end, under a pink arcade that Hazel Marie would've loved.

After parking and gasping for breath in the high humidity, we walked under the arcade, thanking the Lord for that little bit of shade. TUTTLE INVESTIGATIONS was printed in chipped, black letters across the one large window, and under it were the words: AFFORDABLE, EFFICIENT AND DISCREET INVESTIGATIONS.

"He's discreet, all right," I said to Lloyd. "So much so that you can't find him when you want him."

Bitter words, because his door was locked tighter than Dick's hatband. No sign saying when he would return, no secretary to answer my discreet inquiry, and no indication that he'd even been there. In fact, sand had blown up against the bottom of the door and lay an inch thick along the ledge of the window.

"Come on, Lloyd," I said, before dispair over a wasted trip that nobody except Miss Wiggins thought I should've made overwhelmed me. "I didn't come this far to be thwarted by a missing private investigator, who ought to have enough business sense to keep his office open."

Then, to boost my own spirits, I said, "Some people don't know how to run a business, Lloyd, but they can still be good at what they do."

"Yessum, and I sure hope Mr. Tuttle's one of them, 'cause I don't like the looks of this place."

CHAPTER 14

On the way back to the car, it occurred to me to inquire of Mr. Tuttle's business neighbors. "Let's go in here," I said, and pushed through the door of KATHY'S KUT AND KURL HAIR SALON. "I'm going to find that man if I have to sweep this entire town, which, from the looks of it, somebody badly needs to do."

An overpowering reek of hair spray, setting lotion, and permanent-wave solution hit us as soon as we stepped in. But the cool air more than made up for it. The place was filled with more beauty aids than I'd ever known existed, all stacked up on metal shelves and reflected in mirrors, waiting to be purchased by the unsuspecting. Velma would've loved it.

I had another shock when the girl behind the counter asked if she could help us. I had to wet my lips twice before I could answer; her orange, purple-streaked hair made my mouth so dry. I won't even mention her inch-long nails, each painted a different shade — from the palest pink to the deepest burgundy.

"We're looking for Mr. Frank Tuttle, PI. No one's in his office next door, and I was wondering if you would know what time he comes in or where we might find him."

She smiled in a knowing kind of way and said, "Well, I don't know for a fact, but I have a good idea where he might be." She twisted around and yelled toward the back of the row of beauty-parlor chairs. "*Christy!* Where you think ole Frank is?"

"Hah!" Christy yelled back, glancing up from the head of hair she was teasing the life out of, and gave no further information.

"Tell you what," the purple-streaked girl said, "if I was looking for him, I'd go down past the Publix grocery into the next block, to The Strip Hall."

"I thought we were already in the strip mall."

"Yeah, but I'm talkin' about The Strip *Hall,* honey, the name of a bar. It's a coupla doors down from the intersection. You can't miss it."

"He's in a *bar?* In the middle of the *day?* Not that I hold with going to a bar at any time, but it's hardly even lunchtime."

She leaned over the counter and looked out the window. "That's where he probably is, though. See, that's his car parked right over there."

She pointed to a low-slung brown car with a huge dent on the fender. The passenger door was caved in, too. Now, I know that people shouldn't be judged by the kind of vehicle they drive, except sometimes you can't help it, and this was one of those times. From all I'd seen of Mr. Tuttle's locked-up office and beat-up car, I was having my doubts as to the health of his detecting business.

Lloyd walked to the window and looked out. "Why, that's a Crown Vic," he said. "With a mighty poor paint job."

"Yeah," the salon girl said, "it's an old cop car. Or what's left of one. He got it at auction and had it repainted. Anyway, that means he's around somewhere, pro'bly eatin' lunch early. His hours aren't all that reg'lar."

"I'm beginning to see that," I said, through tight lips. Mr. Tuttle was sounding less and less like somebody I wanted to do business with. Still and all, he was a friend of Mr. Pickens, which in one way wasn't much of a recommendation, but in another was the best I had.

"Thank you for your help," I said, turning to go. "We appreciate it, as I'd never have

144

thought to look there."

"Sure, honey. Good luck." She was grinning as we left the hair salon.

Lloyd and I walked down the arcade of the strip mall toward something called The Strip Hall. The heat was awful under the shade, but became almost suffocating when we stepped out into the sun. A block and a half of walking in that tropical glare had me pinching up the placket on my bodice and fanning it, hoping to create a little breeze. The first order of business after locating Mr. Tuttle and setting him off was to check into a hotel and rid ourselves of knits and woolens.

There was no mistaking the place of sin when we reached it. A large, flashing neon sign hung above the darkened windows, depicting a hip-shot young woman slinging an article of underclothing on and off in time to all that twitching she was doing. The low beat of a jukebox emanated from the open doors, which were reached through an indentation of the wall. I stood before them, holding Lloyd's hand and wondering if I dared venture into that iniquitous den.

I looked down into the child's perspiring face, white with anxiety, and squeezed his hand. "What do you think?" I whispered.

He peered into the dark interior, squinched

up his mouth, and nodded his head with a firmness that I couldn't help but admire. "I think we've come too far to stop now." He cocked his head and gave me a sly smile. "Besides, don't you always say I should be open to new experiences? Well, here's one right here."

"Oh, you," I said, giving his hand a quick shake. "But you stay right next to me and look neither to the left nor to the right. There's no telling what's going on in there, and I don't want any of it rubbing off on you. And I'll tell you right now, I am announcing to Mr. Tuttle that as long as he works for us he will have to find a more suitable place in which to eat lunch. Let's go."

We walked into the place, stopping inside the door to let our eyes adjust to the dark paneling and dim lighting. There were a half dozen small tables lined up along the left side of the long, narrow space where a few people scrunched down in the shadows. As well they should. A bar with a few occupied stools was to the right of us. Neon signs over the mirror behind the bar, as well as on the wall, advertised various ways of becoming intoxicated, and a spotlight lit up a shiny pole inside a wire cage in the very back of the room. It crossed my mind that they might feature wild-animal acts in it, except they probably would need a license for that, so no telling what it was for.

Past the empty cage, a door led even farther back, and I could hear the click of pool balls when the throbbing beat of the jukebox ground down into a heavy but welcome silence. The few men eating sandwiches at the tables glanced at us, and two stringy-haired ones at the bar turned on their stools to look at us with glazed eyes. One heavyset man with poor posture and in need of a shave and a mustache trim, his arms surrounding a glass and a bottle, didn't pick up his nodding head. A drunk, I could see at a glance. My lip curled with disgust at the sorry sight. Each and every one of those men should've been out working and making something of themselves. I have no patience with a lack of character and ambition.

"Hey!" A loud voice from behind the bar cut through the room. A burly, bald man with a dirty apron wrapped around his waist threw down a towel and started toward us. He leaned across the bar, barking, "You can't bring that boy in here! He's underage. Get him outta here, 'fore I lose my temper and my license!"

"You're going to lose something worse than that," I said, feeling Lloyd's hand clamp down on mine, "if you don't speak to me in a courteous way." I gripped my pocketbook and stared him down, but I was trembling inside.

"Look, ma'am, I apologize, but this is not a place for a kid. Or a lady, either."

"I'm well aware of that. It was perfectly obvious to me before I set foot inside the door that it's not fit for any decent person. But I've come a long way to see Mr. Frank Tuttle, PI, and I've been told that he frequents this establishment. Point him out to me, please, and I'll be more than glad to shake the dust of this wicked place off my feet."

His eyebrows went up at that, and he modulated his voice. "Why don't you and the boy wait outside, and I'll look around and see if he's here."

"Oh, I expect he's here, so I'll just wait till you point him out."

"Lady," the man said with a huge sigh, "I got a business to run and I don't need this."

"Neither do I, so get on with it."

"Look, I'm askin' you nice as I can. I can't have no minor in here, an' if you don't leave I'll have to call the cops."

"Good. I have friends in law enforcement, one of whom has recently been promoted to sergeant. Maybe the ones you call will be able to tell me which of these sterling patrons of yours is Mr. Tuttle."

"Now, ma'am," he said, almost whining by now, "I won't have no patrons at all, if I go around tellin' who's here and who's not. You don't understand."

"I understand plenty. Your patrons are ashamed of being here, aren't they? They don't want anyone to know what they do when they should be at their jobs, do they? I want to ask you something, sir: How long has it been since you were in church?"

"Well, Jesus, I dunno. Been a while, I guess."

"My suggestion is that you get yourself back to it and into a better line of business. Then you can call on the Lord with a better chance of being heard. And in the meantime, which one of these customers is Mr. Tuttle?"

The heavyset man who was embracing his glass and bottle turned his stool slowly around. He kept himself from listing too far off it by holding on to the bar. He looked at us through red-rimmed eyes, the bristles on his unshaven face glinting in the neon lights.

"Who'n hell wants Frank Tuttle?" He flicked the ash off a cigarette, sending sparks across his none-too-fresh blue shirt. The thick muscles of his thighs bulged under brown polyester pants, and his feet were in black short-top boots, much like those worn by Sergeant Coleman Bates.

"Mrs. Julia Springer Murdoch wants him," I said, straightening my shoulders. "And if you are Mr. Tuttle, I want to see you in your office. We haven't come this far to talk business in a bar."

He started laughing then, ending with a deep, most unattractive cough. I could've told him what was causing it, but I didn't think he'd listen. "How 'bout that, summoned to the principal's office," he said, or slurred, as his elbow slipped off the bar and nearly upended three glasses and himself.

"You're being summoned to do your job, Mr. Tuttle, if that's who you are," I said, just about on the edge of being offended. "Now get off that bar stool and do it. I've come more miles that I care to count to get my property back and, if you're in any shape for it, to engage you to do it."

Everybody in the place had stopped eating or drinking or whatever they were doing, to listen in. I almost lost my breath when a nearly naked woman walked out of the back and leaned on the end of the bar, watching us intently. I turned Lloyd around, ready to move him out.

I glared at Mr. Tuttle. "Well, don't just sit there. Come on."

He glared right back at me, his eyes glittering from deep in his puffy face. We stared at each other a minute longer, then his cigarette burned down between his fingers.

"Goddoggit!" he yelled, flinging the thing aside and sliding off his stool.

"I'll not have that kind of language in my presence, Mr. Tuttle. Nor in this boy's. Get yourself under control."

He slid off the stool and pulled himself up as straight as his extended abdomen would allow, squinched up his face, and opened his mouth to let me have it. Before a word got out, though, he began to sway this way and that as his eyes rolled up in his head. Then he keeled over, falling flat out on the floor.

CHAPTER 15

Lloyd leaned over to peer at Mr. Tuttle's stretched-out body. He pushed up his glasses that tended to slide down his nose. "Is he dead?"

"Passed out," the bartender said, like it was part of the daily routine. "Can't hold his liquor, is all."

"In that case," I commented, "you'd think he'd learn, wouldn't you?" Then, since no one seemed willing to take charge of the situation, I said, "Will some of you gentlemen be kind enough to get him up and put him out on the sidewalk? Lloyd, you stay with him while I go get the car."

The bartender's eyebrows rose up. "You gonna take him in this shape?"

"I certainly am. He's a hard man to find, and now that I've found him, I'm holding on till he's fit to work."

The bartender motioned to the two men at the bar, and between the three of them, they sat Mr. Tuttle up. As they bent him at the waist, a long, somewhat melodious eructation of liquorish fumes floated out of his mouth.

"They Lord," I said, wondering what other uncouth melodies we'd let ourselves in for.

They got him halfway to his feet and began dragging him out to the sidewalk, while I held the door open. "Just prop him against the wall," I said, "and don't go far. We'll need help to get him in the car. Lloyd, stay right by him, but not too close. Don't go anywhere and don't talk to anybody. I'll be right back."

I hurriedly retraced our steps toward the arcade, just about wilted by that time from the heat and the mental exertion of dealing with that seedy specimen, the burden of which I had now undertaken to bear.

After getting the car back onto the highway with the air-conditioning turned up high, I double-parked in front of The Strip Hall. Mr. Tuttle was half sitting, half lying on the sidewalk, his legs spraddled out and his head hanging down, with Lloyd propping him up on one side.

A car behind me blew its horn, so I got out and walked back to the driver. It tries my patience that people can be in too much of a hurry to be polite.

I leaned in at the window and said, "Pardon me, but you can go over or go around, if you're in a hurry. We have an emergency here, and I'll move as soon as I can."

I think I was glad I couldn't understand Spanish or Cuban or whatever he spoke in, but I do believe he got his frustration out of his system, for he stopped blowing his horn.

With the help of the same customers, we got Mr. Tuttle shoved and pushed into our car and stretched out on the backseat. I thanked the Good Samaritans, assuring them that a good deed was its own reward and that they could be proud of themselves.

Once Lloyd and I were in the car and we'd left the environs, I hoped for good, he said, "What're we gonna do with him, Miss Julia?"

"Sober him up, though for the life of me, I don't know how it's done. We'll let him sleep it off, maybe, and get some nourishing food into him. First thing, though, we've got to find a place to stay. I'm going to turn around and go back the other way. This area's not to my liking at all."

So we did, passing several more-than-decent-looking accommodations on the way. Each time Lloyd pointed one out, I shook my head.

"No, that one's too open and public, and that one's several stories high. What we need is a place where I can park up close to the door so we won't attract a crowd of onlookers when we drag an unconscious man inside."

Finally, we came across a motel consisting of several unattached cottages and I pulled in. The Royal Palm Court had a distinctively dismal look to it from the highway, which didn't improve upon closer inspection. "This is not what I'd ordinarily choose even for a temporary stay, Lloyd, but I believe it'll do for our present purposes."

I was less sure, though, when I stepped inside the office to check in. There was a sign advertising rates by the week, by the day, and by the hour, which should've told me something right there. I told the excessively tanned woman behind the counter that I'd take a quiet, out-of-the-way cottage for both a day and a night, and possibly more as the need arose.

"You got it," she said, handing me a key attached by a length of twine to a small strip of plastic that had a room number on it. "No loud parties, no loud music, otherwise nobody bothers you. You better hurry and get your things in. It's about to pour."

Walking back to the car, I noticed that the

day had darkened considerably and a hot, dry wind had picked up, rattling the palm trees overhead. A roll of thunder sounded off in the distance.

As I drove toward the last cottage on the right, Mr. Tuttle let out a loud snore. Then he began to cough, ending with a threatening gurgle down in his throat.

"Uh-oh," Lloyd said, switching around to look over the seat.

I slammed on the brakes and leaned over, too. "Mr. Tuttle, if you throw up in my new car, you'll buy me another one. You hear me?"

He didn't answer, but he subsided. I pulled in to the parking slot in front of our assigned cottage and sat for a minute, figuring how we could best proceed. The wind gusted around a pitiful-looking palm tree — nothing royal about it — beside the cottage, and another roll of thunder warned that I'd better decide something sooner rather than later.

"I don't know how to do this, Lloyd," I said. "It's a settled fact that the two of us can't carry him inside, and he can't manage on his own. What do you think?"

He pondered the matter, then said, "We could lock him in the car and let him sleep it off by himself."

"That's true," I nodded. "But he could

156

suffocate with the windows rolled up, and with all the trouble we've gone through, I don't won't to lose him like that. This heat is unbearable, even with a cloud coming up."

Mr. Tuttle moaned and tried to roll over, one arm flopping down on the floorboard.

"He may be waking up," I said, glancing back at him, "and if he can manage his feet, maybe we can aim him for the door. You stay here with him, and let me get our suitcases inside."

This I did, stepping up onto the small porch and unlocking the door to the cottage. I almost backed out again. Stifling heat rolled out of the cottage, along with a most unpleasant mixture of mildew, stale cigarette smoke, and other things I didn't want to guess at. There was a large bed against one wall, one upholstered chair — damp to the touch — a three-drawer chest with a television set on top, a small table with two straight chairs, a dinky little closet, a smelly bathroom with a rust-stained shower, and the poorest excuse for a kitchenette I'd ever seen in my life. The whole place needed a good scrubbing with Lysol, but with Mr. Tuttle on our hands and the clouds about to open up, we needed an immediate refuge. I turned on the window air-conditioning unit and wondered if any of us would get any sleep with the racket it made.

Setting down the suitcases, I went back out to the car, holding my hair with one hand and my dress-tail with the other against the wind. Lloyd was sitting in the front seat with his feet dangling out the open door.

"Lloyd," I said, "I hate for us to be subjected to such deplorable conditions, but it's probably the best we can do under the circumstances. As soon as Mr. Tuttle's sober enough to walk, we'll move out of here."

"I don't mind," he said. "We came down here to find our property, and I'm willing put up with whatever it takes."

The child did my heart good, seeing evidence again of his many stalwart qualities. I believe in setting a good example, and he had always proved to be an apt student.

Mr. Tuttle groaned again, then began mumbling a string of slurred words that I didn't care to interpret.

"Maybe we ought to try to get him out now," Lloyd said, as another roll of thunder sounded overhead. "It's fixing to rain." He studied Mr. Tuttle from over the front seat, and I could see his mind working at the problem. "I think if we open both back doors, I can get on the other side and push on his shoulders while you grab his feet and pull, then we can get him out."

"Yes, that should work. But what if he can't walk and just crumples up on the ground?"

"Well, either way, in the car or on the ground, I think we ought to get him started."

So we did, with big drops of rain beginning to sprinkle on our backs. I almost changed places with Lloyd, preferring to deal with a man's shoulders than with his lower extremities. But Lloyd did more than push on his shoulders. He lifted them up and shoved himself up under the man's upper torso, pushing and sliding him toward me, the leather seats providing the slippage we needed. All I had to do was guide the man's feet toward the ground, and we had him sitting on the edge of the backseat, half out of the car and leaning against me.

"Mr. Tuttle!" I yelled in his ear. "Can you stand up?"

"Wait, Miss Julia," Lloyd said, slamming his door and hurrying around to my side of the car. "Don't try to pull him out. He'll fall on you."

"Oh, Lord," I wailed, as the rain started pelting down and Velma's set quickly became a thing of the past. I couldn't get the man in or out, and his dead weight was buckling my knees. "What're we going to do?"

"Stand him up, Miss Julia!" Lloyd cried, his

glasses streaked with rainwater. He hitched himself up under Mr. Tuttle to take some of the weight off me.

We pulled and tugged until Mr. Tuttle was out of the car, tottering against the two of us for a minute before he sagged at the knees and took all three of us down to the ground. Lloyd yelped and I shrieked, quickly pulling my dress down to its proper place before scrambling up. And just in time, for Mr. Tuttle suddenly treated us to a noxious flow of everything he'd ingested for the past twelve hours. Let me tell you, if you ever think you'll be throwing up in public, I'd recommend against having a mustache. The combination is not a pretty sight.

"Leave him, Lloyd!" I yelled, my hair streaming in my eyes and the rain soaking my clothes to the skin. "Let him drown, I don't care!" I ran for the cottage, while Lloyd hurriedly closed the car doors before joining me on the little porch.

We stood there, soaked through, as the rain came down in a roar, looking at the pile of sodden humanity beside the car and wondering what we were going to do with him.

Mr. Tuttle stirred, raised his head, and blinked his eyes as the rain came down harder than ever, slicking his dark hair over his face and flattening his mustache. He tried to get up on one hand, but fell back to the muddy ground.

"This is awful, Miss Julia," Lloyd said, jittering around on the porch, wringing his hands. "We've got to do something."

"I don't have an idea in the world what we can do," I said, doing a little hand-wringing of my own, "but I'm about to strike him off my dance card for good."

I was fed up with Mr. Tuttle. If there's one thing I can't stand, it's somebody who won't help themselves, and Mr. Tuttle was a prime example.

"We've got to do something," Lloyd said, then jumped as a streak of lightning cracked around us.

"Look!" he said, pointing at Mr. Tuttle. "That did it!"

And sure enough, Mr. Tuttle was hauling himself up, holding on to the car and cursing worse than anything I'd ever heard. He looked stupefied, shaking his head and wiping the rain from his face. His clothes were soaked through and caked with mud and the lingering aftermath of his vomiting episode.

"I'll get him!" Lloyd cried. Before I could stop him, he ran out into the downpour and took Mr. Tuttle's hand, guiding him to the cottage.

They stumbled inside with me right behind. The rain continued to pour down, but with the door closed the sound of it lessened.

"Gotta get outta here," Mr. Tuttle mumbled and headed straight for the bed.

"Oh, no, you don't." I grabbed his arm and turned him around. "Not the bed we have to sleep on. You get in the bathroom and get out of those filthy, wet clothes before you sit on anything."

He listed to one side as he looked down at himself and his rain-soaked, mud-smeared, and smelly clothes. He took a deep breath that rocked him back on his heels, then almost retched again.

"In the bathroom!" I said, and headed him toward it. He went as meek as you please. I pushed him into the shower stall and turned on the water. Mr. Tuttle slouched against the wall, his head drooping on his chest. "Get out of those clothes," I told him, "and don't come out till you're clean."

Closing the door behind me and hoping for the best, I went back into the squalid room. Looking in the doorless closet and then in the chest of drawers, I finally found a scratchy olive blanket.

"Lloyd," I said, "open the bathroom door, please, and hand him this. Tell him to wrap up in it before putting in an appearance.

Then you go into the kitchen alcove and get some dry clothes on. We're all going to catch our deaths, I don't care how hot it is down here."

CHAPTER 16

I sat on one of the wooden chairs at the table, shivering from the air conditioner blowing on my wet clothes. By this time, I couldn't say much for the state of Florida. If it wasn't suffocating you with stifling heat, it was freezing you with artificial air. Tired from our exertions with Mr. Tuttle, I waited for Lloyd to change his clothes and listened to the shower running in the bathroom. I had high hopes for Mr. Tuttle's return to normal working conditions whenever he got out of it.

"What should I do with my wet things?" Lloyd asked, as he walked out of the kitchenette in a short-sleeved plaid shirt and khaki pants.

"Let me have them," I said, taking them from him. "I'll spread them out over the kitchen counters so they'll dry."

"He still in the shower?" Lloyd stood looking at the closed bathroom door.

"Sounds like it. And I wish he'd hurry. I need to get in there and change my clothes."

We sat at the table, waiting for Mr. Tuttle to finish, and still the shower ran and ran. I looked at my watch, then Lloyd and I glanced at each other. He shrugged his shoulders and we continued to wait.

Finally, he said, "I think I better check on him."

"I think so, too."

He went to the bathroom, tapped on the door, opened it, and stuck his head inside.

"Miss Julia!" he yelled, running inside. "You better come in here!"

"Oh, Lord, what now?" I jumped up and ran into the bathroom, where Mr. Tuttle was scrunched up stark naked on the floor of the shower stall, his head lolling to one side and water spraying down over him.

"Turn off the water, Lloyd! He's passed out again." I grabbed a towel and threw it over the part of Mr. Tuttle that I had no desire to see, although that first unfortunate image was already impressed on my mind.

"Mr. Tuttle!" I yelled. "Get up! Get up out of this shower right now! Watch the towel, Lloyd."

Surprisingly, Mr. Tuttle, groaning and grunting with the effort, got to his feet. We guided him out, stepping on and over his discarded clothes on the floor where he'd left them.

"Where's that blanket, Lloyd?" I held the towel while the boy draped the blanket around Mr. Tuttle. "Hold on to this, you hear me?" I yelled in his ear. It seemed to take a loud, firm voice to get through the haze in his mind. Or maybe he was dense even under normal conditions. "Don't you drop it."

Mumbling and staggering, he let us guide him across the room where he managed to sink onto the bed. A mistake, for the bed commenced to roll and bounce, heaving and undulating under him as Mr. Tuttle's eyes slowly began to cross. He turned white as a sheet and moaned in a most pitiable way.

"Why," I said, in wonder, "it's a water bed. Who in the world would want such a thing?"

Lloyd leaned down to study Mr. Tuttle's face up close and with some concern. "Sir, are you all right?"

"Sick," Mr. Tuttle mumbled, clutching the blanket with a shaking hand. Every time he moved, the bed moved with him. "Sick as a dog."

"I don't doubt it," I said, having no pity for a self-induced illness. "And it serves you right. Watch him a minute, Lloyd, while I put on some dry clothes. Maybe you better set the trash can next to him, just in case."

I went into the bathroom with a change of clothes and stood studying the mess Mr. Tuttle had left. His clothes took up most of the floor, which hadn't been spacious to begin with. Sighing, I picked them up, hating to have to handle the filthy things.

"I'm not going to put up with this," I mumbled to myself. So I went through the pockets of his pants and jacket, removing wallet, change, a set of keys, comb, handkerchief, another thin leather wallet that held his investigator's license, a sodden pack of Winstons, and various and sundry odds and ends that were commonly found on a man's person, and some that might not've been. And they talk about the contents of women's purses. I placed everything on the back of the commode, double-checked to be sure I'd not missed anything, and pulled out his belt, which could likely be salvaged. His boots were in sad shape but, except for the soaked leather and curling toes, they'd come through reasonably well. After setting them and the belt aside, I removed the plastic liner from the trash can and stuffed the rest of Mr. Tuttle's wet and soiled clothing in it, including a pair of what I believe were called

Jockey shorts, which I picked up between my thumb and forefinger, both of which I thoroughly scrubbed afterward.

After changing out of my own wet clothes, I walked back into the room with the plastic liner filled with Mr. Tuttle's discarded clothing. He was still sitting on the side of the bed, either shivering from the air conditioner or shaking from the effects of his morning, and probably all-night, indulgences. Lloyd had brought a chair over and was sitting right in front of him, studying him intently. The boy had an inquisitive mind, and I hoped that he was learning a fruitful lesson from Mr. Tuttle's inability to conduct himself in a dignified manner.

"Lloyd," I said, "the rain has slacked off a little, so get some change from my pocketbook, if you will, and run down to the office where there's a Coca-Cola machine right beside the door. Get us three cans and some ice, if they have it. And come right back, so I won't worry about you."

"Yessum," he said, "and I better get my cell phone and charger out of the car, too."

As the boy started to rise, Mr. Tuttle's hand snaked out from the blanket and grabbed Lloyd's arm. "Need a drink. Anything, a six-pack, a pint. Anything."

"Stop that!" I said, snatching up a phone

book and swatting the man's arm. "You're getting a Coca-Cola and some Bayer aspirin, and that's all you're getting. Now, behave yourself.

"Lloyd," I went on, "take that sack of clothes on your way and throw it in the Dumpster. I saw one behind the office on our way in."

"Yes ma'am," he said. Then he turned around and looked at me. "What's he going to wear?"

"Not a blessed thing. Otherwise, we'd have trouble holding on to him, if he took it in his head to leave. This way, he can only leave when we're ready for him to. And besides, I'm not about to wash those filthy things."

Lloyd grinned, pleased with the way my mind worked, since his worked pretty much the same way.

While Lloyd was gone, I sat down in the sticky upholstered chair to study the pitiful lump that Mr. Tuttle made there on the bed. He sat all slumped over, his head nodding on his shoulders, afraid, I guessed, to lie down for fear of starting the bed rolling again. I estimated his age at somewhere in his late forties or early fifties, mainly from the sprinkles of gray in his brown hair. After studying the lines on his face, I mentally added a few years, then subtracted them out of consideration for the hard living he was apparently engaged in. Regardless of his true age, though, he was certainly old enough to know better than to live the way he was presently doing.

After a while, he lifted his eyelids halfway, frowned, and finally focused on me. "Wha' . . . , where's this place?"

"The Royal Palm Court, Mr. Tuttle, where you're going to stay until you can do the job I want you to do."

That didn't seem to get through, for he mumbled, "Need a drink. Got th' shakes bad." And to demonstrate his needy state, a full body-length shiver ran through him and continued out in a rippling wave under the bedspread.

"Get it off your mind, Mr. Tuttle. Your drinking days are over for the time being, and they're not going to return until I head back to North Carolina. Although if you have any self-respect, you'll swear off that mind-wasting stuff for good."

He glared at me from those deep-set, bloodshot eyes, but I didn't let it bother me. I got up and went to turn Lloyd's clothes over, hoping they'd dry quicker. As soon as my back was turned, Mr. Tuttle was on the telephone, asking the woman in the office to call a taxicab to bring him a pint of bourbon. Any kind, he didn't care.

"Well, they Lord," I said, grabbing the receiver away from him and moving the telephone out of reach. "You just don't learn, do you, Mr. Tuttle? Never in my life have I seen anybody so determined to ruin his life and health. To say nothing of his livelihood."

"Need . . ."

"Need, my foot! You don't need a thing but to get hold of yourself and do your job. Now, listen to me, you may as well make your mind up to it, for you're going to help Lloyd and me find a nest of thieves. That's the kind of work Mr. Pickens says you do, and I know he'd want you to help us. You wouldn't want to let him down, now, would you?"

He huddled up even more inside the blanket, but his eyes were glittering at me. I was glad we'd gotten rid of his clothes, leaving him somewhat defenseless. He might've considered leaving buck naked when soused to the limit, except in that case he wouldn't have been able to put one foot in front of the other. But I didn't think he'd be too anxious to flee in his birthday suit cold sober. From my earlier glimpse of him in the shower and now from the sight of his big, knobby feet sticking out from the blanket, he wouldn't want to put himself on public display. At least that's what I was counting on, along with watching him like a hawk to forestall another stunt like calling for a home delivery.

Lloyd returned with the drinks and a bucket of ice. By the time I'd fixed us each a glass and stood over Mr. Tuttle until he'd swallowed two Bayers, we heard a car horn blow out in front of the cottage. Looking out the window, I saw a taxi sitting out there with its motor running.

Mr. Tuttle started to rise, but I put a hand on his shoulder and, with little effort, pushed him back down. Picking up his feet, I swung them onto the bed, telling him to lie down and let the aspirin work. He did, mainly because the bed set up such a sloshing that he dared not struggle against it.

"Stay inside, Lloyd," I said, "and sit on him if you have to. I'll tend to that delivery out there."

Going out and closing the door behind me, I sat down on one of the damp metal chairs on the porch, pretending I didn't notice the taxi parked right in front.

"Lady," the driver yelled, leaning across the seat to call through his open window. "I got your pint."

"Are you speaking to me?"

"This is number eight, ain't it?"

"I believe so," I said, pointing to the number over the door.

"Well, I gotta call to pick up a pint and deliver it here. So come on and get it."

"I don't know what kind of pint you have, but whatever it is, I didn't order it. You can look elsewhere or take it back."

"Well, look, lady," he said, scratching his head, "all I know's the dispatcher gave me the message and here I am, and I've already paid for this pint and made the run, so what am I supposed to do?"

"I don't have any idea, but I would suggest that you pour it out and refuse to be a party to such goings-on from here on out."

He rolled up the window, put his car in gear, and peeled out. Mad and disgusted, I surmised, which he had every right to be, mixed up as he was in such a disreputable business.

CHAPTER 17

After the taxi left, I continued to sit outside in the metal chair, listening to the last of the rain dripping from the eaves and the palm fronds. Several mud puddles dotted the sandy yard between the porch and the car. I leaned my head on my hand, pondering the mess I'd gotten us into. I'd expected to find another Mr. Pickens — someone capable and trustworthy, someone who would take hold and go to work while we watched from the sidelines. But what had I ended up with? Mr. Tuttle, that's what.

I sighed heavily, feeling sick with disappointment, wondering what to do. I couldn't allow Lloyd to linger in Mr. Tuttle's presence — it wasn't healthy, what with all those bad habits he was being exposed to. Yet we'd come too far just to turn around and go home with empty hands.

I could've strangled Mr. Tuttle. If he'd been half the man Mr. Pickens was, he'd already be on the job. Instead, he was piled up in bed, completely out of commission. What he needed was to be jacked up and whipped into shape, and I didn't know how to get that done.

But I knew someone who did.

So I stopped feeling sorry for myself and went back inside where Mr. Tuttle was snoring away and Lloyd was thumbing his Game Boy. Watching him as I turned his clothes again, I wondered if he'd ever get any height. Short stature was another legacy from his father, which was a shame but couldn't be helped. But the child's inner qualities far outweighed any physical resemblance, for Lloyd was open-minded and intellectually curious. Plus, he had a wry sense of humor and didn't go around criticizing everybody in his path.

But enough about my first husband. "Lloyd," I said, "what do you think about calling Miss Wiggins to come help us?"

"Etta Mae?" He blinked. "I think that's the best idea I've heard."

"Then let's do it. If your phone's charged up, I'll call her right now."

I heard Miss Wiggins gasp in surprise when I identified myself. "Oh," she said with a sudden intake of breath. "Are y'all in Florida? How're you doing down there?"

"Not too well, as a matter of fact. If your offer still holds, we could use your help with a matter of some urgency."

The woman squealed. Excitement does that to some people. "You want me to come down there?" She was hardly able to contain herself. "Really? I mean, to Florida?"

"Yes, I do. If, that is, it won't endanger your job. You see, Miss Wiggins, we have gotten ourselves tangled up with a private investigator who, in spite of being a friend of Mr. Pickens, does not engender a whole lot of confidence in his ability to function without supervision."

"What? I mean, ma'am?"

"I'll explain when you get here. How soon will that be?"

"Well, uh, let me see. I'll have to make arrangements for my patients. But that won't be a problem. One of the girls I work with owes me about a week for when she went to Cancún with her boyfriend. She'll do it, I know she will."

"I do hope so," I said, suddenly worried that I couldn't depend on what was essentially a last-ditch appeal. "I tell you, Miss Wiggins, we're in an emergency situation here, and I was hoping that you could leave right away. Today, in fact."

"Oh-h-h," she said, her breath catching

with excitement. "Then I will. I'll throw a few things in a suitcase and be on my way." She stopped, then resumed in a more sober tone. "I hope my car holds up for the trip."

"Oh, no, don't drive. I want you to take the next plane out. Just let me know your time of arrival so we can meet you."

"You want me to fly?" Her breath caught in her throat. "Oh, my goodness."

"It's perfectly safe, much safer than driving. You'll be all right, Miss Wiggins, and it'll have you here in a few hours. I hope you won't let fear of the unknown stop you."

"Oh, I want to fly, I really do. It's just so exciting I can hardly stand it."

"Well, then, down to business. Forgive me for getting personal, but can you use your credit card to pay for your ticket? I will, of course, reimburse you for all your expenses, including room and meals and whatever else you need."

"Yes, ma'am, I think so," she said, after a second or two. "I have a little in a savings account, too, but don't worry, I'll make do some way. Oh, Miss Julia, I can't get over this. Going to Florida and flying to get there! This is the most exciting thing that ever happened to me. I might even fly over Disney World!"

"You may, indeed. Now, Miss Wiggins,

time is of the essence, and I want you to take the first and fastest plane you can get. We'll meet you at the airport here, no matter what time you get in." I gave her Lloyd's cell-phone number. "Let me know as soon as you have an arrival time."

"I will, oh, I will. And you can call me Etta Mae, if you want to."

When I clicked off, Lloyd, who'd been listening to my end of the conversation, gave me a firm nod and said, "That was a good move, Miss Julia. From what Mama says about her, she'll know how to handle Mr. Tuttle's spells. She's a nurse, you know."

"Well, not exactly," I replied, thinking that the wearing of a white uniform didn't always confer the highest qualifications upon the wearer. "But she'll know more than we do. And she'll be another pair of eyes watching him."

Now that help was on the way, I settled down to wait out Mr. Tuttle's unconscious state, hoping the sobering-up process was taking place during it. Surely by the time he awakened, he'd be fit to talk to. That thought brought to the fore a matter of increasing concern to me. What if I had chosen the wrong path entirely by pursuing this man who, so far, had proven to have so reprehensible a character? The only redeeming quality he possessed was a private investigator's license, and who knew how long he'd keep that? And if he did, was it enough for me to engage him on a matter of some import? Was he even capable of tracking down a criminal ring that had eluded even Sergeant Coleman Bates?

I put my feet up on the ottoman and, resting, closed my eyes for a few minutes. Lloyd quietly took a book from his satchel and commenced to read.

"Lloyd," I said softly, as I came to myself, "we need to eat something. It's long past time for lunch, and we haven't had a bite. And," I continued, pointing at Mr. Tuttle, "it's a settled fact *he* hasn't."

"I could call out for pizza," he said. "Is there a phone in here? I don't want mine to be busy if Etta Mae calls."

"You'll have to crawl under the bed where I hid it from Mr. Tuttle. Order us a big one, please, and whatever else you want. We'll need enough to offer him, if he wakes up."

After reclaiming the phone from its hiding place, Lloyd placed the order in a clear and concise manner, and soon enough, our long-delayed lunch was at the door. When the young man in a paper hat showed up, I was at a loss as to whether or not to tip him. But I was so grateful for a chance to eat that

I went ahead and gave him a dollar.

Lloyd's phone rang just as we sat down at the table, and my heart jumped as I reached for it. "Miss Wiggins? When will you get here?"

"You won't believe this, Miss Julia," she said, "but the next plane out is not till sixten in the morning. Everything's delayed or canceled because of the weather. Then I'll have to change in Atlanta."

"No planes tonight?" She was right: I couldn't believe it. I'd thought this was the space age.

"No'm, and I won't get to West Palm Beach until ten-twenty A.M. Will that be all right?"

It wasn't, but what could I do? Assuring her that we'd be there to meet her and thanking her for flying to our rescue, I hung up with a considerably lighter load of worry. Now, if only her plane wouldn't crash.

Turning to Lloyd, I told him her time of arrival, and we both sat there staring at the pizza and coming to terms with the unforeseeable problems in the hours ahead of us.

With a glance at Mr. Tuttle's inert form, Lloyd said, "It's gonna be a lo-ong night."

"Let's just eat and hope for the best."

After eating and placing the leftovers in the tiny refrigerator, I settled again in the big chair to rest my eyes. Since Mr. Tuttle had hardly moved, I told Lloyd that he could play the television if he kept the sound down low.

It was almost dusk when our guest began to stir, moaning and thrashing around while the mattress swayed beneath him. With all that sloshing, I feared for his safety.

"Mr. Tuttle," I called, leaning over him and shaking his shoulder. "You ought to be still. You're creating havoc with this bed, and that can't do you any good."

His eyes snapped open. He stared at me, frowning. Then his eyes began to dart back and forth. "Where's this? Who're you?" He rubbed his hand across his unshaven face. "I need a drink."

"A motel, Mrs. Julia Murdoch, and you're not getting one. Lloyd, hand me a wet washcloth, please."

Mr. Tuttle took a deep breath and blew it out in a huge sigh. I had to turn aside. He kept blinking and squinching his eyes as he tried to get his bearings. In between the blinks, his red-rimmed eyes appeared somewhat clearer than they'd been before his nap, yet they still had a blank, unfocused look to them.

Lloyd handed me a wrung-out washcloth and I began scrubbing Mr. Tuttle's face. He brushed my hand away and, as he began to sit up, grabbed my arm to slow the motion under him.

"The blanket, Lloyd! Get the blanket back on him." I'd had all the glimpses of naked parts I could stand, for Mr. Tuttle was not what you'd call modest or fastidious about his person.

He swung his feet to the floor, then seemed to lose his momentum as the bed bounced around him. Leaning his head in his hands, he let out an awful groan that would've moved a more tenderhearted woman to compassion. But I knew why he was moaning, and could find no pity in my heart.

"Oh, god," he grunted, "my head." Then, dragging his hand across his stubbled face, he said, "Get me outta this hammock."

"You're on a water bed, which is the best we could provide given the state you've been in. If I were you, I'd be thankful for it. Now, you need to eat something. Your system's all torn up, and you need to get back on a normal schedule. Lloyd, bring us a piece of that pizza pie from the refrigerator."

Mr. Tuttle gave me a look of wonderment, or it might've been of confusion, he was still so addled. When Lloyd handed me a slice of cold pizza, I rammed it up to Mr. Tuttle's mouth.

182

"Eat this," I said. "You'll feel better with something in your stomach."

His eyes crossed as he looked at the slab of crust piled high with onions, bell pepper, salami, sausage, and pepperoni congealed in tomato sauce. He got a big whiff of it, then clutched his stomach. My own began to churn.

"Trash can, Lloyd! Get it up here fast."

Clasping the trash can in his arms, Mr. Tuttle finally subsided, resting his head against the rim of it. Breathing heavily, with sweat running down his face and drool out of his mouth, he was the sorriest sight I'd ever seen. I was again having my doubts as to his ability to investigate anything other than the bottom of the can.

Lloyd stood beside me, enthralled with this evidence of a misspent life. "He looks pure worn-out."

"Yes, he does. That's what strong spirits will do for you, Lloyd. So, as disgusting as this sight is, I want you to remember it, in case you're ever tempted to indulge."

"No, ma'am," he said, his eyes big behind his glasses. "You don't have to worry about me. If this is how you end up, I'm not ever going to drink that stuff."

I patted his shoulder, commending him for having good sense and strong moral fiber. I just hoped he kept on that way, for we committed Southern Presbyterians don't believe in any kind of drinking, social or otherwise. Of course, there are a number of uncommitted Southern Presbyterians who don't share the same conviction, but I didn't have to stand over them with a bucket in my hand.

I washed Mr. Tuttle's face again, and this time he was too weak to stop me. Handing him a glass of foul-smelling beachside water and two more Bayer aspirin from my pocketbook, I yelled in his ear, "Take these, and then lie back down."

He swallowed the aspirin, as meek and obedient as a child, then clasped the glass of water with both hands and drank it down. "More," he whispered, like a perishing man in a desert.

Lloyd refilled it not once, but twice again, and by that time, Mr. Tuttle's not inconsiderable abdomen was sloshing as bad as the bed. With our guidance he lay back on the pillow, which thank the Lord was normal and not water-filled, and fell into a deep sleep.

"I don't know how much more of this I can take," I told Lloyd. "He's got to come to himself sooner or later, but who knows when that'll be." I stopped and considered for a moment. "I wish we'd brought Miss Wiggins with us in the first place."

Lloyd nodded. "I do, too. We'll need her if he gets fractious on us. We might have to call a doctor."

"If he's not closer to normal by morning, we might have to. The problem is, though, we don't know what normal is like for him. We may be seeing it now."

"It's got to be better than this," Lloyd said as he gazed soberly at Mr. Tuttle. "All he's done is sleep and throw up, sleep and throw up, and I don't think that's normal for anybody."

I nodded, marveling again at how incisive his mind was. He could cut through to the gist of a problem as quickly as Sam or Lillian could.

I swiped at Mr. Tuttle's face again with the washcloth and he didn't move a muscle, not even a flutter of his eyelids. "He's out like a light," I said. "I think it's safe for us to go get a decent meal somewhere."

"And leave him by himself? What if he wakes up and decides to go off?"

"We're going to do everything we can to prevent that. Your health is more important than Mr. Tuttle's, and you need a proper meal. I saw a cafeteria back a little ways when we drove here, so we can get a balanced meal there and be back here in less than an hour. And don't worry, there's no way Mr. Tuttle can get his bulk through any of these tiny windows, so we're going to lock him in. And remember, he doesn't have any clothes."

Lloyd smiled at the thought. Then he said, "But he could call somebody to bring him some."

"Not if he doesn't have a phone. Get your cell phone." I followed the cord of the room phone to the outlet and pulled the plug. Then, wrapping the cord around the set and getting my keys and my purse, I said, "He's not going anywhere. Now, let's us eat while we have the chance."

And that's what we did. Twice in one week I found myself eating in a cafeteria, a phenomenom I didn't intend to repeat any time soon. In addition to our own meals, I purchased three extra rolls and a slice of ham to wrap up and take back with us, in case Mr. Tuttle was able to eat during the night. The ham looked suspiciously like the canned type, not having any of the deep, rich color or salty taste of good country ham, but it would have to do.

On the way back to the Royal Palm Court, I took a further chance and stopped at a convenience store. We moved through it like Sherman through Georgia, selecting cereals, milk, sugar, coffee, orange juice, napkins, butter, and jelly, getting breakfast purchased and bagged in no time at all.

As I was paying, Lloyd snapped his fingers. "Hold on, Miss Julia. I just thought of something."

He ran back down the aisle and came back with a large can of V8 vegetable juice. "You like that?" I asked, surprised since I'd never seen him drink it.

"No'm, not especially." Then, crooking his finger for me to lean down, he whispered so the checkout girl couldn't hear. He'd learned from me that you don't tell every Tom, Dick, and Harry your personal business. "I think it's good for hangovers, which Mr. Tuttle probably has."

"I think you're right," I said and added the can to our purchases.

When we pulled into the space beside Cottage Number Eight, all was quiet and undisturbed. Holding my breath while unlocking the door, I prayed that I'd not miscalculated by leaving Mr. Tuttle alone and unguarded.

CHAPTER 18

It was with some relief that I heard Mr. Tuttle's rumbling snores as soon as I opened the door, and saw the blanketed mound he made on the bed. I don't know what we would've done if he'd managed to leave, but I was glad we didn't have to visit every juke joint in the area to find him again.

Our sleeping arrangements, which I was more than ready to make by this time, were the next thing to worry about. Since Mr. Tuttle had taken over most of the bed, we had a problem. I considered going over to the office and requesting an adjoining cottage, but quickly discarded that idea. Mr. Tuttle could do nothing but improve as time went on, and as his system reactivated itself and began to demand what it craved, we had to keep a close watch.

We turned on the two small lamps in the room, leaving the overhead light off. Lloyd switched on the television, and all through that, Mr. Tuttle snored on and on. I wondered if so much sleep was good for him.

"Miss Julia," Lloyd whispered, as I handed him his robe and pajamas, "where're we going to sleep?"

"I've been thinking about that, so let's walk over to the office and see if they have a couple of cots we can rent."

That's what we did, skirting puddles of rainwater as we went and braving the damp heat left over from the thunderstorm.

"I got one bedroll left," the bewhiskered man behind the counter told us. "Lotsa families checked in tonight, an' they took all my cots. Bedroll'll be ten dollars. Sheets're extra."

We took the bedroll and sheets, because they were better than the floor, but not much. The bedroll was little more than a pallet, so thin that you could feel the ripples in the linoleum through it.

"I'm sorry about this, Lloyd," I said. "But I'll make it up to you tomorrow, if you don't mind camping out tonight."

He studied the pallet, then grinned. "It's better than crawling in with Mr. Tuttle. But what about you? Where're you going to sleep?"

"Oh, I'll just stretch out on this chair and ottoman. It'll do for one night."

He studied the stained brown chair for a minute. "You'll be all cramped up by morning if you sleep in that thing. Why don't you take the bedroll, and let me sleep on the chair?"

"That's thoughtful of you, Lloyd, but believe me, I'd rather have the chair. I might never get off the floor if I got down there."

He studied that for a minute, then said, "Oh." Then after a minute's thought, he said, "I still don't feel right, having a bed while you don't."

I looked at the skimpy pallet and laughed. "It's not much of one, so you're welcome to it."

"You know," he said, "I keep thinking this is going to be fun, but to tell the truth, it's getting old in a hurry."

"It is for me, too. But I'm counting on tomorrow being better. Now, let's get ready for bed and try to make the best of it."

"Okay, but I'm scooting my pallet over to the corner. I don't want to get stepped on if Mr. Tuttle decides to get up."

After I lined the commode seat with toilet paper, we took turns putting on our nightclothes in the bathroom, and without a word being said, we kept our robes on throughout the night, which was the longest one I'd ever spent. I would've tossed and turned all night if I'd had any room to do it in.

By morning I was so stiff I could hardly get out of the chair, to say nothing of the crick in my neck that required some of the aspirin I'd been dosing Mr. Tuttle with.

I rose early, about dawn, preferring to be up and stirring than to spend another minute in that uncomfortable position. I let Lloyd sleep on while I made a pot of coffee.

By the time it stopped perking, I was dressed, and Lloyd was sitting up, rubbing his eyes.

"Wash your face, honey," I said. "I'll have some cereal and toast ready for you in a minute. How'd you sleep?"

"Not too good," he said. "But probably better than you did." He yawned until his jaws creaked. "I hope we're going to move to a better place today, one with a real bed."

"We will, even if we have to trundle Mr. Tuttle in with that blanket wrapped around him. After last night, I'm past worrying about being a spectacle. Hurry up now, Lloyd. We've got to get Mr. Tuttle moving, so we can meet Miss Wiggins. I hope he knows where the airport is, and is in good enough shape to tell us."

While we were eating our breakfast at the little table, Mr. Tuttle commenced to waken, coughing and hawking and clearing his throat until my appetite was all but gone.

I went over to the bed and shouted in his face, "Mr. Tuttle! Do you need the trash can?"

His eyes popped open, staring up at me. "What? Who're you?"

"I am Mrs. Julia Murdoch, and I've come some eight hundred miles to put you to work."

He groaned from the depths of his empty stomach and tried to turn over.

"No, you don't," I said. "You've had enough sleep and enough time to get over your moral lapse. Now get out of that bed and keep that blanket around yourself. There's a child here who's seen quite enough of you. To say nothing of myself. Now, get up. We have business to tend to."

"Water," he gasped. "I need some water."

"You can have it, but only if you're sitting up by the time I get it."

I brought a glass of water, filled with ice to cut the taste of what came out of the tap, and a glass of the V8 vegetable juice that Lloyd had recommended.

Mr. Tuttle was sitting on the side of the bed, the blanket bunched around his hips, but lapped over what it was intended to cover. Holding his head in his hands as the bed rippled under him, he continued to moan with each breath.

"Here's your water. Don't spill it."

He drank all the water without once coming up for air, and held out the glass for more. "Drink this first," I said, handing him the vegetable juice.

He started to drink, but gagged when it was about halfway down.

"Stop that!" I said. "I want you to drink it and keep it down. The time for pampering is over, Mr. Tuttle, so get hold of yourself. We have work to do."

After a fit of coughing, he managed to croak, "Am I under arrest? I want my cigarettes. I'm entitled."

"At this moment, Mr. Tuttle, you're not entitled to one thing. But, for your information, there are no cigarettes to give you and you are not under arrest. Which isn't to say that you don't deserve to be."

A shudder ran through him, setting the bed in motion again. He turned slightly green and said, "I need to get off this thing. It's making me sick."

"That's not all that's making you sick, but all right. Sit on this chair over here."

He stood up, swaying and listing to one side, but he had the presence of mind to hold the blanket where it needed to be held.

I guided him to the chair, and Lloyd, who'd been watching from the table, brought him a cup of coffee.

After drinking several big gulps of it, Mr. Tuttle looked up at both of us. "Where's my clothes?"

"Probably at the county dump by now. They were fit for neither man nor beast after you came out of them. But I'll get you some when you and I come to terms on how we're going to proceed."

He rubbed his unshaven face with his hand, making a scratching noise that set my teeth on edge. Then he shook his head to clear it. His eyes were so bloodshot that I wondered about the state of the brain behind them. "Proceed with what?" he asked. "Bring me up to date here."

I sat down on the ottoman to look at him face-to-face. "Mr. Tuttle, if you would keep up with your business like any normal professional would do, you would already be up to date. I left detailed instructions for you with your answering service, and the fact that you don't even know who am I proves that you have been out of commission for far too long. Listen carefully, for I don't intend to repeat myself again. I am Mrs. Julia Springer Murdoch from Abbotsville, North Carolina, and this is Lloyd Puckett Springer.

We are close friends and associates of Mr. J. D. Pickens, under whose auspices we have come so far to find you. He himself, to my everlasting regret, is unavailable to undertake the important job I am now here to give to you." I took a deep breath and went on. "Mr. Tuttle, I have it on good authority that there's a bunch of criminals in this area. They've gone through many towns and cities stealing precious jewels right from under the noses of the owners. No law enforcement agency has been able to stop them, but they didn't know who they were fooling with when they went into my home and took my wedding rings. And Hazel Marie's jewelry, too. I intend to get every last piece back and I want you to help me."

Mr. Tuttle had the most confused look on his face, and I wondered if he had gone so far as to have pickled parts of his brain. But I continued on, hoping something would get through.

"We came here expecting to find a private investigator of Mr. Pickens's stature. Instead, we found you. I will tell you, Mr. Tuttle, I am extremely disappointed that my expectations were not met. We had to remove you from that sleazy bar, and spend time we could ill afford in sobering you up. Your clothes were ruined when you fell down in the mud and threw up all over yourself, which is the reason they got thrown in the dipsy Dumpster. That brings you up to date as far as the recent past is concerned. What we have to talk about now is where we go from here."

Lloyd said, "Yeah."

Mr. Tuttle looked from one to the other of us, lingering on Lloyd, who was still in his blue plaid robe with his hair sticking up. Lloyd stared right back at him through his thick glasses, not at all intimidated by him.

"Pickens sent you?" he asked, then shook his head. "Hellava note's all I can say."

"It's going to be worse than that if you don't watch your language," I told him. Lloyd nodded in agreement. "Now I'm going to fix you a bowl of cereal, although I caution you not to expect to be waited on much longer. We need to decide how to locate and recover my property as soon as possible."

"I can't eat anything," he moaned. "Can't even think about it."

"Don't try playing on my sympathy at this late date. I don't have any for people who bring their troubles on themselves. You have a choice of Raisin Bran or Froot Loops. Which will it be?"

"You're a hard woman," he said, wrapping

the blanket tighter around him. "I'll take the Froot Loops."

"I'd recommend the Raisin Bran from the condition your system is likely to be in, but so be it." I fixed a bowl and took it to him. Then I sat in front of him until he'd eaten as much as he could get down. "Here's some dry toast. That should set well."

He shook his head. "Can't."

Shoving it at him, I said, "Eat it." He did, and looked the better for it.

"Now," I said, "get back in the shower and let's hope it clears your head enough to talk business."

He was able at last to get to his feet and totter to the bathroom, but he had to be pointed toward it or he would've walked into the closet.

As soon as the door closed behind him, Lloyd said, "I don't know if he's in any shape to talk business or not, Miss Julia. He still looks awfully bilious."

While Lloyd dressed, I cleaned the kitchen, throwing out most of the food we'd bought the night before. By then Mr. Tuttle re-emerged from the bathroom, draped in the only covering available to him. I gave him a cup of coffee and drew up a chair beside him. "Now that you've regained use of yourself, Mr. Tuttle, what's the first order of business? I bow to your superior knowledge of how to go about apprehending criminals."

"First order is getting me some clothes."

"That's way down on the list, and not until I'm sure that you're not going to go running off to one of those juke joints again. Here," I said, handing him a comb. "Do something with your hair."

"I need a razor, too," he said, rubbing his bristly chin.

"You've been needing one long before I came on the scene, but don't worry about it. I'll get what you need when I'm sure of your cooperation."

"Look," he said, as a shrewd glint lit up his eyes. "I'll cooperate and I'll do whatever it takes to find your missing property, but we have to come to terms first. You don't know what it costs to run down leads and hook into official lines of communication. High technology requires specialized techniques, which is what you'll get from me. It takes money for that, and besides, as long as I'm concentrating on working for you, I have to turn down other clients. I have a business to run, you know."

I rolled my eyes, pleased that he was showing enough sense to negotiate with me, but recalling a similar bargaining session when I first engaged Mr. Pickens. No telling what he would've charged me, if a picture of Hazel Marie hadn't held out rewards other than monetary ones. I had no such lure in this case, for I certainly wasn't going to offer Mr. Tuttle a piece of recovered jewelry.

"Yes," I replied, nodding my head as if in agreement and giving him a shrewd look right back. I knew where he was going with this. "I know the kind of business you run. But I'm willing to listen and I'm willing to talk. What you should understand right up front, though, is that I am a woman who gets her money's worth. Let's hear your terms."

"Well, let's see," he said, mopping his hand across his face, "I don't expect you and the boy have money to burn, so I'll give you rock-bottom prices. I get seventy dollars an hour, plus expenses, and the first expense is a suit of clothes."

Lloyd leaned over and whispered in my ear, "That's an awful lot. I bet he'd take less, the shape he's in."

I nodded, pleased that the boy had such sharp negotiating skills. He would need them when he came into his half of Wesley Lloyd's estate.

"No, Mr. Tuttle," I said, shaking my head. "You'll get clothes similar to the ones you ruined and not a thing more. And if seventy dollars an hour is rock-bottom, I'd hate to hear what your going rate is."

"Okay, sixty plus expenses, with three days' advance."

"No advance. I don't trust you with it. I'll agree to sixty, but you'll be paid at the close of each day, and only if you've put in a full day and have the evidence of it in hand." I waited a few seconds, then slapped the finishing touch on him. "And for your information, I understand there's a sizable reward waiting for whoever brings these criminals to justice."

He thought about it for a minute, undoubtedly remembering the twelve lonely dollars I'd found in his pocket. If I'd been a betting woman, I'd've bet that his bank account was in similar straits.

"Deal," he sighed, like he'd given up hope of getting a better one. Which he had, for I was sure that there were more investigators available in the area, though none who were personally known by Mr. Pickens.

"Just a minute," I said. "Before we close this out, I need to know what you're going to be doing to earn this money. So far, all we've discussed are my responsibilities. Let's hear yours."

"I'll find your property, if it's here to be found. Which is not likely, but I can do it if anybody can." When he saw the expression on my face on hearing that unsubstantiated claim, he went on. "Listen, lady, when I was with the Tampa PD, I had the best clearance rate of anybody on the force. They don't come any better than me, and it's lucky for you that I'm between cases right now."

"Uh-huh, and I notice that you're no longer with the Tampa Police Department. But we won't go into the reasons why. Lloyd, hand me that Gideon Bible on the nightstand, please."

When the boy brought it, I said, "Mr. Tuttle, put your right hand on this Bible and swear to me that you're going to use every minute that you're in my employ toward finding my rings and Hazel Marie's valuables, and that you're going to use every technique and device available to accomplish same, and that you're going to leave absolutely no stone unturned."

His right hand crept out from a fold in the blanket, as he placed it on the Word of the Lord. He glanced blearily at Lloyd and then at me. "I so swear."

"So help you, God," I said.

"So help me, God. Now get me some clothes."

CHAPTER 19

"Look at the time," I said, tapping my watch. "We better hurry or we'll be late."

Mr. Tuttle glanced up with a hopeful look. "You going somewhere?"

"We're meeting a young woman who's capable and energetic and another pair of eyes to watch you." As he sulled up at that, I began to gather our things. "Let's get everything packed and ready to go, Lloyd."

"Now, Mr. Tuttle," I went on, as I folded Lloyd's pajamas, "there're two ways we can do this. We can drive you home, and you can get your own clothes — if you don't mind slipping in wrapped in that blanket. Or I can run out to the KMart and buy you some."

"KMart! No way. You said you'd replace what you threw away, and they didn't come from KMart."

I smiled to myself, for I knew polyester knit when I saw it. "Don't be so touchy. I simply meant as a stopgap measure. I'm not about to go to a men's store and lay out money for something that might not fit. And you're in no condition to go in and try them on. All we need to do is get you publicly presentable until you can get your own clothing."

"Well," he said with a sullen frown, "I'm not going to forget about 'em."

"I don't intend for you to. Now tell me what you want to do."

"You got a car?"

"Certainly I do, right outside. How do you think we got here? And no, we didn't fly."

"Then take me home. I'll get something there."

"Like that?" I pointed to the blanket, which he now had wrapped tightly around himself.

"There's a garage under the building with an elevator. If I run into anybody, they'll think I've come in from the beach."

"Of course," I said, perking up considerably at this evidence of Mr. Tuttle's knowledge of disguise. In a beach town, it wouldn't be unusual for a person to walk around in a blanket, and I was glad I hadn't thought of that the night before when I'd assumed that nakedness would keep him inside.

"That's what we'll do, then," I said, as I went into the kitchen to begin discarding the rest of the food. "Lloyd, honey, would you put the suitcases in the car?"

He followed me into the kitchen and whispered, "What about Etta Mae? She'll be scared if we're not there to meet her."

"Don't tell him, but we'll get her first," I whispered back, glancing at Mr. Tuttle to see if he could hear me. But he was back in a state of befuddlement and not aware of much of anything.

Taking a plastic grocery bag with me, I went into the bathroom for Mr. Tuttle's belongings. "I'm putting your personal things in this, Mr. Tuttle, along with your belt and boots. So, see, I didn't throw everything out."

"Lemme have the boots. I got sensitive feet."

He struggled with the black ankle-high boots, having a difficult time getting them on without socks. When he stood up, Lloyd turned away, his hand over his mouth to keep from laughing. I permitted myself a restrained smile at the sight Mr. Tuttle made when he wrapped the blanket over his shoulders like a toga and stomped toward the door in his boots with his bare white legs twinkling above them.

"Just hand in the key," I said, as I locked the cottage door and gave the key to Lloyd. "We're all paid up. Now, Mr. Tuttle, ordinarily I'd put you in the front seat in deference to your age and your position as our guest. I'd appreciate it, though, if you'd sit in the back. No insult intended, but I need to concentrate on my driving, and I can't risk a distraction if you get careless with that blanket. Lloyd, you get in front with me."

Mr. Tuttle mumbled something about not caring how he got away from this place, as long as he got away. He stumbled out into the weedy yard, squinching up his eyes against the glare of the sun. Lloyd guided him to the car.

When Mr. Tuttle got there, he stopped and backed up, looking at the machine from one end to the other.

"Whoa here, a minute. This yours?"

"Yes, it is," I said, unlocking the doors with the punch of a button.

"Maybe we oughta renegotiate our terms."

"Not on your life. What I can afford and what I can't is nobody's business, and has nothing to do with what you've agreed to work for. Now, get in."

He did, but he wasn't too happy about it. Then, as I turned the ignition, I glanced back at him sitting there like a draped Buddha. "I need directions. How do I get to the airport?"

"Airport? I'm not going to the airport. I'm going home for some clothes."

"All in good time," I assured him as I drove past the Royal Palm Court's office. "Now, which way do I turn?"

I had never in my life received such grumbling and resentful instructions on how to go and where to turn, but what else could he do? It's remarkable how a lack of clothing can make a man amenable to whatever you want.

As I turned in to a parking slot at the airport, Lloyd said, "I was getting worried, but looks like we're right on time. Is Mr. Tuttle going in with us?"

"Oh, I wouldn't think so."

Mr. Tuttle chimed in then. "Well, what am I going to do while you're traipsing all over the place?"

"Just stay right here. I'll leave the windows down, and as soon as we get Miss Wiggins, we'll be back. I wouldn't try to go anywhere if I were you. We're too far from the beach, and you might end up in jail if anybody sees you like that."

Miss Wiggins came bouncing out of that airplane like she'd flown it all on her own, and as thrilled as she was, she might have.

My eyes rolled just a little bit at her skintight jeans stuffed into high boots and her T-shirt with somebody's face on it. The heavy coat that she'd left the mountains in was slung over her arm, and she was ready for balmy Florida.

"Miss Julia!" she screamed, heading for me with open arms. As I edged away from her embrace, she veered to the right. "Lloyd!" She grabbed him in a big hug, chattering away about the flight and the breakfast she'd had thousands of feet up in the air. "I met all kinds of people, the nicest you'd ever want to know. You should've been with me, Lloyd."

"Miss Wiggins," I said, finally breaking in since I was anxious to move away from all the people smiling at her enthusiasm. "We have a guest in the car, and we'd better get back to him. Let's get your luggage and be on our way."

She had only the one suitcase, which soon came rolling out on the conveyor belt. Lloyd insisted on carrying it, although she put up a fuss at first.

As we approached the car, I slowed and said to Miss Wiggins, "I'm going to ask you to sit in the back with Mr. Tuttle, if you don't mind. He's been in a bad way, but he may be coming out of it. Just consider him your patient for the time being, and keep your eye on him."

"Oh, I will," she said, her face glowing with excitement. "I'm used to cranky old men."

Lloyd put her suitcase in the trunk, and I opened the back door for her. She leaned over and began to crawl in, then she abruptly backed out. "Whoops," she said. "That man's naked."

"Uh, well, that's part of the problem. But we're taking him home to get his clothes. Can you put up with his state of undress for a little while?"

"Oh, sure. I'm pretty used to that, too." And in she went, as Lloyd and I got in the front.

I turned to be sure that Mr. Tuttle was covered, and not only was he wrapped tightly in the blanket, he was cowering in the corner, looking trapped and embarrassed.

"Miss Wiggins," I said, beginning the formal introductions, "this is Mr. Frank Tuttle, who is going to help us recover our stolen goods. Mr. Tuttle, this is Miss Etta Mae Wiggins. She's a friend of the family who will help you get back on your feet."

For once, Mr. Tuttle had nothing to say, but as he took in Miss Wiggins's attributes through slitted eyes, he straightened up and tried to suck in his stomach.

"Hi," Miss Wiggins said cheerily. After her initial shock, she was as composed as she would've been if he'd been fully clothed. "We're gonna get along fine, aren't we?" She patted his thigh and, even though it was well covered, I had to turn away quickly and start the car. There's such a thing as too much familiarity, even if he was her patient.

Mr. Tuttle hardly knew what to make of Miss Wiggins. He sat quietly, except for giving me directions to his home and cutting his eyes at her, while she and Lloyd chattered away at all the sights. Finally, we came to a peeling blue block-shaped building without any architectural features to lift it out of the ordinary. I could almost understand why Mr. Tuttle might prefer a more convivial place if that was what he had to come home to every night. But far be it from me to criticize anyone's taste in housing.

"Pull in there," Mr. Tuttle said, pointing to a concrete driveway, "and go under the building."

I parked in an empty space that he said was his, and we sat for a few minutes while he swiveled around to see if anybody else was in the garage.

"Be back in a few minutes," he said, opening his door.

"We'll *all* be back in a few minutes," I said.

I opened my door, and Lloyd and Miss Wiggins followed suit.

Mr. Tuttle gave me a frowning look. "Be quicker if you wait here. I won't be long."

"I know you won't, but we're making every step you make until we know we can trust you."

"*Trust* me! Whatta you think I'm gonna do, run out on you?"

"I don't have an idea in the world what's on your mind, but I'm taking no chances. You have to admit that your performance to date hasn't been exactly stellar."

He rolled his eyes and got out of the car, with Miss Wiggins right behind him. "You mind if I call you Frank?" she asked, as she skipped to keep up with him. He just grunted, while she kept on. "You can call me Etta Mae, if you want to."

Frank? Etta Mae? My guard immediately went up. How much help would she be if I had to worry about leaving her with Mr. Tuttle? In his weakened state, he'd be no match for her boldness. I hoped I hadn't made a mistake by calling her.

Lloyd and I followed them to the elevator and crowded into the small space. For my benefit, Mr. Tuttle wrapped himself in the scratchy olive blanket with the air of an offended Roman senator. But his eyes kept wandering to Miss Wiggins whenever he thought nobody was looking.

When we stepped out on the fourth floor, he thrust out his hand, palm up, and gestured for his keys. Poor manners, but I dug them out of the plastic grocery bag and gave them to him.

His apartment was what I assumed was called a studio, since it consisted of one room, a bath, and a kitchen nook. I don't know why he was so anxious to leave the Royal Palm Court cottage, since what he had was not that much of an improvement. There was a pullout sofa bed that was still pulled out, with dingy sheets rumpled up on it. A pair of trousers were draped over a recliner with no effort having been expended to preserve the crease. An empty pizza box was on the coffee table, along with several empty and half-empty glasses. Other glasses and smelly beer bottles and piled-up ashtrays were scattered around on the yellow dinette table and on the floor. A television set and a stereo set were on bookshelves, plus an inordinate number of paperback books and magazines stacked up all over the place.

"Have a seat," he said, ungraciously, "if you can find one."

"Wow, Frank," Miss Wiggins said as her head swiveled around. "You've got a really nice place here. A little messy, but that can be fixed. Let's pick up a few things, Lloyd."

"You don't have to do that," I said, but she assured me she liked to stay busy. While she and Lloyd puttered around, I pulled out a chrome chair at the dinette table and carefully sat down. Mr. Tuttle went into a large walk-in closet where we heard hangers being shoved aside. In a few minutes, the blanket came sailing out into the room. Lloyd raised his eyebrows as he looked at me. I shrugged. It was already clear that Mr. Tuttle was not a neat person.

He came out of the closet wearing a pair of light blue linen-looking pants and a white undershirt. Carrying a white short-sleeve shirt, a yellow tie, and a blue plaid jacket, he headed for the bathroom.

"Why, Frank, you're a right good-looking man with your clothes on," Miss Wiggins said, but he ducked his head and ignored her.

"Help yourself to whatever's in the refrigerator," he said, before closing the bathroom door.

"Anybody want anything?" I said, almost under my breath.

"Not from this place, I don't," Lloyd whispered back.

Miss Wiggins wrinkled her nose. "I'll pass, too."

I nodded. So we sat there listening to Mr. Tuttle's shaving ritual and looking around at the room that was barren of all photographs, wall art, and personal knickknacks.

Lowering my voice again, I said, "I wonder how reliable he's going to be."

"Me, too," Lloyd said, leaning close to me. "He may not be worth the trouble we've already had with him. But then," he went on, frowning, "we're not supposed to pass judgment. Maybe we ought to witness to him, Miss Julia. I know that's what Mrs. Ledbetter would do."

I nodded. Emma Sue Ledbetter could grind a person into the ground with her witnessing, but that wasn't my way.

"Sometimes, Lloyd," Miss Wiggins said, surprising me no end, "what we do gets through better than what we say."

"That's quite true," I agreed. "So, maybe if Mr. Tuttle sees how committed we are, some of it will rub off on him." I sighed, knowing how infrequently that happened. "Let's just hope that we can turn him around, because unfortunately, he's all we have."

Lloyd said, "I wish he'd hurry up. We need to get him looking for those crooks."

Just thinking of how difficult that was

going to be almost overwhelmed me. I had not planned on having to nurse Mr. Tuttle, or to have Miss Wiggins do it, either.

Mr. Tuttle stepped out then, all shaved, shirted, tied, and jacketed, and Miss Wiggins said, "Woo, woo, don't you look nice."

As much as her comment distressed me, I had to admit that he had made himself fairly presentable. If you could overlook the bloodshot eyes, the bags that hung under them, the tiny piece of toilet paper over a razor nick, and a distinctively greenish tint around the gills. Also the slight trembling of his hands.

"Go on ahead and get the elevator," he said, putting his wallet, keys, comb, and so forth in his pockets. "I just need a glass of water."

We started for the door, but when I heard the second cabinet door close in the kitchen, I marched right back in there.

"Mr. Tuttle!"

"What! Goddoggit, woman, don't sneak up like that!" He turned his back, wrapping his arms around a suspiciously shaped bottle.

"I'm not having that, Mr. Tuttle. Etta Mae," I called. "Come make him put this thing up or, better still, pour it out."

"Come on now, Frank," Miss Wiggins

said, as she saw the problem and stepped right up to take control. "Believe me, the hair of the dog is not going to help."

"Look," he said, "I just need a little nip to get me up to speed. See." He held out a quivering hand. "One drink's all it takes to stop this."

"Yes," Miss Wiggins said, "and one leads to another and then another. Let's go now, and get busy finding Miss Julia's rings. You won't notice it once you start working."

"Don't pamper him, Miss Wiggins," I said, steaming at Mr. Tuttle's attempt to sneak another drink. "That trembling will stop on its own. And if it doesn't, why, he can do his work shaking from one end to the other, for all I care."

I couldn't interpret the look he gave me, as he stood there hugging that little flat bottle to his chest. He wanted to be mad, I could tell, but he had about run out of gas in his present weakened state.

His shoulders slumped in defeat, and he meekly put the bottle back in the cabinet. Then he drew a glass of water from the tap and drank it down. With an awful shudder, he turned from the sink with a beaten look on his face.

CHAPTER 20

His smoldering eyes told another story, however, and I girded myself to keep a vigilant watch over him every minute. I hoped that Miss Wiggins recognized what we were up against and stayed on her guard, as well.

"I'll drive," Mr. Tuttle said as we stepped out of the elevator into the garage. He had that hand out again, palm up, wiggling his fingers for the keys to my car.

"There's not enough insurance in the world for me to let you take the wheel in the shape you're in. But you can ride in the front seat, now that you're decent and don't constitute a hazard to me and everybody else on the road."

He gritted his teeth and accepted my decision with poor grace, crawling into the front seat and slamming the door. Miss Wiggins and Lloyd exchanged smiling glances as they got into the back.

Turning toward them, I said, "You two

buckled up back there? Are you, Mr. Tuttle? I wouldn't want to lose you."

"Ought to have a helmet, too," he mumbled under his breath. "Considering."

"Save your comments," I told him, as I backed out of the narrow space, then pulled up and backed out again. Mr. Tuttle clasped the armrest, as I braked and turned and pulled up and backed out another time, finally getting the car out on the street.

I breathed a sigh of relief when we were going in a straight line. "You would think they'd make those parking areas big enough to turn around in."

Mr. Tuttle buried his face in his hands. He came up for air with a deep breath and said, "Pull in at that convenience store up there."

Immediately on my guard, I demanded, "For what?"

"Cigarettes! Do you mind?"

"Well, yes, I do, but I'm not without some compassion. Breaking you of one bad habit is probably all you can handle at one time."

"I'll go with him," Miss Wiggins said.

As they got out of the car, Mr. Tuttle took another one of those long, exasperated breaths, but Miss Wiggins just grinned at him and slipped her arm through his.

When they came out of the store a few

minutes later, Mr. Tuttle crammed one pack of Winstons into his coat pocket and tore into another pack. He stopped and lit a cigarette, cupping his hands around the flame. Taking a deep drag that nearly put him on the ground, he leaned on Miss Wiggins's shoulder to keep his balance. Then he took another drag and flipped the thing away.

Getting back in the car, he said, "I figured you wouldn't let me smoke in here."

"You figured right. Where to now?"

"My office. Turn right out of here, then left on the Dixie Highway. I'm going to find your missing jewels and get you off my back."

"Believe me," I assured him, "it can't come soon enough. It's too hot down here for me."

"Me, too," Lloyd said.

"Not for me," Miss Wiggins chimed in. "I love it."

As we continued on toward Mr. Tuttle's office, Lloyd began filling in the blanks of the sorry tale concerning our loss and how we'd come to be in Florida. "Sergeant Coleman Bates told us the crooks could be here, so that's why we're here, too."

Mr. Tuttle grunted in response.

Back under the pink arcade, he unlocked

218

his office door and plowed on in, leaving the three of us to follow on our own. I pinched up my mouth at his rudeness, but didn't say anything even though Lloyd glanced up at me, surprised that I hadn't.

Since Mr. Tuttle had left us in his wake, we stood and took in the waiting room. I couldn't say much for his taste in decorating, but so far I hadn't been able to say much for his taste in anything. There was a black Naugahyde sofa against one wall and a number of armless and chrome-legged chairs by the others. A leaning floor lamp stood in one corner, and in front of the sofa there was a coffee table with an ashtray on it. A dusty artificial palm tree drooping over a brass pot and two sailing pictures were the only attempts at accessorizing the room, and, for my money, they both failed in the effort.

But Miss Wiggins was still in her wonder mode. "This is so nice," she said. "A bit dusty, though."

"Don't look at me," Lloyd said, backing away. "Let's just leave it. Besides, we need to get a place to stay."

"That's next on my list," I said, heading toward the office. "And we need some lunch, too."

Walking down a narrow hall toward the office light, we passed a dark and unoccupied secretarial nook and the open door of a bathroom. My mouth tightened as I closed it on my way.

At least his office, small and cluttered as it was, looked as if some work at some time had been done in it. A large metal desk with two of those chrome-legged chairs in front of it took up most of the space. File cabinets lined one wall, and a narrow table extended the desk to hold a computer, a printer, and a copying machine. Stacks of file folders filled every available surface, and crumpled papers littered the floor.

Maybe I was wrong. If any work could get done in all the clutter, it would be a marvel.

"How're you feeling, Mr. Tuttle?" I asked, trying to be considerate of the previous day's effects.

"Oh, just dandy," he said, as he began shuffling through the papers on his desk.

"Come on, now, Frank," Miss Wiggins said. "Be nice."

I took one of the seats across from him and sat my pocketbook on my lap. "We'd get along better if we all stopped resorting to sarcasm. I intend to follow my own advice, and it would be so much more pleasant if you'd do the same, Mr. Tuttle. And, since I'm on the subject, I might mention that a little gratitude for taking care of you would not be amiss."

I took no notice of the bleary-eyed stare that he gave me. "Now, Mr. Tuttle," I went on, my hands firmly on my pocketbook as I leaned toward him, "just how do you plan to go about this? We need a strategy for finding those thieves. Lloyd and I have already done the hard part by tracking them here to your town, so all you have to do is find their hideout."

He rubbed his hand across his face and took a deep breath as if to calm himself. "I'll make some calls. See where the cops are on this thing. They may already know where they are." He leaned over the desk and hunched his shoulders. "*If they're here.* I remind you that we don't know anything for sure, but if they are here, the cops may be gathering evidence and waiting for the right time to bust 'em."

"Well! We certainly don't want to miss out on that."

"Well!" he said in a feeble attempt to imitate my enthusiasm. "We certainly do. No way am I gonna get between a SWAT team and their target. You can forget that."

"I will not forget it. The thing to do, Mr. Tuttle, though far be it from me to tell you your business, is to get to them before the police do. I want my property back, and I don't want it to end up in police custody for an untold number of years while they try to prosecute crooks who have clearly stolen it."

Lloyd and Miss Wiggins looked as if they were at a tennis match, the way their heads were turning from one to the other of us.

With absolutely no expression on his face, Mr. Tuttle sat and stared at me. So I gave him a stiff nod to punctuate my words, and said, "You can go ahead and make your calls now, so we'll know how to proceed. And, Mr. Tuttle, I know that you feel so much better, now that you're back doing productive work, making a living, and helping people who are in distress. Let this be a lesson to you whenever you're tempted to make a return trip to that gin mill I found you in."

"Ah, God," he moaned, burying his face in his hands. Then with a martyred sigh, he said, "Why don't you all go get some lunch. Come on back later this afternoon, and we'll see what we have."

"Good idea," Lloyd said, as Miss Wiggins began to rise.

I twisted my mouth, studying Mr. Tuttle. Yes, he seemed eager to work, and yes, he was behaving in a professional manner, but his hands still shook, and he was in too much of a hurry to get rid of us.

"We'll do that," I said, rising and tucking my pocketbook under my arm. "Lloyd, you can come with me. We'll let Miss Wiggins stay here, if she doesn't mind. One of those fast hamburgers for you, Mr. Tuttle? And a milk shake to settle your stomach?"

"Yeah, Lord," he said, his eyes rolling up to the ceiling. "If that's the choice."

When I unwrapped a double cheeseburger and placed it in front of Mr. Tuttle, he went white as a sheet. Sweat popped out all over his face.

"Give it to the boy," he said, his voice strangling in his throat.

"You need to eat something, Frank," Miss Wiggins urged.

"That's right," I said. "We can't have you giving out on us, now that we've got you working. Try the milk shake. It's good for you."

"Just get that greasy thing away from me." Turning his head, he pushed the cheeseburger to the edge of the desk.

So we ate our lunch in the waiting room in deference to Mr. Tuttle's delicate stomach, listening all the while as he made and received telephone calls and clicked away on his computer.

"At least he sounds busy," Miss Wiggins said.

When we finished, I put the wrappings and empty cups into a bag and walked back through the hall to gather up Mr. Tuttle's leavings.

Surprised to find that he'd closed his office door, I tapped once and opened it. He sat behind his desk, holding some papers up as if he were intent on his work. But he couldn't hide the bloom on his nose and cheeks, and he couldn't dispel the fumes in the air that greeted me.

I walked right up to his desk and pinned him with an indignant glare. "Where is it? I declare, if a man isn't trustworthy, he's not worth a thing. Let's have the bottle."

He had the grace to look a little sheepish, then he leaned down and fished an empty bottle from a trash can. "There was only a little sip left."

"It doesn't smell like a little sip. I am surprised and disappointed in you, Mr. Tuttle. I thought you'd given your word to stay away from that stuff."

"Well, but," he said, eager now to appease me, "I got some news for you. Your thieves may be here, sure enough, only over on Palm Beach. I may be able to pin 'em down a little more when I make contact with a buddy of mine."

I opened my mouth to say something, but

the phone rang and he quickly answered it. While I listened to his grunts and monosyllabic replies to his caller, I tried to tamp down my anger by studying the contents of the frames on the wall.

When he hung up the phone, he leaned so far back in his swivel chair that it creaked and crackled under him. As he put his head back and closed his eyes, I tiptoed over and looked down at him, wondering if he was thinking or dropping off to sleep.

Careful not to break his concentration, if that's what he was doing, I murmured, "I see from these commendations that you were a fine officer in your time."

He cocked one eye at me. "My time's not over."

"I'll give you all the credit you deserve when you find my rings. I'll not only praise you to the skies, I'll give you a bonus."

That brought him straight up in his chair. "How much?"

"Don't you worry about that. I'm a generous woman when it comes down to it. You just stay away from juke joints and hidden bottles and stick to your knitting, and I'll see that you're a happy man when we leave."

"Won't need a bonus for that," he mumbled, but he started in on his papers again. Then with a wheedling smile, as if we were back on good terms, he said, "Why don't you take everybody and drive around a little. See the sights. Go out to the beach, do some shopping."

When I didn't immediately take him up on his suggestions, he turned away and grumbled, "One thing I miss about the Tampa PD is the authority to keep the public off my back."

"You're not in the best of health, you know," I reminded him. "You might be glad to have someone around in case you have a relapse. But I do need to get us checked into a hotel, so we'll go do that."

"Good!" he said with an inordinate display of enthusiasm. "Come on back around six, and I might have something to report. And," he went on with a sideways glance at me, "you'll owe me a check."

"I'm aware of that. And you keep it in mind, too, in case you have the urge to sneak off to some place you shouldn't be."

Then, with a pleasant smile, I said, "I'll just leave Miss Wiggins to keep you company."

CHAPTER 21

Taking Lloyd with me, I drove around until we found more suitable accommodations than the Royal Palm Court. It was immediately apparent from the liveried doorman to the number of valets that the Crestview Hotel, which had neither a crest nor a view, was more in keeping with my expectations. Lloyd was thrilled because it had a swimming pool, and I was pleased because of its in-house restaurant and room service. I chose it, too, for the sake of convenience, since it was about halfway between Mr. Tuttle's apartment and his office. We could get to either one in a few minutes if the need arose, which, if past experience was any guide, it very well could.

I took two rooms right across the hall from each other, one with a king bed for Miss Wiggins and one for Lloyd and me with two double beds. When we were led to it, I saw that it was spacious and well-appointed, with a sitting area, a cabinet stocked with all kinds of snacks and drinks that I intended to keep locked, and a clean, rust-free bathroom filled with towels, soap, lotion, shampoo, and two kinds of tissue.

Relieved to be settled in a place with all the amenities, and grateful to have Mr. Tuttle in Miss Wiggins's capable hands, I sank back into a comfortable lounge chair. Intending only to rest a few minutes while Lloyd unpacked his clothes, the previous miserable night almost caught up with me.

But there was no rest for the weary, for my eyes popped open at the recall of what I'd left undone. Reaching for the phone, I said, "We better call Lillian and let her know where we are."

Lloyd said, "I was just thinking that."

But when Lillian answered, I could hardly get a word in edgewise. As soon as she heard my voice she started in.

"Where you been? Me an' Latisha settin' up here waitin' to hear from you, not knowin' a thing an' Mr. Sam, he call long-distance an' I had to make up something real quick so he won't fly home to see about you. An' I don't like tellin' stories to nobody."

"Slow down, Lillian. What'd you tell him?"

"I say you doin' something at the church

with Miz Ledbetter 'cause I couldn't think of nothin' else."

"That's perfect, Lillian. If he calls back and wants details, tell him I'm attending a seminar with Emma Sue entitled 'Good Wives Create Good Husbands.' "

"Title what?"

"That's probably too much detail, anyway. Just tell him I'm out learning how to be a good wife."

"Well, I hope so," she said, sounding somewhat appeased.

Wanting her off that subject, I proceeded to change it. "You'll be glad to know that Etta Mae Wiggins is with us now."

"She is? Well, thank the Lord. Now I feel better, 'cause she got a head on her shoulders."

After telling her where we were staying and giving her our phone number, I handed the phone to Lloyd so he could assure her that he was safe and getting enough to eat.

Pleased that I'd done all I could for the time being, I put my head back against the chair and napped for a few minutes. When I woke up, Lloyd had on fresh clothes and was combing his wet hair in front of a mirror.

"I used that spa tub, Miss Julia," he said, when he saw me sit up. "It's really something. You ought to try it."

"Maybe I will. What time is it?"

"About five."

"Oh, my goodness." I sprang up as fast as my stiff joints would let me. "We'd better get over there and check on Miss Wiggins. I'm sure she's had enough babysitting for today. Why'd you let me sleep so long?"

"I was about to wake you. I'm a little worried about her, too. She might think we've forgotten her."

After a quick freshening up, I rushed Lloyd out the door and down the elevator to the car, more and more concerned about having left Miss Wiggins on duty so long. If I'd had a decent night's sleep the night before, I wouldn't have succumbed to the temptation of a nap.

Relieved to see Mr. Tuttle's car parked in the strip mall lot and a dim light in his office, we parked and walked under the arcade. I quickened my steps, eager to hear what he'd learned. Maybe he'd already beat the bushes and found the crooks. Wouldn't that be a wonder? I couldn't wait to get inside.

"Etta Mae," Lloyd called as we entered. "We're back."

She poked her head out of the office, still with a cheery smile on her face. Things couldn't be too bad, if she was so undaunted.

"Hey," she said. "Did you get moved? We've been having a grand time. Frank's been working away, and I've read every two-year-old magazine in the place. And look, Lloyd," she said as we came toward her. She held out her hands, her freshly painted fingernails wiggling in front of him. "I ran next door and got this new polish. It's called I'm-Not-Really-A-Waitress Red. Don't you love it?"

He looked them over. "Real nice," he said, but he didn't sound all that impressed. Nor was I, even when she offered to paint my nails the same red.

Mr. Tuttle sat behind his desk, right where we'd left him, ignoring our entrance. He had the telephone cradled on his shoulder while scribbling on a notepad.

"Yeah," he said into the receiver, reaching over to stub out a cigarette. "I got it. And that's it? Okay, bud, I owe you one." He listened, then grinned. "Yeah, same to you." And hung up.

"Well," he said, giving us a quick glance while he stirred the papers on his desk, "That was the last call, so I'm wrapping it up for the day."

My heart sank, for it was clear that he'd gotten no closer to our goal. I stood by his desk, clutching my pocketbook. "It seems to me that, instead of sitting here and talking on the telephone all day, you would've been out looking for that nest of vipers. I expected more from you."

"Mrs. Murdoch," he said tiredly, as if he was almost at the end of his rope, "I need to know where to look. You want to wander around the streets and on the beach trying to figure out who's a thief and who's not, then be my guest. What I'm doing is eliminating as many leads as I can, so I'll know what to investigate. Can you understand that?"

"I understand this," I said. "People who get snippy are most unattractive."

"Well, Lord preserve us," he said, rearing back and raising his arms in mock alarm. "I sure don't want to be unattractive. That's my number one priority."

There was that sarcasm again. I glared at him and, not giving an inch, he glared right back. As we battled back and forth, neither of us willing to break off, my mouth began to twitch and an uncontrollable urge swept through me. It was all I could do to keep a straight face. Then Miss Wiggins chimed in.

"O-o-oh, Frank," she said brightly. "I can help you with that. I love to do makeovers."

Our staring contest broke apart as his eyes darted to her and his mouth dropped open.

Mine did the same.

"See, Frank," she said, walking over to him, "you'd be more attractive in a solid color instead of all that plaid. Maybe all gray or all brown. A block of color would tone your complexion down. It's a little on the ruddy side, don't you think? You ought to have your colors done, so you'd know what to wear."

She began smoothing his hair, then leaned over and peered at his face up close. His mouth closed, then opened again with nothing coming out. "You ought to be using a serum product, too," she went on. "It'll do wonders for your skin. And your eyebrows, Frank! You need to pluck those strays. Want me to do it for you?"

Cringing from her close inspection, he held up his hands. "It was a figure of speech! I don't care what I look like."

But I was too far gone by that time. The thought of a pair of delicate tweezers in Mr. Tuttle's hands hovering over his heavy eyebrows had set me off. I started laughing and couldn't stop. Bending over and covering my mouth with my hand, I tried my best to regain control. But the more I tried, the funnier Mr. Tuttle's number one priority became.

I was laughing so hard that I needed a

Kleenex to mop my eyes. And every time I looked at Mr. Tuttle's bewildered face, I lost control of myself again.

Miss Wiggins immediately came to my aid. "Are you all right, Miss Julia? Maybe you better sit down."

She guided me to a chair while Lloyd watched with baffled concern. "What's so funny?" he asked.

"Nothing," I said, waving my hand as I tried to compose myself. "Just a passing thought." But as that thought passed by again, another full-body laugh erupted.

"I'm sorry, Mr. Tuttle," I finally managed to get out. "I got carried away there for a minute. Too much stress, I expect." I dabbed at the last of the tears on my face, took a deep breath, and went on. "I apologize for speaking so sharply to you earlier. This theft has unnerved me and affected my manners, which are normally above reproach." Fanning my face, I made an effort to get back to business. "Now, I'd like an update on what you've accomplished today. And we need to discuss how to proceed tomorrow, although if there's anything that can be done tonight, I don't see why we can't do it. I know you want to see this matter to a happy conclusion as much as I do."

"Probably more," he mumbled, without

the least acknowledgment of my apology. Then he called his answering service, saying, "I'll be at Maxey's Seafood."

Then he got his jacket and started out of the office. "Well, come on. I'm locking up."

"Where're we going?"

"I'm going to eat."

"Oh, good," Miss Wiggins said. "I'm starving, aren't you, Lloyd?"

"Wait, Mr. Tuttle," I said, hurrying after him. "You can't stop working this early. You've barely put in a full day."

He stopped, took a deep breath, and said, "Look, I'm taking a West Palm PD detective out for a . . . taking him to dinner. To see if he's heard any talk, anything funny or unusual going on in South Florida. You don't mind if I eat at the same time, do you?"

"Not at all. We'll go with you."

"No, ma'am, you will not. Trust me, it's no place for you and the boy." He glanced at Miss Wiggins. "Etta Mae might enjoy it, but it's business for me."

"If you're taking someone to dinner, it must be a restaurant, isn't it?"

"Well, yeah. It qualifies."

"Uh-huh, but it's mostly a juke joint, isn't it?"

He rolled his eyes so far back that I doubted they'd ever be straight again. "All right, Mrs.

Murdoch, it has a bar, okay? But I have to go where the information is, don't I? So if you want me to find your valuables, you'll let me do what it takes to find them. Although I'll tell you right now, I think you're on a fool's errand."

"We'll go with you. There's no telling how much information we can pick up just by listening. Now, Mr. Tuttle, if you roll those eyes one more time, they're going to be locked in your head, and then where would you be?"

Gritting his teeth, he managed to say, "All right, but I'm warning you, you're not gonna like it."

"Let me worry about that. If it takes hobnobbing with drunks and alcoholics and beer drinkers and the like to find my property, why, I'm willing to bear it. Etta Mae," I went on, "I'd like you to go with him, and Lloyd and I will follow in my car. We'll pull in at the Crestview Hotel first and get Lloyd settled in the room, then go on together."

Before Lloyd could object, which he was about to do, I forestalled him. "I'm not taking you into a bar. For one thing, they'd evict all of us. But while we're gone, you can rent a decent movie and order room service. Won't that be fun?" Turning back to Mr. Tuttle, I said, "You and Miss Wiggins can wait in the car while I make sure he's all right."

"I'm not waiting for anybody," Mr. Tuttle said.

"Oh, please do. You might need help with the bill."

I could see his mind working, counting the twelve dollars in his pocket. "We'll take your car."

But even as he conceded, Mr. Tuttle made a noise down in his throat that sounded like he was choking.

To make him feel better, I said, "Remember I'll be paying you for your day's work tonight, plus paying for your friend's dinner. So, see, you'll be glad we came along."

"It'll all go on expenses anyway," he said, but so low that I could hardly hear him. He was gradually learning not to argue with me but, like Lillian, he had to have the last word, even if it did him no good.

Since I was getting my way, I began to feel a little more kindly toward him. Until we walked out to my car and he marched right around to my door. "I'm driving," he said, "and no back talk."

"I am not accustomed to being spoken to that way. But," I said, quickly changing my tune at the expression on his face, "if you feel that strongly, maybe you better drive."

With Mr. Tuttle at the wheel, we were soon turning in to the Crestview, where he parked in a loading zone and put his investigator's license on the dashboard.

"Golly, Frank," Etta Mae said, "I didn't know you were official."

He shrugged. "It works sometimes."

The doorman opened our doors, and Lloyd and I prepared to crawl out. As we left, I heard Miss Wiggins say, "Would you look at all that gold braid on him? And the lights, Frank, they've got this whole place lit up. Lights under the trees. Lights on the trees. I can't believe I'm going to get to sleep here."

I hurried Lloyd upstairs, all the while telling him what he could do and what he couldn't. "Be careful of the movie you select. Order a balanced meal, and don't let anybody in but whoever delivers it. Stay in the room until I get back, and keep the door locked with the safety latch on. But don't go to sleep if you can help it. I'll need you to let me in." The boy wasn't happy about being left out and grumbled a bit about it. But, in another instance of the difference between him and his father, keeping on and on about something wasn't in his nature.

Even so, I briefly considered staying there with him, since I didn't like leaving him

238

alone. On further thought, though, I didn't see how I could. I still didn't trust Mr. Tuttle, especially in a bar, and I wasn't sure I could trust Miss Wiggins, known at home as a fairly loose woman, with him.

"All set," I said, getting back into the car. "Let's go have a nice dinner together."

Mr. Tuttle cut his red-rimmed eyes at me, and I do believe he snorted. "You might as well know that the place we're going to is a cop hangout. It'll be loud and crowded and, whether you like it or not, Mrs. Murdoch, people're going to be drinking."

"Sounds like my kinda place," Miss Wiggins giggled. "Just kidding, Miss Julia." But I wasn't sure she was.

Mr. Tuttle went on with his instructions to us. "I want you both to walk right through the bar on into the back, where there're tables. Sit down, order something, and stay outta my hair. I've got people to see and things to do, and I don't want any comments about the way I go about it. Are we clear on that?"

My, he was in a cranky mood. I said nothing for a while, marveling as he maneuvered my car through the traffic like he'd been driving it all his life. I wondered if cars could sense when a seasoned driver was at the wheel. It seemed so to me, because it never behaved so docilely when I was driving it.

"Please don't worry about Etta Mae and me," I finally said. "We won't bother you in the conduct of your, well, *my* business. If, indeed, that's what you aim to conduct. But I am telling you that I am not going to put up with another unseemly episode on your part. You stay away from the stuff that put you in such a condition, and you won't have any problem with me."

I glanced at Miss Wiggins in the backseat, who leaned up, grinning, and poked Mr. Tuttle on the shoulder. "We'll be watching you, Frank."

Mr. Tuttle didn't say a word, just swung that big car into a parking lot, jerked it to a standstill, and got out. Slammed the door, too.

CHAPTER 22

It was almost full dark when the three of us walked through the packed parking lot toward Maxey's Seafood, Bar & Grill, and even darker when we got inside. I stopped in my tracks right inside the door, so taken aback that I couldn't take another step. Etta Mae and Mr. Tuttle crowded up behind me as I stood stock-still, amazed at the congested mass of humanity milling around in that loud, smoke-filled room. There were the biggest, burliest men I'd ever seen hanging on to the bar and the loosest, most wanton women hanging on to them. The crowd rippled and eddied and swirled in on itself, smoke hung in a hazy cloud, the odor of alcohol assaulted my senses, the blaring beat of the jukebox throbbed under the yelling, talking, and shouts of laughter, and every last one of those merrymakers had a glass or a bottle in hand. Out of the midst of the din, an occasional curse word pierced the commotion, and even worse, I do believe that every man and half the women had a handgun on a belt or under a shoulder. Mr. Tuttle had been right: It wasn't my kind of place.

Miss Wiggins stopped close behind me, and standing on tiptoes to look around, she said, "Oh, Toby Keith, I love him! You like to dance, Frank?"

He didn't answer, just jabbed a finger past my head and growled, "Dining room's that way. Go straight through and stay there."

"This is awful," I said. "You can't hear yourself think."

"Don't complain to me," he said, surveying the crowd and speaking from the side of his mouth. "I warned you. Now move out of the door and go find a table."

I straightened my shoulders, took a grip on my pocketbook, and let Etta Mae lead the way. She cut a swath through the crowd as every male eye turned to follow her.

We marched through that roiling mass of men and women, silencing them as we passed, me in my lavender crepe and off-white Naturalizer pumps and Etta Mae in her tight jeans. I looked neither to the left nor the right, telling myself that it was no worse than walking into church when every member, including the pastor, turned to see who was coming in late.

It was considerably quieter and less crowded in the back room, but there was no lessening of the number of beer bottles and suspicious-looking glasses on the tables. And, would you believe, some of the clientele hiding out in the back room were wearing law enforcement uniforms? I thought of writing a letter to the editor, complaining about such blatant disregard for the dignity of the profession. You would never see such a thing in Abbotsville.

Etta Mae and I took the first empty booth, sliding in opposite each other, since I was in no mind to wait to be seated. Good thing, too, for I never did see a hostess.

"Here's the menu, Etta Mae," I said. "It seems limited, but order whatever you want."

We both had steaks, which were quickly served on sizzling platters. While I ate, I worried about what Lloyd was having. I was uneasy for having left him to his own devices, but he was in a better place than we were.

While I picked at my meal, Etta Mae went at hers wholeheartedly. In between bites, though, she craned her neck to watch what was happening in the front room, her eyes sparkling with the wonder of it all. "This place is really rockin'," she said. "Reminds me of the Delmont Roadhouse back home, except it only gets revved up on Saturday nights."

I turned around to look toward the front, too, worried about what Mr. Tuttle was up to. I couldn't imagine that any kind of decent work could transpire in such a raucous atmosphere. Even more, I worried about Mr. Tuttle himself. What if he started drinking again? How would we get him home? How would we find our jewelry if he lost another day or so, vomiting and sleeping, sleeping and vomiting?

"Miss Wiggins. I mean, Etta Mae," I said. "I'm concerned about getting back to the hotel at a reasonable time. I don't like leaving Lloyd so long, and if Mr. Tuttle gives in to temptation, we could be here half the night."

She swallowed what was in her mouth. "I don't think he'll go on a toot tonight. Yesterday scared him. It was his first blackout."

"That's what it was?"

"Yes, ma'am, he doesn't remember a thing."

"I wish I didn't," I said, the picture of his prostration vivid in my mind. "Well, I guess if we need help with him, there're plenty of police officers we can call on. Although from the looks of most of them, I'd almost rather put my trust in your average man on the street. I'm sorry you're being exposed to it."

"Oh, I don't mind," she said, her fingers tapping on the table in time to the pounding music. "I just hope Frank can find your jewelry. Listen, Miss Julia," she said, as she leaned across the table, "I think there's more to him than we've seen."

Well, she would, wouldn't she? But, so far, I wasn't convinced.

Mr. Tuttle, looking bright-eyed and flushed in the face, suddenly slid into the booth beside Etta Mae. "You two have dinner?"

I pursed my mouth, registering my disapproval as a wave of beery breath wafted across the table. "Yes, thank you, we have. Now, I'd like a report on what you accomplished today, and tonight, as well. If you're capable of giving it."

"Let up, Mrs. Murdoch," he said, smearing his hand across his face. "What you saw yesterday was an unusual occurrence. I was between jobs."

"I accept your apology," I said, and thought he was going to get up and leave right then. "Sit down, Mr. Tuttle, I owe you for the day, and I'll pay you as soon as you give your report."

He sank back in the booth and, propping his elbow on the table, hid his face in his hand. "Aw, God," he said, then he pulled himself together and took a small spiral notebook from his jacket pocket. "Okay, here's where we are. Word's out that there is a jewelry ring operating throughout the southern states. They hit private homes, mainly in small towns, then move on before the owners know they've been robbed. Local police look first at the usual suspects, while the real ones are doing it again miles away. So the cops end up a day late and a dollar short. That's why it's taken so long for them to put it together. Local forces thought they were the only ones involved."

"We already know that," I said.

Mr. Tuttle didn't like being interrupted. He gave me a quick glare, then turned a few pages in his notebook. "Well, maybe you don't know this. A suspect in another case let something slip about Palm Beach being the central drop for loads of jewelry coming in from all over the place." He closed his notebook and looked around for the waitress. "That's it."

"That's it? Why, Mr. Tuttle, you haven't learned one thing that Sergeant Coleman Bates in Abbotsville hasn't already told us. I expected a good deal more from you."

He leaned his arms on the table and stared at me. "Listen, what I've done is *confirm* what you brought to me as rumor. Do you think I just jump up and act on anything that walks in the door? No, I don't, and I've already told you that this is like looking for a needle in a haystack. And now, I've put in a full day of work for you, and I want to be paid."

"And I want you to know that Sergeant Coleman Bates is an excellent deputy sheriff, and he doesn't deal in rumor. All you've done is go back over the same ground as he has. But," I said with a sigh, "to show good faith, I will pay you for duplicating his work." And I wrote out a check, knowing that he couldn't cash it and get into trouble during the night.

Handing it to him, I said, "You'll be happy to know that you'll have more help tomorrow."

"Oh, good," he said, folding the check and putting it into his breast pocket. "I hope it's that ace of a sergeant you've been throwing up at me."

"No, you're going to have Etta Mae, Lloyd, and me working with you all day. Now that we're settled, we can devote the whole day to whatever you need us to do."

I gathered my pocketbook, readying myself to leave. "And I hope after a good night's sleep, you'll have a better disposition. Are you ready to go?"

He took no notice, motioning instead to a monstrous man who appeared at our booth. At Mr. Tuttle's invitation, the man crammed himself in beside me, as I moved as far into the corner as I could.

"This is Mac McGruder," Mr. Tuttle said. "He's a detective with the West Palm sheriffs, and he's heard a few things you might be interested in."

I estimated Mr. McGruder's height at close to that of Lieutenant Peavey back home, with an additional fifty pounds or so on his frame. His shoulders were massive, straining his pale green jacket. Under it, he wore a yellow polo shirt, open at the neck to reveal a gold chain glinting in the half-light. I wouldn't have thought him the jewelry type, but then I'd rarely been around the type that was. His face was fleshy, the kind that would fold into wrinkles if he lost weight. Sunburned scalp peeked through his thin, sandy-colored hair. All in all, not what I'd had in mind to direct us toward our goal. But I'd been wrong before.

"Will you have some dinner, Mr. Mc-Gruder?" I asked. "The selection here isn't the best, but perhaps you'll have something?"

"No, ma'am," he said, his voice surprisingly soft and high-pitched for such a large-chested man. Then again, I've often found that the larger the man, the squeakier his voice.

Giving Miss Wiggins a speculative glance, he picked up a salt shaker and began turning it around in his hands. "Frank tells me you got some jewelry missing."

"That's correct, and it's worrying us to death. If you know the whereabouts of those home invaders who stole it, I would appreciate hearing it. We don't intend to leave here until we've found what we came for."

"What'd I tell you?" Mr. Tuttle said under his breath. Then in a normal tone, he went on. "Help us out here, Mac, if you can."

"Well, I tell you," Mr. McGruder said, looking at me from under eyebrows that were thicker than the hair on his head. "Frank has done just about everything that can be done already. I've helped by running a few databases that he can't access, but there's not much there. I want you to know, though, that Frank's good at this business, real good. We worked together some years back, and they don't come any better. If he can't find your thieves, I'd bet they're not here."

"Thank you for the testimonial," I said, getting my back up at the thought that Mr. Tuttle had primed him to brag on his investigative prowess. "But the proof is in the doing. If Mr. Tuttle is so good, where is my jewelry? Just saying it's not here is not telling me where it is."

Mr. McGruder smiled at the salt shaker, then at Etta Mae. "It's a mystery, all right. We've been getting word of a lot of jewelry thefts around the state, but none here. That's the only lead I have for you, if it qualifies as one."

"But doesn't that tell you something?"

"Maybe," he nodded. "It could mean that they don't want to . . . well, mess in their own backyard. There's only one other possibility I can think of, but it won't help you."

"I'm open to any and all possibilities," I said. "Let's hear it."

"Yeah," Etta Mae said, quivering with anticipation. "We're ready for some action."

In the midst of the din coming from the barroom, a buzzing noise began sounding on Mr. McGruder's person. He flipped his jacket back, revealing a holstered pistol. As Etta Mae's eyes glittered, Mr. McGruder fiddled with a pager on his belt.

"Gotta call in," he said, heaving himself out of the booth. "Sorry I couldn't be more help. Frank'll fill you in." And with a nod to Mr. Tuttle and a wink at Etta Mae, he left, weaving his way through the tables and disappearing into the mob in the next room.

"Well," I said, leaning back against the seat. "That was sudden and not very polite."

"He's Homicide," Mr. Tuttle said, as if that explained anything. "You two ready to go?"

I nodded, my shoulders slumped at our lack of progress. I was disappointed, but not yet defeated.

"I want to know what Mr. McGruder's one possibility is," I said, stopping Mr. Tuttle's move from the booth in midslide.

"It's not much," he said, in a begrudging way. "But if you must know, there're a few rumors floating around that might be worth checking out. Everybody gets real tight-lipped when something like this is up."

"Come on, Frank," Miss Wiggins urged. "Don't be so secretive, and tell us what's going on."

He leaned across the table and lowered his voice, looking first at her and then at me. "The feds're in town."

CHAPTER 23

After quickly checking the figures on the bill, I left money on the table and hurried to catch up with Mr. Tuttle and Etta Mae, anxious to hear more. We edged between first one and then another reveler, as Etta Mae again drew attention, until we finally gained the comparatively fresh air outside. I had stopped expecting the most minor of courtesies from Mr. Tuttle, although you would think he'd have walked us to the car instead of going ahead and waiting beside it. Especially after that bombshell he'd just dropped.

"Feds?" Miss Wiggins whispered to me as we stumbled across the gravel lot. "We better watch our step around them."

Mr. Tuttle unlocked the car and opened the doors for us, then walked around the car, tossing the keys up in the air and catching them. Except when he dropped them twice and had to feel around in the dark to find them.

He got into the driver's seat and immediately started the car. "I'm going back to the office for my car. Then you and Etta Mae can go to bed."

"We are not going to bed until you explain about those feds you mentioned. Who are they, what are they doing, and what do they have to do with us?"

I thought he wasn't going to answer, but when he stopped for a red light, he said, "Maybe nothing. But there's a house over on Palm Beach that the locals've been told is off-limits. That could mean that the feds have an eye on it."

My heart jumped. "And it could mean that they've cornered those sneak thieves and are just waiting to jump in and arrest them."

"We don't know that," Mr. Tuttle said as if he had to explain the way of the world to a simpleton. "Don't jump to conclusions. It could be something entirely different, something that has nothing to do with you, if you can believe that."

"Don't be snippy, Mr. Tuttle. I'm not in the mood. Just tell me what you plan to do. Let's find out about that house, for one thing — who's in it and, most particularly, what's in it. I tell you, I want my one-of-a-kind, well, *two*-of-a-kind engagement ring back before they cut out the stones and send them out of the country. And my wedding band, too."

"I don't blame you," Miss Wiggins said from the backseat. "Come on, Frank, tell us about those feds. Are they T-Men or G-Men, DEA, FBI, ICE, or what?"

He shrugged. "I don't know what they are, and I don't plan to find out. All I'm doing tonight is see that you get back to the hotel and stay there. Then I'm going to scope out a certain block on Palm Beach and see what I can see."

"Oh, good," I said. "We'll go with you."

"No, you won't."

Miss Wiggins bounced in her seat. "Oh, please, Frank. I've always wanted to go on a stakeout."

"Let's not argue, Mr. Tuttle," I added. "The reason we came down here was to recover our property, and if it's right across that river out there, I want to know about it. But first, please drive us to the Crestview."

Mr. Tuttle took his eyes off the road to stare at me. "You're going to bed?"

"No, we're going to pick up Lloyd. I can't leave him for however long a stakeout will take. You'll be surprised at how much help he can be."

"I'll be surprised, all right," he said in a tight voice. "All I've had here lately is one surprise after another. First you show up, then Etta Mae bounces in, and now this. Don't surprise me anymore. I can't take it."

Fearing he'd hurt Miss Wiggins's feelings, I said, "Etta Mae's here for one reason and one reason only, and that's to help you. If anybody can break you of your bad habits, she can."

I could almost feel him steam up as he gripped the steering wheel hard enough to snap it in two. "Look," he finally said, after he abruptly braked at a stop sign. "You don't want to go on a stakeout. Believe me, you don't. It's long, it's boring, and it may not tell us anything. On top of that, you have to stay quiet, which I know you can't do."

"Now, you look," I said, rubbing my shoulder where the seat belt had cut into it. "I know you had something to drink at that bar, and I know you didn't have a bite to eat. That's a deadly combination, Mr. Tuttle, because you'll be asleep two minutes after you get to that house. But with us there, you'll have three extra pairs of eyes to take up the slack."

He made a strangled noise in his throat, but by that time we were at the Crestview. He parked in the same spot with the same bad grace, crossed his arms, and sulked.

Miss Wiggins said, "Stay here, Miss Julia.

I'll go get him."

Happy to let her make that trek, I remained beside Mr. Tuttle, enjoying blessed silence. I was tired of the constant arguments with him. You'd think he'd be tired of them, too, especially since he hadn't won one.

Lloyd and Miss Wiggins came revolving out of the door of the hotel and tumbled into the backseat, chattering with excitement. Mr. Tuttle heaved an injured sigh and cranked the car, letting it idle while he tried one more time to discourage us.

He jerked a thumb at the backseat and said, "They ought to be in bed, and you know it."

"I'm not sleepy," Lloyd said.

"Me, either," Miss Wiggins said. "I am *ready.*"

"See," I said, "they're not sleepy."

"Do you even know what a stakeout is?" Mr. Tuttle's agitation showed in the way he gripped the steering wheel.

"We certainly do, and there's no need to raise your voice."

"I do," Miss Wiggins chimed in. "I have a friend who's a deputy sheriff."

"Ah, God," Mr. Tuttle said, leaning his head against the door. "Don't tell me. It's that wonder of wonders, Sergeant Coleman Bates, again."

"No," Miss Wiggins said, frowning. "I mean, I know him, but I meant somebody else."

"All right," Mr. Tuttle conceded, which would've saved considerable time if he'd done so in the first place. "We'll go, but here's what you're going to do. You're going to sit in this car as long as I tell you to, and you're going to keep quiet while you're doing it."

"Are we going to sit here all night?" I asked, a couple of hours later as we sat in the car, parked between streetlights on a side street in Palm Beach. We were somewhere between the ocean and the Intracoastal Waterway, but I wasn't sure exactly where.

Mr. Tuttle had driven us from the Crestview through the night-lit city and across the bridge that spanned the waterway onto the island of the rich and famous. Miss Wiggins had gasped and moaned at all the sights along the way, being particularly impressed with the tall palms that lined the streets and the massive hotels, and disappointed that high walls and tall hedges kept her from seeing the mansions. She'd kept pointing out the side window, saying, "Look at that, Lloyd. I can't believe I'm actually here."

Mr. Tuttle had made several turns, and

took us to what seemed to be the middle of the island, into a residential area. He'd parked on the street, several houses down from our target, which he'd grudgingly pointed out to us.

The small houses, at least in comparison to those on the beachfront, were lined up fairly close together on lots that I was sure would make me go white in the face if I'd had to buy one. Most of the two-story homes looked to be made of stucco, painted various pastel colors. The one we were watching was some shade of pink. At least, it seemed so from what I could see of it. Palm trees and hedges and vines and blooming shrubs hid almost all the houses — and that one in particular. I had to strain to see it, noting that whoever was in it had most of the lights on.

"Don't complain to me," Mr. Tuttle said, showing no sympathy at all for the hours of tedium we were enduring. "I told you."

He'd pushed his seat back so he could stretch out his limbs, but now he sat all scrunched up, leaning against the window. I was still sitting upright, my eyes glued to the house where I was more and more convinced that my precious rings lay waiting for me. Lloyd and Etta Mae had watched intently for a while, but I had heard the occasional whisper and muffled laugh. For some little while, though, there'd been silence from the backseat. It was long past our bedtime, and the warm night air wafting over from the ocean a few blocks away drifted through our open windows, making my head nod and my eyes grow heavy.

Now and then, when a car turned in to the street, Mr. Tuttle would say, "Get down," and we'd all scoot down in our seats so that four people sitting in a car during the wee hours of the morning would not draw unwanted attention.

After one such episode I sat back up just as a light went out in one of the upstairs rooms of the house.

"You think they're going to bed?" I whispered.

Miss Wiggins giggled and said, "Lucky ducks."

I ignored her, and turning to Mr. Tuttle, said, "Maybe they're coming out and going somewhere else."

I could feel his eyes on me in the dark, saw him stretch and change his position. "We don't even know if that's them. We're operating on rumor here. For all I know, they could be in Timbuktu or, Lord help us, back robbing houses in that hick town you come from."

"I doubt it, Mr. Tuttle, and if I came from

a place like West Palm Beach I wouldn't be casting slurs on somebody else's hometown. From what I've seen of it so far, your town has little to recommend it."

Lloyd said, "Now, y'all." I had to smile in spite of the fact that Mr. Tuttle tried my very soul.

We watched another light go out in a downstairs room, but one front room stayed lit behind drawn curtains, and another toward the back that I figured for the kitchen.

"Looks like somebody went to bed and some others are staying up," I said, trying to see my watch and failing.

"If it's who we think, they'll keep a lookout all night." Mr. Tuttle yawned wide enough to make his jaws creak. Then he settled back again.

"Miss Julia?" Lloyd leaned close to the back of my seat. "I have to go to the bathroom."

"Me, too," Miss Wiggins whispered.

The logistics of such a maneuver, given our present company and circumstances, hit me full force. As did the realization of my own urgent need.

"Come to think of it," I said.

CHAPTER 24

"Aw, God!" Mr. Tuttle muttered, jerking himself upright. He started the car, bounced us up into a driveway, slammed it into reverse, and swung us out into the dark street. He gunned it around the corner with a screech of tires, swerving to miss a parked car. I grabbed the armrest, and Miss Wiggins yelped from the backseat.

"What're you doing!" I cried.

"This was a mistake from start to finish," Mr. Tuttle snarled, his face tight and frowning as he finally turned on the headlights and swung onto A1A.

He slowed as we crossed the bridge into West Palm, offering no other word for his extreme behavior.

Picking up my pocketbook that had been flung to the floorboard, I said, "Surely you're not upset because some of us have a call of nature. That is something completely beyond our control."

I think his teeth were grinding together, but he managed to say, "Somebody was moving through the hedge. Weren't you watching?"

"No! When? I didn't see anybody."

"That's because you're not trained to see. He went around the back and slipped into the next yard. We were either spotted by somebody in the house, or it was a routine check by a federal agent. I didn't turn on the lights because I didn't want your license plate to be seen. He could've made the car, though, so I'm getting you back to the hotel where you'll be tourists and nothing else."

My heart thumped in my chest at our close call, but then I wondered why. Miss Wiggins wondered, too. "What would've happened if we'd been seen?" she asked. "Parking on the street's not a crime, is it?"

Mr. Tuttle made a sound between a laugh and a snort. "You'd be surprised. In fact, it's a wonder a PB squad car hadn't moved us out long before this. The island's swarming with them." He concentrated on his driving, then went on. "That's one more reason to think the feds have the area off-limits, and dogged if I want to be picked up for interfering in a federal investigation."

"Wait a minute!" I said. "Are you saying that house was full of federal investigators? I thought we were watching a bunch of crooks who stole my jewelry."

"I'm not saying either one, 'cause I don't know. But I am saying that we might not've been the only ones watching, and it's a wonder somebody didn't catch us at it. Especially with all the talking and complaining and calls of nature I've had to put up with." He took another one of those long, rasping breaths, as if it took all his effort to hold himself in. "Ought to have my head examined for trying a stakeout with civilians." He said the word with distinct distaste.

Wanting to make him feel better, I said, "Don't blame yourself, Mr. Tuttle. At least we know something's going on in that house, which is more than we knew before we started."

"The whole thing was a fiasco from the start," he said, apparently taking no comfort from my words. "We weren't even equipped. Should've had some coffee and a coupla fruit jars. With lids."

I frowned at the kind of equipment he seemed to think necessary for house-watching.

"Don't ask," he said. "Just think."

Miss Wiggins giggled and Lloyd said, "Oh," understanding the reference before I did.

Lloyd slid back onto the backseat. "I sure would use a fruit jar right now. If I had one."

"Well," Miss Wiggins chimed in, "Miss Julia and I couldn't." And I finally got the picture.

Mr. Tuttle turned in to a slot next to his car at his office. "That's just one more reason this whole thing was a mistake." He put my car in Park and opened the door. "Come on around, Mrs. Murdoch. I'll follow you to the hotel to be sure nobody's tailing this car. I want you to go in that room and I don't want you to come out till daylight. If anybody comes by and asks where you were tonight, tell them you went out to dinner and that's all."

"You think somebody's after us?" I had visions of blank-faced men — either in masks or in gray suits — banging on our doors scaring us half to death.

"What I think is if your thieves were in that house and they spotted us, they'll move out as soon as they can. And if federal agents were monitoring the house, your goose might be cooked. I'm just glad I was driving your car and not mine."

"You mean they might confiscate my new car?"

"No telling what they'd do if we burned

a surveillance. Just let the valets park this thing and hope nobody'll spot it. Now listen to me and don't give me any back talk. Go straight to the hotel and stay there. I'll let you know if I find out anything."

I was so distressed that I didn't even call him down for giving orders to the one who paid him. At the time, I was more than willing to do what he said. At least until I could think of something better.

"My goodness," Miss Wiggins said, as I meekly came around and slid into the driver's seat. "I didn't plan on getting arrested down here."

When we got back to the hotel, I showed Miss Wiggins the room that I'd reserved for her. It was right across the hall from ours, and Lloyd and I walked in with her.

Miss Wiggins stopped two feet inside the door and stood looking around. "Oh, my," she said, "this beats my single-wide by a mile, and it's so *nice.*"

Well, of course it was. I make it a practice to try to replicate the amenities of my home whenever I travel. Excepting the Royal Palm Court, of course, which was a special case and couldn't be helped.

"Sleep well, Etta Mae," I said, preparing to take my leave. "Nobody will bother us.

I've already come to the conclusion that Mr. Tuttle just wanted to be rid of us, so he'd be free to do whatever he wants. But," I went on grimly, "that can work both ways."

Lloyd showed Etta Mae the air-conditioning controls and how to double-lock the door. Then we left her and crossed the hall to our own room, where Lloyd immediately went to the bathroom and I followed thereafter. He was asleep almost as soon as his head hit the pillow, but my mind was so exercised that it took a few more minutes for me to fall into slumber.

I was up and dressed before Lloyd awoke the next morning, my mind full of details that needed to be implemented. It was all I could do to stay calm. As Lloyd stumbled into the bathroom to get dressed, I called Miss Wiggins and asked what she wanted to order for breakfast.

"You mean room service? Oh, anything. Whatever you order will be fine with me."

"Well, get yourself together and come on over. We have things to do this morning."

By the time breakfast arrived, Miss Wiggins had joined us, as wide-eyed and expectant as she'd been the day before.

"Just look at this," she exclaimed, lifting one cover after another and surveying the food that had been brought on a cart covered with white linen. "And it's all still hot."

"Uh-huh," Lloyd said, "but they didn't send any grits, did they?"

"This may be South Florida," I said, "but they don't have grits. Now let's sit down and eat. I have some plans I want to go over with both of you."

As we ate, I tried to ignore Miss Wiggins's delight with the tiny jars of jelly, the carnation stuck in a bud vase, and the darling little cream pitcher that had come on the cart.

"Here's what we're going to do," I said. "Lloyd, I hate for us to be apart again, but I don't see any other way around it. I'm going to take you to Mr. Tuttle's office and let you stay with him until I get back. The man is put out with us, well, probably just with me, so he may try to show his independence today. Somebody needs to be with him, so he won't get himself into trouble again."

"Well, I'll try, but what if he goes to that bar?"

"You go right along with him, but not inside because they won't let you. And if Mr. Tuttle goes in by himself, you sit outside right in front of the door until he comes out again. Which won't be long, because the bartender's too afraid of losing his license."

Lord, I hated to have the child do a thing

so fraught with peril for his spiritual well-being. But I'd gone over and over it in my mind during the night and could see no other way.

Miss Wiggins, noting my distress, spoke up. "I could do that, Miss Julia. Then you won't have to leave Lloyd with him."

"I don't mind doing it," Lloyd said, reaching for another piece of toast. "I bet he won't even go to that bar if I'm tagging along."

I smiled at him, gratified that he was willing to take on the tedious job of babysitting Mr. Tuttle without a moan of protest. I would never have put him in such a position if I hadn't had plans for an even more perilous expedition for Miss Wiggins and myself.

He looked up at me. "What will you and Etta Mae be doing?"

"We," I said, with a determined nod, "are going shopping."

CHAPTER 25

I sent Miss Wiggins back to her room, telling her that shorts and a T-shirt were perfectly acceptable attire for tourists, but walking on the beach was not on the day's itinerary. When I explained what she should be wearing, she was willing to make the effort, but wasn't sure if she'd brought, or even owned, anything close to what I described.

When she returned, I looked her over, then had her remove the belt from her dress so that it hung loose and longer than its accustomed length. Then I asked her to take off all her makeup and to put on tennies with socks. She did it all without hesitation or complaint, but with a lot of sideways glances at me. Gradually, though, she began to emerge fairly close to my idea of a mousy, unassuming woman who might be under the thumb and authority of some head of a household somewhere. Except her hair was too short, and there was nothing to be done about that. I tried to smooth out her natural curls, but had to give it up as a lost cause.

Looking at herself in the mirror, she said, "I feel like I'm in a costume, getting ready to be in a play."

"And so you are," I said.

Lloyd watched all this with some bemusement, but I just went about my business without explaining what I was up to. That business consisted of searching through the Yellow Pages and making two phone calls.

Then I looked through my suitcase and got out a pair of white gloves and the one hat I'd brought in case we decided to attend a Florida church.

Centering the hat on my head, I said, "Now, Lloyd, I want you to stick to Mr. Tuttle like glue. Etta Mae and I should wind up our business in a couple of hours, and we'll meet you at his office. Don't let him get away from you."

"No'm, I won't. I'll cry if I have to." He gave me a conspiratorial grin, and I gave him one right back. "But don't have too much fun without me."

"Just shopping, Lloyd, just shopping." I looked at my watch and took up my pocketbook. "We'd better go."

Miss Wiggins was unusually quiet as the elevator took us down to the lobby. She seemed hesitant and ill at ease, unaccustomed as she was to appearing in public without makeup and the short, tight clothing she normally wore. In both looks and manner, she was naturally as bold as brass, but in her current getup she edged behind me and kept her head down.

As we walked out of the lobby, one of those small Oriental cars pulled right up to the door.

"Good timing," I said, and then took care of the necessary forms with the man who'd delivered the vehicle.

As we got into the rental car, Lloyd said, "Well, I was wondering how we were going to get around since Mr. Tuttle told us not to drive our car. You think of everything, Miss Julia."

"I try to," I mumbled, as my mind went over and over the plans I'd made. I didn't want to tell Lloyd about them for fear that Mr. Tuttle would worm it out of him. Not that Lloyd would slip up and tattle, but investigators can be sneaky interrogators.

Then Lloyd said, "I'm surprised you didn't rent us a bigger car. This sure is a change from ours."

"We won't be doing that much shopping," I told him. The real reason, though, was that the play Miss Wiggins and I were going to be in required an inexpensive and nondescript car. It would've been completely out of character to drive up to our destination in a top-of-the-line automobile, and I had no intention of giving ourselves away in such a careless fashion.

As we approached Mr. Tuttle's office, I glanced at Miss Wiggins, who wasn't quite as perky with her assets hidden away as they were.

I drove straight to the parking area at the strip mall and was relieved to see Mr. Tuttle's former police car parked right in front. I pulled up behind it and stopped.

"Now, Lloyd, I'm in no mind to speak with Mr. Tuttle this morning. So you run in and be sure he's there. Then come back to the door and let us know. I want to be sure I'm not leaving you by yourself."

"Yessum." And out he went, straight into the office. I kept my eye on him all the way, hating to leave him in the dubious care of a man already noted for his lack of discipline and self-restraint.

I kept the engine turning over so we could be off on our mission as soon as I was sure Lloyd was in Mr. Tuttle's company. I also wanted to be ready to peel out of there before Mr. Tuttle could raise a fuss. Although he couldn't have had much to say, even if I'd given him the chance. After all, he'd been the one to urge us to go shopping.

As soon as Lloyd waved to us from the door, I took off. Then, giving Miss Wiggins the directions I'd written down from one of my phone calls, I asked her to help me find the area I wanted. So far, she'd been pleasingly willing to do what I asked of her, without demanding explanations for my actions.

"All will become clear," I told her, and she nodded, content, it seemed, to simply be a part of our own private task force.

After finding the store I wanted and parking almost in front of the Bethel Bible Bookstore, I left her in the car and went inside. In just a few minutes, I was back at the car with my purchase of two Bibles — the King James Version. On my way out of the store, I'd also picked up a handful of tracts on the Ten Commandments that were being offered free with purchase.

"You drive, Etta Mae," I said, opening the car door for her. "I need to concentrate on our next move."

"Oh, goody," she said, hopping out and running around to the driver's side.

Between the two of us we found our way across the bridge onto Palm Beach. After one or two wrong turns, we turned onto the residential street in question. Pointing to the curb some two blocks from the house we'd watched the night before, I said, "Pull in right there, Etta Mae, and let me tell you what we're going to do."

Her face lit up as I divulged my plan. "Oh, wow, Miss Julia, I'd never have thought of that. I hope it works."

"So do I, but whatever happens, at least we'll get a glimpse of who and what is inside that house. Now, Etta Mae, take one of these Bibles and hold it close to your chest. I want it to look as if you're ready to whip it open at a moment's notice. And smile. Smile like you're happy to be doing the Lord's work."

She gave me a big grin as I smoothed the gloves on my fingers and adjusted my hat pin again. "I can do that," she said. "I always get the giggles anyway, when I'm nervous."

"It'll be just like going on an Every Member Canvas for your church. That's how we're going to act — friendly, but very firm. We aren't asking for pledges or donations, though, so that ought to put them off their guard right away." I tapped my fingers on the armrest, wondering if I'd forgotten anything and what we would encounter when we rang that doorbell. "You know," I went on, "it wouldn't surprise me if those people were unchurched, and I don't know how you feel about it, but I don't believe in asking people like that for money for church missions and upkeep. Christians ought to be able to support themselves. But," I said, girding myself to tackle what we'd come for, "that's another subject."

"Yes, ma'am," Miss Wiggins said. "Maybe we ought to go on and do it. People'll wonder about us if we sit here much longer."

"Yes, you're right. All right, here's what let's do. Let's hit this one first," I said, pointing to the house on the corner. "In case anybody's watching, we want to appear to be going door-to-door all up and down the street."

"Good idea," she said, opening her door. "Let's do it." She giggled. "Before I lose my nerve."

I needed her enthusiasm right then, for the plan I'd hatched in the middle of the night didn't seem quite so perfect now that we had to implement it. We walked along the sidewalk and turned in at the opening of the head-high hedge leading into the courtyard of the house a few doors from the one we were interested in. The courtyard was enclosed with all kinds of tropical greenery. A fountain gurgled over in a corner, and the ocean breeze rattled the palm fronds. We walked up to the door, and Miss Wiggins rang the doorbell. She had a smile plastered on her face and her Bible clasped to her forefront. I cut my eyes to the target house, hoping someone could see us through the thick hedges, and thereby determine that we were harmless. Annoying, but harmless, which was what I was aiming for.

After a few minutes, the door was opened by a maid in a black nylon uniform with a white frilly apron. "Yes?"

Not having thought this far, I waited for Miss Wiggins to say something. When she just stretched her smile wider, I had to think of something. "Is the lady of the house in?"

"No'm," the maid said. "She's not receiving this morning."

"Then may we leave a tract for her and one for you?"

She accepted the tract, frowned at it, and began to close the door. "Soliciting's not allowed here, ma'am."

"Oh, really?" That almost stopped me, and I glanced around to see if the police were after us. "Well, we're not actually soliciting. We don't want anything from you, we want to give you something. And also to show you these lovely Bibles, complete with index, concordance, and gilt-edged pages, all for a mere pittance."

The maid shook her head and began backing away from the door. I quickly poked Miss Wiggins and said, "Show her, dear."

Miss Wiggins held out her Bible with shaking hands, and I realized there would be little help from that quarter. So I jumped again into the breach. "But perhaps you already have a number of Bibles, although you can't have too many, can you? I hope you'll forgive us for disturbing your work, but Scripture tells us to go tell it on the mountain. There not being any around here, however, we're doing the next best thing and covering the flatlands. So let us leave these with you and we'll be on our way." I thrust two more tracts at her, which she gingerly accepted. "I'm sure you keep every one of the Ten Commandments, but it doesn't hurt to look them over again. Especially since they've been so much in the news lately."

I stepped back, taking Etta Mae's arm to turn her with me. Still frowning at the tracts, the maid closed the door. We walked away and down the sidewalk, toward our target house.

Giving Miss Wiggins's arm a little shake, I said, "You can stop smiling now. I declare, Etta Mae, you have to do better than this. You should've jumped in and helped me out. I hardly knew what to say, and the next house is where we have to be at our best." I peered closely at her, looking for some evidence that she could give her best. "Maybe we should do another rehearsal before tackling it."

She took a deep breath, pushing out the Bible she was holding close to her chest another few inches. "No'm, I think we better get to it before that maid sics the cops on us. I was scared silly when she said soliciting isn't allowed. But I think I've got the hang of it now. Let's hit it, then get the heck out of here."

"I couldn't agree more. Let's go." Then I slowed down. "Wait, Etta Mae, I know what we can do. All these houses're closed off with hedges and shrubs, so nobody can tell what we're doing once we turn in. We can walk up and just pretend to ring the doorbells. That way, if anybody's watching, they'll think we're Jehovah's Witnesses, which, in a way, we are."

"Okay, I guess that'll work." As we started toward the next house, she said, "We're not really going to ring the bell, are we?"

"No, just pretend to, that's all. Then we walk to the next one, looking disappointed but still committed to our mission."

And so we did, getting ever nearer to the house we were aiming for. But just as we reached the sidewalk after pretending to find no one home at a neighbor's house, a car started up in the driveway next door. I pulled Miss Wiggins back into the yard behind the hedge. "Wait, don't let them see us."

I flipped open my Bible and thrust it toward Miss Wiggins, as if I were explaining something to her, all the while cutting my eyes toward the sound of the car. As the car backed out into the street, I said, "Peek out, Etta Mae, and see who's in it."

She did, then shook her head. "It's a big black SUV, maybe an Expediton or a Yukon, something like that. Could be an Escalade, I guess."

"I don't know one from another."

"Me, either, when they get that pricey." She squinched up her eyes, staring after it. "Anyway, it's going the other way. Couldn't see who was in it, because it's got tinted windows." She drew back and fanned her face with a tract. "Well, I guess nobody's home over there, so we might as well go back to the car." Still fanning furiously, but with a look of relief on her face, she added, "It's hot as you-know-what down here. Let's go, Miss Julia."

"Indeed we will," I said, taking off down the sidewalk away from our car. "They won't leave that house unguarded if it's full of stolen goods. So it's the perfect time for

279

us, when some of those crooks are off some-where else. Come along, Etta Mae."

I think she whimpered, but she fell into step and we walked down the sidewalk and turned in to the opening of another high hedge that bordered the yard. Without hesi-tation, for fear one or both of us would turn and run, we marched up the short brick walkway toward the heavy wooden door that gave a Spanish look to the pink house.

I glanced this way and that, getting the lay of the land around the house. There wasn't much to see except tropical shrubbery, but one quick glance down the driveway revealed a closed garage, backed by a thick growth of bamboo. As we approached the front door, I shook my head at the overgrown bushes and flowering vines that grew along the founda-tion of the house, shutting out any sounds from the street and the neighbors. Some-body needed to take some hedge clippers and clear out the place.

I had to brush aside some tendrils flapping around in the breeze when they threatened to unseat my hat. As shady as the yard was, the heat and humidity were high enough for me to make a mental note to buy air-conditioning stock when we returned home.

"Hold your Bible where they can see what it is, Etta Mae," I said, as I clasped my pocketbook and hefted up my Bible along with the Ten Commandment tracts.

Then I put on a big smile, letting my little light shine, and rang the doorbell.

CHAPTER 26

Nothing happened for several minutes, making me wonder if Mr. Tuttle had been totally wrong about this house. Would federal agents, if they were watching, let us walk right up to the door like this? I didn't know, but it was all we had, so with a quick glance around to see if government men were hiding in the bushes, I pushed the doorbell again.

When the door opened a crack, a bushy-headed man with black-rimmed glasses perched on a sunburned nose stared out at us. I had to look down on him, for he wasn't tall, getting a good view of a head of hair badly in need of a trim. He peered up at us around the edge of the door. Then he sidled into the opening, blocking our view of anything inside, but giving me a glimpse of thin, hairy legs sticking out of baggy shorts.

"What?" he said in a whispery voice, sounding almost as fearful as I was feeling.

Stretching a smile across my face, I said, "Good morning, sir. I hope we're not disturbing you, but we're visiting all the houses on the street, passing out a little hope and joy at every door. How are you this morning?"

"Busy," he said. "Whatever you're selling, we don't want."

"Oh, my goodness," I said, with a titter of laughter. "We're not selling anything unless, of course, you'd be interested in purchasing one of these fine Bibles. But that's only a sideline, not our main mission at all. No, we're here to bring you the blessing of the Lord, and all you have to do is pass that blessing on to ten other people. When you do that, something unbelievably wonderful will happen to you. You will be astounded at the blessings that will return to you tenfold."

Not having planned what I was going to say, I myself was astounded at what had come out. But in for a penny . . .

I took a deep breath and went on. "I know that may sound like a chain letter, but you don't have to write a thing. Just give a blessing to the next ten people you meet, and that's it. May we come in and tell you about the blessings we've received? We'd love to give our testimony of how this mission has spread all over the country and how you can be a part of it." I reached up with a gloved finger and mopped a trickle of sweat from my temple. "May we come in for a minute? It's quite warm out here."

"No, no," he said, inching the door closed, "I don't want any. You have to go now. I'm working."

"Well, but . . ." I put out a hand, hoping to stay the door, but he pursed his mouth and shook his head. "Let me leave you one of these," I said, slipping a tract through the narrowing crack of the door. "It tells all about the Ten Commandments, and I would recommend that you pay particular attention to the eighth one. Observing it, along with the other nine, of course, could pay rich dividends." Hearing myself say such an obviously ironic thing stunned me. "Or maybe not."

"Oh-h-h," Miss Wiggins suddenly wailed, startling me so bad that I almost stepped off the stoop. She began rocking back and forth, bending over with her arms clutched across her stomach. She let out another wrenching groan, as her Bible and a dozen tracts splattered on the stoop.

"Miss Wiggins!" I cried, dropping my Bible and reaching for her. "What's wrong with you?"

As she swayed against me, I had to grasp the door frame to steady myself as her full weight fell on me. She was a little thing, but heavier than she looked, and it was all I could do to hold her.

The man looked as shocked as I felt, but there was no pity in him for Miss Wiggins's plight. He flapped his hand at us. "You have to go. I can't have this."

Miss Wiggins finally staggered upright, one hand feeling around for support. Emitting the most piteous groan I'd ever heard, she suddenly lurched forward onto the door, popping it open, and falling right onto the little man. He yelped in surprise, stumbling back with Miss Wiggins hanging onto him. He sat down abruptly on the hall floor with Miss Wiggins sprawled all across him, his glasses dangling from one ear as one skinny leg waved in the air.

"Oh, my Lord!" I cried, dashing into the hall after them, fearing the worst. "Etta Mae! Are you hurt?"

"Get her off me!" the little man cried. Then he yelped again and began pushing at her and scooting backward with his feet.

She was like a dead weight, as I pulled and tugged to get her off him. Rolling her over onto the floor, I finally managed to lay her out and get him loose.

"Sunstroke!" I shrieked. "She's dying of sunstroke. Call a doctor! Call an ambulance!" Lord, what would I do if she ended up in the hospital? More to the point, what would federal agents do?

"Help me, mister," I pleaded, as I patted her face, trying to bring some life back to the stricken woman. I could see the whites of her eyes as they rolled back in her head, and feel the tremors that rippled through her body as her heels drummed on the floor. "She's going into convulsions! Oh, Etta Mae, don't die on me." Turning to the man who still sat on the floor, staring in horror out of one lens at his uninvited guests, I said, "Don't just sit there, do something!"

He scooted away and scrambled to his feet. "I can't have this! You have to get her out of here."

"Can't you see she's ill? You've got to help me. She could die right here in your house." Leaning over Miss Wiggins, I loosened the clothing around her neck, thinking how pitiful it would be if she died without the makeup she loved so much. Reaching for an errant tract, I fanned her pale face.

"Cold towels! That's what she needs." I pointed to the man, ignoring his shocked look. He was no worse off than I was. "Go wet some towels and bring some water. Hurry!"

He scurried down the hall as I smoothed Miss Wiggins's hair out of her face. "Etta Mae? Can you hear me? You're going to be all right, honey. Open your eyes for me. Can you do that?"

She opened one of them. "Look around while he's gone," she whispered. "Hurry."

I jerked back, stunned at her sudden recovery. Then I smiled, patted her shoulder, and slid on my knees to where I could peer through a wide arch into what I took to be the living room. But it was like no other living room I'd ever seen. Tables lined the wall with several secretarial chairs in front of them. On the tables were more computers than I had time to count, all of them up and running. Too scared to get nearer, for I could hear water running in the back of the house and knew the man would soon return, I stayed on my knees, trying to see what was on the screens.

"Newspapers, Etta Mae!" I hissed. "They're reading newspapers on every one of those things."

"What things?" she whispered back.

"*Computers!* I'm going to try to get closer."

She clamped a hand on my leg, of all places, and dragged me back to her side. Not only was she heavier than she looked, she was stronger.

"He's coming back!" And she started groaning and writhing on the floor and, to my amazement, heaving in the most realistic manner possible.

"Quick," I commanded as the man came into view. "Give me the towel. She's in a bad way."

He handed over a sopping towel and squatted down beside us, but not too close. "She can't stay here," he said, not liking the situation at all, but not knowing what to do about it. "You have to take her somewhere else."

I swabbed the towel over Miss Wiggins's face, then draped it over her forehead. The cold water seemed to have a calming effect, for the patient's moans began to die down and the spasms in her body began to ease off. "Maybe we should call an ambulance," I said, cocking an eye at the man to see how he would take that suggestion.

"No!" he snapped, then calmed himself. "I mean, it would disturb the neighborhood. They have strict laws around here. Can't you get her to your car? That'd be quicker. You could take her right to a hospital."

"I guess I could try. Etta Mae? Are you feeling better?"

She answered with a threatening gurgle down in her throat. The man jumped back in alarm, and I moved out of the line of fire, just in case.

Taking the towel from her forehead, I spread it out and covered Miss Wiggins's face. Water dripped from it into her hair and onto the floor. "Let me try something," I said. "If this doesn't work, we'll have to call for help." With a commanding glance at the man, I said, "Bow your head.

"O Lord, we ask for your mercy upon this poor woman who has been struck down by the sun and the heat. Give her strength, we pray, and restore her to health so we can get out of this man's hair and back safely to our motel room. And we ask your blessings upon this kind gentleman, a Good Samaritan in almost every sense of the word. In your name we pray. Amen."

With that, I gave Miss Wiggins a pinch in the side and she rose up, fully recovered. Snatching the towel from her face, she sprang to her feet. "I'm healed!"

I clasped my arm around her waist and pulled her to the door. "Not fully, so calm down." I hurried her outside, and with a glance over my shoulder, said to the man, "Thank you so much for your help. I'm sure we can manage now. Sorry to've bothered you. Don't give us another thought. I believe we might've misread our mission statement.

We're supposed to be in Palm Something-Else in California. Have a nice day!"

We fled down the walkway, out on the sidewalk, and headed as fast as we could to our car. "Wait for me, Etta Mae," I puffed. "I'm about to have a heatstroke, myself."

Hurrying down the sidewalk, heedless of watching eyes, we finally reached the car. Slamming the car doors behind us, we were nearly suffocated by the built-up heat inside. "Crank this thing up, Etta Mae, and get the air-conditioning going," I said, panting in the airless car. "I hope you're able to drive, because I don't believe I am."

She giggled as she turned on the ignition and fiddled with the air vents. "Oh, I'm all right. Had you fooled though, didn't I?"

Before I could answer, a sharp rap on my window startled me so bad that I almost went through the roof of the car. I looked through the window straight into the eyes of a hard-faced man in a gray suit and tie glaring in at us. He motioned me to roll down the window. So authoritative he appeared that it didn't occur to me to disobey him. I put the window partway down.

The man, dark-skinned with the shadow of a beard around his chin and a deep frown between his glaring eyes, said, "You ladies have business around here?"

"No, sir, officer sir," I stammered. "We've completed our business. We're just now on our way." Lord, his very presence shook me to the core. If he took us to jail, we'd have to hope Mr. Tuttle would bail us out, and that was a futile hope if there ever was one. I'd seen the contents of his wallet.

"Then be on your way," he said with no attempt to be courteous even though, for all he knew, we were tourists bringing in revenue to the city. "And don't come back. This street is restricted. It's not open to traffic."

"Oh, I'm so sorry. We must've missed the sign. But, since we've had the good fortune of meeting you, I'd like to give you this." I thrust a Ten Commandments tract through the window. Since it was the one I'd fanned Miss Wiggins with, it was a little the worse for wear. And having been crumpled in my hand during our dash to the car hadn't helped it, either. "It's our very last one, so we have no need to linger. We'll just be on our way, and thank you, officer, for working in this hot climate. You must be suffering out there in the heat."

He glanced with some skepticism at the tract, then banged his hand on the top of the car. "Move on out of here."

"Yes, sir," I said, rolling up the window before he could change his mind. "Hit it, Etta Mae." And she did.

She drove us down the street and stopped at the corner. "Where did he come from?"

"I don't know. But he nearly scared me to death."

"Look back," she said, "and see if you can see where he goes."

Craning around, I saw that the gray-suited man had crossed the street and was about to be swallowed up by another hedge. "He's going to a house across the street and one down from the one we were at. Mr. Tuttle was right, Etta Mae, that house is under surveillance. Let's get out of here."

She mashed the gas pedal, squealed the tires, and moved us out. When she turned onto the main thoroughfare, I finally began to feel safe, and safer still when we headed onto the bridge that would take us off the island.

Able at last to breathe easily, I said, "I was sure we were in big trouble. Thank goodness I held on to that last tract."

Miss Wiggins giggled with a faint trace of hysteria in the sound. Strands of wet hair hung around her face and dripped on her shoulders. "I thought he was one of the crooks," she said, "and I nearly wet my pants. I mean, we'd just escaped from one tight spot, then there he was, looking mean enough to do worse than rob us." She maneuvered the car into the traffic in West Palm Beach, then gave me a quick glance. "How'd you know he was a cop? He didn't have on a uniform."

"Yes, but he had on a suit and tie. A gray suit, which was a dead giveaway, if you ask me. And in all that heat, too. So he wasn't a police officer, Etta Mae. No, he had to be one of those federal agents Mr. Tuttle told us about. Besides, he didn't deny it, did he?"

"No, he didn't, but I'd say we've had a successful day even if we almost got arrested. You saw newspapers on those computers, which plainly show how the crooks knew who and where to rob."

"I don't know, Etta Mae," I said, mulling over my quick glimpse of the electronic display. "They could be telemarketers of some sort. I just wish we'd gotten a better look. No telling what we could've found."

Squirming around to straighten my skirttail, I went on. "But you got us inside, which was more than I could do. And Lord, Etta Mae, you gave me a fright when you fell on that man. I thought you'd had a heart attack or something." I adjusted the air vent a little, and sighed. "Too bad your quick thinking didn't get us any real proof."

She glanced at me, her eyes sparkling, then back at the street. "Who says it didn't?"

CHAPTER 27

As Miss Wiggins took a westward turn, the sun streamed through the windshield with a glare strong enough to blind us and hot enough to dry the wet strings of hair around her face. She reached up and flipped down the visor. Something in her hand caught the light and sparkled along the dashboard. Then she held it out for me to see.

I squinted at it. "What is it?"

She laughed in a way that told me she was quite pleased with herself. "Here. Take a look."

I took it from her and caught my breath as I recognized the pendant on a thin gold chain. "Why, it's Mildred Allen's mother's lavaliere! Isn't it? Don't you think it is?"

"I don't know. I've never seen Mrs. Allen's mother's jewelry. Or hers, either."

"Well, it is. I know it is, because, look, it has all this gold filigree around the stone. It's a yellow diamond. Very old-fashioned and made in the twenties, I think. I remember because Mildred wanted to give it to Tonya, and Tonya said it wasn't her style." I turned the pendant over and saw 22K stamped on the back. "Hurt Mildred's feelings, too. How'd you get this, Etta Mae?" I stared at her, my heart leaping as a dozen possibilities opened up. "It was in that house, wasn't it? How in the world . . . ?"

"I picked his pocket."

"You what?"

"When I let myself fall against that goofy guy, he was so surprised he didn't know what was happening. He kept pushing at me and trying to scramble away, and that gave me a chance to feel him up." She giggled. "Gave him a little pinch while I was at it, too. Didn't you hear him yell?"

"Well, I did, but I didn't know it was because you were invading his privates. My word, Etta Mae, that was a bold move."

"I had to distract him so I could rummage around in his pockets." She laughed again. "Worked, too."

"I'll say it did," I said, holding up the lavaliere as it spun on its chain. "This is all the proof we need. That house is the command post of a national, or a seminational, jewelry ring. And speaking of rings, I want mine back. Turn around, Etta Mae. I'm going right back over there and face that little runt down. And he'd better hand them over, too."

"Uh-uh, better not, Miss Julia. No telling what he'd do if we showed up again, especially if his buddies have come back. And that government man will be on the lookout for us, too. We wouldn't get in the yard good before they grabbed us."

"Well, we have to do something. What's going to happen when that man realizes this thing is gone? And the first time he puts his hand in his pocket, he'll know it. Oh, my word!" I sat up straight, struck with a startling thought. "They're going to pack up and leave, that's what they'll do. Etta Mae, we have to get back there, government agents notwithstanding. If they leave, we'll never track them down again."

I clasped Mildred's mother's lavaliere in my hand, thinking to myself how lucky we had been so far. Who would've thought that we could come into the state of Florida with its millions of residents and be fortunate enough to locate one particular house with one particular set of criminals living in it? One chance in a million, or several millions, is what it was, and so unlikely as to be scarcely believed. Yet it had happened, so I knew that it was meant for me to get my rings back. And Hazel Marie's things, too.

I nodded my head, feeling justified in having undertaken this mission, in spite of the improbability of a successful conclusion. Sometimes we just have to challenge the odds and rest on the promise that all things work together for good to them who wait long enough. Or something like that. My memory wasn't what it once was.

"Hurry, Etta Mae," I said. "Let's get Mr. Tuttle and see what he says. And he better be right where we left him and not out following up leads that lead nowhere."

"I'm hurrying, but this traffic is awful."

I braced myself with a hand on the dashboard as she came to another abrupt stop. But my mind was still on Mr. Tuttle and his poor showing thus far. "I've a good mind to adjust his pay. I mean, we're the ones who found the thieves' hideout, and you're the one who found this necklace. And that's irrefutable evidence in my book."

Miss Wiggins gave me a quick glance as the car surged ahead with the flow of traffic. "I don't know, Miss Julia. We haven't gotten your things back yet, and we may need him. And didn't you say it was his friend who told you about the house? And Frank took us to it on the stakeout. That ought to count for something."

"Well, yes, I guess you're right. Maybe I better hold fire until we see how it works out." I bit my lip as I tried to imagine just how it could work out. "I hope Lloyd is all right. Lord, I hated to leave him in that man's care. Hurry, Etta Mae, I'm getting awfully antsy all of a sudden."

When we finally turned out of the traffic and into the parking lot of the strip mall, I breathed a sigh of relief at the sight of Mr. Tuttle's low-riding Crown Victoria. At least he was still in the vicinity, since it was unlikely that he would've walked far. The pavement was shimmering with heat, and the humidity was high enough to suffocate a normal person. Of course, that bar he frequented was fairly close by.

I started calling Lloyd's name as soon as we opened the office door and walked in. "Lloyd! We're back. Where are you?"

"In here," he called from the back office, and my anxiety fell away. "What'd y'all buy?"

We hurried down the narrow hall to find him sitting behind Mr. Tuttle's desk fiddling with the computer, and Mr. Tuttle nowhere to be seen. It took me a minute to recall that we were supposed to have been shopping, but far be it from me to keep important matters from the child, since his incisive mind had been of considerable help to me in the past. So Miss Wiggins and I filled him in on the morning's activities and displayed the lavaliere that Miss Wiggins had been so adept at finding.

His eyes grew big with wonder and perhaps envy as we told him of our escapade. "Oh, wow, I wish I'd been there. Etta Mae, you really picked his pocket? And he didn't feel you doing it?"

"Well, he felt something," she said, laughing. "But not that."

"Oh, wow," he said again. "I thought you were going shopping."

"I'm sorry about that, Lloyd," I said. "But we did shop a little. You know, for the Bibles we needed. I just didn't want to put you in harm's way, and besides, we needed you here to watch out for Mr. Tuttle. And where is he, by the way?"

"Gone to get some sandwiches for lunch." The boy looked at his watch. "But he's been gone awhile. I hope nothing's happened to him."

Miss Wiggins and I glanced at each other. "We don't have time for leisurely lunches," I said. "And I don't intend to hang around much longer waiting on him. Where did he go?"

"I don't know," Lloyd said. "He just said

for me to answer the phone and he'd be back soon. I told him if he went to the place where we first found him, you wouldn't like it."

Etta Mae grinned. "And what did he say?"

Lloyd squinched up his mouth, his eyes darting from one side to the other. Then he bit the bullet and told the truth. "He said there were a lot of things Miss Julia wouldn't like, but that wouldn't stop him from doing what *he* liked."

"Did he, now!" I said. "I'll tell you one thing, that man's going to be left out in the cold if he doesn't straighten up. Etta Mae, I'll bet he doesn't have lunch on his mind. I'll bet he's in that bar, drinking instead of eating. And what did he think this child was going to do for lunch? I have about had my fill of this. Let's go back to the hotel and make some plans."

"Suits me," Lloyd said, as he switched off the computer and came out from behind the desk. "I'm getting tired of just sitting around."

"I guess we ought to do something," Miss Wiggins said, although she sounded a little hesitant about it. "I just wish we had somebody to depend on besides ourselves. I don't want to end up in jail or shot by criminals."

"Shot? You think they'd shoot us?" That

kind of danger hadn't occurred to me. I never thought anybody would have the nerve to point a gun at me.

"Look, Miss Julia," she said, "they've gone to a lot of trouble locating good jewelry in out-of-the-way places, and they've put a lot of money into doing it. Remember all those computers you saw? They're not cheap, and they must have several gangs that're spread out everywhere breaking and entering and looting and all that. It could be a big operation and may be run by a criminal mastermind or something. They're not going to just fold up without a fight, and it could get dangerous. Depending, of course, on what you plan to do."

"Well, I hadn't thought of it quite like that," I said, wondering why I hadn't. "Actually, I haven't thought of it at all. Too intent on locating them, but now that we've found them, it would behoove us to plan the next step very carefully." I tapped my fingers on my pocketbook, thinking it through. "Etta Mae, what do you think of going back over there and looking up that government agent?"

She smiled somewhat wryly. "I don't think we'd have to look him up. We could just park, and he'd find us."

I dismissed that with a wave of my hand.

"Well, what we could do is show him the lavaliere and testify that it is stolen goods. I'd think that would be all he'd need to raid the place right then and there."

As she thought about it, I did, too. Then I had to readjust my thinking. "Well, no, that wouldn't work. If the agents raid the house, I'd never get my things back because it'll be held as evidence. And you know how slow the government is. No, we have to think of something else and keep them out of it."

"Miss Julia?" Lloyd said. "We'd think better on a full stomach. I'm about to starve."

"Me, too," Miss Wiggins said.

"Then let's go back to the hotel," I said. "We'll get something to eat, and see what we can come up with. Whatever we decide on will be better implemented after dark, anyway. Unless, of course," I said, stopping to calm my rising fears, "they decide to leave this afternoon."

Etta Mae turned to face me. "They could," she said, nodding, "but there's no way we can watch the house in the daylight. Those agents would see us and run us off. Or worse. And, remember, that goofy guy can't leave until the rest of his gang gets back. And even then, I bet they'll wait till after dark. I mean, they'll have to make arrangements of some kind as to where they'll go and how they'll get rid of whatever's in the house."

I held my head, moaning at the thought of them getting rid of my precious rings. "They wouldn't just throw it all away, would they? I mean, so they would't get caught with it?"

"No, not after what they've been through to get it." Miss Wiggins's decisive manner reassured me. "What I meant was they'll probably pack everything up and move to another location. Or, maybe try to get to a port where they can ship it out."

Well, *that* wasn't very reassuring, but she'd convinced me that we had enough time to make some arrangements of our own. So I nodded my head and headed down the hall.

As we reached the front door, it opened to let a blowzy and reeking Mr. Tuttle stumble in. I was stunned at his sudden and garish appearance, for he had lapsed not only morally, but sartorially, too. Gone were the tie and plaid jacket he'd worn earlier, and in their place was a loose Hawaiian shirt, replete with flamingos and palm trees. If he was taking Miss Wiggins's advice about steering clear of plaid, he'd badly miscalculated with its replacement.

He reeled backward when he saw us, but quickly righted himself with a hand against the wall. "Well," he said, blowing out a miasma of alchoholic fumes. "The prodigal ladies have returned."

"Prodigal, my foot!" I said, rearing back from the overpowering stench. "Look who's talking. Mr. Tuttle, I am both disappointed in you and fed up with you. Make out your final bill, and I'll consider paying it. But as of now, our professional association is over and done."

"Uh, Miss Julia?" Miss Wiggins tugged at my sleeve. "Let's not be hasty. We might need him."

A silly grin spread across his face, which was already blooming with a liquorish glow. "She sure gets on her high horse, don't she?"

I had the urge to smack him right back through the door, but Miss Wiggins was pleading his case. "I can sober him up, really I can. Let's take him with us."

I gave her a long, calculating look, then gave in. "All right, if you think you can manage him. But he better sober up fast, or he's going to get dumped by the wayside." I grabbed Lloyd's hand and sailed past Mr. Tuttle, unwilling to give him the time of day. "And I don't mean maybe, either."

CHAPTER 28

Lloyd and I got into the rental car, while Miss Wiggins led Mr. Tuttle to the passenger side of his. She got him buckled in, swatting away his feeble attempts to commandeer the car keys. Then she walked over and leaned down to my window.

"I figure we might need two cars," she said, "so I'll follow you to the hotel. Then we'll get him upstairs and go to work on him."

I nodded, impressed with her foresight. If it'd been up to me, I'd have left Mr. Tuttle's car and his unreliable self right where they were.

Still fuming at how he had let us down, I drove carefully to the hotel. As we neared it, Lloyd said, "Your hat's on crooked, Miss Julia, if you don't mind me saying so."

"Well, my word," I said, reaching up to push it into place. "Though it's no wonder after all we went through this morning. But that reminds me, Lloyd, I'll call the rental people to come pick up this car, since it's been seen and is of no more use to us. So don't let me forget my gloves."

"I'll put 'em in my pocket," he said.

"I just thought of something else. I hope nobody at the hotel sees us with Mr. Tuttle. He is a flat-out embarrassment in the state he's in, and people might think the less of us for the company we keep."

Lloyd thought for a minute, then said, "We can pretend he's not with us. Just, you know, happen to be riding in the same elevator."

"I guess so," I sighed. Then, bypassing the valets and turning in to the parking lot beside the hotel, I went on. "I don't want to encourage you to be disrespectful of Mr. Tuttle, Lloyd, which I may have inadvertantly done. Mr. Pickens said the man has problems, so maybe there's something in his life that drives him to drink. Although I can't understand anybody who won't exercise enough self-discipline to restrain themselves from doing what they ought not do." I pulled into an empty spot and turned off the ignition, heaving another aggrieved sigh as I did. "But I'm willing to give him the benefit of the doubt for now, just as long as it doesn't interfere with what we need to accomplish. So, I want you to remember that it reflects well on you to accord respect toward your elders. Even if some of them don't deserve it." I pushed my hat into place again, got out of the car, and slammed the door behind me. "And at this moment, Mr. Tuttle is one of them."

"Yes, ma'am," Lloyd said, hurrying after me.

Meeting Miss Wiggins and Mr. Tuttle at the elevator, I was relieved to see that he was submitting to her guidance without complaint. Of course, the grip she had on his upper arm was tight enough to make anybody amenable to directions. He didn't seem to mind, though, for a silly smile was plastered on his face. As if his fall from grace was just a little misstep that we would overlook.

He was in for a surprise.

We crowded into the elevator and rode up to the third floor with no stops for other passengers. Walking docilely beside Miss Wiggins, Mr. Tuttle followed Lloyd and me to our door.

"Where we goin'?" Mr. Tuttle asked, looking around as if he'd never seen a line of doors in a hallway before.

"In here," I said, opening the door and preceding him. "Sit down over there." I pointed to a large chair by the window, and Miss Wiggins led him to it. "Now, Mr. Tuttle, there's a lot I could say to you. But I won't, because in your present condition it would just go in one ear and out the other."

He flared up at that. "My preshent condision is jus' fine. All I had was a coupla beers, and I'm perfe'lly cabable of doin' my job." He stared up at me. "I'll have you know."

"And I'll have you know that your present condition is unacceptable to me. Etta Mae," I said, turning to her, "he's your responsibility. Do whatever it takes to sober him up. I wash my hands." And to prove my point, I turned away and took off my hat, glad to be rid of it and him.

"Food and coffee, lots of it," she said, as Lloyd picked up the phone to call room service. "Aspirin and maybe some Alka-Seltzer. Then a shower and a nap. He ought to be all right after that. You want me to take him to my room? So you and Lloyd can get some rest?"

That was tempting. He'd be out of my hair and my sight while he underwent Miss Wiggins's ministrations — something I wasn't eager to witness. But on second thought, it might not do to have them alone together in a hotel room. No telling how rambunctious he might get with her.

"No, let's all stay here for the time being,"

I said. "You might need some help with him, although I will say that he's not in as bad a way as when Lloyd and I first found him. At least he can walk on his own, whereas then he could hardly put one foot in front of the other. Maybe he'll come to his normal self fairly soon, and we can make our plans for tonight."

"Okay," she said, "but if you don't mind watching him a few minutes, I'll run over and get into some decent clothes."

Before long, she was back, dressed in low-slung pants and a high-slung top, between which too much skin revealed itself. Her idea of what was decent was not the same as mine. But I overlooked it as the room service waiter delivered our order, and Miss Wiggins set about force-feeding Mr. Tuttle. He balked at the turkey sandwich she thrust into his hand, but she said, "Eat!" and he tried. Lloyd and I found our appetites, too, and if we'd just had pleasant company and stimulating conversation, it would have been a fine meal.

Instead, we had to listen to Mr. Tuttle moan that he was too full to drink any more coffee, and besides, he didn't care for coffee, and on top of that, this particular coffee was too bitter to drink.

Miss Wiggins dumped a spoonful of sugar in his cup, said, "Drink it!" and he did. I was beginning to admire her forcefulness, for he soon learned that his pleading and groaning wouldn't move her. After a while and after downing a pot of coffee at her urging, he begged to go to the bathroom.

"Make him close the door, Etta Mae," I said, as I took Mr. Tuttle's chair, which was the only comfortable one in the room.

"It's closed," she said, coming back into the room. "I told him to take a shower while he's in there. Lloyd, you have enough to eat? Let's push this cart out into the hall and make some room in here."

Coming back in, Miss Wiggins said, "Miss Julia, what're you planning for tonight? Frank ought to be sober by then, so you can go ahead and include him."

"I've been thinking about it," I said, leaning my head against the back of the chair.

"Me, too," Lloyd said, "and I think we ought to go stake 'em out again. If we could sneak up close enough, we might find out what they're doing."

"I don't think we can get near the place," I said. "Those agents know my car and the rental car, both."

"But we have Frank's," Miss Wiggins

pointed out. "They don't know that one, do they?"

"Maybe not. But the thing's hardly fit to ride in."

"It drives better than it looks," Miss Wiggins said. "Lots of power under the hood. But that agent said the street's restricted, so they'll run us off." She stopped and thought about it. "Or run us *in,* regardless of what car we take."

"Well, what about this?" Lloyd said, leaning forward eagerly. "How about if we park on another street and walk over? There'll be plenty of bushes we can hide in because the whole island is covered with them."

"It certainly is, Lloyd," I said, "and there's a whole thicket of bamboo behind that house and garage." I smoothed my mouth with my hand as I tried to think it through. I could hear the shower running and tried not to picture Mr. Tuttle in it. "Well, I don't know what else we can do. Except, do they arrest people for walking around after dark? That place has so many rules and regulations, they might."

"Oh, I wouldn't think so," Miss Wiggins said. "You and Lloyd can walk together and I'll walk with Frank. We'll look like any normal family out for an after-supper stroll."

"Except when we cut between houses and

start making our way through the foliage," I said. "And what if those crooks decide to leave, how're we going to get back to the car in time to see where they're going?"

"Let me think about it," Miss Wiggins said. "I might have an idea."

As the bathroom door opened, she jumped up and headed for Mr. Tuttle, who was dressed, but not entirely. His shirt was untucked and unbuttoned. His belt wasn't buckled, and his feet were bare — not a pretty sight. His hair was wet and slicked back, proving he'd done more than turn the shower on.

"All ready for a nap?" Miss Wiggins asked brightly.

"I don't need a nap," he said somewhat sullenly, not meeting her eyes. But she grabbed his arm and led him to the bed. He sat down on the edge of it, and looked at her for his next move.

"I want you to take a couple of aspirin," she said, shaking out two from the bottle and holding them out to him.

He did, and to my dismay, started to put his wet head on the pillow where I would have to put my own.

"I've changed my mind, Etta Mae," I quickly said. "Let's put him to bed in your room. That way, we won't disturb him while we have our discussion."

"Good idea," she said, pulling him upright and walking him to the door. "I'll be right back. Come on, Frank," she said, guiding him out of the room, "you'll feel better in a little while."

He went docilely enough, but we could hear him mumbling all the way across the hall about needing neither a shower nor a nap. And he didn't know why he had to take not one, but both.

Miss Wiggins came back in after a few minutes, smiling half to herself. "He's down for the count. But I'm going to leave this door open a bit, in case he decides to get up. One good thing at least, he's not a belligerent drunk."

"Belligerent enough," I said, unwilling to give Mr. Tuttle any credit at all.

Miss Wiggins pulled up a straight chair near mine, and said, "Tell me what you think of this." And she proceeded to outline a plan that seemed to answer our most critical needs.

"That's the best idea I've heard, Etta Mae," I said, as I pulled out a couple of bills from my billfold. "I'd never have thought of such a thing. If you know what we need, why don't you take Mr. Tuttle's car and go buy them. Lloyd and I will look after him, and maybe get a little rest ourselves."

"Okay, I shouldn't be long." Miss Wiggins picked up Mr. Tuttle's keys, threw a kiss at Lloyd, and went on her merry way.

"Lie down, Lloyd, if you want to," I said as my head sought a comfortable place on the chair. "We may have a long night ahead of us, and we need to be at our best."

"Yessum, I was thinking about doing that. But we might ought to call home and see how things are there."

"Lord," I said, sitting upright. "I have let the time get away from me. We haven't called in so long, Lillian'll be beside herself. Slide that phone closer, please, and dial it for me. I'm too tired to move."

CHAPTER 29

"What y'all doin' down there?" Lillian demanded as soon as she heard my voice. "Where you at, anyway? Is Lloyd all right? I been waitin' an' waitin' for you to call, an' worryin' an' frettin', an' all this time go by an' you not callin', I tell you, Miss Julia, you got to do better'n that."

"I'm sorry, Lillian, I really am. It's just that we've been busy and out and around, trying to get our ducks in a row. And we've had some problems to deal with, too," I said, picturing Mr. Tuttle out like a light across the hall. "But, Lillian, we have found where those crooks are. And even met one of them, which of course is good, because now we know one of them. But not so good because now he knows us, too, so we're trying to decide what to do next. They may be getting ready to move, which means we'd have to look for them again. Anyway, how are things there? How's the weather? Have you heard from Sam or Hazel Marie?"

"Things is fine, 'cept for Latisha drivin' me crazy. School been out, 'cause they's ice on the roads, an' all she want to do is make cookies all the time. An' Miss Hazel Marie, well, I guess no news is good news. But, I tell you, Miss Julia, Mr. Sam gettin' worriet 'bout you. He done call three times since you been gone, an' I don't think he believe me when I say you at church. He say you sure got religious all of a sudden. An' he ast me jus' las' night if I holdin' out on him, an' you know I don't do good tellin' stories, 'specially to him."

"I know, Lillian, and I appreciate it more than I can say. It's for his own good, though, because he'd be worried to death if he knew what we're doing."

"Well, look to me like you ought to call him back," she said. "Jus' so he know you not in the hospital or something, 'cause he ast me that las' night, too. He say if he don't talk to you soon, he got a good mind to come home, so you better call him up."

"Call Russia? Why, Lillian, I wouldn't know how to start. What city is he in, anyway?"

"He say Saint Something-or-Other. I don't know. Peter's, I think." She stopped and thought for a minute. "You reckon he might be turned up down there somewhere? Don't they have one of them, too?"

"I believe they do, but he'd be in the original, which is across the world from here. Listen, Lillian, the next time he calls, try to calm him down. We only need a day or two more, and we'll either have our things back or have to accept the fact that they're gone forever. So right now, I don't have time for distractions."

She didn't say anything for a while. Then she said in a chiding tone, "Don't look like to me Mr. Sam ought to be one them."

"Well, of course he's not, except right now, I have to keep my mind on what we're doing. It's coming down to the wire, Lillian, and I need you to reassure him before he jumps on a plane and gets home before we do." Not wanting to argue with her, especially since she was right, I said, "You want to talk to Lloyd? He's right here."

Before relinquishing the phone, I gave her the name of our hotel and the phone number. "But don't give it to Sam, Lillian, whatever you do. It's for your use alone, because I don't want to worry him."

She mumbled something about wishing I didn't want to worry her, either. I handed the phone to Lloyd, relieved that I'd done my duty and could put my mind to figuring out the night's work.

After several minutes of "Yes, ma'am's" and "I will's," Lloyd hung up. "She sure is worried about us."

"I know, but I can't help it." I fidgeted in the chair, picturing my precious rings only a few miles away. Less than that, if we could go straight across the waterway. The afternoon stretched out before us, and I could hardly sit still for fear that those crooked thieves would be gone before we could sneak back over there.

"I declare, I don't think I'll be able to rest a minute," I said. "I need to be up and doing something, not sitting around here while they could be getting away." So I got up and paced the room.

"I sure wish I'd brought some shorts or something," Lloyd said. "These long pants're too hot for this weather, and it won't even cool off after dark like it does at home."

"Neither of us is dressed for it," I said, pushing at my long sleeves, which kept sliding back down. "I just couldn't imagine how hot it would be when I was packing, not with snow coming down."

"Well, you know, Miss Julia," the boy said, "if we want to look like we belong over there tonight, we ought to dress the part. I haven't seen anybody in long sleeves, and hardly anybody in long pants."

I flashed on that gray-suited federal agent, and how I'd immediately known that he didn't qualify as either a tourist or a Palm Beach resident. Clothes do make the man, and pretty much reveal the man's occupation, too.

Lloyd pushed his point. "I think we need to have on something that will make us look like we belong, and I sure am hot in these things."

"I'm not too comfortable, myself," I admitted, recalling the sweltering heat of the morning. "All right," I went on, making up my mind, "why don't we go look for some clothes that'll make us fit in better. I'll leave a note for Miss Wiggins while you run look in on Mr. Tuttle. I don't want him waking up and getting it in his head to take off. Although I wouldn't be exactly devastated if he did."

Finding a pen and pad by the telephone, I proceeded to write a note for Miss Wiggins, mumbling all the while to myself. "We'd do just as well without him, for my money. But Miss Wiggins is convinced that we need his help. Such as it is."

Lloyd turned back. "You think it's safe to take our car? Mr. Tuttle said we ought to leave it parked."

That gave me pause, but only slightly. "I

think he was only trying to keep us here. Nobody's looking for it or for us."

Having reassured him and myself, I took my pocketbook, considered my hat but left it where it was, and followed Lloyd out of the room. He had one of the card keys to Miss Wiggins's room, which she'd left behind, and he carefully inserted it into the slot on the door. As soon as he opened the door, I could hear the rumbling snores of a man deep in slumber.

Lloyd stuck his head inside, then eased back out. "He's dead to the world. I bet he won't wake up for hours."

"We won't be gone that long. Come along now. We'll stop by the desk in the lobby and ask where the best place to purchase temporary clothing is."

We did and were directed to one of the last places I ever thought I would shop for clothing, temporary or not. After parking what seemed to be a half mile from the entrance, we trudged toward the double doors of a Target store, perspiring every step of the way.

"I don't know about this, Lloyd," I said, panting and puffing in the heat that engulfed us. "It looks like another Wal-Mart. What kind of clothes do they have here, anyway?"

"They have just what we need, Miss Julia," he said, wiping the sweat from his eyes. "Mama gets some of my school clothes at the Target in Asheville, so it'll be fine. Besides, we don't want to spend a lot of money on something that we'll be hiding in the bushes in."

The boy's fiscal responsibility put shopping in a superstore in an entirely different light, and I patted his shoulder approvingly. And luxuriated in the cold air that surrounded us as we walked inside. Lloyd got a cart and started pushing it into the maw of the great store. Accustomed as I was to shopping in small shops with personal attention by the owners, I felt totally lost, not knowing where anything was and unable to find anybody to ask.

"Come on, Miss Julia," Lloyd said, pointing the cart toward the right rear of the store. "I think I know where the clothes are. These stores are set up pretty much the same everywhere."

When we got to the boys' clothing area, there wasn't a soul to help us find what we were looking for. It was every shopper for her- or himself, and I began looking through the garments hanging on circular racks.

"Here's the shorts," Lloyd said, as he sorted through the folded stacks on a table.

He held up a pair for me to see. "These look like my size."

"Why don't you get a couple of pairs and try them on. If we can find the fitting rooms. And some T-shirts, too. Whatever will be cool and look native enough to get us by."

I waited outside the men's fitting rooms while he tried on what he'd selected, taking note of everybody who came and went. You can't be too careful these days. But soon he came out in a pair of navy shorts with his knobby knees on full display. A striped short-sleeved T-shirt completed his ensemble. "I think these'll do," he said. "And the other outfit is the same size, so I'll wear these and take the other one. Let's find something for you now."

"Well, I don't know," I began, but he took off toward the women's department and I followed along.

"Look for something easy to move around in," he said, as we stood surveying rack after rack of every kind of casual wear one could conceive of — except the kind I wore. "I think you ought to get a pair of pants. You want long or short?"

I laughed. "You know I'm not going to wear a pair of pants, much less a pair of shorts."

"But you have to, Miss Julia. Nobody

wears dresses and pumps down here. We'll get you some sandals or maybe some tennis shoes. Then you'll fit right in. Let's find a bunch of things, and you can try on till you find what you like."

I didn't say anything, but if we looked around until I found what I liked, we'd be there all night and then some. None of the offerings came anywhere near my usual choice of apparel, but Lloyd gathered things from one rack after another and shooed me toward the dressing room.

An officious-looking woman suddenly appeared before him. "Only three garments at a time in the fitting rooms," she said, looking suspiciously at the armload of women's clothing in the boy's arms.

"He's with me," I said, "and he's helping me, since nobody else is. Here, Lloyd, give me three of those things and wait out here with the rest of them. I'll exchange with you, if these don't work." Then, smiling pleasantly at the woman, I went on. "Will that comply with the store policy?"

"I guess," she conceded, "but he can't go in the ladies' dressing rooms."

My head came up at that. "He wasn't intending to. And I'm surprised that you'd think such a thing. But if you want to keep your eye on us, that's fine with me. We could use the help."

She soon sidled off because helping customers wasn't her job. So I went behind a curtained cubicle and began to remove my clothes. Lloyd had given me a variety of sizes, and it didn't take long to discard two pairs of pants right away. One pair I could hardly get past my knees, and the other had enough room for two of me. A pair in bright green polyester knit with an elastic waist fit well enough in spite of being skintight, but somebody had cut some corners on them.

Hearing a saleslady in the next cubicle, I poked my head out at the edge of the curtain and snared her. "Excuse me, but these things're defective. They've got a flare down here on the bottoms, but they're about four inches too short. They don't even reach my ankles. You should report this and stop buying from the manufacturer."

She gave me an openmouthed look, swallowed hard, and said, "Ma'am, that's the way they're supposed to be. They're cropped."

I let the curtain fall back, dismayed at my lack of current fashion sense. But I wasn't about to go out in public in something so revealing, top, bottom, and behind. Even though the narrow confines of the fitting room didn't allow for a rear view, there was no way in the world I'd let anyone else get that view, either.

Sticking my head out from behind the curtain again, I called to Lloyd. "You still out there, Lloyd? I've decided to stick with a dress. I don't feel right in trousers."

"Don't they fit?"

"Well, this pair did," I said, giving him a partial view of the green pants. "They have a lot of give to them, which is fine for now. But after a little wear, they'll start to droop in unsightly places, and I can't have that. Besides, I'm not the slacks-wearing type."

"But, Miss Julia, we may have to run for our lives tonight. You need something you can scoot around in. Here, try these tops on with them." He held out two shirts.

Lord, I tried one on over the green pants, and would you believe that it was so short and stretchy that it showed the naked flesh of my midriff? I peeled it off over my head and picked up the other one. It was of a loosely woven cotton with Mexican embroidery around the neckline. The only fit it had was across the shoulders, so that it fell several inches below the waistband, giving some cover to what needed to be covered. As unfitted as it was, the least little breeze would be able to waft its way inside, and I admit I was tempted. But I decided I'd rather be hot and miserable in a dress than cool and miserable in an inappropriate costume.

So I redressed and left the unsuitable clothing in the fitting room.

"I'm sorry, Lloyd. I know you mean well, but those things aren't for me. I'd be so self-conscious I couldn't watch those crooks — too aware of who was behind me getting an eyeful. Let's go to the shoe department. I think I can manage some flats."

On our way to look at shoes, I continued to justify my decision. "I'm just not built for beachwear, Lloyd, and I don't want anybody laughing at me."

"Nobody would laugh, Miss Julia. You'd just look like everybody else." Which was no comfort at all, since I'd noticed what most people in the tropics wore and wasn't all that eager to follow suit.

Putting my foot down against buying tennis shoes, which Lloyd urged me to do, I finally settled on a pair of sandals with thick rubber soles. They were quite comfortable, but I had to remember to lift each foot up higher than normal when I walked. The thick soles had a tendency to trip me up.

"I think you ought to get these flip-flops," Lloyd said, teasing me as he held up a pair of shiny gold ones. "They have a lot of 'em for sale, so people must like them."

"Well, I don't. Those thongs make your

toes sore. I've heard your mother complain about that. No, Lloyd, these plain sandals are as far as I'm willing to go. Besides, you can't wear stockings with that strap between your toes."

He grinned. "I don't think you'd wear stockings with sandals, would you?"

"Some people might not, but *I* would."

CHAPTER 30

We put the sandals in the cart along with the purchases that Lloyd intended to make and began strolling along toward the check-out counters. There were ever so many items on display, many of which would've lured a less responsible person than I to overbuy. It seemed to me that these huge stores that carry everything one could conceivably want had method behind the seeming madness of selling for less. They could easily afford to cut their prices a few pennies on each item, because their customers ended up buying what they didn't need, and didn't even know they wanted, until they saw it.

These thoughts were running through my mind as I ran my hand over a stack of towels that were of surprisingly good quality. In fact, as I looked around I was more and more impressed with the array of bedding and all manner of dry goods, as well as home-decor objects. I was sure I could use any number of things if a Target store were to open in Abbotsville.

"Miss Julia," Lloyd said, "I know what we need. We ought to have some sunglasses. Let's see if we can find them."

I looked at my watch, not wanting to be too long away from the hotel. Miss Wiggins would be returning soon, and Mr. Tuttle remained to be dealt with. Figuring that we could spare a few more minutes, I followed him as he pushed the cart toward another section of the store. He slowed as we neared the electronics display, which could detain him all day if we'd had time for it.

But he knew our time was limited, so he continued on. As we passed an aisle in the housewares department, I glanced down it and thought my heart would stop. Grasping Lloyd's shoulder, I brought him to a halt. "Wait! Back up, quick!"

He quickly backpedaled a step and looked up at me, his eyes big behind his glasses. "What is it? What's going on?"

I leaned down and whispered fiercely, "I saw somebody!"

"Who?"

Instead of answering, I grabbed the front end of the cart and whirled it around. "Keep your head down," I whispered, hurrying with the cart back the way we'd come.

Moving as fast as I could without attracting attention, I glanced up and down each aisle as we passed, looking for a straight shot to the check-out counters.

"What is it, Miss Julia?" Lloyd asked. "What's wrong?"

Still keeping my voice down, I said, "I saw the man who was in that house this morning! He was with another man, and we almost ran right into them."

Lloyd cast a frightened glance behind us. "Did he see us?"

"I don't think so. Lord, I hope not." By this time, I was hurrying past each display and slowing down before crossing an aisle, giving the space an anxious look before proceeding past.

"We better get out of here," Lloyd said.

"That's what I'm trying to do, but I saw another man in the front aisle, heading this way. He may be with them."

"But only that one man knows what you look like. Let's just leave my stuff and get on out."

By this time, we were back in the women's department where I felt a little safer, especially behind a triple rack of pink nylon step-ins.

I was still trembling from our close encounter, but I tried to pull myself together

331

and think strategically. "We could do that, but you know he's told his cohorts what happened this morning. I mean, he'd have to explain the loss of Mildred's lavaliere, if nothing else. And I must say, Lloyd, that any description of me would be unique and easily recognized. I don't have on my hat and gloves, but this is the very same dress."

Lloyd squinched up his mouth, giving our cornered situation deep thought. "You're sure it was the same man?"

"As sure as I'm standing here. Once seen, nobody could forget him. It was him, all right. I just can't figure out what they're doing in Housewares."

"Okay, here's what let's do. Go back in the fitting room and put on those green pants. And here're your sandals. They don't know me, so I'll run and get a few more things."

The green pants and loose top were lying on a counter waiting to be rehung, so I snatched them up and hurried back to the fitting room. Stripping off my dress, I quickly pulled the pants onto my lower parts and the top onto my upper. Who would've ever thought I'd be eager to wear something with spandex in it?

Reluctant to appear in public view, I stuck my head out of the door and found Lloyd waiting for me. He handed me a floppy straw hat with a kerchief attached that tied under the chin. I put it on without benefit of a mirror, not wanting to see what I looked like.

"Put these on, too," he said, handing me a pair of sunglasses. "Nobody'll recognize you now."

"I doubt I'd recognize myself," I said, slipping on the glasses under the brim of the hat and tying the kerchief. I felt like Greta Garbo, but hardly resembled her. But nothing would help the mortification I felt at displaying myself in public, knowing I didn't have the shape to justify a pair of stretch pants. "Let's go, Lloyd, but don't walk behind me. It's not an edifying view."

"You fit right in," he said, with an approving nod. "You look just like somebody who's retired from up North."

That didn't exactly reassure me, but I put my discarded dress and my Naturalizer pumps in the cart, clasped the handle, and began pushing it toward the front of the store. Unable to play the part of a shopper, though, my eyes kept flitting here, there, and yonder, watching for the one person who might see a door-to-door missionary underneath the trappings of a Florida retiree.

"Wait, wait, Miss Julia," Lloyd said, pulling at my sleeve. "Let me get these tags off.

We have to pay for everything or they'll arrest us for shoplifting."

"I've already taken some off. Oh, my goodness, Lloyd, wonder if they have many people wearing what they buy out of the store before they even buy it? I didn't think of that."

"Make up something," he said, thinking ahead as he always does. "Say that you spilled something or, no, I know." He took my wadded-up dress from the cart and with a mighty tug, ripped the thing from hem to waist. "See? No way you could wear it now." Then he turned in a complete circle, eyeing the store as far as he could see. "It looks clear. Let's head on out."

Of course, we had to wait in line since there were only two lanes open when they could've opened eight. We edged along, waiting our turn, while I held my head high, daring anyone to give me a second glance. Fortunately, there were, just as Lloyd had foretold, any number of aged women in equal or worse ill-advised ensembles.

As our turn neared, I put Lloyd's extra selections on the conveyor belt and laid the sales tags in a neat row beside them.

"What's this?" The checkout lady pointed at the tags. Well, actually, she was hardly a lady, more a woman with hard-living lines creasing her face.

"They're for what I'm buying," I told her. "See? I have it all on. Here're two tags for what the boy has on, and a tag for my top, and one for the slacks, and for the glasses, and for the hat. And this one's for the sandals." I lifted up a foot for her to see.

"You're wearing everything?"

"Yes, I am, and I assure you that the number of tags matches the number of garments I'm wearing. You see, I had an accident in your store. My dress — hold it up, Lloyd — got snagged on one of the display units and it ripped from one end to the other. I couldn't walk out of here like that, could I?"

The woman eyed the torn dress, and me, with narrowed eyes. "How do I know you don't have something on that you're not telling me about?"

Mortally offended at the suggestion of theft, something that would never happen in Abbotsville, I drew myself up. "Would you like to see? I can assure you that my undergarments did not come from this store, nor from any store like it."

By this time, others who were waiting in line were beginning to take an interest in the delay. One old man in Bermuda shorts and black socks craned his head and said, "I'd like to be sure about that."

"Keep out of this," I snapped, anxious to bring this transaction to a close. Any minute, those jewel thieves would be appearing to check out their purchases. I took a quick look behind me, then opened my pocketbook. "I want to pay you for what we're buying. Please ring it up."

I handed her a credit card, which she proceeded to study with some skepticism. "I'll have to have this verified," she said, turning as if to call for help.

I quickly pulled out a roll of bills to hurry the transaction along. "We'll just pay cash," I said, wanting her to know that we were not in reduced circumstances and had no need to resort to shoplifting. "If you have any doubts as to my veracity in this matter, I suggest that you call Detective McGruder of the West Palm Beach sheriff's office, homicide division. He's a friend of mine." When in doubt, always play the law enforcement card.

"Well, I guess it's okay," she said, as if she weren't quite sure of it. And, to my relief, she handed back my credit card and began running the loose tags across the scanner.

We took the plastic bags filled with Lloyd's new clothes and my old ones, and, trying not to run, headed for the pneumatic doors. Neither Lloyd nor I said a word to each other, so intent were we to appear relaxed and unconcerned about being recognized by thieves or being waylaid by the store manager and a security guard. If I had to prove my innocence by undressing in front of strangers — being strip-searched, if you will — I would never get over the humiliation.

Actually, though, I would get over it — at the very point that I sued the pants off whoever dared accuse me of stealing, and of stealing such tacky merchandise, at that.

CHAPTER 31

I dove into the car, slammed the door behind me, and scooted onto the leather seat — and almost scooted off. As spandex slid across baked leather, I grabbed the steering wheel and levitated.

Lloyd threw our purchases in the backseat, buckled himself in, and screamed, "They're coming out! Hurry, Miss Julia, they're coming this way."

My heart thumped in panic as I took a quick look across the parking lot. Three men straggled out of the store, each of them carrying merchandise too large for shopping bags. "It is them, Lloyd! At least one of them is, that little runty one. And look what they bought. Suitcases!" My hand shook as I turned the ignition. "Oh, my word, they're going to pack up and leave. I knew they would. I just knew it."

Jittering around as much as the seat belt would let him, Lloyd said, "Don't look, Miss

338

Julia, they'll see you. Pull your hat down on that side."

I snatched the brim over to one side, skewing my sunglasses to such an angle that I had a cockeyed view of the parking lot. But I'd driven in worse conditions, and didn't stop until I was halted at the exit by a stop sign and oncoming traffic. I took the time to readjust my glasses, then proceeded on to the hotel, hoping I hadn't been recognized.

"My, that was a close call," I said, trying to steady my inner trembling. "Who would've thought they'd be shopping in Target's, too? Did you see what kind of car they had?"

"No'm, you got out of there too fast," Lloyd said, as he dried his sweat-streaked glasses on his shirttail. "Thank goodness."

"I just hope that bushy-headed one didn't see me. He'd surely think it odd to run into me twice in one day."

"He wouldn't've recognized you if he had. I don't think anybody would."

"I hope they wouldn't." I steered the car into the hotel parking lot and looked in vain for a shaded spot. Leaving the car in the hot sun, we hurried toward the hotel.

He smiled without looking at me. "You look fine, Miss Julia. Really, nobody would give you a second look."

"It's the first one I'm worried about. Let's

get to our room so I can put on something decent."

As I slipped the card key into the slot on our door, Miss Wiggins opened her door. "Hey, Lloyd," she said in her usual cheery manner. "Who's . . . ? Oh, Miss Julia, I didn't know that was you."

"See, Lloyd?" I said, pushing open the door and hurrying inside. "I look a fright."

"Oh, no, I didn't mean that," Miss Wiggins said as she followed us into the room. "I meant with the shades and all. You look terrific, Miss Julia. I love those platform soles and cropped pants. They're very trendy these days."

I untied the kerchief, threw the hat and sunglasses on the bed, and started rummaging in my suitcase for a skirt of some kind. "Trendy," I mumbled. "Just what I wanted. Listen, Etta Mae, we just came from a Target store where I got this getup, and you won't believe who we almost ran into."

"A movie star?"

"What? No, for goodness' sake, not a movie star. Worse than that. We saw that bushy-headed man whose pocket you rummaged through this morning. And he was with two other men, and they came out of the store loaded down with suitcases and satchels. . . ."

"And duffel bags," Lloyd added.

"Yes," I said, nodding, "and duffel bags, everything they need to pack up and leave."

Miss Wiggins's eyes widened. "Oh, my. They're going somewhere, aren't they?"

"Yes, and taking all their ill-gotten gains with them. So we've got to be there to stop them."

Miss Wiggins's head suddenly jerked around. "Oh, good grief!" she screeched, and tore out of the room and across the hall.

I stopped my search and looked at Lloyd. "What is it?"

"Mr. Tuttle, I think," he said, and hurried after her.

Lord, if he was awake and creating a commotion, we could be thrown out of the hotel. After a quick look up and down the hall, checking for spectators, I went across, too.

The most awful retching sounds were coming from the bathroom. Miss Wiggins was yelling, her voice echoing in the tiled area. "Lean over, Frank. Lean farther over."

"He's throwing up," Lloyd said.

"So I hear." I resigned myself to listening to the sorry result of self-indulgence and took a seat where I could see across the hall to the door we'd left open. "I declare, Lloyd, I could wish we'd never gotten mixed up with him. We ought to take him back to his apartment and just leave him. I am sick and tired of taking care of somebody who won't take care of himself."

"I don't know, Miss Julia," Lloyd said with a far-off look on his face. "We're supposed to love our neighbor and be Good Samaritans and all that, and maybe he's been put in our path so we can help him. I'm wondering what Jesus would do in this situation."

"They Lord, Lloyd, I doubt Jesus would be in this situation in the first place." I didn't just doubt it, I knew it, and it had nothing to do with tending to Mr. Tuttle. Jesus would still be in Abbotsville, not running around Florida trying to steal from thieves what they'd stolen from us. I knew that because he'd said if a man takes your cloak, let him take your coat along with it. Which, if I'm not mistaken, would mean that I ought to not only wave my stolen rings good-bye, but I should chase those crooks down and give them what they'd missed.

But I didn't bring up such knotty theological problems to the boy, seeing no need to lay any additional burdens on him. Still and all, he'd made me rethink my attitude toward a man who had been of some minor help to us and who was now stumbling, white-faced and shaky, out of the bathroom.

"Sit here," Miss Wiggins said, guiding him to a chair. "Take it easy for a while. I'll fix you a Coke."

As she did that from the supply she had on hand, Mr. Tuttle cut his eyes at me. Then he buried his face in his hands and groaned, "I think I'm gonna die."

"You're not going to die," I told him. "At least not today. But you are killing yourself with that stuff, and if you don't know it, I'm telling you straight-out."

"Two beers," he moaned. "That's all I had, but, man, something hit me like a ton of bricks. I don't understand it."

"Well, I do," I said. "You've poisoned your entire system with alcohol. I wouldn't be surprised if your liver and everything else isn't saturated with it. The thing for you to do, Mr. Tuttle, is stop it, just stop it cold and not get yourself in this fix again."

"She's right," Miss Wiggins said, handing him a glass of Coca-Cola. "But I know it's hard. Have you tried AA?"

"I'm not an alcoholic," Mr. Tuttle said, taking immediate offense. "I just ate something bad, maybe that hamburger I had for lunch."

"How can you say such a thing?" I said,

looking at him in amazement. "The first step to conquering a vice is to admit to it. But before you even do that, you have to stay out of that Strip Hall and find a better place to eat. Then you need to get yourself in church. I can assure you that you won't be tempted to drink in church." I thought about that statement for a second, then said, "Unless you go to one that serves wine at communion. Of course, wine is biblically recommended, but you'd be safer going to one that uses grape juice, like a good, sound Presbyterian church."

Mr. Tuttle leaned his head against the back of the chair, unable to respond. Miss Wiggins and Lloyd kept silence as well. Perhaps I had gone into too much detail, but the man needed to keep better company than what he'd been associating with.

"Well," I said, preparing to rise, "it's getting late and we need to eat something. And make our plans. Etta Mae, did you get all the gear you went after?"

"Yes, ma'am, I got it, but I had to go on the other side of the interstate before I found a Circuit City. You want to look at it now or wait till after we eat?"

"Let's have room service again. I don't feel like dressing and undressing a dozen times."

Lloyd's head came up at that. "You decided to wear those pants tonight?"

"I think I might. They're certainly easy to get around in, and I don't expect to see anybody I know. Besides, it'll be dark."

"Where dark?" Mr. Tuttle mumbled, but he could've been talking to himself for all the attention he got.

Miss Wiggins grinned at me. "They look real good on you. Who knows, you may start a trend in Abbotsville."

I rolled my eyes and sidled toward the door. I might've considered it if I could've kept my back turned all the time. "Let's go across the hall. Our room is a little larger."

Miss Wiggins pulled Mr. Tuttle out of his chair and headed him out. "We'll order you some soup, Frank. And some Alka-Seltzer. Then you'll feel better."

After ordering and receiving a cart of food, we sat around eating and waiting for Mr. Tuttle's head to clear. Miss Wiggins began to show us the purchases she'd made.

"They're supposed to work up to ten miles," she said, as she unboxed them. "Guaranteed, too, so if they don't, I'm taking them back."

I twisted my mouth. "It'll be too late by the time we find out they don't."

"Oh, look," Lloyd said, reading the instructions, "they've got all kinds of special features. Automatic squelch, backlit LCD, silent vibrate, voice scrambler, and a belt clip-on. Why, we can even get weather alerts, in case it clouds up. Man, you got some good ones, Etta Mae."

"What you got there?" Mr. Tuttle asked, frowning at the electronic gadgets that Miss Wiggins and Lloyd were examining.

"Walkie-talkies," Miss Wiggins said. "See, Frank, we're figuring we can't all get up close to that house. Somebody has to stay with the car, and we can't park too close or we'll be run off."

"Who says?"

"Oh, I forgot you don't know," she said. "Me and Miss Julia went over there today. And the house we staked out last night is the right one, all right. And we know they've got jewelry in it, because I got a piece of it back. Show him that lavaliere, Miss Julia."

I took it from my purse and handed it to her. "See?" She dangled it front of Mr. Tuttle's eyes, which slowly began to cross as he tried to focus on it. "This came from Abbotsville, and it belongs to one of Miss Julia's friends. So we know we're on the right track."

"Y'all went over there?" Mr. Tuttle couldn't seem to take in what she was saying, so maybe his head wasn't so clear after all.

"Yes, we did," I chimed in. "And we did it while you were out drinking your lunch and getting into your present fix."

He gave me a cold glare, but what's true is true, and pretending otherwise doesn't help a thing.

"So anyway," Miss Wiggins went on, "when we were about to leave, some man who Miss Julia pegged as a federal agent told us that the area is restricted, and not to come back. So that means we have to park some ways away, but near enough to get there if any of us needs help. See?"

Mr. Tuttle still wasn't following too closely. "How'd you get that necklace?"

"Well," she said with a sly grin, "I just did."

"She picked his pocket," Lloyd said. "I sure wish I'd been there to see it, too."

Mr. Tuttle shook his head, then held on to it with a shaky hand. "Maybe you better start at the beginning."

I sat back and listened while Miss Wiggins started at the beginning of our morning escapade. It sounded exciting and quite successful to hear her tell it. And I suppose it was, but she left out the high level of courage we'd displayed by taking matters into our own hands, as well as the flat-out fright that had propelled us away from there.

Now we were proposing to go back under cover of darkness, and as the time drew near, I felt a ripple of excitement and fear. But my precious rings were within reach — at least I'd convinced myself they were — and neither federal agents nor common thieves were going to deter me from getting them back.

"Let's figure out who's going to do what," I said, concerned again about putting Lloyd in danger. "As much as I would like to see into that house, I think Lloyd and I ought to stay with the car."

"But I want to creep through the bushes," Lloyd said. "I'm real good at it, and if I got caught they wouldn't do anything to me. I mean, either the crooks or the federal agents, would they? I could say I was playing hide-and-seek or something. Besides, nobody on either side has ever seen me."

"No, Lloyd, I can't let you do that. I want you to stay with me and operate this walkie-talkie thing. Let's let Etta Mae and Mr. Tuttle do the creeping, and you and I will be their backup."

"Okay, I guess, but I bet I could get closer than anybody. And not get caught, either."

Mr. Tuttle decided to step in then. "Wait a minute here. What's the big rush? If you've identified a piece of jewelry, we can call Mc-

Gruder and let him handle it. He can coordinate with the feds, and we can stay out of it altogether."

"I've told you, Mr. Tuttle," I said, "and I don't want to have to tell you again. I'm not going to let my things get confiscated and put in federal custody. I want my rings back where they belong and not in an evidence locker somewhere."

"Yeah," Lloyd said. "And Mama's, too."

"And another thing," I went on, "those crooks're getting ready to move. Lloyd and I saw them at Target today, and they were buying suitcases. That means they're packing, and packing means they're leaving. So the big rush is to get to them before they do, or at least to see where they're going."

That stopped the planning session again while Lloyd told about our shopping trip and how we almost ran into the one man who could identify me.

"And that's why," I summed up, "I'm dressed as I am, and why we have to do something tonight."

CHAPTER 32

Mr. Tuttle's eyes rolled back in his head. "Why did I ever get mixed up in this?"

"I've wondered the same thing," I said, "and it's because I hired you to, and you didn't turn me down. So stop complaining and pull yourself together. If this is going to work, we all have to know what we're doing." I turned the walkie-talkie set around in my hands, looking at the dials and the antenna. "And the first order of business is to show me how this thing works."

It was Lloyd who read the directions and adjusted the dials on the two handsets — to put them on the same frequency, he said. It was remarkable how quickly the child could pick up on technology and figure out the most garbled instructions.

"Etta Mae," he said, handing a set to her, "why don't you go over to your room and close the door. Then we'll see if these things work. Oh, wait," he said as she started out of the room. "We need some code names so if anybody gets on our wavelength, they won't know who's talking. You can be One-A, and Miss Julia, you be Two-B."

"To be?" I asked.

"Yessum, and Mr. Tuttle'll be Three-C, and I'll be Four-D. That suit everybody?"

Miss Wiggins was delighted with the idea of secret codes and security measures. She skipped out of the room, closing the door behind her. Mr. Tuttle just shook his head.

Lloyd put the set close to his mouth and said, "Four-D calling One-A. Come in, One-A. Over."

"This is One-A. Hello?" Miss Wiggins's voice blasted out and reverberated through the room. Mr. Tuttle grabbed his head, and I did the same but for different reasons.

"Oops," Lloyd said. "I better turn the volume down." He fiddled with the dials until we could hear only a whisper of Miss Wiggins's voice as it demanded an answer.

"Lloyd, are you there? Is this thing working? Hello?"

"Ah, One-A, this is Four-D. We're receiving. Are you receiving us?"

I put my ear next to the set that Lloyd was holding and heard her say, "I sure am, and probably everybody in the hotel is, too. How do you turn this thing down?"

"Return to base, One-A," Lloyd said. "I'll fix it here. Over."

"Okay," she responded, then after a second, she said, "Over."

As soon as I opened the door for her, she said, "Man, this thing is loud. I hope you can turn it down, Lloyd, because it'll wake up the whole island."

"Oh, yeah, I can." He took the set from her, looked at the directions again, and adjusted the dials. "It's fine now," he said, handing it back to her.

"You're all crazy," Mr. Tuttle said, pursing his mouth and shaking his head. "This is not gonna work."

"And pessimism," I told him, "is not at all helpful. If you have a better idea, now's the time to trot it out."

"I've already told you my idea," he came back. "Call McGruder and let him handle it."

"And I've already told you why we're not going to do that. So you can either help us or stop trying to hinder us."

"Frank," Miss Wiggins said, as she sat on the arm of his chair and leaned close to him. "We really need you. Miss Julia's determined to do this, and so am I. How would you feel if something awful happened, and you weren't there to help us out?"

"Yes," I chimed in, "and if those agents catch us, the first thing I'm going to tell them is that I hired you to find my jewelry and that you left us in the lurch. How would that look in the newspaper?"

He glared at me, and not for the first time, either. I stared back at him, not giving an inch.

Then, in the rudest manner possible, he said, "Just what're you gonna do when you get there? Knock on the door?"

"We've already done that," I said. "No, what we're going to do is sneak up on them and see what they're doing."

"And how're you gonna do that? You think they'll have the windows open? You think you'll get close enough to hear what they're saying? You'll be lucky if you get within two blocks of that place. And luckier still if you don't end up in jail. The feds'll have that house locked down tighter'n a tick. No way you're gonna get anywhere close to it."

"You are the most negative person I've ever met," I said, drawing myself up. "If you'd looked at that house like you should have, you'd have seen that there's a bamboo thicket all across the backyard. It reaches up and over the garage, and there's no reason in the world we can't sneak in from the other street and get right up to the garage without a soul seeing us. And if they're leaving, they'll be going in and out the back door, right in front of us, and we won't have to get close to the house at all.

"Now let me ask you something, Mr. Tuttle. Does it make sense to you, if those crooks leave tonight, that they'd load up their cars in full view of the neighbors and federal agents, even if they don't know they're there? I mean, from the front of the house? No, they wouldn't. They'd load up from the back, and from what Etta Mae and I saw, the garage is right close to the back of the house. If we're in the bamboo, we'll be able to see them going and coming. How's that for a plan?"

Mr. Tuttle snatched the handset from Miss Wiggins. "Gimme that thing. If you're gonna do it, do it right. First thing, don't go over there till after dark, but not too late. About ten-thirty or eleven. I'm bettin', if they leave tonight, it'll be around midnight, so you'll have plenty of time. You oughta take one car — yours, Mrs. Murdoch. It'll fit in better'n mine."

I nodded, agreeing that my large, new car would look more like it belonged on that wealthy island than his rust-covered police reject.

"Second off," Mr. Tuttle went on, "park

away from the house, maybe three or four blocks away. Look for a house that's having a party or something and pull in along with the guests."

"What if nobody's having a party?" Etta Mae asked.

"Somebody's *always* having a party on the island," he said. "It's the season. Only problem is, Palm Beach police're always around, too. And let me tell you something else, as soon as anything happens, they close the bridges to the mainland. So if you're caught on the island, *you are caught.* You got that?"

I wasn't sure I appreciated Mr. Tuttle's return to sobriety. He was about to get too big for his britches, giving orders and talking down to us.

"I notice you keep saying *you*," I said. "Does that mean you're not going with us?"

"You got that right. I could lose my license."

He could lose it for his way of living, too, but he didn't mention that. I didn't, either, but he knew what I was thinking.

Miss Wiggins got up and walked across the room, motioning me to follow. She leaned her head close and whispered, "I'm worried about this, Miss Julia. We got away with a lot this morning, but we might not be so lucky again. I'm thinking that if he won't go with us, maybe we ought not try it."

I whispered back, "Are you backing out on me?"

"No, not really. I'm pretty much game for anything, but what about Lloyd? I sure wouldn't want anything to happen to him."

Well, of course she'd put her finger on it right there. After thinking about it for a minute and casting an angry glance at Mr. Tuttle, who was spoiling all our plans, I said, "I'm worried about Lloyd, too. We could leave him here in the room. He wouldn't like it, but he'd be safe."

"But what would he do if we can't get back?"

"Lord, Etta Mae, don't even think that. Of course we'll get back." Then, with another glare at the stumbling block sitting in the only comfortable chair in the room, I went on. "That settles it. Mr. Tuttle has to go with us, that's all there is to it. Come on, Etta Mae, I may have just the thing to get him up and moving." As we walked back across the room, I whispered to her, "But I'll tell you the truth, he was more amenable when he was under the influence. At least then, he didn't try to run everything."

She grinned and nodded. "But he has

some good ideas, don't you think? I'd feel better if he's with us."

I didn't think I would, but I kept reminding myself that he was Mr. Pickens's friend and that said something right there. I wasn't too sure what it said, but Mr. Tuttle seemed the best we could do. I only wished that Mr. Pickens could've been with us. As frisky as he was in some ways, he could be counted on, whereas if we let Frank Tuttle out of our sight, we'd have to go looking for him instead of my rings.

I went across the room and stood over Mr. Tuttle. "Mr. Tuttle, I'll make a deal with you. If you'll go with us and give us the benefit of your expertise, I'll write out a check to you right now. And I guarantee it will more than cover the little time you've already given us, plus tonight's activities, and a sizable bonus for hazardous duty. And, believe me, it will be enough so that if we're caught, it'll bail you out of jail and set you back up in business."

"Let's see it."

"Not so fast. That's one part of the deal. The second part is this: If, in spite of federal agents and thieving crooks, we happen to recover our jewelry, I'll hand you another check."

"As big as the first one?"

"Bigger. That's how important my rings are."

He started to rise, but I held up my hand. "Sit still. There's a third part to this. Not only will you go with us tonight, but, because Lloyd is concerned for your soul, I want you to consider getting yourself in a church. And if you will, I will pay you for every Sunday that you go for a solid year, and at the same hourly rate you normally charge. I'm not even asking you to give up your destructive habit. All you have to do is give church a try, and if that doesn't take, I don't know what will."

"Oh, for God's sake," he said, slinging his head around like he'd never heard anything so outlandish.

"That's exactly what I'm saying. It's for God's sake and your own. Is it a deal?"

"Oh, hell, yes, if that's what you want." Then he gave me a sly grin. "I think I got the best end of it. I get paid regardless of what happens tonight. Right?"

"Right. Only not as much if I don't get my rings."

"And going cold turkey is not part of the deal?"

"Right again. I don't care if you have to stagger into church every Sunday that rolls around. I'm counting on what you hear there to do the rest of it. And don't worry about having a makeover before you go. You can go just as you are, and you'll be welcome." At least, I hoped he would.

"And you don't care what kind of church I go to?" Mr. Tuttle was feeling better and better about my proposal.

"No, I don't. You can go to a storefront church, if you want to. Or to the Salvation Army or to a downtown cathedral, if you can find one. Even to a drive-in church, it doesn't matter to me. I'll tell you one thing, though, you'd be better off in a Presbyterian church." I stopped and caught my lip with my teeth. "But I may be prejudiced."

"Write your check," he said with a great deal more enthusiasm than he'd hitherto shown. He stood and hitched up his pants. "I need something else to eat. That soup's not gonna last me all night. I guess you know they don't have room service in jail."

CHAPTER 33

Lloyd had been listening wide-eyed to all this. He sat on the edge of his chair with his eyes going back and forth between us, listening to the ins and outs of our transaction. I hoped he was learning a lesson, which is, when circumstances call for it, money can be quite useful in getting your way. People are all too willing to throw up hindrances for no other reason than to be obstinate. But some of them, in fact all of whom I'd had dealings with, could be bought. But, as Lloyd had just witnessed, it wasn't all that pretty a sight. So the main lesson I wanted him to learn was this: Before you begin waving money around to further your own ends, you ought to be totally convinced that your ends are worthwhile. And when you're sure of that, then whip out your checkbook.

Which I did and wrote out a sizable check, tore it out, and handed it to Mr. Tuttle. "It's too late in the day to make a deposit, and we don't have time for personal business anyway. But you may be sure it's good, and if I get my rings back, the next one will be even better."

Mr. Tuttle's eyes widened as he looked at the check. Then he puckered up his mouth in a silent whistle. A flash of pure pleasure crossed his face as he folded the check and put it in his nearly empty wallet. "Let's get this show on the road," he said, rubbing his hands together.

"Wait a minute," Miss Wiggins said. "Tell us what you want us to do, first."

He nodded sagely. "You're already doing what I want you to do — listening to me and following orders. I don't want anybody going off on their own. We could get in big trouble over there one way or another, so there has to be one person in charge. And that's me."

I rolled my eyes, but didn't say anything. Since I'd paid for his services, I might as well get the benefit of them. But he sure was bossy.

"First thing we're gonna do," he went on, looking stern and serious as he took up the burden of command, "is scout out the area and find a good place to park. By then the sun'll be down, and time for a nice, normal family to take a leisurely stroll."

361

"What if we don't find a good place to park?" I asked, and got a exasperated look in return.

"We will. We can always park in a hotel parking lot. Or at a restaurant. Don't worry about it, I know what I'm doing."

My head came up at that short answer. I had a good mind to tell him that it was only by the grace of Miss Wiggins that I was putting up with him in the first place. But fomenting sedition in the ranks was hardly a good way to start, so I kept my thoughts to myself.

Mr. Tuttle started looking over the food cart and picking through the remains of our supper. He ate a quarter of a sandwich that Lloyd had left and finished off Miss Wiggins's salad. Then he forked up the cold mashed potatoes from my plate and ate the last two rolls in the basket.

"That's better," he said, after emptying all three tea glasses. "If anybody has to go to the bathroom, better go now. We've got a long night ahead, so get with it."

I could've done without his crude way of referring to the normal functions of the body — matters that a well-bred person would never mention — but I also remembered the miserable state we'd been in on the stakeout. Everybody else did, too, for Lloyd dashed to

362

the bathroom and Etta Mae took off for her room.

Mr. Tuttle called after her, "Better take off your shorts and put on some long pants." Then he grinned at me. "Wouldn't want to mess up them pretty legs. That bamboo may be tough to get through."

Seeing my glare of disapproval, he straightened up and said, "That could be another problem. If the bamboo's old and thick, we won't be able to get into it. On top of that, we got to worry about going through the yard of the house that backs up to the garage." He shook his head. "Every house over there is wired to the gills, and if they have motion-sensor lights, then we've had it."

"Why, Mr. Tuttle, those crooks wouldn't call the police, I don't care how wired they are."

"I'm not worried about the crooks. I'm worried about the neighbors." He mopped his forehead with Lloyd's napkin. "If we get arrested, they'll throw the book at us. Talk about your obstruction of justice and interfering with an official investigation. To say nothing of trespassing and stalking and everything else. Man, I just don't know."

"Don't lose your nerve now, Mr. Tuttle," I said and, as Miss Wiggins came back in the room, went on. "Her bathroom's empty, so do your business over there. And pull your-self together while you're at it."

As he left, Miss Wiggins said, "He getting cold feet again?"

"He's just worried about getting arrested," I said, waving that concern away. "But we have two good lawyers on call — Sam and Binkie — so I'm not. Of course," I went on quickly, "being stuck in jail would sure put a crimp in getting my rings back, so that's not in my plans."

"I thought Mr. Sam was off somewhere," Miss Wiggins said, rubbing a hand nervously on the low-slung jeans she'd put on.

"He is, but he'd be back in a hurry if I made my one civil-rights-guaranteed phone call to Russia. And, you know Binkie'd be here in a flash. Of course, she'd have to find a babysitter first, and that could prove wor-risome. But . . . oh, there you are," I said as Lloyd came out of the bathroom. "My turn next."

I allowed Mr. Tuttle to drive my car, even though I wasn't convinced that he was in the best of health, considering the ills he'd suffered earlier in the day. But he'd made a good case for doing so, pointing out that the charade, as he called it, required him and Miss Wiggins to be the mother and father of this make-believe family.

"And the mother and father," he said, turning on the ignition, "ride in the front seat, and the father drives. The little boy sits in the back with his granny." He pointed his finger at me. "That's you."

"If I'm the grandmother," I said, smoothly correcting him, "whose mother am I?"

"Hers," he said, jerking his thumb at Miss Wiggins. "And if you don't like 'granny,' how do you like 'mother-in-law'?"

I declare, the man could make the most innocuous words sound like the worst of insults, but since actually being his mother-in-law was not in my future, I let him get away with it.

Settling into the backseat as Mr. Tuttle guided the car onto the street, I said, "Well, either way, I don't expect anyone'll ask what kin we are."

"No, they won't," he came back, "but if we're gonna walk the sidewalks, Etta Mae'll be holding my hand, like a normal married couple, and you and the boy'll come along behind us."

I thought about that for a minute, then said, "Are you all right with that, Etta Mae? Pretending to be married to him, I mean?"

"Oh, sure," she said, grinning at me over the backseat. "I know how to look like a married couple. I've had lots of practice."

Indeed she had, if half of what I'd heard about her was true. At least two husbands, with half the men in Delmont trying to be her third.

As we crossed over the bridge, I was again taken with the tall palm trees that lined the main thoroughfare on the island, as well as with the restrained and well-landscaped commercial buildings we passed. Then we came up on a huge, brightly lit hotel with a magnificent fountain out front and the Atlantic Ocean for a backdrop. The sight almost took my breath away.

"Look, look," Miss Wiggins cried. "Limos and chauffeurs and doormen and everything. They must be having a party. Look at the evening dresses! Oh, I wonder if Donald Trump is there."

"Who's he?" Lloyd asked, pressing his face to the window as we passed.

"Just somebody who lives down here," I said. "Part of the time, anyway."

Cruising at low speed to stay within the posted limit, we passed the hotel and rode along the wide streets of the island. The streetlamps gave off a soft glow, just enough to provide glimpses of large houses and spacious lawns. And on the other side, off in the distance, I could see waves cresting on the ocean, their whitecaps gleaming in the dark.

"Look at that ocean," Lloyd said, wistfully. "It's so close, and we can't even go in it."

Miss Wiggins's soft response drifted over from the front seat. "I feel the same way about Disney World."

"It's all right, sugar," I said, patting Lloyd's arm. "We'll come back sometime in the summer when you can go in."

Then I leaned up toward the front seat and tapped Mr. Tuttle's shoulder. "You need to turn somewhere along here," I said, in case he'd lost his bearings.

"I know it. I'm going all the way down, then come back up on the street that parallels this one. We'll keep working our way down until we get as close as we can. Now, listen," he said, with a quick turn of his head toward me, "if for any reason we're stopped, we're just tourists, okay? Taking in the sights of Palm Beach."

Well, that didn't take a lot of private detecting expertise. We'd thought that up a long time ago, and anybody who looked at us would immediately think the same thing. I mean, the way we were dressed and all, who could imagine that we were anything but tourists? There I was in an outfit I wouldn't be caught dead in, Miss Wiggins in low-riding jeans and tight T-shirt, Lloyd in baggy shorts, and Mr. Tuttle in a Hawaiian shirt, the likes of which hurt my eyes to look at. Who in the world would wear such getups in their own hometown?

After several long minutes of cruising up and down the streets, Mr. Tuttle finally pulled to the curb where a string of cars was parked. The residents of a house several doors down seemed to be having a get-together, which was what Mr. Tuttle had been looking for.

"This is good," he said approvingly. "We're between streetlights, too, and it's as dark as it's going to get. Check the handsets and be sure they're on the same frequency, and put 'em both on vibrate. Lloyd, leave yours in the car, and give me the other one." He stretched himself up so he could clip the set onto the belt under his shirt. "Okay, everybody ready?"

"But we're not anywhere near where we want to be," I told him. "That house must be three or four streets over."

"I know what I'm doing," he said, sounding as if he was gritting his teeth. "But we're gonna walk now and come back on the street right behind it. I want to get a look at that bamboo thicket you say you saw. For all I know, it was a clump of weeds."

"I didn't just say it. I saw it, and so did Etta Mae. Didn't you, Etta Mae?"

She nodded and opened her door as Mr. Tuttle did his. Lloyd and I followed, turning our faces to the ocean breeze that whisked through our hair and rattled among the palm fronds.

"Wait a minute," I said. "I want to put my pocketbook in the trunk."

With a sigh, Mr. Tuttle popped the trunk, then snapped his fingers. "Hold on. Let me see what you got in there." He leaned into the trunk and rummaged around until he found and opened a toolbox that Ralph Peterson must have provided. Or maybe it came with the car. Mr. Tuttle took something from it and stuffed it in his pocket.

"Don't ask," he said, as I opened my mouth. "Tricks of the trade."

"I was just going to say that I know bamboo when I see it, and you can count on that."

He slammed the trunk closed, his face a study in anger management, then took Miss Wiggins's hand and led her out. Lloyd and I fell in behind. Before long, we were ambling along the sidewalk as if we were a happy little family out for an evening stroll. But like many families, there were some of us who were doing it under duress, and others who'd rather have been doing something else, and at least one who was mortally offended at having her word doubted.

CHAPTER 34

I might've enjoyed the walk if I'd been better able to manage the platform soles on my sandals. As it was, it was all I could do to lift each foot high enough to keep from stumbling, and Lloyd had to steady me more than once.

But I'll tell you the truth, I'd had my fill of walking by the time we'd gone up one street, down the next one, and back up another, circling ever nearer to the target house. We passed several people out for evening constitutionals, just as we were. Some were walking leashed dogs, others were strolling leisurely along, and some were running for their health, slinging off sweat as they passed. So even though I was getting more and more tensed up at the thought of what we were about to do, I was comforted by the thought that, so far, we were fitting right in.

As we walked from one pool of light from

a streetlamp to another, I noticed that Mr. Tuttle had gone from holding Miss Wiggins's hand to putting his arm around her waist. He might've thought that was a normal and unremarkable gesture by a husband toward his wife, but in my experience, it was not. In fact, if Wesley Lloyd Springer had ever done that to me, I'd have thought he was suffering from an attack of some kind and needed help to stand up. Sam, of course, had to be watched all the time, for he had no qualms about showing affection in public, but at least he restrained himself from inappropriate displays of it.

But when Miss Wiggins's arm crept across Mr. Tuttle's back, so that they were practically melded together, they were going too far. Such postures might be forgivable, though tasteless, in young couples, but not in couples who'd supposedly been married for some time.

I stepped up behind them and said, "If you don't want to attract attention, you'll step apart. Remember you're supposed to have a half-grown child back here, and no decade-long married couple of my acquaintance would put on such a show as you're doing."

Miss Wiggins immediately broke contact. "Oh, you're right. Sorry, I forgot myself." She wrinkled up her face, I suppose to let me know that she'd been playing a part and not cuddling up to Mr. Tuttle because she liked it.

Mr. Tuttle, on the other hand, showed his displeasure by grabbing her hand and saying, "Will this be too much? Or do you want me on the other side of the street?"

"Mr. Tuttle, you know what I'm talking about. Just don't go overboard with your playacting. People will notice."

"And you don't think they'll notice we're standing in the middle of the sidewalk snapping at each other?"

"Of course they will, if anybody's looking. But what could be more normal than family members having words? Now, let's go on. If we don't do something soon my feet're going to give out."

At the next corner, we turned onto the street that was a direct parallel to the one where Miss Wiggins and I had solicited for the Lord earlier that day.

"How many houses from the corner is it?" Lloyd asked.

"I'm not too sure," I said, worriedly. "Two or three, anyway. Just look past the houses until you see a bamboo thicket across the backyard."

"It's kinda dark," he said.

I'd noticed the same thing, and so had

Mr. Tuttle and Miss Wiggins, who were trying to look to their right without turning their heads. Unfortunately, the houses on this street were just as surrounded by thick hedges and tropical vines and dense shrubbery as the ones on the other street. This was going to be more difficult than I'd imagined.

Mr. Tuttle suddenly stooped down and began to tie or rather, retie, his brown oxfords — a nifty distraction, I thought. We gathered around to wait for him.

"All right," he said out of the corner of his mouth, "which house backs up to it? Which one of these yards do we stumble through to get to that blasted bamboo?"

"Mr. Tuttle," I said, "please don't take that attitude. Can we help it if people let their landscape plantings run rife and take over their yards? I can't tell which one it is, but we can't be far off."

Lloyd said, "It all looks like a jungle to me."

Mr. Tuttle finished his shoe-tying pretense, stood up, and looked at me. "You ought to be able to pinpoint the house, since you were over here just this morning. But I guess you didn't think of that."

"No," I said, and right sharply, too. "I was thinking of other things. Like gathering evidence. Besides, you were over here, too, when we staked it out. And with your supposedly trained skills of observation, I'd think you could walk right up to it, regardless of how many yards you had to go through."

"Let's walk," he said, and taking Miss Wiggins's hand, started off again. But he muttered just loud enough for me to hear, "I still don't like it. And no amount of money's gonna change that."

"Lloyd," I said, just loud enough for Mr. Tuttle to hear, "when a person says he'll do something, he should just do it, and not keep whining about it."

"Yessum," the boy said.

Nobody had anything more to say until we reached the corner two blocks from where Mr. Tuttle had had the shoelace-tying episode. My feet were killing me.

Mr. Tuttle crossed the street, passed the streetlamp, and stopped in the middle of the block where it was dark. "Here's what we'll do," he said, lowering his voice. "Mrs. Murdoch, you and the boy go on to the car. Be sure the handset is turned on when you get there and that the volume is way down. Stay in the car. Do not get out. And if you see a cop car, get down below the windows. But if anybody does see you, you want to look like you've come from the party that's going on, and just getting ready to drive off. Everybody got that?"

Lloyd nodded, but I said, "What will you and Etta Mae be doing?"

"We'll strike out through one of the yards — take your pick, Etta Mae, your guess is as good as mine. If we're lucky, we'll end up in the bamboo, and that's where we'll stay. I'm not going up to that house, and I'm not taking any chances, I don't care how bad you want your rings back. If I see anything that tells us what they're doing, we'll slip back out and come to the car."

"Well, I guess that'll be something, at least," I said. "But it seems to me that after all the trouble we're going to, you'd be prepared to do more than just hide and look."

He ignored me. He reached under his Hawaiian shirt and unclipped the second handset. "I'll be leading the way, Etta Mae, so you take charge of this. But no talking, understand? That goes for you, too, Lloyd. The only time anything is said is if we need the car. And you," he said, turning to me, "you be ready. We'll come out on the street behind the house, right where we're going in, and that's where I want you to be — along where I tied my shoe. So, if we call, it'll mean we need to be picked up, and I mean quick. Got that?"

"I believe I do," I said. "It's not all that hard to understand."

I think he growled, but I couldn't be sure. As we started to turn away, I thought of something else. "Mr. Tuttle, I hate to bring this up, but what do you want us to do if you and Etta Mae get caught? I mean, how long should we wait for you?"

Miss Wiggins whimpered and clutched Mr. Tuttle's arm.

He took an inordinately long time to gather his thoughts, but finally he said, "If we're arrested, call McGruder and get us a lawyer. If the crooks find us, you'll hear a commotion, because I'll be making tracks."

"What about me?" Miss Wiggins asked, hugging herself even though it was hot as blazes.

"Don't worry, Etta Mae," Lloyd said. "We won't leave you. We'll come after you, won't we, Miss Julia?"

"You can be sure of that," I said. "I didn't ask you down here only to abandon you. Besides, Mr. Tuttle will look after you, won't you, Mr. Tuttle?"

"Yeah, sure. But, Etta Mae, you got to look after yourself, too. I've been sick, remember? And I ought not be doing anything strenuous."

"Sick, my foot," I said, shaking my finger

at him. "If you come back without her, Mr. Tuttle, you better keep on going, because I'll hound you to the ends of the earth."

We parted ways then, as Lloyd and I proceeded on toward the car, and Mr. Tuttle and Miss Wiggins turned back to creep through somebody's yard.

As we walked away, I felt more and more anxious about Miss Wiggins's welfare. I was letting her walk off into the jaws of danger, and all for my personal benefit. One thing I admired about the woman: She might be scared to death about doing something, but that wouldn't stop her from doing it. She could be depended on, as Hazel Marie had so often said, to do anything in the world for you, but this suddenly seemed too much to ask.

"Wait, Lloyd," I said, my hand on his shoulder. "I can't do this."

I turned around and hurried after Miss Wiggins, with Lloyd following me, asking, "What? What? Where're we going?"

"Etta Mae," I said in a loud whisper, as she and Mr. Tuttle stopped and turned to me. "I've changed my mind. You go on back to the car with Lloyd. I'm going with Mr. Tuttle."

"No, you're not," Mr. Tuttle said, as if he had a say in the matter.

"Shush," I told him. "You and Lloyd go on to the car, Etta Mae. And look after him for me."

"Oh, no, Miss Julia," she said in real distress. "You can't go sneaking through a yard. You could break something."

"Listen to me, both of you. I don't know what I was thinking before, but this is the best way. Etta Mae, you're at more of a risk than anybody. You're young and pretty, and if those crooks corner you, well, they might not stop at stealing jewelry. No, you're my responsibility just as Lloyd is, and I don't want either of you put in danger. Besides, you drive faster than I do. In case we need to leave in a hurry."

"Just a minute, here," Mr. Tuttle said. "I can't be saddled with somebody that'll hold me back. This is crazy."

"I've thought it all out, Mr. Tuttle, and I'm telling you that this is the way it's going to be."

He threw up his hands. "Forget it. I'll go by myself."

"No, you won't. For all I know, you'd sit under a palm tree for thirty minutes and come back and tell us those crooks were in bed and sound asleep. Somebody has to be with you, and that somebody is me."

"Yeah," he said, glaring down at me. "And

what're you gonna do if you have to run? What're you gonna do if you get picked up?"

"I've already thought it out. If anybody catches me — I don't care if it's crooks, federal agents, or wired-up neighbors — I'll just be a confused old lady who doesn't know where she is. And you, Mr. Tuttle, could be out looking for me. Think about it. That's a better excuse for wandering around somebody's yard than what you or Etta Mae could come up with."

Nobody said anything for a minute, as the truth of what I was proposing became obvious.

"Of course," I went on, "I'll have to put on a really good act, because this outfit I have on probably makes me look ten years younger."

Lloyd said, "No, it doesn't, Miss Julia. You look just like yourself."

I didn't know whether to be reassured that I looked old enough to pull it off or be insulted that it made no difference. But he meant well, so I gave him a weak smile and took the handset from Miss Wiggins.

CHAPTER 35

After a few more minutes of convincing Miss Wiggins that Lloyd would be safer in her care than mine, we parted company again, but with different partners. Mr. Tuttle and I started to retrace our steps toward a house — any house — that backed up to the bamboo thicket.

"Slow down, Mr. Tuttle," I said, trying to keep up with him. "These sandals aren't made for a footrace."

"Shoulda thought of that before," he said, as we crossed the street that put us on the block we wanted. Then he started mumbling and complaining. "Craziest thing I ever heard of. Here I am, half-sick, and about to get arrested or shot. I am stressed all to hell. And I don't like it, I don't like it at all."

"I wish you'd stop that," I told him. "You're making me nervous. You have to remember that we all do things we don't like. It's a sign of maturity, so act your age."

"I could sure use a drink," he mumbled.

"Get your mind off of it and on to what we're doing." Slowing as we approached two dark houses side by side, I whispered, "What about between these two? Looks like nobody's home in either one." I craned my neck, trying to see through the foliage. "It's awfully dark down in there. I wish we had a flashlight."

"Yeah, and wouldn't that keep anybody from seeing us." Mr. Tuttle was looking up and down the street, keeping an eye out for strollers, walkers, and runners. So far, we were the only ones in sight.

"I'm just saying," I said. "I know we couldn't use one."

"Let's go." Mr. Tuttle suddenly dove into the hedge that divided the yards and was gone.

"Wait, don't leave me." Squinching up my eyes, I pushed aside fronds and branches, getting scratched in the process, and followed him into the dark recesses of a landscape badly in need of a good yardman.

After popping out on the other side of the hedge, I could see only a vague outline of Mr. Tuttle's back as he stooped over and looked around. Grabbing a handful of his shirt so he wouldn't get away from me, I followed him as he edged from one clump of shrubs to another. I couldn't see a thing.

Mr. Tuttle suddenly pulled out of my grasp, falling a foot or more, as water splashed on my new cropped pants. With a muffled cry, he almost fell over. "Dang it all!"

"What is it? What happened?" My eyes had gradually become accustomed to the dark, and I saw that he was standing in water up to his knees.

He stepped out, his oxfords squishing with water, and started cursing under his breath. "Dad blast it. Fell in a damn swimming pool! I coulda drowned."

"Oh, for goodness' sake, Mr. Tuttle," I hissed. "It's a fish pond."

I was feeling somewhat better as we skirted the pond and continued on toward the dark line of what I was sure was a thicket of bamboo. If Mr. Tuttle's attempt to walk on water hadn't brought the law or the neighbors down on us, I figured we were pretty much in the clear. So far, at least.

We slithered in and around one ornamental plant or tree after another. I brushed against one shrub that gave off a scent like honeysuckle, but it probably wasn't. Finally reaching the back boundary of the yard, we came up against a thick growth of bamboo. I reached out and ran my hand down one of the tall stems, feeling the ringed joints that distinguished this rapacious plant. We knew better than to plant it in Abbotsville, even if we'd had the climate for it. Our lesson had been learned years ago, when somebody set out the first sprigs of kudzu.

"Mighty thick in there," Mr. Tuttle whispered as he stuck his arm in as far as it would go. "Don't know if we can get through it."

"Try it sideways," I whispered back, as I wedged myself between two thick stems. Something swarmed around my face, and I swatted at it, wondering if we'd be eaten alive by mosquitoes. I tried not to dwell on what manner of spiders was lurking among the leaves that flipped across my face.

Mr. Tuttle bent some stems enough to slip in beside me. "If we can't get any closer than this, might as well pack it in."

"Push on through," I urged, following my own advice. But it wasn't easy going. The ground was so soft and mushy that each platformed step I took threatened to wrench an ankle. Feeling with my hands out in front of me, I twisted this way and that as I slipped through the woody stems. I couldn't see a thing.

"Wup." Mr. Tuttle suddenly stopped. He grabbed my arm and whispered, "Be real quiet."

I immediately quit flailing through the undergrowth and came to a standstill. "What is it?"

"I see a light."

"Where?"

"Right through there."

I twisted toward him to get his line of sight and was able to see a dim glow beyond the corner of a building right in front of us. I had hoped there would be a yard light so we could get a good view. But from the little we could see, the glow seemed to be coming from a streetlight. Whatever it was, it wasn't in the yard we were aiming for. All it did was outline the roof of a house and the edge of a small building directly in front of us.

"That may be the garage," I whispered right up close to his face. "Let's get up behind it."

He hesitated, then adjusted his path and headed for the back of what I was convinced was the garage we were looking for. I slid in behind him, wondering why I hadn't let him blaze the path before this. It was ever so much easier to follow his lead.

As we reached the back of the small structure, Mr. Tuttle squatted down beside it. I followed suit, but we weren't in a position to see around it.

"Scoot up to the edge," I whispered, poking at him. "We can't see anything back here."

Mr. Tuttle's breath was loud and wheezing, and mine wasn't much better. Just as he started to slip closer to the edge, we heard low voices and the sound of a car door opening.

"It's them!" I whispered. "They're in the yard."

"Sh-h-h," Mr. Tuttle came back at me. "Listen."

I did, but all I could hear was the low rumble of men's voices, without any words clear enough to understand. From the sound of it, one was giving orders and at least one other responded shortly in agreement. Then we heard a house door opening and what sounded like a muffled curse. Footsteps came and went, accompanied by a few grunts now and then. I flinched as we heard a number of soft thumps and the sound of leather shoes on gritty pavement. Then more rumbling talk, but all so low that I couldn't make out word one.

But as Mr. Tuttle and I hugged the wall of the building, trying to keep our breathing under control, I was able to distinguish a variety of footsteps, seeming to come out of the house, walk a ways, then go back in.

Then, I clearly heard a voice coming nearer and saying, "That it? Okay, put some empties in this one."

The owner of the voice seemed almost on top of us, only a few steps from where we were huddled behind the garage. I clutched at Mr. Tuttle's shirt and felt him hunker closer to the building. From then on, the footsteps going in and out of the house came closer to us than they had at first. After listening to one or two trips back and forth, I heard the thunk of car doors locking automatically. I wondered why we didn't see the flash of headlights that usually accompanied locking a car, but then realized that they'd been smart enough to disconnect some wires. Finally we heard the house door close and no more footsteps.

"They've gone in," I whispered, nudging Mr. Tuttle with the handset. "Peek out and see what they were doing."

I didn't think he was going to do it, but finally, with a rasping breath, he scooted to the edge of the building and parted some leaves. I was right beside him, parting my own leaves to see what was in the yard.

Two dark SUVs were parked side by side in what looked to be a paved courtyard behind the house. The cars, or trucks, or whatever those road monsters qualified as, were so dark that it took me a while to make them out. And when I did, my heart skipped a beat. They sat there, two sleek hulks crouching like panthers in the night. There were no lights on in the back of the house, although as my eyes adjusted, I could see soft light spilling onto the driveway from a few windows in the front.

I leaned close to Mr. Tuttle and murmured, "What do you think?"

He edged away from the corner and said, "I think we oughta get out of here while the gettin's good."

"Not yet. I want to know what they're doing. It sounded like they were loading up. And if that's the case, I want to know where they're going."

"They might not leave for hours, and we can't stay here all night."

Well, no, we couldn't, I thought, picturing Lloyd and Miss Wiggins waiting anxiously for our return. We had to do whatever we could here and now, or forever lose our chance.

What to do? What to do? I lifted the tail of my Mexican tunic and wiped the sweat from my face. I was hot and grimy and feeling as if every bug and spider in the thicket had found a home on me. But we had come this far, so . . .

"Mr. Tuttle," I whispered as close to him as I dared, for he was sweating profusely, too. "Slip out there and see what's in those cars."

"No way."

"Oh, go on. We need to know what's in them. We've come too far to leave empty-handed."

"Listen to me," he said, sticking his face right in mine. "If they're the thieves you think they are, they'll have a lookout. You think they'd pack them cars with whatever they've hauled in, then just walk off and leave 'em?"

"But they haven't left," I whispered right back. "They're right there in the house. Probably going to the bathroom one last time. I'm telling you, I think this is our only chance to be sure. Why, Mr. Tuttle, my rings could be barely ten feet away from me right this minute, and they could be on their way somewhere else."

"If they move out, the feds'll be on 'em. They won't get away."

"Those agents can't see what's going on back here. They're in a house across the street and down a ways. All they can see is the front, and it looks normal from there."

"I don't care," he said, stubbornly resisting me. "For all we know, agents could be here in this thicket with us."

"Yes, and if they were, they'd've already caught us. Besides, from the one I met, they're not dressed for creeping through bushes. Go on, Mr. Tuttle. Then we'll get out of here."

"It's too dangerous. Let's go back to the car and wait. We'll see 'em if they leave."

Well, we could do that, but what if they left and we followed them, and they led us to a Taco Bell or McDonald's where we'd have no chance to look inside?

Mr. Tuttle, apparently thinking that my silence meant agreement, started pushing his way back through the bamboo stalks on his hands and knees. I hesitated, not wanting to be left on my own, but not wanting to leave when it was all so close, either. Besides, with both SUVs between me and the house, how perilous could it be?

So, I took a deep breath and crept to the edge of the thicket, looked around, and crawled out onto the paved courtyard. I heard Mr. Tuttle's frantic whisper to come back, but I scrambled toward the nearest black SUV. I stopped a couple of feet from it and looked up at it with a sinking heart. It wasn't just the night that was dark; so were the windows. They were as black as pitch, something that I'd thought was illegal, but apparently not illegal enough.

Then, scaring me half to death, Mr. Tuttle was suddenly by my side. "Get back," he said. "I'll handle this."

I watched as his shadowy figure crept to the back of the nearer vehicle and fiddled with something he drew from his pocket. Then, duck-walking to the other one, he fiddled around at the back of it. A few quick motions later, he scooted back toward the thicket, whispering as he passed, "Get outta here."

I could've wrung his neck. He'd been right beside both cars and had passed up a chance to look inside. There was nothing for it but to press up close to a window and see what I could see.

I crept closer and reached for a door handle to pull myself up. Just as I clasped the handle, the most awful wailing noise blasted the air, blaring out loud enough to wake the dead.

Jerking my hand away, I almost fell backward, so frightened that I couldn't think straight. The house door slammed open, and more than one rapid pair of footsteps approached as I scrambled away from the car. I dove for the bamboo, feeling Mr. Tuttle grab me and pull me inside.

I wasn't the only one scrambling, though, for several dark figures flitted around the cars, until finally one of them stopped the wail of the antitheft device. As Mr. Tuttle pulled me deeper inside the thicket, I clearly heard one of the men say, "Hinson, you and Taylor check the yard. Artie, you take off, and do it the way I told you."

Mr. Tuttle leaned in. "Call the car!" he rasped under his breath. "Tell 'em to hurry."

Fumbling, even as I stumbled through the thick stems, I finally found the Send button and put the set up to my mouth. "Etta Mae! Lloyd! We need you. Come to the house where Mr. Tuttle tied his shoe. Hurry!"

Lord, my heart was going a mile a minute, and I thought we'd never get out of that thicket. We pushed and scraped and clawed our way through, and all the while I was transmitting an urgent signal for rescue.

"They're not answering!" I gasped. "It's not working."

He barely slowed down. "Just get out of here."

As we popped out into the neighbor's yard, I sent another SOS, this time demanding a response. Still not getting one, I whacked the set against my hand. "What's wrong with it?"

"Gimme that thing," Mr. Tuttle said, snatching the set from me. "They can't answer when you're sending."

And sure enough, as soon as he took it, we heard Lloyd's voice, faint and frantic.

"We're coming! We're coming!"

Then a harsh voice barked something unintelligible except for the word, "Over."

"Goshamighty!" Mr. Tuttle yelped. He threw the handset into the thicket and started running for the street.

"Wait!" I panted, trying to keep up and dodge the fish pond, too. "Who was that?"

"I don't know, and I'm not waitin' to find out."

We tore through the yard toward the street, the sounds of motors revving and roaring behind us and the screech of tires somewhere beyond us.

"Stop!" Mr. Tuttle's arm flew out before me, bringing me up short beside the front hedge. "Scrooch down. We'll wait till they get here."

I squatted beside him, trying to get my breath and praying that Miss Wiggins would hurry. A squeal of tires and the shriek of metal on metal ripped through the night, as a number of lights flashed on in houses up and down the street. The roar of several motors resounded from a side street, and all I could do was moan, "Oh, Lord. Oh, Lord."

Then a car scraped along the curb almost in front of us and stopped, its motor still running. I peeked through and saw my car, with lights out and an open door. Lloyd's urgent whisper pierced the hedge. "Miss Julia, we're here. Where are you?"

"It's them!" I barreled through the hedge, ripping polyester as I went. Lloyd was out of the car, holding the back door open, and I went in headfirst with Mr. Tuttle so close behind that he landed on me.

Lloyd jumped into the front seat, his teeth chattering as he slammed the door. Miss Wiggins stomped on the gas and sped us away down the street. She crossed two more, then pulled to the curb.

"Get off me!" I pushed at Mr. Tuttle until I had enough room to sit up and see what was going on. "Why're you stopping, Etta Mae? We need to get out of here."

"There're cars all over the place," she said, checking the rearview mirror. "They're coming from everywhere and speeding like crazy."

"Yeah," Lloyd said, excitement bubbling up in his voice, "and two of 'em scraped each other! I thought we'd have a wreck."

"Oh, me, too," Miss Wiggins said, leaning her head against the steering wheel. "A big SUV just missed us. He was in the middle of the street, then two or three other cars were right behind him. Two of them clipped each other and just missed us."

"Turn the ignition off," Mr. Tuttle said.

As she did, he went on. "We'll wait here till the smoke clears. Sounds like the feds're on their tail."

We sat in silence for a few minutes. Then I thought of something. "How many SUVs did you see, Etta Mae?"

"One, I think."

"Yeah," Lloyd chimed in. "It was one. The other cars were sedans of some kind. Was that the crooks in the SUV?"

"I'm convinced it was," I said, looking out the back window. "And furthermore, I'm convinced that there's another one doing the same thing we are. Waiting till the smoke clears."

CHAPTER 36

"We're OK here, I think, so let's wait and see." Mr. Tuttle was twisted around so he could watch through the rear window. "If you're right, the other one'll be coming out pretty soon."

"So the first car was a distraction?" I asked, trying to think like criminals on the run. "I mean, to fool the agents into chasing it?"

"Right. No way those guys didn't know they were being watched. Both sides sitting around waiting to see what the other would do. You heard the commotion they made when they left, like they were hightailing it outta there. And the feds fell for it."

Lloyd said, "Maybe the agents left somebody, too. You know, in case the crooks pulled a stunt like that."

"Maybe," Mr. Tuttle agreed somewhat dubiously. "But there's usually only a couple standing watch at a time."

Miss Wiggins straightened up and managed to join the speculation. "There were at least two cars chasing that SUV, maybe a couple more. Though, who knows, the extra ones could've been people just trying to get out of the way." She took a deep breath. "They were all coming straight at us. On both sides of the street, too. I just dodged 'em. I didn't count 'em."

"You did a good job, Etta Mae," Lloyd said. "You should've seen her, Miss Julia. She really knows how to handle a car. I wasn't even much scared."

"See, Etta Mae?" I said, reaching up and patting her shoulder. Then I reached down and scratched a place on my ankle that was itching me to death. "I knew you were the best one to drive. Now we have to decide what to do. Shall we wait for the other car, or shall we ease on out of here and see what's going on?"

Mr. Tuttle didn't like that. "I'll tell you what we're not going to do. We're not going to ease on anywhere. The safest place is right here where we are. The PBPD'll have every man out and that bridge'll be closed, so nobody's gonna get across."

"You mean we're stuck over here?" I didn't like the sound of that. I badly needed a bath and a change of clothes. And so did Mr.

Tuttle. The air in the car was heavy with the reek of overexerted bodies. "Etta Mae, I think we need some windows down, if you don't mind. I'm about to suffocate."

As she lowered the windows, she said, "How long will they keep the bridge closed?"

Mr. Tuttle gave a little laugh. "I'm thinking, right now, they've got that SUV stopped, and whoever was in it is flat out on the ground, looking at five-to-ten. It won't take the cops long, though, 'cause they don't want to keep traffic tied up. People complain, and part of their job is keeping people happy."

"Well, I declare," I said. "Looks to me as if catching thieves would be their first priority."

"They'll catch 'em," Mr. Tuttle said smugly. "But that other truck just might slip through while they're processing the guys in the first one."

"Wait a minute," I said, struck almost, but not quite, dumb. "Did those crooks deliberately send out the first car, knowing it'd get stopped? I mean, *knowing* that the people in it would be arrested and their goods confiscated?"

"That's my guess," Mr. Tuttle said. "And I'd bet there was only a driver in that truck, and not a blessed thing of any value."

"That's cold," Miss Wiggins said. "Wonder if the driver volunteered or they made him do it." She switched around in the seat and looked at me. "I bet they made the one we saw this morning do it. Just to teach him a lesson."

"Don't worry about him," Mr. Tuttle told her. "If the cops don't find anything in the truck, they'll have to let him go."

"Oh, I'm not worried about him," she said. "He's a thief, and I hope they find something on him."

But they won't, I thought. So my rings were still on the loose or, if the second SUV pulled out, still on the run, and likely to end up who-knew-where, as soon as the police opened the bridge.

Lloyd was kneeling on the front seat, helping Mr. Tuttle watch through the rear window. "I hope we don't miss it when it comes out. Once it gets in traffic, we won't be able to tell one from another."

Mr. Tuttle gave a pleased-with-himself chuckle. "Oh, yeah, we will. I put a strip of duct tape on a taillight of both of 'em. We can follow either one anywhere it goes."

"Why, Mr. Tuttle," I said, "how clever of you. I must say that that little trick was worth setting off the alarm like you did. Although at the time, I could've smacked you for it."

"Me?" Mr. Tuttle stared at me. "I didn't set it off. It was you trying to open the door."

"I wasn't trying to open the door. I know better than that. I was only trying to see through the windows, and just looking is not enough to set off anything."

Mr. Tuttle looked as if he wanted to argue the point, but at last he shrugged and said, "Etta Mae, I got a better idea. Swap places with me, and let me drive."

"Gladly," she said. "I'm still shaking like a leaf."

"Lloyd," I said, as Miss Wiggins and Mr. Tuttle opened their doors, "why don't you let Etta Mae sit in the front and you come back here with me?"

So the three of them played musical chairs without the music, and when everybody was settled, Mr. Tuttle started the car. Before I could ask what his better idea was, he whipped the car into a U-turn and headed us back down the street.

Lloyd's head snapped around. "We're not going back there, are we?"

Mr. Tuttle didn't have the courtesy to answer, just drove on toward the cross street that led to the house, passing the yard we'd so recently explored. At the corner where Etta Mae had barely evaded the chase scene, he slowed, looked to the left and the right, as we all did too, and pulled out. He drove toward the main thoroughfare that paralleled the Atlantic Ocean, turned right on it, and headed toward the street that led to the bridge.

"Are we just leaving?" I asked, feeling the pull of my rings as the distance between them and me lengthened.

Mr. Tuttle compounded his rudeness by ignoring my question. Miss Wiggins glanced back at me, her eyebrows lifted in consternation, while Lloyd whispered, "What's the matter with him?"

I patted his hand to assure him that I had matters well in control. "Mr. Tuttle, I don't know what's wrong with you, but we want some answers. What are you doing and where are we going?"

"Right here," he said, swinging the car to the side of the street and parking. "See that intersection down there? Every vehicle that's aiming to cross the bridge has to turn onto it, whether they're coming from the north or the south. Sitting here, we won't miss the one we're looking for, even if it wiggled around us and came a different way."

"Oh, what a good idea," Miss Wiggins said. "And with streetlights on all four corners, we can't miss it."

Lloyd thought a minute, then asked, "What

if it's already come and gone?"

"Listen," Mr. Tuttle said as he lowered his window. "Hear the sirens? And look over there." He pointed ahead of us at the blue and red flashes of light reflecting off the clouds. "That's at the bridge. Nobody's gotten off the island yet."

He was right, for just then two cars came from the south and several more from the north, all turning onto the street toward the bridge. The street must have been full, for those cars stopped, as a line of cars began to back up into the street we were on. It was starting to look like a major traffic jam.

"Be on the lookout," Mr. Tuttle said. "I figure the one we're after will try to blend into the traffic and get over the bridge that way."

I nodded, though nobody could see me. But that's what I'd do, if I was trying to sneak off an island.

"There it is!" Lloyd cried out, pointing out the back window.

"Where?" I twisted around but couldn't see anything but bright headlights on a line of cars two blocks long.

"I don't see it," Miss Wiggins said, as she strained against the glare of the lights.

"Just keep your eye on it," Mr. Tuttle said. "It's not going anywhere for a while. You sure it's a black SUV?"

"Yessir, pretty sure," Lloyd said. "But it could be dark blue or maybe green. Oh, look, it's pulling out and passing."

"Go after it, Mr. Tuttle!" I urged, but he just sat there.

As the dark car sped by the line of cars waiting to cross the bridge, Mr. Tuttle said, "That's not it. Both taillights are okay."

"Are you sure you could see the taillights?" I asked, becoming more and more anxious, as it seemed that Mr. Tuttle wasn't all that eager to find the car. "It went by so fast, you could've missed it."

"I saw both of them, and there was no duct tape on either one. Keep watching."

Mumbling to keep from starting something up again, I said, "Yes, and maybe they saw that duct tape and took it off."

Miss Wiggins chimed in then. "The line's moving," she said. "At least a little."

And, sure enough, the cars in the lane beside us were inching toward the intersection.

Mr. Tuttle said, "Probably opened one lane to relieve the congestion. Keep watching. If you see it, I'll have to try to cut in, if anybody'll let me."

Well, there was something else to worry about. What if the car passed by, and we had to sit and watch it out of sight because no one was gracious enough to let us in the line of traffic?

"Here comes another one!" Lloyd sang out.

Mr. Tuttle craned his neck as a dark, truck-like car passed us, but even I could see that both taillights were bright and unencumbered with identifying duct tape. "They're a dime a dozen down here," he said.

I leaned back against the seat, tired of staring into headlights and trying to distinguish one dark car from another. After trekking through the wilds of an unkempt yard and struggling through a privacy screen filled with stinging and crawling insects, as well as having to put up with Mr. Tuttle, I had about given up hope of ever recovering my precious rings.

Sighing at the futility of our efforts so far, I had to admit the possibility that I was just too old to be running around Palm Beach, chasing thieves and looking for duct tape. Sam would kill me if he knew what I was doing.

But, of course, he didn't, so I could keep doing it. I got a grip on myself, deciding that if he could bounce around Russia, I could certainly do the same in Florida.

CHAPTER 37

Lloyd, still on his knees so he could look out the rear window, suddenly bounced on the seat. "Another SUV's coming!"

"I see it," Miss Wiggins said. "It's almost right beside us."

I pressed up close to the side window and there it was, barely an arm's length away, moving at a snail's pace in the line of bumper-to-bumper traffic. I peered as hard as I could to see who was in it, but its windows were as black as the night. It could've been moving all on its own, for all I could tell.

"Check the taillights," Mr. Tuttle said.

"It's them!" Lloyd screamed, as the dark vehicle inched past us. "See? The left taillight's half covered."

"Oh, Mr. Tuttle," I said, my nerves tingling, "you figured it all out. I apologize for ever doubting you. Mr. Pickens himself couldn't've done any better." I reached up and poked his shoulder. "Now crank this thing up and get after them."

"We don't want to get too close," he said, turning on the ignition like he had all the time in the world. "We'll let a few cars go by, so they won't know they're being followed." He turned the wheels sharply, flipped on the blinkers, and eased away from the curb, ready to cut into the stream of traffic as soon as a place opened up.

But a place didn't open up. The cars moving slowly past us stayed nose to rear end, with hardly a gap between them.

"Pull on out, Mr. Tuttle," I urged. "People do it all the time. Somebody'll stop and let us in."

Mr. Tuttle had his neck twisted around, one arm hanging out the window, trying to motion to some kindhearted soul to let us in.

"They're getting away!" Lloyd cried. "Oh, my goodness, if they get across the bridge, they'll be gone."

By this time, Miss Wiggins was doing a little bouncing, herself. "Ease on out, Frank," she said. "If you get far enough out, they'll have to let you in. Or run into you."

"Yeah, and if we get hit, we'll be tied up here all night with the cops. I'll get in sooner or later."

Well, I wasn't willing to wait for later. I opened my door and stepped out on the street.

"Miss Julia!" Lloyd yelled. "What're you doing?"

I closed the door behind me and watched the line of cars easing along beside me.

With his dangling arm, Mr. Tuttle grabbed at me. "Get back in here. You'll kill yourself."

I barely looked at him. "You just be ready. I'm stopping this traffic any minute now."

I stood just beyond Mr. Tuttle's reach, waiting for the least little gap so I could run out between two cars. One of them would have to stop, if I could only get up the nerve to do it. It was a little like jump rope, you never know the exact moment to jump in.

As I prepared to take my life in my hands, I heard a car door slam, along with Mr. Tuttle's yell. "Come back here!"

Miss Wiggins ran up beside me and took my arm. "They won't hit two of us. Bunch of selfish people, I've never seen the like. Come on."

The cars beside us slowed even more for some holdup farther down the street, and Miss Wiggins took that as a sign. Still holding my arm, she ran right out behind a dark Lincoln Town Car and turned to face a red sports coupe. I could feel the Lincoln's rear bumper behind my knees, and feared that I'd soon feel the front one of the coupe.

My nerve restored by Miss Wiggins's intrepid actions, I held up both hands and yelled, "Stop!"

The brakes on the little red coupe squealed as the car slid to an abrupt halt, almost standing on its front wheels. More brakes shrieked on the pavement behind it, and impatient horns started blowing. With the grille of the little sports car staring me in the face and a line of stopped cars as far as the eye could see, I felt a little like Moses holding back the Red Sea.

The coupe's driver, who was wearing one of those flat berets with a bill that some people play golf in, leaned out his window, yelling his head off. "Are you crazy! Get outta the street!"

Miss Wiggins, with a grim look on her face, stood firm. And so did I, although the headlights only inches from us were about to blind me. Just then, the Lincoln pulled away, but we kept our hands up and the coupe could do nothing but wait. He couldn't even pull out and go around, for the far lane was filled with cars. More horns blared up and down the line of traffic, so Mr. Coupe Driver got the same idea. He flashed his lights at us and banged on his horn. But it gave out only a melodic tootle.

He kept it tootling away, as he got angrier and angrier, finally displaying his feelings with a rude gesture that had never been aimed at me before. "Move it!" he screamed. "Get outta my way!"

"Etta Mae," I said, "you stay right here so he can't go anywhere."

I marched over to the driver's window and said, "Young man, where are your manners? Does your mother know you act like this? We are on an urgent mission, so you can just hold your horses and keep your fingers to yourself."

As I rejoined Miss Wiggins in front of the coupe, the Lincoln rolled far enough from us for Mr. Tuttle to pull into its place in the line.

"Let's go, Etta Mae," I said, and dashed for the door that Lloyd was holding open. I got squashed for the second time that night as Miss Wiggins landed on top of me in the backseat.

Mr. Tuttle straightened the car and took a rasping breath. "Damnedest thing I ever saw," he said. "You two are crazy."

"I keep hearing that," I told him, as Miss Wiggins and I settled ourselves in the backseat with Lloyd. "But it worked, didn't it?

We'd've still been sitting there if we'd waited on you."

Lloyd took my hand. "I was scared you'd get run over," he whispered.

"I was, too," I whispered back, squeezing his hand. "But the cars weren't going that fast, and I knew they'd stop. I'm sorry I frightened you, though." Then, remembering why I'd taken such a chance with my life, I leaned up toward Mr. Tuttle. "Do you see them? Have we lost them?"

"They're up there somewhere. Probably already made the turn toward the bridge."

"Well, we need to get closer. Once they're over the bridge, they could go in a dozen different directions."

"How am I gonna get closer?" Mr. Tuttle asked with just a hint of exasperation. "You see this traffic?"

I sat back, resigned to going with the flow, which was all we could do at the moment. Finally, Mr. Tuttle was able to make the turn onto the street leading to the bridge. The flashing lights of police cruisers lit up the night, and we all craned to see what they were doing.

"Oh, my goodness," I said, "what if they've stopped the second SUV? All our efforts will be for naught."

"Look!" Lloyd said. "They're putting one

on a tow truck."

We passed slowly by a large flatbed truck that, with the help of a half dozen police officers and the wide-eyed stares of passers-by, was winching up what I hoped was the first, and not the second, SUV. Steam boiled up from its hood, and the right front fender was smashed in. Whoever had been driving it had not stopped peaceably, but he had certainly distracted the police. And not only the police, but as Lloyd pointed out, federal agents, too, for he recognized two sedans pulled to the side that had been chasing the SUV.

"I don't see but one," Miss Wiggins said. "I bet the other one is over the bridge and gone."

"Oh, don't say *gone*," I said, feeling despair overtake me again. "Please hurry, Mr. Tuttle. I mean, if you can."

As if that was all he needed to hear, he hunched over the wheel and the car spurted up and over the bridge, as the traffic divided into two lanes.

"All right," he said, "we're in West Palm now, so which way do we go?"

"We don't know this city, Mr. Tuttle," I said. "That's why we hired you. Which way do you think?"

He eased the car over to the side of the

411

street. "We better decide something quick. You got your U.S. 1, north or south, and you got your Dixie Highway, north or south. Then there's I-95, north to Daytona and Jacksonville or south to Miami, and the turnpike farther to the west, and it's north or south, too. Take your pick."

"How can I pick?" I wailed. "I don't know where they'll go, but let's do something besides sit here. They're getting farther away by the second."

"They might be going to Miami," Miss Wiggins said, "but there're so many ways to get there."

"I think they'll go whichever way is the fastest," Lloyd said. "They'll want to get away from here as quick as they can, 'specially with one of them already arrested. Who knows? He might even tell on 'em."

Mr. Tuttle pulled back out on the street and kept going straight, making good time. "I think you're right," he said, "so I'm picking the interstate. But north or south? Somebody decide before we get there."

But we were almost at the entrance of the north ramp already, and for the life of me I didn't know which direction to take.

"There it is!" Lloyd screamed, waving his pointed finger and practically bouncing in my lap. "See it? See the taillight? It's at the

top of the ramp. Up there! Up there!"

"North," Mr. Tuttle muttered, as he stomped on the gas and swung onto the ramp. "They're goin' north."

Once on the interstate, Mr. Tuttle hit the speed limit, or rather the speed that other cars were going, which was somewhat over the limit. "Keep your eyes peeled," he said, "because I'm not getting too close."

"It's staying in the fast lane," Lloyd said, holding on to the back of the front seat so he could see. "But they're all fast, seems like."

"Yeah, well, I'm staying at least four cars back and outta their lane. That way, they won't see us on their tail."

I rested my head on the back of the seat, content now to let Lloyd keep watch and Mr. Tuttle drive. We had the thieves in sight and my rings within grabbing distance, unless we'd figured wrong and they'd been in the other truck or, Lord help us, already shipped out and on their way to a foreign land.

Still, this was what we had, so I closed my eyes for a little rest, thinking how remarkably things had worked out so far.

Here we were, headed in the general direction of home and fast on the heels of thieves with a car full of stolen jewelry. Who knew where they were going or what we would do when they got there? Maybe it would be

413

time then to call in the authorities and take my chances with them. Given the choice, I'd prefer my rings in an evidence locker rather than in a duffel bag on the way to South America.

So, just for a few minutes, I could rest on the laurels of what we'd already accomplished.

"Mr. Tuttle," I said, rousing myself, "have you ever seen anything like this? Just think about it — how it's all worked out better than anybody could've hoped. I think it was meant for me to get my rings back, don't you?"

Mr. Tuttle grunted, then said, "It ain't over yet."

Oh, ye of little faith, I thought, and tried to shore up mine.

CHAPTER 38

I came awake with a start. A monstrous 18-wheeler decked out with dozens of lights rumbled past us, the car swaying in its wake. Any number of other vehicles zipped by as well. All was quiet inside the car, though, because both Lloyd and Miss Wiggins were curled up beside me, deep in slumber.

I leaned forward and tapped Mr. Tuttle on the shoulder. "Where are we? Are they still in sight?"

"Yeah, they're up there, about three cars ahead in this lane." He yawned, his jaws creaking. "Right on the speed limit, too, taking no chances on being stopped. That's why everything on the road's passing us." He scrunched his shoulders to relieve the tension of driving. "We're about a hundred miles from West Palm."

"A hundred miles, my goodness. You don't think they'll drive all night, do you?"

"They better not," he said, trying to stifle

another yawn.

"Why? Are we low on gas?" I hadn't thought of having to stop before our prey did. We'd lose them for sure, if we stopped and they didn't.

"Not yet," Mr. Tuttle said. "Still got about a half a tank. But I'll tell you one thing, if they don't stop soon I'm gonna have to pull over, irregardless."

"Oh, don't do that." I could picture the chased car miles away by the time we got off an exit ramp. "We'll help keep you awake."

"I got no trouble staying awake. My trouble is all that tea I drank before we left. I'm gonna pop if we don't stop soon."

"Oh, my," I murmured, realizing that all of us could be in the same fix. And what a pity it would be to lose my rings forever, all because our kidneys had to act. "Well, hold on as long as you can, Mr. Tuttle. Too bad you didn't think to bring a fruit jar."

He didn't answer, so I fell back against the seat and looked out the window, wishing he hadn't brought up the subject. Once something gets in your mind, it stays there and gets bigger and more urgent all the time. Mr. Tuttle squirmed in his seat, his shoulders hunching up and relaxing. With the tires humming along on the pavement and Lloyd and Miss Wiggins sleeping away, I decided to spend some time in prayer.

"Hey!" Mr. Tuttle said. "They're coming off. See 'em?"

I slid up on the seat and looked out the front window. Sure enough, there were three vehicles on the exit ramp about a half mile away, heading for a brightly lit rest area. Staring hard, I could make out three pairs of taillights, but only one pair with a cockeyed look to it.

"Thank the Lord," I said, reassured again that prayer is a mighty instrument.

"They're getting gas," Mr. Tuttle said, as he flicked on his blinkers and pulled onto the ramp. "We better, too."

Driving toward the countless number of gas pumps, he pulled up beside one of them. Turning off the ignition and opening his door, Mr. Tuttle said, "They're on the other side, with a couple of cars between us. Keep your head down and don't stare at 'em. Just get us filled up, and I'll be right back."

"Wait! Take Lloyd with you." I shook Lloyd awake and told him he needed to go to the bathroom. As Lloyd rubbed his eyes and stumbled out of the car, I said, "Keep your eye on this boy, Mr. Tuttle, and don't come back without him. Etta Mae," I went on, "wake up, honey. I need you to put gas in this thing."

She woke up, blinking and scratching her head. "Gosh, I didn't mean to go to sleep. Where are we?"

"At a rest stop, a hundred miles or more from where we started. Hurry, now, those crooks're getting gas, too, and we need to be careful."

"I'm on it," she said, hopping out and tackling the gas pump as if she had done it every day of her life. And she probably had.

While she unscrewed the gas cap, I opened the trunk and rescued my pocketbook, having felt lost without it near. "Keep your head turned, Etta Mae, in case the thief that knows us comes walking by. Here, use my credit card, and hurry. I'm about to die to go to the bathroom."

"Oh, me, too."

Just as the nozzle clicked off, Mr. Tuttle and Lloyd, looking mightily relieved, got back to the car. "Hurry up," Mr. Tuttle said, sliding under the wheel. "They're pulling out."

Lloyd walked to the front of the car, staring off across the wide rest area. "I think they're stopping at the restaurant place."

"Oh, my, are you sure?" Anxiety was stressing out my nerves again. "They could be back on the interstate any minute."

"No," Mr. Tuttle said, "I see 'em. They're

418

parking at the far end down there. We got time."

Miss Wiggins quickly tightened the cap on the gas tank, and we piled back into the car.

"Point them out to us, Mr. Tuttle," I said, hanging on to the back of the front seat. "I want to be sure they're still here."

He let the car roll slowly toward the huge building that housed every fast-food enterprise you could think of, plus reasonably well-kept ladies' rooms. "Look down past the cars parked along here," Mr. Tuttle said, pointing a finger of the hand holding the steering wheel. "That last one down there at the far end all by itself."

"Well, I see some kind of vehicle, but with their lights off, I can't be sure of the tail-lights."

"It's them," he said, with more assurance than I was feeling. "I watched 'em all the way. I'm parking, too, but nowhere close. You and Etta Mae might want to take advantage."

"I do," Etta Mae said, opening her door as soon as the car nosed into a parking spot.

I slid out behind her. "We'll hurry. Keep an eye on that car, but don't leave without us."

Miss Wiggins and I ran toward the entrance, along with a multitude of other road travelers. We edged our way inside the huge open space, breathing in the odors of a dozen different offerings of food, and headed for the ladies' room.

Women always take longer than men because of the innumerable buttons and snaps and zippers that we have to contend with. But I found that elastic in the waistband of polyester trousers cuts the time in half. I waited by the door for Miss Wiggins, who had to struggle with her jeans.

We dashed back to the car, dodging more travelers who had stopped to rest and eat. Jumping into the front seat, Miss Wiggins asked, "Are they still here?"

"Yep, you passed two of 'em on your way out."

"We did? Where? What'd they look like?"

"Like your normal, run-of-the-mill jewel thieves, wearing ski masks and running shoes."

Lloyd laughed. "No, they didn't, Etta Mae. He's just teasing you. They looked just like anybody else. We wouldn't've known who they were if we hadn't seen them get out of their SUV and walk up here to go inside."

"Just think," I said almost to myself, "we walked right past them and didn't even know it." Then, after a minute or so, I asked, "Just two? That's all you saw? Etta Mae, we figured on at least four, and with two here and one in custody back in Palm Beach, where's the other one?"

Mr. Tuttle had the answer. "They wouldn't leave the truck unguarded. I figure somebody's still in it." He suddenly opened his door. "I'm goin' in. If they're taking time to eat, I'll get us something, too. I could use some coffee.

"Whoa!" He slammed the door closed as quickly as he'd opened it. "That's one of 'em coming out now."

We all scooted up to see the man that Mr. Tuttle was indicating. I declare, he didn't look anything like a jewel thief. He had on a short-sleeved plaid shirt with jeans, his combed-back hair a tad on the long side, like he'd missed his last appointment with a barber, and he was carrying a sack of fast food.

The man stood beside the entrance for a minute, his eyes raking the cars in the parking lot. I scrunched down instinctively, while Mr. Tuttle reached for Miss Wiggins and hugged her. Then the man switched the toothpick in his mouth to the other side and moved off into the shadows toward his car. He was a fairly tall but slightly built man with ropy-looking muscles. He walked along easily with a gliding motion, seemingly unconcerned that he had burgled houses right and left all over the place. He reminded me of a, well, a cat burglar.

We watched as he approached the driver's side of the SUV, where another man got out to speak with him, then that man walked away toward the building. The interior lights hadn't come on when he opened the door.

"See?" Mr. Tuttle said, releasing Miss Wiggins. "They're taking turns, always leaving somebody with the car, but one guy's still inside. Getting something to eat, I bet. Okay," he said, opening the door again, "I'm going in. I'll get sandwiches and coffee and whatever else I can grab. This may be the last stop of the night."

When he slammed the door, the car settled back into darkness except, of course, for the glow coming from all the lights on the restaurant building and along the sides of the parking area, and from the headlights of incoming and outgoing cars. We watched Mr. Tuttle enter the building, then quickly turned our attention again to the last car parked at the end.

"Oh, look," Miss Wiggins said, "he's getting out."

So he was, and as the driver's seat was on the far side of the car, we couldn't see what he was doing. But it looked strange, for all we could see was his head bobbing up and down in a rhythmic fashion.

"What's he doing?" Lloyd asked.

"It looks like . . . ," Miss Wiggins started. "Oh, I know. He's exercising. Knee bends or something, after all that driving."

"You think he's alone?" I asked, my mind filling with possibilities. "I mean, that there are only three all told?"

"I think he is, Miss Julia," Lloyd said. "They let him go in and get something to eat. But looks like they're making him eat it in the car."

"That's probably it," Miss Wiggins said, nodding in agreement.

I leaned back in the corner, considering the situation. The more I considered, the more I was consumed by the thought that this could be the last stop before they got where they were going, and when they got where they were going, they could well be joining a dozen more crooks, who thought nothing of taking what didn't belong to them. But right now, this very minute, there was only one slightly built man between me and my beautiful rings. And Hazel Marie's things, too.

CHAPTER 39

"Etta Mae?"

"Ma'am?" She turned in the seat to look back at me.

"Are you thinking what I'm thinking?"

"Um, I'm not sure. What're you thinking?"

"I'm thinking this is the only chance we'll get. I'm going over there to look for my rings."

Lloyd bounced so hard he almost hit the roof of the car. "No, Miss Julia, you can't! He might get you."

"Sh-h, Lloyd. That man won't do a thing to me. There're too many people around. And all I want to do is get a quick look at that car. Etta Mae, are you with me?"

"It depends, I guess."

Lloyd said, "I don't think you ought to do anything."

I patted his arm. "I want you to distract him, Etta Mae. Do something like you did at their house. Just get him out of the car so I can look inside."

"Well, I don't know if that'll work again, but I can try. You don't want to wait for Frank?"

"No, because if the man saw Mr. Tuttle walking toward the car, well, you can imagine what he'd think. But a young woman like you, maybe in distress or something, why, that wouldn't concern Mr. Jewel Thief at all."

Lloyd said, "Okay, I'm going with you."

"No, Lloyd," I said, giving him my full attention. "This is women's work. Besides, I have a job for you. I want you to stay right here in the car and let us know if the other two come out. Do whatever you have to — blow the horn, yell bloody murder, anything to let us know that they're on the way. Will you do that?"

"Yessum, but what do I tell Mr. Tuttle when he comes back? You know he won't like it."

"Oh, well, tell him we're walking around stretching our legs. Which will be the truth, just not all of it." I opened my door before my nerve began to give out. "You stay in the car now. Come on, Etta Mae, let's go."

We walked off side by side, going around the back of the parked cars, heading toward the SUV at the far end. I wasn't able to manage my thick-soled sandals any better after all the experience I'd had with them, and I thought to myself that once I was able to get out of them, I'd never in my life step into another pair.

"Etta Mae," I said, lowering my voice as a family of sleepy children and irritable parents trooped in front of us. "How about this? Why don't we separate and you walk down the sidewalk over by the building so he can see you coming and not be surprised or anything. Pretend like you don't notice him, you're just taking a little stroll. While he's watching you, I'll walk along here and come up to the back of his car."

"That'll work," she said. "I guess."

"I know this isn't a Christian thing to do, but if you can somehow lure him away from the car, that'd be perfect. And, Etta Mae? We only have a few minutes before the other two get back, so work fast, okay?"

She nodded, her lip held in her teeth. "I'll think of something. You be careful, though."

I stood at the back of a pickup truck with a camper on top, watching as she slipped between the cars and began ambling down the sidewalk beside the building. She was still some ways from the man in the car, but she put a little swing in her hips, weaving in and out of the clusters of people headed inside. Getting in practice, I surmised.

As she neared the empty parking spaces, I knew she'd draw the man's attention. She was the only one of the multitudes of people here in the middle of the night who was wandering away from bathrooms and food. He'd watch her, no doubt about that, and she was giving him something to watch.

I slipped behind the pickup and edged on toward the next car, trying to appear unremarkable. I lost sight of Miss Wiggins when a family with three screaming children tumbled out of a van right beside me. Taking a cue from Mr. Tuttle, I bent over to adjust a sandal strap, waiting for them to go inside.

"I'm gonna pop you if you don't stop that," a woman said to a wailing child. The child screamed louder.

I glared at the woman, but she didn't notice. She swept the child up and walked toward the entrance, the rest of them trailing in her wake.

Moving toward the back of another car, getting ever nearer to the dark SUV, I was able to catch sight of Miss Wiggins. She was walking right in front of it by this time, but she never turned her head. She seemed engrossed in thoughts of her own, which I thought indicated Miss Wiggins's knowledge of male psychology. Having their presence ignored is always attractive to men. I saw her lift her arms to brush up her hair for a cooling breeze on her neck. The gesture seemed natural enough, given the humid night air, but some people might easily construe it as provocative. However it appeared, the man in the car was certainly getting an eyeful.

Then, as I rounded the back of the last parked car in the line, I saw her trip and fall, her arms flailing as she went down. I gasped and had to hold myself back from running to her aid. Just as I almost revealed myself, the man hopped out of the car, leaving the door open, and hurried to her. He leaned down just beyond his front fender where Miss Wiggins had fallen, so I couldn't see what was happening.

Taking a deep breath and hoping that Miss Wiggins's fall had been intentional and not accidental, which would've been an ironic twist to this little escapade, I walked purposefully across the empty spots to the back of the SUV. With his attention focused on Miss Wiggins, he wouldn't expect a sneak attack from the rear.

Peeking around the back of the SUV, I saw the man lift Miss Wiggins to her feet and heard him say, "You got to be more careful, little girl. You could damage something."

She moaned and clung to him, swaying like she couldn't get her balance. I heard her thank him for coming to her rescue.

Hiding behind the back of the car, I listened and waited for the chance I hoped would come.

The man said, "You okay now? That was a pretty nasty fall."

"I don't know. I think so," Miss Wiggins said in a plaintive voice. "I don't know what happened. I must've stepped wrong or something." She kept her hand on his shoulder and he kept his around her waist. She looked up at him. "I'm just so thankful you were here to help me."

"Anytime," he said. "Anytime. Think you'll be able to get back to your car? Where're you parked?"

"Way back up there." Miss Wiggins waved her hand in a vague manner. "It's my ankle or my foot, or something," she said, as she lifted one foot and balanced on the other one. She teetered for a minute, which required her to clutch at the man again. His back was to me so I couldn't see his face, but from his motions I could tell that he didn't mind holding on to Miss Wiggins.

"I'd walk you to your car," he said, "but I have to stay here. Boss's orders, you know.

Watch the car, that's my job."

"Oh, that would be too much to ask," Miss Wiggins said, sounding so small and hurt. "I'll be all right in a few minutes. You go on and watch your car. I'll just lean against the fender till my foot feels better and try . . ." She winced as she put her foot down. ". . . and try to make it on my own."

"Well, shoot, baby," the man said, "I can't just walk away with you suffering like this. You're too pretty for that."

She gave him a melting smile and rubbed a hand across his chest. "That's so sweet. Maybe . . . maybe if you'd walk with me out that way a little." She nodded toward the darker part of the lot, where there were no cars and no people. Still holding on to him, she leaned down to rub her ankle. "You know, to kinda loosen it up and work the kinks out. That way, you can keep an eye on your car. I'm a nurse, so I know walking will help."

Hardly a nurse, I thought, but under the circumstances I couldn't find fault with pushing the truth a little.

"A nurse?" the man said. "Well, that's good to know. I thought you might be, well, working the rest stops, but I knew I was wrong soon as I got a good look at you. My name's Tim, by the way."

430

Miss Wiggins put her arm around his waist as they turned and walked away from the car, her limping and hobbling and holding on to him every step of the way. "Mine's Tammy," she said.

As they went off, I could hear Miss Wiggins chattering on, keeping his attention on her and away from the car. Since he'd left the driver's door open, I hopped in there, hoping that the dark windows would hide me if he decided to look back. But both front windows were down, putting me in full view of anybody who looked, so I pushed my way between the bucket seats and crawled into the backseat. Looking into the rear cargo hold, I saw it was jammed full of suitcases and satchels.

I leaned over the backseat and quickly unzipped the nearest one. Thrusting my hand inside, I expected to pull it out dripping with gold and diamonds and jewels of all kinds. Instead, I felt solid stacks of something that was nothing like the mass of rings and bracelets and necklaces I was hoping to find.

Feeling and pushing around, I was finally able to lift a section of the tightly packed contents. When I pulled it out, my breath caught in my throat. I was holding a wrapped bundle of U.S. currency. Thoroughly disappointed, I threw the bundle back in without determining the denomination. However much it was, the satchel was full of it, and so was the next, and the next one after that. I didn't take time to rezip or relatch as I went, just stretched myself over the backseat and kept scrambling for every bag I could reach.

Frantically opening one satchel after another, I found stacks of bound bills in some and loose bills crammed into others. Money, money everywhere, but not a single, solitary ring in sight.

Taking a quick glimpse over my shoulder to check on Miss Wiggins and the custodian of all this wealth, I saw them still walking arm in arm some little distance away. But it hardly mattered if they came back or if I was caught, for those crooked scoundrels had already turned my rings into a car full of hard cash.

CHAPTER 40

I could've cried, if I'd had time. There I was, sifting through bag after bag of bound bills, stacked bills, and loose bills, totaling an untold amount of ready cash. But what good did it do me?

Well, in for a penny, I thought, with another quick glance over my shoulder. I stretched myself full length across the satchels behind the seat, reaching for the last three right up against the back hatch. I could barely touch them, so I wiggled farther in, my feet dangling in the air, and was able to unzip the nearest one. Money again, nothing but money. I declare, I was going to report this, and I hoped those crooks spent the rest of their lives in jail.

Unable to reach the farthest two, I squirmed my way across the baggage until I was sitting on top of it, thankful again for the darkened windows of the SUV. Nobody could see me, and unless Tim, Miss Wiggins's rescuer, returned, I was safe enough. Quickly un-latching the next-to-last bag, I crammed my hand inside and felt the same filthy lucre as I'd found in all the others.

Twisting around to get to the last one, I fumbled for the zipper tab, something that's always on the opposite side. Finally getting it unzipped, I plunged my hand in just as the blast of a car horn ripped across the usual noises of a busy way station. It blared out over and over, and it didn't stop.

"Lloyd!" I thought. The other men were on their way back. Mr. Tim would be, too, and he was closer. My hand was still stuck in the bag, and now it was fingering links of chains and the smooth roundness of pearls and the heaviness of gold and little round circles that could be rings.

Lloyd's voice sounded faintly over the horn that was blasting away. "Miss Julia! Help! Help, Miss Julia!"

Lord, the child was as good an actor as Miss Wiggins. You would've thought he was being kidnapped. But there was no time to revel in his theatrical ability, for it was already drawing attention. People were stopping all over the parking lot, and some were pushing out of the entrance doors to see what the trouble was. Mr. Tuttle, who had both hands full of take-out food, was among them. And so were the two men I figured I was being warned about. They'd stopped about halfway to the car where I was perched on top of their ill-gotten gains. They were looking back toward the ruckus that Lloyd was creating, but showing no interest in investigating its cause.

Just then I heard the pounding of feet coming from the other direction and Miss Wiggins, experiencing another miraculous recovery, yelling, "He's coming! Get out, get out!"

I was trying to do just that, as I fumbled with the latch to the rear door, hoping to hop out and be on my way. With the loaded satchel, too, for I had no intention of leaving it behind. My rings might be in it. I knew they could be miles away on another woman's finger or stashed in a lockbox somewhere, but I'd come for jewelry and I intended to leave with jewelry.

Finally getting the window of the hatch unlatched, I pushed at the heavy thing until I got it partially open. Swinging one leg over the door, thankful to be wearing trousers even though they weren't the most becoming, I felt the car tilt as Miss Wiggins's rescuer jumped into the front seat.

"Hey!" he yelled, twisting under the steering wheel to fling himself at me.

I nearly fell out of the window, he scared me so bad. But teetering on the door as I clutched the jewelry bag to my breast, I leaned over and snatched a handful of cash from another bag. Ripping off the binding, I slung the money out of the car. The breeze took it and swirled it around the parking lot, and as the bills floated here, there, and yonder in the air, tires screeched and people began yelling and running to find their fortune. I strewed out more, dipping into one satchel after another time and time again, flinging money far and wide.

As Tim, the rescuer, scrambled between the front seats, Miss Wiggins leaned in the door and grabbed his feet. "Help, somebody!" she screamed. "Help! Help!"

I think I've mentioned that Miss Wiggins is a strong little thing, and she latched on to that man and practically pulled him out of the car. I saw him fling her off, then start around to the back of the car where I was straddling the door, half-in and half-out. Throwing myself back into the car, I sprawled over the bags, clutching the jewelry satchel as I headed for the front seat, grabbing loose money as I went. I threw out another handful from the side window, the warm ocean breeze lifting it up and sweeping it over the heads of people who were snatching and grabbing and chasing it all over the parking lot. One woman, on her hands and knees, her bottom up in the air, was trying to crawl under a van after some errant bills; a car left idling when its driver abandoned it rolled into another; people screamed and shrieked; one man punched another in the face; and Lloyd kept blowing the horn.

The dark SUV that we'd chased all the way from Palm Beach had become a magnet for every soul who'd stopped for a bathroom break.

I got the passenger door open just as Miss Wiggins's rescuer reached for me. Squirming away from him, I felt myself suddenly being lifted up and out. My sandals barely touched the pavement, for Mr. Tuttle had me in a grip like steel and was running me across the parking lot toward our car.

"Etta Mae!" I screamed, struggling to get loose as Mr. Tuttle rounded the rear of the parked cars. "Run!"

Mr. Tuttle was huffing with the load he was carrying — me and the satchel. "She'll make it. Just keep going."

There wasn't much I could do but keep going, the way he was moving on, my head bobbing with each stride. My lower limbs were running along with his, but even with the thick sandal soles, only my tiptoes were touching the ground.

"Stop!" I yelled, as he plowed on. "We can't leave her."

"Get in the car," he said, jerking the back door open as we reached it.

"Miss Julia!" Lloyd screamed, as I was thrown into the backseat.

"Get in, boy!" Mr. Tuttle puffed. "Lock the doors and stay there." He turned and ran back toward the mob of people still scrambling, and now fighting, for free money.

I pulled myself up, stashed the jewelry bag on the floorboard, and looked out to search for Miss Wiggins. "Do you see her, Lloyd? Oh, Lord, what if they have her."

Lloyd was shaking as he leaned over the front seat. "I thought they got you, Miss Julia. When I saw the other two come out, I was so scared I didn't know what to do."

"You did the exact right thing," I said, reaching up to hug him. "Without you, they'd've surely caught me." I pressed my face close to his, thankful that I'd been mindful of his safety. Releasing him, I said, "Where'd those two men go? Do you see them?"

He stretched to look out the window over the parked cars. "I can't see a thing. Oh, I hope Etta Mae's all right. And Mr. Tuttle, too."

Tucking my feet over the jewelry bag, I realized that Lloyd wasn't the only one shaking. I was in a state of mortal recrimination, myself. Yes, I'd recovered some stolen goods, which might or might not include my rings, but if I'd done it to Miss Wiggins's detriment, what did it profit me? There was only one answer: Not one solitary thing.

"Lloyd, I've got to go look for her."

"Okay, let's go."

"No, you stay here. I can't afford to lose anybody else. This bag back here is full of jewelry, and I need you to stay with it." I opened the door. "Lock up, and don't let anybody in."

Standing outside until I heard the locks engage, I turned toward the end of the parking lot where so many were congregated, including some of the restaurant workers. I could tell by their little paper hats. Something different was going on down there by this time, for people were to-ing and fro-ing and milling about in the vicinity of the dark SUV. Just then the SUV cranked up with a roar and a plume of exhaust that had no effect on the men struggling around the open hatch at the rear. They were reaching in and grabbing as they pulled and pushed each other, grasping at loose bills fluttering in the air.

"Get me some!" A woman with bleached hair and no brassiere jumped up and down, yelling in my ear.

"Call the police!" somebody screamed.

"Gimme that," a man said, snatching at a young woman's handful of bills. She bunched up her free fist and socked him silly, then hurried on her way.

I twisted around, looking and looking for some sign of Miss Wiggins or Mr. Tuttle. So many people were in my line of sight, stooping and rising and flitting from here to there, that I couldn't tell one from the other. I held on to the rear fender of a car, trying to stave off the ebb and flow around me.

A hundred-dollar bill floated across my vision and came to rest on my bosom. I brushed at it just as an old man with yellow teeth and bristly chin reached out and clamped down on something that wasn't his to clamp.

"Why, you old goat!" I smacked him good, but it didn't stop him. He just scampered away, chasing another bill.

Just then, the crowd around the back of the SUV began to fall apart. Somebody inside was whaling away at the grasping hands, as the vehicle began to inch backward. One man jumped up and clung to the rear window and two more leapt onto the hood. The

SUV came to a stop as a fat man took a tire iron to the windshield.

I couldn't help but marvel at how far people will go when something valuable is at stake. It was enough to make you despair for the human race, if you thought about it.

The passenger's window whizzed down, and one of the men inside snatched at the tire iron. He almost came out of the window as he and the fat man twisted and struggled for it.

Taking my chance, I dashed behind the fat man, trying to peer inside. "Etta Mae! Are you in there?" Bobbing back and forth both to see and to avoid being hit, I screamed as loud as I could.

Kicking at a hand that was fumbling around my ankles, I kept yelling for Etta Mae, trying to find her. Some idiot gave a sudden yank on my cropped pants, pulling the elastic waistband down around my hips. I jumped back, clasping my arms around my bared middle. Well, not quite bare, but I'm not in the habit of displaying my undergarments. Ready to flail into whoever had been so bold, I snatched my pants back up and nearly fell over. There, with her head sticking out from under the idling SUV, Miss Wiggins was frantically motioning to me.

"Under here, Miss Julia," she hissed.

"Quick, nobody's on the other side."

Just then the crooked thief who was struggling for the tire iron popped his door open and came out fighting. I dropped to the ground and slid under the car, ending up on my stomach and nose to nose with Miss Wiggins.

"Etta Mae! What're you doing under here?"

"Sh-h-h, keep your head down and scoot on out."

I stayed as close to her as I could as she edged toward the far side of the car's underbelly, which rumbled above us. I could hear the scuffle of feet around the car and feel the thud of bodies thrown against it. It was an all-out melee and I was glad to be out of it, temporary though our hiding place was.

Suddenly, the SUV's motor revved up with a horrific noise and an overpowering odor of gasoline exhaust. I raised up in alarm and banged my head on the undercarriage.

"Oh, *God* . . . bless it all!" I pressed my face onto the pavement, my head pounding and my eyes full of tears.

"What's the matter?" Miss Wiggins whispered. She was almost out from under the car, peering around.

"I hit my head," I moaned. "On the differential thing."

"The *what!* The *differential?*" She began to laugh, burying her head in her arms, her shoulders shaking.

"Stop that," I hissed, "and get us out of here. They're going to run over us." Or gas us to death, for fumes were chugging out of the exhaust pipe and billowing around us.

Miss Wiggins slid out from under the car, reached for me, and pulled me out, too. We squatted beside the car, hugging it in the hope of staying out of the driver's sight. Waiting for her signal to run, I glanced at her. Her face was streaked with dirt and her T-shirt was stretched all out of kilter. The neck of it was so wide that it was almost falling off her shoulder.

I leaned back against her, thankful to be breathing fresh air again but dreading to stand up and run. Which we were going to have to do any minute.

Then a huge figure loomed over us, and my arm was nearly pulled out of its socket. "What're you doin'! Get outta here!" Mr. Tuttle jerked us to our feet and pushed us through the roiling crowd at the back of the SUV. A mob was still reaching and grabbing at the satchels, while somebody inside tried to beat them off. With Mr. Tuttle's hand on my back, I was again rushed toward our car, Miss Wiggins running along beside us.

As Lloyd unlocked the doors, we fell into the car, our breath coming in loud gasps.

"Is everybody all right?" Lloyd jittered in his seat. "Anybody hurt? What happened? What happened?"

"We're all right, honey," I managed to get out, although I wasn't sure about all of us. I, for one, was still seeing stars. "Calm down now, and let me see to Etta Mae." I tapped Mr. Tuttle's shoulder. "You can leave anytime, Mr. Tuttle."

He cranked the car, as I turned Miss Wiggins's face to examine it. "Did that man hurt you?"

"No, not really. I'm all right. I just fell kinda hard when he pushed me. But he about ripped my shirt off when I pulled him out of the car." She gave a little laugh. "Sliding around under it didn't help, either. Did you get hurt?"

"Not in the least, thanks to your quick actions. And," I continued, giving credit where it was due, "Lloyd's warning and Mr. Tuttle being Johnny-on-the-spot."

"And speaking of spots," he said, turning in the seat to back the car out. "I spilled coffee all over myself when I came out and saw what was happening. I'm wet from one end to the other, and probably scalded, too."

"All in a good cause, Mr. Tuttle," I said.

"Yeah, well, I told you to stay in the car," he said, backing into the traffic lane. "Twice, I told you to stay in the car, but . . . Will you look at that?" He stopped the car and pointed to the crowd of people who were running after the SUV as it sped down the entrance ramp toward the interstate. "Bet they won't get far."

"Well, I don't care," I said. "I'm through chasing them. I got what I came for, although probably none of it's mine."

Mr. Tuttle looked at me through the rearview mirror. "You only got one bag? How much you reckon's in it?"

"I have no idea, but it's heavy enough to have all the jewelry from Abbotsville and several other towns, besides."

"*Jewelry!* You didn't get a money bag?" Mr. Tuttle had the car rolling toward the ramp, but he brought it to a sudden stop.

"Of course not," I said. "I'm not a thief. But whether any of the contents are mine or not," I went on, trying to make the best of what I'd found, "some people will get their treasures back. Thanks to us. You've put in a good night's work, Mr. Tuttle. You can be proud of yourself."

He bowed his head and groaned, as the car moved on toward the ramp.

"Etta Mae, you sure you're all right?" I

was worried, since the woman wasn't entering into the general expressions of relief. She was being too quiet, all scrunched up in the corner of the seat.

"Oh, yes, ma'am, I am. I was just thinking."

"About what?" Lloyd asked.

"Well, that Tim guy was awfully nice." The car spurted forward as we merged into the interstate traffic. "At first, I mean."

They Lord, I thought to myself.

CHAPTER 41

"Give me some directions back there," Mr. Tuttle growled. "Back to West Palm or keep going north?"

Before I could answer, a wail of sirens split the air, and looking back, I saw a cluster of pulsing blue lights speeding toward us.

"Oh, no!" Lloyd wailed. "They're coming for us."

Miss Wiggins sat up in a hurry. "You think?"

Mr. Tuttle glanced down at the speed-ometer. "They're not after us. Just watch. They're after those guys with the money. Somebody at the rest stop called it in."

And sure enough, three of Florida highways' finest blasted past us, rocking the car as they went. We watched as the blue lights flashed in the distance and listened as the sirens grew faint. Mr. Tuttle drove sedately on.

"Where to?" he asked again. "Make up your mind."

"Well, I don't know," I said. "How far are we from Abbotsville?"

He glanced at me in the rearview mirror. "'Bout five or six hundred miles, give or take."

"Goodness," I said. "What do you think, Etta Mae? Shall we go back or go on?"

"All my summer clothes are in the hotel," she said, "but I guess I could get some more."

"Ours are, too, Miss Julia," Lloyd said.

"Well, we can't just leave them. I'll have the hotel pack them up and ship them to us. Mr. Tuttle, do you have any urgent business that you need to get back to?"

"Am I still on the clock?"

"As long as you're with us, you are."

"Then I don't need to get back." He settled himself deep in the seat, prepared to keep on driving.

"That being the case, we should stop for the night, or for what's left of it. I don't want you falling asleep at the wheel."

"Oh, look!" Lloyd cried out.

Mr. Tuttle slowed as we approached a line of cars inching along beside a covey of highway patrol vehicles parked along the side. Blue lights strobed across the scene, flashing eerily in the darkness. The dark SUV, its doors wide open, was skewed against the guardrail. Patrolmen swarmed around it, and I saw the head of someone in the backseat of one of the patrol cars.

Serves you right, I thought with grim satisfaction. Anybody who'd sneak into a person's home and steal that person's valuable personal items deserved to be tracked down like a dog and put under the jail.

"Don't let 'em see us!" Miss Wiggins crouched down as we neared the scene.

I ducked down, too, then thought better of it. "There's no need for that, Etta Mae. The police don't know who we are, and those crooks aren't about to tell on us. We didn't take their money, and they'd hardly confess to having stolen goods, especially since they no longer have them. They have enough explaining to do as it is. In fact, I'd say we've done them a favor, wouldn't you?"

"I guess," Miss Wiggins said, peeking out the window as we passed.

I could see Mr. Tuttle shaking his head, but he offered no comments. He sped up as the traffic thinned, and soon we were cruising well away from any entanglement with the law.

"Miss Julia?" Lloyd chimed in from the front seat. "If the crooks stole that jewelry, and we stole it from them, who does it

449

belong to now?"

"No, Lloyd, it's not stealing to take back what's been stolen in the first place. My conscience is very clear on that. What we'll do is go through it and see if any of it belongs to me or your mother or anybody we know. If it does, why, then, it'll be back where it belongs. We'll turn the rest over to Coleman, and let him deal with it."

Mr. Tuttle heaved a mighty sigh. He was probably thinking of all that loose money floating around that he'd been too busy rescuing us to get any of.

"Mr. Tuttle," I said, leaning up close, "I want to thank you for putting aside any thought of personal gain during that altercation back there. Instead of enriching yourself, which you could've easily done along with all the other grasping people, you looked after us. That was an unselfish thing to do, and I commend you for it."

He just groaned, an unseemly response, it seemed to me, to a compliment.

"Now," I went on, "when we're far enough away from that arresting scene, you can pull off whenever you see a nice motel. I want to get some sleep before the sun rises."

He continued to press on for some little while. I was just at the edge of sleep when he took an exit ramp, and after a few turns, pulled up in front of a well-kept motel, though not a nationally known one.

"How're we gonna do this?" he asked as he turned off the ignition.

"Get two rooms, please," I said, handing him a few bills. "We want two double beds in each, and an adjoining door. There's safety in numbers, you know. And," I went on as he got out of the car, "get them on the first floor so we can park right outside our doors, just in case."

By the time we got to our rooms, Mr. Tuttle had to carry Lloyd inside to their room. The child was dead to the world, and I was on my last legs. Miss Wiggins trudged to our room, her arms wrapped around her waist like she was suffering from a stomach ailment.

Mr. Tuttle knocked on the connecting door, opened it, and proceeded to take a seat beside the bed I intended to get into. He kept eyeing the satchel, while I kept waiting for him to leave so we could get some sleep.

"Let's see what's in it," he said.

So I made sure the outside doors were locked and opened it up. I was fairly curious, myself. Mr. Tuttle dipped his hands in and brought them out dripping with gold chains and ropes of pearls.

"Man alive," he breathed. "Would you look at this. No tellin' how much it's worth."

"It's just jewelry," I said, as Miss Wiggins swayed beside us, glassy-eyed with fatigue. Or maybe she'd really injured herself. "But there's too much to go through now. Besides, as long as I don't look, I can still hope my rings're in there."

Mr. Tuttle let the ropes and chains dribble through his fingers as they fell back into the satchel. He snapped the latch closed and straightened up with a pensive look. "They will be," he said. "This has been the strangest case I ever been on. Everything from start to finish has been out of whack." He wagged his head from side to side, like he didn't know what to think. "Nobody, I mean nobody, would believe it. *I* don't believe it."

"Don't believe what?"

"That you could come down here on nothing more than something a deputy sheriff threw out and find the very thieves you were looking for, and believe me, that's unheard of 'cause we got so many of them. Then you just happen to find one particular necklace you recognize and *steal it back*." Mr. Tuttle seemed stunned at how we had so unerringly found our quarry. He smeared a hand across his face and flopped

452

back into the chair.

"And then," he went on, shaking his head in disbelief, "you just happened to see them buying suitcases, and *then,* we see them loading up to leave, just in time to follow them."

"And don't forget," I said, getting into the recount of amazing coincidences, "I just happened to find the one satchel with jewelry instead of money."

"No, Lord, I'm not forgetting that. I'll tell you what's a fact, I don't know how you managed it. I mean, I've never had a case where everything worked out like this. Downright eerie, if you ask me. Almost like, well, like somebody was telling you what to do and where to do it."

I smiled to myself, for I'd been thinking along the same lines. "Somebody was, Mr. Tuttle, and I'm glad you've taken note of it. When you live right and do right, why, things just work out for you."

Miss Wiggins mumbled, "Amen."

Mr. Tuttle turned his hands out, palms up, like he didn't know what else to do. "Okay, so why wouldn't your rings be in there? I don't see it stopping now."

He stood up and headed toward the connecting door, shaking his head as he went. I hefted the satchel off the bed and tucked it beside the lamp table, where I could keep my hand on it for the rest of the night.

Miss Wiggins threw herself on one of the beds, shoes and all. I wasn't far behind, for both of us were worn to a frazzle.

CHAPTER 42

Well, we made it home, obviously, since we're here and not too much the worse for wear. I must admit, though, it took an entire day of bed rest for me to feel like myself again, but that day had to wait awhile before I could get to it. I declare, touring Florida is not for the infirm or the faint of heart.

Lillian, of course, was happy and relieved to see us, squeezing Lloyd to her bosom until he nearly suffocated and hugging Miss Wiggins and telling me over and over that I ought to know better than to be gone so long without letting her know where we were.

I was so tired from our long trip that I could hardly lug in the satchel that had been my constant companion ever since I'd relieved it from those thieves. But I let it fall in my surprise at seeing Hazel Marie and Mr. Pickens already back from their illicit vacation, which they'd never admit to. Strange that it had rained in Las Vegas at the same time it poured in Mexico, so they both had to come home.

Mr. Pickens and Mr. Tuttle had an old-home week reunion, shaking hands and grinning all over themselves. Lillian had obviously told Mr. Pickens everything she knew, so he wasn't all that surprised to see his old friend come walking in with us. I think he was surprised to find him sober, though.

"So how do you like working for Miss Julia?" Mr. Pickens asked him.

I shot Mr. Tuttle a warning glare to remind him that he hadn't yet received his final payment, but I needn't have worried. He didn't crack a smile, just shook his head in a wondering kind of way and said, "Changed my life, is all."

But Mr. Pickens couldn't leave it alone. "She's known for doing that," he said. "Or at least for trying to."

But in the midst of all the exchange of greetings, I had to undergo another crushing hug from Hazel Marie while evading one from Mr. Pickens.

"Did you get our things back?" Hazel Marie squealed. "What's in the bag? I couldn't believe we'd been robbed. Lillian told us all about it, and oh, Miss Julia, I can't believe you went after them."

"Somebody had to," I said, hurrying toward the fireplace, where it was warm. We were still in our Florida clothes and had almost frozen to death coming up the mountain even with the heat going full blast. "Since," I went on with a dark glance at Mr. Pickens, "some people were out of town when they were needed."

"Love your outfit," he said, with a wicked glint in his eyes.

Having forgotten my ill-chosen attire since I'd been in it so long, I sat down abruptly and determined to stay that way until Mr. Pickens had his mind on something else.

After all the welcoming was over, Miss Wiggins said that she really needed to get home and check on her job. We all urged her to stay for dinner and for the retelling of our journey, but she couldn't be moved. Mr. Pickens volunteered to drive her to the airport where she'd left her automobile.

I hated to see her go, having become accustomed to her company, but she still didn't look well, nor did she act well. Wouldn't even take a seat in the living room, just stayed stooped over with her arms across her middle, like she was in pain. I thanked her profusely for all she'd done and insisted on paying her for her time.

"After all," I told her when she tried to refuse any remuneration, "you left your job the minute I called, and it's only right that I pay you at least for your expenses and your time. I don't know what I would've done without you, Etta Mae. You saved our bacon more than once. And," I went on, "I don't care what anybody says, you conducted yourself with admirable decorum where Mr. Tuttle was concerned." Having closely observed her actions on our trip, I had begun to think that perhaps her reputation for loose behavior was not entirely warranted, and I wanted to commend her for it.

She finally accepted payment and left, still with that strange hunched-over posture. I suggested that she might need to see a doctor, since I'd also noticed that she looked a little thicker around the midsection. But she assured me she was fine and that it was not unusual for her to put on a pound or two periodically.

After Mr. Pickens and Miss Wiggins left, I thought I could rest and readjust myself to being home. But there was no rest for the weary, for Hazel Marie couldn't sit still until we'd seen what was in the satchel. "Oh, if our things aren't in it, I'll just die. I mean, after all you went through to get it. Oh, Miss Julia, what if everything in it belongs to somebody else? What if all our things are gone?"

Well, of course, that had been my worry ever since I'd come down from the thrill of getting the satchel in the first place. But I'd come to this conclusion: If my rings, and Hazel Marie's things, too, weren't in the satchel, I would accept the fact that they'd been converted to cold cash that had either fluttered in the breeze of a parking lot or been confiscated by law officials. I wasn't up for another wild-goose chase, even if we had an inkling of where they might be. I'd just have to face Sam with a ringless hand and live with the knowledge that they were gone for good. Maybe another woman somewhere — no telling where — was flashing killer sapphires and diamonds on her finger.

"All right, Hazel Marie," I said, knowing that putting it off wouldn't help anything. "Let's see what's in here. We'll dump everything out on my bed."

And that's what we did. It made a glittering pile on my Martha Washington spread, and Hazel Marie could hardly wait to get her hands in it. Lillian's eyes widened at the sight, and Lloyd whistled in amazement.

"Stand by the door, if you will, Mr. Tuttle," I said. "You're still on the clock, and we don't want another theft attempt."

"Oh, my goodness," Hazel Marie said, as she began digging into the pile. "It's like a pirate's treasure. Oh, I'll tell you what let's do. Let's separate it and put all the necklaces in one pile, bracelets in another, and so on. That way we can see what we have. Help me, Lloyd."

"Okay," he said and dug his hand into the heap, pulling out gold pieces that he began to separate.

"Try to find the rings first," I said.

"Yessum," he said. "I'm looking for them."

"Oh, look!" Hazel Marie squealed. "It's my Judith Ripka necklace! I'd know it anywhere. Look, Miss Julia, can you believe it?"

My spirits lifted considerably at her discovery. Maybe we had gotten to the thieves in time. Maybe this haul had been their last and they hadn't been able to turn it into cash. "Keep looking, Hazel Marie," I said, trying to calm the excitement I was feeling. "I don't think I'm able to."

She fell to it, spreading out the jewelry and rapidly separating it. "The rings are the hardest," she said. "They're so small and they get tangled up in all these chains and pearls."

She gave a sudden gasp. "Here's my pin!

Oh-h-h," she said, clutching it to her breast and closing her eyes in thanksgiving. "And look, I think this is Mildred's ruby earring. Oh, I hope the other one's in here. I'll tell you what, though. We're going to have a time with these pearls. They're so much alike, we may not be able to tell which belongs to who."

I sat on the edge of the bed, reluctant to go through the pieces and not find what I wanted, what I'd endured so much to recover.

"Miss Julia?" Lloyd said it so quietly I almost didn't hear him. "Is this it?"

My heart skipped a beat as I saw what he held. There it was, my precious engagement ring, held up in his grimy little hand, whole and safe and back home where it belonged. I thought I was going to cry.

Instead, I took it from him and clutched it in my hand as a wave of gratitude swept over me. Then I put it on my finger, determining that it would stay there forever. I couldn't stop smiling, for that which was lost was found.

"Mr. Tuttle," I said, for he was watching all this from his stance by the door, "and you too, Lloyd, we must never put too much emphasis on material things. There are other things much more important. But, oh, I am so thankful to have this one material object back where it belongs."

As I held out my hand, admiring the beautiful ring, I thought to myself that I'd never ask the Lord for another thing. Then, rummaging through the mass of precious jewels, I said, "But it looks a little lonesome all by itself. Let's see if we can find my wedding band."

Well, we never did find it, even though we searched through everything again. So I had to be content with getting back only half of what I'd lost. But it was the better half by far. Hazel Marie found her diamond watch and the pearls I'd given her, but her tennis bracelet was among the missing. Somebody had helped himself to a number of things, just as that little bushy-headed runt had with Mildred's lavaliere. There is no honor among thieves.

"I think we've got everything that belongs to us," Hazel Marie said, as she surveyed the separate piles of bracelets, necklaces, rings, pins, pearls, earrings, and one lone diamond stud. "At least from what's here. I don't recognize anything else. Why don't we ask Mildred to come over and see what else is hers?"

"Yes, we'll do that. Tomorrow. I can't face anything else tonight." I held up my hand to admire my ring and happened to catch Mr. Tuttle's eye. I smiled at him, wanting to include him in my happiness. "Can you believe this, Mr. Tuttle?"

He didn't smile back. He just gave me an abrupt nod and said, "I can believe anything now."

Lillian had hardly known what to make of Mr. Tuttle, who felt the same way about her.

I'd introduced him to her as soon as she'd released Lloyd and dried her eyes. "Mr. Tuttle's been ever so much help to us, and I think we've been a help to him. He's turning over a new leaf, aren't you, Mr. Tuttle?"

He'd mumbled something in response, but after we'd gone through the jewelry and Mr. Pickens had gotten back, we sat down to eat. Mr. Tuttle eagerly attacked the roast beef and rice and gravy that Lillian set on the table. And no wonder, for the man had for too long neglected solid food in favor of a liquid diet. By this time, he'd been without his usual intake for some few days, so he had a healthy appetite.

Since we arrived home late on a Saturday, I saw to it that Mr. Tuttle started fulfilling his part of our agreement by going to church with us the next morning. I showed him how

I expected him to keep a church attendance record, so he could submit it for payment. I was quite pleased that his first time would be at a fairly evangelical Presbyterian one.

"I'm keeping track, Mr. Tuttle," I told him, "and you may be sure that I will pay your going rate at the end of each month."

He hadn't balked at the suggestion, other than wondering about wearing the same clothes he'd been in for two days, which still bore the snags and rips of his mad dash through a bamboo thicket. A suit of clothes from Sam's closet fit him fairly well after I taped up the hems and told him to keep the jacket buttoned to hide the gap at the waist of Sam's pants.

Once we were settled in our usual pew, Pastor Ledbetter gave one of his better sermons, I was pleased to note, for Mr. Tuttle needed help about as bad as anybody I'd ever known. I was quite proud of the pastor, and I sat there beside Lloyd and nodded approval of every sound point, occasionally glancing at Mr. Tuttle to see if any headway was being made.

Just as the pastor was winding up his sermon with the standard altar call, although we don't actually have an altar in the Presbyterian church, I felt a stir in the pew as Lloyd switched his knees to one side. Hazel

Marie, on the far side of Lloyd, suddenly switched herself around, and lo and behold if Mr. Tuttle wasn't climbing over Mr. Pickens (who was in church only as a courtesy to Mr. Tuttle, while I feared that lightning might strike) and was sidling toward the aisle.

Lord, everybody in the sanctuary was stretching and craning to see what the disturbance was. I clutched Lloyd's arm as Mr. Tuttle shuffled past us and reached the aisle, where he jerked his borrowed jacket down, took a deep breath, and headed for the front.

I couldn't believe it. Nor could Pastor Ledbetter. A look of awe spread across his face, and he almost stumbled as he hurried down from the pulpit to meet and greet his convert. Most Presbyterians have an aversion to making public displays of themselves, and it'd been so long since anyone had answered the call that a great murmuring swept across the congregation. We were so accustomed, don't you know, to using the time of the pastor's altar call to find the page in the hymnal for the closing hymn.

Of course, we were late eating lunch afterward, for we all had to stream forward to extend the hand of fellowship, even though Mr. Tuttle wouldn't be staying around long enough to increase the church roll. But Pastor Ledbetter didn't know that, and he positively glowed at the success of his sermonizing. And rightly so, for it isn't often that a little lost lamb with the age and hard living Mr. Tuttle had on him is brought into the fold.

All the way down the sidewalk and across Polk Street, as we headed for the house, Mr. Tuttle beamed quietly to himself, unaware that the tape on the hem of one pant leg had come undone and was dragging on the ground. Not wanting to disturb that beatific smile on his face, I didn't mention it.

Fact of the matter, I knew I should make some comment about his decision for the Lord, but I didn't know what — Congratulations? Welcome to the church, even though he wasn't staying? Bless you? Or, About time?

Everybody else was in the same predicament, and I wished for Sam, who is rarely at a loss for words. Mr. Pickens kept a wry smile on his face and solved his problem by turning on a football game while Hazel Marie and I heated the meal that Lillian had left. We began the meal as we always did, with Lloyd offering thanks for what we were about to receive, then proceeded to eat it.

Deciding that somebody had to say something because ignoring the miracle that had taken place in Mr. Tuttle's heart was not the thing to do, I said, "Have some more green beans, Mr. Tuttle. And I must say, if I'd known that you intended to go forward this morning, I would've seen to it that you had a better suit of clothes. Some that fit, I mean."

"It don't matter," he said, still with that heavenly glow about him.

As we began to rise from the table, Mr. Tuttle suddenly said, "That preacher said I ought to get on the right track by having daily devotions. Could somebody say a Bible verse?"

It seemed to me that more than an hour already spent in church would've qualified as his daily quota, but I asked Lloyd to run get the Bible. I saw a swift look of humor cross the boy's face and knew what he was thinking. His favorite verse whenever he was put on the spot was, "Jesus wept," the shortest verse in the Bible. But that would hardly be appropriate in the circumstances.

"What do you want me to read?" Lloyd asked, as he returned with a Bible and took his seat.

"Start at Ephesians 5:18 and read a couple more," Hazel Marie said, then ducked her head as everybody stared at her. "That was our Sunday school lesson this morning."

As Lloyd read the verses, I was floored at how felicitous they were — absolutely perfect for the occasion and indicative of our continued guidance from above. The Lord must've really wanted to get Mr. Tuttle, and I was gratified to have been an instrument in the getting.

We were finally able to leave the table, as Mr. Tuttle seemed satisfied with his devotions, but later in the afternoon he asked if I knew anybody who was sick so he could go visit them. I told him that since I'd been out of town a few days, I didn't know anyone who craved a visitation on a Sunday afternoon. Then he went to the evening service over at the church, by himself I might add, and came back lecturing all of us about honoring the Lord's day. We'd read the Sunday paper.

There's nothing worse than a reformed drinking man, unless it's a reformed sinner who suddenly sees sin everywhere. And when it's one and the same man, well, let's just say that the following morning I was happy to put him on a plane, thinking, *Better him than me,* and send him off with my thanks and a check that put another beatific smile on his face.

Well, I've gotten ahead of myself, so taken up with Mr. Tuttle's conversion experience that I've overlooked some important matters. I've already said that Hazel Marie was home from Mexico, and wouldn't you know that Mr. Pickens was right there with her. Every time I turned around, he was underfoot, making some mention of the law enforcement meeting he'd attended at the exact same time she'd been in Mexico, as if that would fool anyone. And he kept saying, "Would you believe that?"

I'd finally had enough of it, and said, "No, I wouldn't."

But he had the effrontery to hug her right in front me, saying, "Don't go off again, sweetheart. I missed you too much." At least she had the grace to blush at such an outrageous and blatant inversion of the truth.

One morning a couple of weeks after we'd all returned home, Hazel Marie accosted me in the living room. "Guess what, Miss Julia. Etta Mae Wiggins has a brand-new car. I saw her yesterday in the parking lot when I was making hospital visits for the church, and there she was in a bright red Camry. I'm so happy she was able to get it. You've seen the one she was driving, haven't you? It was practically falling apart."

I made the appropriate comments, but privately I had to think about this turn of events. So, Miss Wiggins had suddenly come into money? Not from me, that was clear, for even though I'd paid her well, it hadn't been that well. So, where had she gotten it or, more to the point, *when* had she gotten it? I went over all our escapades in my mind, and finally came to the conclusion that it had to've been when she was under the SUV. It became clear as a bell to me — that's what she'd been doing under there, scooping up and collecting stray bills and stuffing them in her T-shirt.

Well, could I blame her? Everybody else at the rest stop had done the same thing. Not that that excuses anything, but at least Miss Wiggins had kept her wits about her, in spite of all the money that was there for the taking. In fact, at the same time she was taking some for herself, she'd hauled me to safety, even though she almost yanked my cropped pants off doing it.

All things considered, especially some of my own actions, I decided that it wasn't my place to pass judgment.

Still, I couldn't help but wonder if my newfound respect for Miss Wiggins, in spite of her reputation, hadn't become just the least bit downgraded. Then I determined that I wouldn't allow it to. Finders are keepers, as they say, and it wasn't as if she'd *stolen* it. It was my considered conclusion that if any-body deserved a windfall, it was Etta Mae Wiggins.

"Well," I said to Hazel Marie, "I'm pleased for her. She certainly needed a new car."

And Sam? Well, I've saved the best for last, since having him home has made everything else fall into place. I'd tried to talk Mr. Tuttle into staying on a few days so he could meet Sam. And what a meeting that was — I'm talking about mine and Sam's, not his and Sam's, but Mr. Tuttle had been anxious to get back to Florida. I declare, he is such a handsome man — Sam, that is — and my heart lifted when he stepped off that air-plane. I could do little more than smile as we drove home, especially since Sam was so full of his trip, telling of the wonders he had seen.

"Julia, you should've been with me. The only wrong note of the whole trip was think-ing of you back here with nothing interest-ing to do."

I would've smiled and let it go at that, but too many people knew of our exploits. Hazel Marie, for one, could never keep a secret, and I couldn't ask Lloyd to practice any kind of deception.

So I had to tell him, although I skirted gingerly around a few of the more perilous moments of our ocean-side adventures. And if I left out a few minor details, why, it was because they would've upset him. It behooves a caring wife to shield her husband from matters that would only serve to distress and disturb him. Besides, what he doesn't know won't hurt him, and far be it from me to do anything that would hurt my dear, trusting Sam.

Needless to say, Sam was astounded to hear the tale. In fact, he could hardly take it all in. He kept starting and stopping, saying, "You mean you . . . ?" and "You didn't really . . . ?" and so on.

Finally, he put his hands on my shoulders and gave me a serious eye-to-eye. "Julia, what in the world am I going to do with you?"

I answered him by taking a lesson from Mr. Pickens: "Just don't go off again, sweetheart." I ran my hand across his chest and smiled at him. "I missed you too much."

That wasn't entirely true, of course, since I'd been too taken up with my Palm Beach mission to dwell all that long on his absence. But, as I pointed out to Sam, he couldn't be too upset with me, for he was the very reason that I'd had so much to fill my time while he was away. As I'd told Lillian, it had been because of him that I'd undertaken such dangerous actions in the first place, not wanting to lose the rings he'd given me.

The thought of Sam had been behind every action I'd taken, for how would he have felt if he'd returned home to a wife who'd been so careless as to allow such a meaningful and precious gift to get away from her?

And speaking of rings, my recovered engagement ring now has a mate, which Sam insisted on getting for me. They're both on my finger and that's where they'll stay, arthritis or no arthritis. If anybody tries to steal them again, they'll have to take me with them.

And if anybody is wondering, the jewelry bag that I'd relieved from the dark SUV had contained most, but not all, of the valuables stolen from Abbotsville, as well as stashes from Asheville and several towns in South Carolina and Georgia. After Mildred Allen went through the contents, finding some of her mother's pieces as well as a few of her own, I virtuously turned the rest over to Coleman with as little explanation as I could get away with.

We were fortunate to have gotten immediately on the trail of the crooks, for they hadn't had time to convert the local haul to cash. That's a lesson I intend to take to heart from now on: When something needs to be done, just go on and do it. Don't dither around and let them get away with it.

Like I always say, if you don't strike while the iron is hot, you might as well not strike at all.

The employees of Thorndike Press hope you have enjoyed this Large Print book. All our Thorndike and Wheeler Large Print titles are designed for easy reading, and all our books are made to last. Other Thorndike Press Large Print books are available at your library, through selected bookstores, or directly from us.

For information about titles, please call:

(800) 223-1244

or visit our Web site at:

www.gale.com/thorndike
www.gale.com/wheeler

To share your comments, please write:

Publisher
Thorndike Press
295 Kennedy Memorial Drive
Waterville, ME 04901

3 3656 0368758 5

LARGE TYPE
Ross, Ann B.
Miss Julia strikes back